MURDER
SUPERIOR

JANE HADDAM

BANTAM BOOKS
NEW YORK • TORONTO • LONDON • SYDNEY • AUCKLAND

MURDER SUPERIOR
A Bantam Book / May 1993

All rights reserved.
Copyright © 1993 by Orania Papazoglou.
Cover art copyright © 1993 by Chuck Wilkinson.

ISBN 0-553-56084-0

Published simultaneously in the United States and Canada

Bantam Books are published by Bantam Books, a division of Bantam Doubleday Dell
Publishing Group, Inc. Its trademark, consisting of the words "Bantam Books" and the
portrayal of a rooster, is Registered in U.S. Patent and Trademark Office and in other
countries. Marca Registrada. Bantam Books, 1540 Broadway, New York, New York 10036.

PRINTED IN THE UNITED STATES OF AMERICA

OPM   0 9 8 7 6 5 4

MURDER
SUPERIOR

PROLOGUE

1

It was six o'clock on the morning of Monday, May 5, and Norman Kevic was on the air—and in the air, too, in a way, since he'd been flying higher than a statocumulus cloud ever since he'd snorted four lines of pure Peruvian crystal in the men's room of the Philadelphia Baroque Rococo Club at five minutes before closing just a few hours ago. Of course, those four lines weren't the last lines Norm had snorted, just as the Baroque Rococo wasn't the last club he'd visited. The Baroque Rococo was a gay bar Norm liked to go to just to see if he could get thrown out of it—which he couldn't anymore, because they knew him. He'd spent the rest of the night in a place called Bertha's Box, about which the less remembered the better. It didn't matter, because Norm never could remember what he'd done in Bertha's, except for more lines. There were always more lines.

It was six o'clock in the morning and Norm had to

go to work—in spite of the fact that he owned a piece of the station and wasn't about to fire himself. Long before he'd owned a piece of the station he'd been The Voice of WXVE, the King of Philadelphia Talk Radio, the Man of the Morning. He'd taken three days off with the flu back in 1984 and nearly been lynched. There were heads out there who stoked themselves up all night just to be cruising fast enough to take him in between six and ten. More to the point, there were heads out there who weren't very stable. Norm's mail was a steady stream of unidentified flying objects. A dead mouse with a bright purple satin ribbon tied in a crisp bow around its neck. A lifetime subscription to the neo-Nazi rag called *Black Storm Rising: The Truth About the Second World War.* An absolutely awful home-made carrot cake with a flic knife buried inside. The fans would send him anything. They were out there. And they had teeth.

The chair in front of the mike Norm was supposed to use had arms, and that was a no-no, because Norm was much too fat to fit into a chair with arms. He'd been fat all his life, to an extent, but lately it had gotten worse. Who said cocaine made you thin? There was a pile of books on the pull-out shelf next to the microphone and a note: *steve says don't say asshole on the air again it's going to get us in trouble.* Norm stared at the punctuation in "it's" for a good half minute, then crumpled the note. It was Sherri who was the asshole as far as he was concerned. It was Sherri who ought to have been fired, except that he couldn't fire her, because she was Steve's assistant. In the old days, girls like Sherri didn't punctuate words like "it's" even if they knew how, because they knew *better.* They didn't wear jeans to the office, either, unless the jeans were tight. They certainly didn't stand in the open glass door to the broadcast booth in L.L. Bean baggies and overflowing flannel shirts, wearing no makeup and wire-rimmed glasses, looking at him as if he were a slug. *It's.* God. What had he been thinking of? Why? He had to stop doing those lines.

Sherri had taken her glasses off and was tapping

them on her chest. The red light over the microphone was lit. Somewhere out there, a boy named Dig Watter, whose sole job was to make sure there was no dead air on WXVE for any reason short of the Rapture, was probably getting an ulcer.

"Listen," Sherri said. "Just one second before you start. Steve wanted me to tell you—"

"Not to say asshole," Norm said.

"That, too. To lay off the dead Jap jokes. That's what. There's a big Japanese-American community in the suburbs around Philadelphia. You're getting a lot of people pissed off."

"That's what I do for a living. I get people pissed off."

"Just pay attention," Sherri said.

"You ought to lose some weight," Norm said. "You really should. You'd be a very attractive woman if you only lost a little weight."

"You'd be a very attractive man if you just grew a bigger dick," Sherri said.

Then she stepped into the hall and let the door swing shut behind her.

Norm stared after her, furious, the red light blinking, nothing to be done about the goddamned chair right away, furious. What had gotten into these women anyway? It was all that crap with Clarence Thomas and Anita Hill. Sexual harassment. They were the 1990s version of those old maids who used to see rapists under their beds. Christ.

Red light.

Pile of books.

Big hand-lettered sign on his bulletin board:

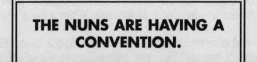

THE NUNS ARE HAVING A CONVENTION.

He grabbed the mike, snapped it open with his thumb and said, "Good morning Philadelphia, this is Cultural Norm, the free-form house worm coming to you from the studios of WXVE radio—any minute now I'm going to turn into the voice of radio past—the living dead—no, I can't be the living dead, I'm not a Republican—I'm not a Democrat, either—if politics gets any sillier I'm going to have to vote for Yeltsin—I wish I could vote for Yeltsin—this is the wrong chair I have in this studio, Sherri sweetie, go get me another one—and I've got news for the lot of you out there, yes I do, before we get down to business. Business today is a good long discussion of that ancient question: can masturbation be good for you? And how? We've got a number of guests coming in, including the Right Reverend Thomas Willard, pastor of the Paoli Pentecostal Church. I think the good reverend's answer to our first question is going to be no—but you can't tell, ladies and gentlemen, you really can't tell. I mean, look at Jimmy Swaggart. Anyway, before we get into all that, we've got more religious news."

He could see Sherri through the glass door, down the hall in the small office where she sat typing letters with a radio on, monitoring the broadcast. When he said that about the chair, her hair snapped up and she leaned over to speak into her intercom. Now a young boy Norm had never seen before was scurrying in from the wings, dragging an armless side chair that was almost as tall as he was and twice as heavy. Norm kicked open the glass booth door and motioned him inside.

"Just a minute ladies and gentlemen, this is my chair, let me sit down in it. Sherri sweetie didn't bring it, though. She sent a boy. What she thinks I want with a boy is beyond me. He doesn't have anywhere near as nice a chest as she does. His is flat. What's your name, kid?"

The kid blushed. "Mike," he said. "Mike Donnelly."

"Right. I want Mike off my mike and out of my booth right now or I'll ask him what he thinks of masturbation and whether he ever commits it. There he goes. Into the hall. Into the sunset. What the hey. Now for that religious news I promised you. The Sisters of Divine Grace—you know, the ones that have that big college and academic conference center out in Radnor—well, the good Sisters have decided to have a convention of their own. That's what I said. A nun's convention. The Sisters of Divine Grace is the largest active Order—that's a Church term for you pagans out there, an active Order goes out and teaches or nurses or whatever instead of staying in a cloister and praying all the time—anyway, they're the largest active Order in the United States, with three thousand nuns in the contiguous forty-eight and another fifteen hundred between Hawaii, Alaska, Puerto Rico, and the Virgin Islands. They also have a number of houses—religious houses now, convents to you bozos—in foreign countries, including what's probably an obligatory one in Rome. Don't quote me on that. I haven't been to church since I peeked up Sister Bonaventure's dress and found out she ran on wheels. Anyway, this convention is going to take place in our own fair ADI, right there in Radnor, for a week beginning the Friday before Mother's Day and running through the Sunday afterward. The Sisters run Catholic schools for the most part, and this year they've coordinated their school schedules to get their vacations all at the same time. And here they'll be. Little skirts. Little veils. Little prayer books. Thousands of them. Maybe I should have saved the masturbation program for them. What I'm trying to say here is that this is a major invasion, *major,* so major all the patent leather shoes in Philadelphia may disappear before our eyes in the next two weeks. We've got to be prepared. We've got to have a war plan. I don't have one yet, but I'm working on it. Stay tuned. Or take on protective coloration. Anyone wearing a Miraculous Medal with a blue glass bead in it is probably safe. And now, just one more thing before we bring in our first guest."

Down the hall, Sherri's head rose slowly and swiveled in his direction. Norman Kevic smiled.

"Ladies and gentlemen," Norm said, "do you know

how to save a Japanese from fugu poisoning? No? Well, *gooooood.*"

Down the hall, Sherri picked up a big glass paper-weight and threw it on the floor.

2

"... do you know how to save a Japanese from fugu poisoning? No? Well, *gooooood.*"

Sister Scholastica Burke looked vaguely at the radio she had pushed up on the top shelf of the pantry when she'd first come in and frowned. Fugu poisoning. Mas-turbation. Pantry. Socks? She knew something about fugu, anyway, because they had several pounds of it down in the cold pantry, frozen solid and shipped from Japan, the gift of a friend of the Order's Tokyo house. Sister Scholastica wasn't worried about poisoning, though, because along with the fugu—which, if she understood it correctly, was an extremely poisonous fish people wanted to eat anyway—the friend of the Order was sending along his own personal fugu chef. That was supposed to help. Sister Scholastica had de-cided that the safest course was to skip the fugu alto-gether, which she intended to do by saying she didn't like fish. She was a tall, red-haired, solidly middle-class product of traditional Irish-American, Irish-Catholic parents, still a couple of years shy of forty. In the old Church, she would have been a mere foot soldier for many more years to come. This being the new one, she was Mistress of Postulants at the Order's Mother-house in Maryville, New York, and one of the two or three women expected to end up Mother General in the long run, as a matter of course. In the short run, Reverend Mother General was just who she had been for the last seven years, and Scholastica had no inter-est in stepping into her shoes. Sister Scholastica didn't have much use for anything at the moment. It was just after six o'clock in the morning. She'd been up long enough to chant office with her postulants and unpack seven cases of glazed fruit from Fortnum & Mason, gift of a friend of the Order's in London. She had three more cases of glazed fruit to go, and then a big pile of something or the other that had been sent from Sydney, Australia. She was dead tired.

She was also feeling a little queasy. There was something about that joke about the fugu that she hadn't liked, something about the way the man had said it, as if he meant it—but she had to be exaggerating, or exhausted, or something. Overreacting, most likely. Her best friend had been murdered a few years ago, and by someone she would never have expected. It preyed on her mind sometimes. She would have felt better if she'd been in Maryville. It had been Reverend Mother General's idea to send her down here with her postulants to "help set up." What Reverend Mother General really wanted her to do was spy. Scholastica wasn't sure who she was supposed to spy on, or for what. Reverend Mother was never that direct unless she was talking to Cardinal Archbishops.

When Fortnum & Mason glazed fruit, they did it right. They glazed entire pears and flawless apricots. Scholastica checked out the apricots, shook her head, and put the box on the nearest clear shelf space she could find. Then she looked across the pantry at Linda Bartolucci. Linda Bartolucci was a postulant, complete with black dress and little short veil. She was supposed to be unloading a large crate full of pâté de foie gras from France. Instead, she was sitting on the crate, reading something. Linda Bartolucci was always reading something. If she'd stayed in the world, she would have turned into one of those thick-ankled women who buried themselves in romance novels on the bus.

Stayed in the world. Where had *that* phrase come from? How long ago was Vatican II?

Scholastica wiped her hands on the sides of her habit skirt and said, "Linda, for heaven's sake, at least pretend to get some work done."

"Work?" Linda looked confused. Then she flushed. "Oh. Sister. I'm sorry."

"Don't be sorry," Scholastica told her, "just unload. We've got Mass at seven thirty."

"I know. I just—I found this, you see. It's a schedule."

"Schedule?"

"For the convention. You know. Somebody was talking about it at dinner last night—I don't remember who. But they're putting a schedule together and they're going to have it printed up and it's going to be just like a real convention."

"But they haven't printed it up," Scholastica pointed out. "That's not until next week."

"Well this isn't printed. It's typed and this is a photocopy anyway. I mean, it wouldn't be a secret, would it? The schedule?"

"I suppose not." Actually, although Scholastica had heard about the printed schedule, she hadn't given it much thought, because thinking about it made her uncomfortable. It was odd the way that worked. Scholastica had joined the Order just far enough back to have gone through formation under the old dispensation—long habits, long silences and all. She remembered the days when a meeting, no matter how large, would have had to depend on daily announcements in refectory for a schedule. It made her very nervous to think that the Order was now modern enough to go to the expense of getting schedules printed in advance. And yet, there were dozens of more substantive changes, even a handful of drastic reversals, that didn't bother her at all. Big clunky shoes replaced by these cute little tie things from Hush Puppies. A Little Office exchanged for a revamped Divine Office that was chanted in English instead of Latin. Sisters who carried money and wandered around by themselves without supervision or companions. Sister Alice Marie said the only thing she couldn't get used to in the changes in the Order since Vatican II was the withdrawal of the rule that every Sister had to take at least one spoonful of every food served at every meal, personal taste notwithstanding. Sister Alice Marie loathed macaroni and cheese. Under the new rules, she didn't have to eat it. She ate it anyway, because she couldn't make herself stop.

Linda was holding out the photocopied schedule.

Scholastica took it and looked down the long list of items meant to span more than a week. Opening reception, Friday, May 16. "Spirituality and the African Cultural Tradition," a seminar, given by Sister Francis Mary, Mistress of Novices, St. Mary's Provincial House, Nairobi, Monday, May 19. Picnic, Wednesday, May 21. Scholastica handed the schedule back.

"Too much to do," she said, "and I won't get to do much of it anyway, because I'll be too busy chasing your lot around this campus. Will you please get back to the pâté? If you make me unload it, I won't let you eat it."

"Virginia Richards said that stuff was made out of goose livers," Linda said. "I don't want to eat it."

"Work," Scholastica told her.

Linda held the schedule out again. "It's the one under Friday I'm interested in. The one at the bottom, for the evening session. See? 'Gregor Demarkian: Investigating the Catholic Murder.' See?"

"What?"

" 'Gregor Demarkian: Investigating the Catholic Murder.' It's right here. Didn't you know about it?"

"Of course I knew about it," Scholastica said. That was half true. She had known Gregor Demarkian was to speak. She had suggested it to Reverend Mother General in the first place, and she had telephoned Gregor herself to extend the invitation. She had not, however, suggested the title, "Investigating the Catholic Murder." She couldn't imagine who had. She couldn't imagine what Gregor Demarkian was going to think about it when he heard about it, either. The best she could hope for was that he'd be polite. She took the schedule out of Linda's hand again, read the offending line, and sighed. "Incredible," she said.

"I was thinking," Linda said.

Scholastica bit back the urge to tell her it was a bad idea. "About what?"

"Well, about this Gregor Demarkian. He's the private detective, isn't he? The one the *Inquirer* calls 'The Armenian-American Hercule Poirot'?"

"Yes, he's the one. But I don't think he likes to be called that, Linda."

"I won't call him that to his face. I was just saying, he's the one who solved the murder of that postulant that Shelley Corrigan's got the room of now, isn't he?"

"You've figured out which room Bridget Ann Reilly was in? What do you do, hold séances?"

"Of course not. That wouldn't be Christian. But we know, Sister. I mean, we'd have to. It was in all the papers."

It had also been in *People* magazine and on *60 Minutes*. Scholastica supposed the girl had a point. Murders in convents did not happen every day, never mind right before St. Patrick's Day, and the country had a certain amount of interest. Excessive, morbid, and totally out of line, according to Reverend Mother General, but interest nonetheless.

Scholastica stowed away a box of glazed chestnuts. "If you want to know if you can go to hear his speech, you can. It's being set up so that everyone can hear him. In the main auditorium. The one they use for convocation."

"Oh, I know about that. It says so right here. What I want to know is . . ."

"What?"

"Well."

"Well, what?"

"Well," Linda said, "I thought, I mean, since he is in the business of investigating murders, not giving talks, and the Order had all that trouble before, you know, I thought maybe he was coming out here because, you know, because something was wrong."

"Wrong? Linda, what are you talking about?"

"Wrong," Linda said doggedly. "You know. Maybe there have been threats, or someone's been acting funny, or you—"

"Don't. Don't say 'you know' even one more time."

"I didn't mean to get you angry, Sister. I just—I mean, there was his name, and there were all the things they said about him when Bridget Ann Reilly died, and now here we all are together like this, like sitting ducks if some nut out there wanted to, ah, you—um—"

"Never mind," Scholastica said. The next box had glazed pineapples in it. "Look," she said. "Nothing is wrong, except for the title they're giving his speech, which he isn't going to like. But there isn't anything wrong. That's the point."

"I don't get it."

"All that happened last year at the Motherhouse," Scholastica said slowly, "and we tried to get the information out to as many people as possible, about what happened, and how it happened, and how it was cleared up, but it isn't always that easy. And so we thought—since Gregor is right here in Philadelphia anyway—we thought that we'd ask him to come and tell the Sisters everything they could possibly want to know, and then everybody would calm down a little. At last, if you ask me."

"You called him 'Gregor,' " Linda said. "Is he a friend of yours?"

"Not really. He asked me to call him Gregor."

"Will he have slides with pictures of blood?"

Scholastica stood. "Go back to work," she said. "Sometimes I wish we still maintained the old discipline. I'd have you begging your soup at dinner for a week on the strength of that. What kind of a question—"

"Maybe somebody will get murdered," Linda said mischievously. "Maybe one of the postulants will just get fed up, and then Mother Mary Bellarmine—"

"Linda."

"You'd kill her yourself if you got half a chance," Linda said. "I heard you say so to Sister Alice Marie."

"I think in the old days, eavesdropping got you thrown in a dungeon."

"I'd just rattle my chains and sing Madonna songs at the top of my lungs absolutely off-key until nobody could stand it anymore and they had to let me out."

"Elvis Presley. Madonna hadn't been invented yet. Get back to work."

"Yes, Sister."

For once, Linda seemed to mean that "Yes, Sister."
She bent over the box at her feet and began to take
out tins of pâté de foie gras. Scholastica watched her
for a moment, then went back to work herself.

It was odd, she thought again, what you minded and
what you didn't. Short habits. Dead postulants. Knowing a private detective well enough to call him by his
first name. It was ridiculous to take anything Linda
Bartolucci said seriously. Linda didn't know how to be
serious.

The pantry opened onto a small back hall. Scholastica drifted out there, to the window that overlooked
the kitchen garden and the narrow stone path down to
the Virgin's grotto, erected by nuns of a different era
to celebrate the piety of a different century. Sister
Scholastica Burke was not one of those people who
pined for the resurrection of the Tridentine Church.
As annoying as the post–Vatican II Church might be in
many of its particulars, she found it preferable to what
the old Church had degenerated into in the years just
before the change. Still, sometimes she wondered if it
might have been better if nothing had changed at all.
Postulants didn't end up murdered in the old days, and
nuns didn't get entangled in murder investigations.
That was an experience Sister Scholastica Burke
would just as soon never have to repeat.

The path to the grotto was cracked. Thick shoots of
bright green grass popped through it in unexpected
places, making it look decorated. Scholastica told herself she had to stop being silly. Gregor Demarkian
didn't cause murders. He only investigated them. It
was idiotic to feel that something awful was going to
happen just because he was going to show up to give
a talk.

In the old days, Sister Scholastica's spiritual adviser
would have called what she was thinking a form of su-
perstition, and sent her off to meditate on the true nature of the risen Christ. If she went looking for a
spiritual adviser now, he'd probably nod a lot and insist
on helping her to explore her feelings. That was some-

thing else to be said in favor of the pre–Vatican II Church.

Scholastica turned around and went back into the pantry. Pre- or post-, it didn't matter much.

These boxes still had to be unpacked.

3

Sister Joan Esther had a lot of unpacking to do herself, although not of boxes. What she had to unpack were suitcases, and right now, standing in the main foyer of St. Elizabeth's Convent, she thought she might have all the suitcases on earth. St. Elizabeth's Convent was the house that had been built to house the Sisters who ran this small college, the only one in the United States run by the Sisters of Divine Grace. It was a big old house, drafty and damp, erected when the supply of vocations had seemed endless and the supply of devout young Catholics looking for a liberal arts education had seemed even larger than that. Looking at places like this made Sister Joan Esther's head ache. She wasn't very old—she had been in Sister Scholastica's formation class; she had entered the convent just out of college while Scholastica had entered out of high school—but she was old enough to remember not only flowing habits but Saturday afternoon confessional lines that extended all the way to the church foyer, parishes so dedicated to the Catholic way of life they provided parish school educations to every child of every member free of charge, devotion to Mary so strong that every young girl dreamed of becoming a nun. If Sister Joan Esther had been asked to name what had changed with Vatican II, she would have said "attitude." Attitude. All the rest of it—the changes in the Mass; the new habits; the bishops who no longer wanted anyone to kiss their rings—seemed entirely superfluous to her. As far as Sister Joan Esther was concerned, the Church could decree that Mass should be said with the priest standing on his head. That wouldn't matter. What did matter was how many people took it all seriously, from the Virgin Birth to the

Resurrection to the establishment of Peter in Rome. What did matter was that, these days, nobody took it seriously at all.

That wasn't fair. That was just the kind of sweeping generalization Joan Esther had been at such great pains to train her students out of, back when she had had students. Sister Joan Esther had a doctorate in theology from Notre Dame. For many years, she had been one of the shining lights in the theology department at this college. It had been Aquinas College then, like a hundred other small Catholic colleges across the country. With feminism had come a name change, and it was now St. Teresa of Avila. Sister Joan Esther liked St. Teresa of Avila. She even credited St. Teresa with giving her her first small feminist insight, at the age of nine. Those were the days when Teresa of Avila and St. Catherine of Siena were described in the missal as having done work "equal to a Doctor of the Church," which always made Joan Esther wonder why, if they were equal, they weren't doctors. Apparently, it had made other people wonder too. One of the first things that had happened in the wake of Vatican II was that Teresa and Catherine were named Doctors of the Church. You couldn't blame Vatican II for everything.

You couldn't blame Vatican II for a radical loss of—what?

Every one of the suitcases on the floor was black. Every one had an oaktag tag tied to its handle with a name printed on it with black felt pen. Every one contained five sets of clean underwear, five pairs of clean black panty hose, two plain white clean cotton nightgowns, one terry-cloth bathrobe, two terry-cloth bath towels, a toothbrush, a tube of toothpaste, a scentless stick deodorant, and a spare habit. Sisters these days could have other sorts of personal items—Stephen King novels and miniature cassette players with Beach Boys tapes were big—but no Sister would pack any such thing in a suitcase meant to be unpacked by another Sister. Sister Joan Esther had asked to be in charge of the unpacking. It was a good job for someone who wanted to be left strictly alone. Unfortunately, it was also going to be unutterably boring.

At one side of the foyer was a wide staircase, leading first to a landing and then to the second floor. Mother Mary Bellarmine was standing on the landing with her arms folded across her chest, looking down in disapproval. She had been there since just after Joan Esther had come in—it had to have been coincidence, in spite of the fact that Joan Esther kept feeling that it had been *meant*—and she was standing there still, not saying hello, not saying anything, just giving off a miasma of poison fog that filled the foyer and made Joan Esther's lungs feel ready to crack. Of course, Mother Mary Bellarmine didn't really give off a miasma of poison fog. Only the Devil could do that, assuming he existed. Joan Esther no longer found it easy to assume that he existed. She wondered if she ever had.

She counted up the suitcases—seventeen, two short—and then went back out the front door and down the steps to the convent station wagon that had picked her up at the airport. At the time, the station wagon had been driven by Sister Frances Charles, an impossibly cheerful young nun who talked nonstop about the wonderful spiritual healing that was going on in the battered women's shelter where she worked. Joan Esther had to bite her tongue to keep herself from asking if any healing of the nonspiritual kind was going on, like job training or help with Pennsylvania's notoriously convoluted human services system. Joan Esther had to bite her tongue a lot these days. It was a gift from God that Frances Charles hadn't been able to hang around to help after they'd come back to the convent. Frances Charles had breakfast duty. She had parked the station wagon in front of the front door and disappeared.

Joan Esther got the last two suitcases out of the backseat—they'd been shoved down to the floor and partially covered with the car's lap blanket; that was why she hadn't seen them—and dragged them back inside where they belonged. Once she was sure she had the whole lot, she could start dragging them up the stairs.

When she got back to the pile, Mother Mary Bellarmine was there, right next to the suitcases, down from her perch. Mother Mary Bellarmine had gone to a modified habit with the rest of them, back in 1975, but she always gave the impression that she was still clothed head to toe in robes. She always gave the impression that she was about to pronounce the death sentence on someone who deserved it. You.

Joan Esther got the list out of her pocket and began to check off oaktag tag names against it. Mother Mary Bellarmine stepped back a little. She had always been a thin woman. Now she looked skeletal. And very, very old.

"Well," she said, after a while. "You don't look any different. I thought Alaska would have changed you."

"Changed me into what?" Joan Esther said, to the suitcases, to the floor. She never looked at Mother Mary Bellarmine if she could help it. "I teach catechism to twelve-year-olds. I teach Catholic doctrine to potential converts. I teach the basics of prenatal nutrition to mothers who are interested. I'm not doing anything much different from what I was doing before I went to Alaska."

"When you were with me, you were teaching in a seminary," Mother Mary Bellarmine said. "And you were in California."

"I know you like California."

"You like California," Mother Mary Bellarmine said. "You did it to spite me. You did it to make me look bad with Reverend Mother General."

"I did it to get some peace and quiet." One of the tags was marked "The Gingerbread Lady." That would be old Sister Agnecita, who made gingerbread houses for the children's ward of the hospital in Fairbanks. Joan Esther hoped that none of the Sisters from Canada went in for things like that, because she didn't know any of the Sisters from Canada. She was just traveling with their luggage, which had turned out to be cheaper to send on ahead in bulk.

"The thing about Alaska," she said slowly, "is that everybody I meet up there knows what he's doing. Nobody is wandering around looking confused and trying to figure out what she's doing in a habit. And I like the bishop."

Mother Mary Bellarmine sniffed. "You did it to get away from me. You told Reverend Mother General you did it to get away from me. Moving away in the middle of the term like that. Giving me less than three days' notice."

"Of course I wanted to get away from you," Joan Esther said. "You were driving me crazy."

"I was trying to turn you into a nun. A nun, Sister. Not—whatever it is you girls are these days."

"I'm forty-two years old, Bellarmine. I'm hardly a girl."

"You're hardly a nun, either. You're soft, just like all the rest of them. You have no stamina."

"I had the stamina to put up with you for six years. Trust me, that was enough."

The Canadians had all been polite enough to mark their suitcases clearly. Now all Joan Esther had to do was get them upstairs to the hall where these women had been assigned, parcel the suitcases out to the correct rooms, and unpack. She had to get the suitcases upstairs and parceled out fairly quickly, but she had more than a week to get them unpacked. That was good. She'd leave them where she dumped them for today. Then she'd go find herself a little food.

Somewhere up above, what sounded like a heavy iron bell rang five times.

"That's the call to Mass," Mother Mary Bellarmine said. "In the old days, you'd have dropped whatever you were doing and gone immediately to church."

"These aren't the old days," Joan Esther said. "I can go to the twelve o'clock Mass."

"I wonder you go to any Mass. I wonder you bother to wear the habit. You don't believe in religious obedience anymore. I don't even think you believe in God."

"If you stand that close to the stairway, I'll knock you over going upstairs."

"You'll probably find some way to blame it on me, too. Going to Alaska. Leaving my house—my house—with less notice than I'd have a right to expect from a cleaning lady. Telling Reverend Mother General—"

"I told Reverend Mother General the truth," Joan Esther said. "I told her you were an evil old woman who was impossible to work for. Does that make you happy? It was three years ago, Mary Bellarmine. God didn't strike me dead and Reverend Mother General didn't relieve you from your post. It's over and done with. Let me by."

"If you really wanted to get by, you could go around me."

"So I could."

"You don't really want to get by me. You want to assassinate me. That's been your plan from the beginning."

The Gingerbread Lady's suitcase was heavier than the one in Joan Esther's other hand. Maybe the Gingerbread Lady had had the good grace to pack something interesting. Joan Esther backed up a little, the only way to get around Mother Mary Bellarmine without doing a complete circle of the suitcase pile. Assassination, for heaven's sake. Mother Mary Bellarmine had always been fond of self-dramatization.

From the bottom, the stairs looked endless, steep, and unforgiving. Joan Esther got a better grip on the suitcases she was carrying and started up.

"You'd better go to Mass," she said to Mother Mary Bellarmine. "It's halfway across campus, from what I saw on the map. You're going to be late."

"Maybe I ought to offer to help you with the bags."

Mother Mary Bellarmine had never offered to help anyone with anything, as far as Joan Esther knew. She didn't think there was any danger that Mother Mary Bellarmine would take up philanthropy now. Carrying the suitcases, she walked steadily up the steps to the landing, turned the corner and walked up some more. When she got to the second floor and out of sight of anyone in the foyer, she put the suitcases down and leaned against the wall.

It had been such a small incident, really, such a nothing, over before it had really begun—and three years ago on top of that. She had taken her stand and won. What more could she possibly want?

It was just that it seemed like a bad omen really, that the second person she should see at this convention would be Mother Mary Bellarmine.

She picked up the suitcases again and headed for the east-wing hall.

4

Sarabess Coltrane had come to that point in her life where she no longer trusted anyone who didn't snap to attention at the mere mention of the name of John Beresford Tipton. It was a very good point to come to, with advantages she would not have dreamed of at twenty, because it limited the number of men she had to talk to for longer than twenty minutes. Sarabess Coltrane didn't hate men. In Sarabess's metaphysically reconstructed universe, hatred was the inevitable waste product of late capitalism run amok. Sex was the perversion of love, what the market did to the deeply felt human need for a socialist reality. Love was the outpouring of the cosmic unconscious. Greed was a neurosis that would disappear with the abolition of property. It went on and on. Sarabess had gone to visit the revolution in Cuba just after Castro had come to power. She had been visiting revolutions ever since, from Chile to Nicaragua to Angola to El Salvador and back again. She had evolved—she was always evolving—from an unthinking species chauvinist in cow leather sandals to a friend of the earth in cotton espadrilles that always seemed to be unraveling into threads and leaving red dye stains on the bony tops of her feet. She had had a vision in the reeking communal kitchen of a Franciscan mission in San Luis Alazar that showed her the face and the magnificence of God. She had had the good luck to find this job in the Registrar's Office of St. Elizabeth's College. Her life was working out perfectly, really, in spite of the fact that the world didn't seem to make sense anymore. That was her Catholicism. Sarabess Coltrane believed that God was the engine of history that was driving the world inexorably in the direction of an international communitarian utopia. She was sure the gates of Hell would not prevail against it.

Sister Catherine Grace believed that God was a big white man with a beard who sat on clouds and looked after people's pet kittens—but Sarabess liked her anyway. Sister Catherine Grace couldn't be more than twenty-two years old—the one time Sarabess had mentioned it, Sister had guessed that John Beresford Tipton was a kind of tea—but she had enthusiasm and energy and, best of all, a big mouth. It was the one thing Sarabess didn't like about working at St. Elizabeth's, that the place was so well stocked with nuns. Most of the Orders Sarabess had come into contact with in South America had been hemorrhaging. It figured that this one, where the Sisters still wore habits and everything was so conservative, would have more nuns than they knew what to do with. The problem with conservative nuns was that they didn't talk, and if they didn't talk you never found out anything. With Sister Catherine Grace you found out everything, because she hadn't shut up since she opened her mouth and let out a wail in the delivery room.

Sister Catherine Grace was lettering a poster she was supposed to have finished the night before. Her veil was hoisted behind her shoulders so that it fell over the back of her chair. Sarabess was pretending to go through the files that had been taken out the day before but not put back where they belonged. The first thing she did every morning was return errant paper to its proper bureaucratic place. What Sarabess was really doing was trying not to look in the small wall mirror that sat above the grey metal file cabinet marked "Student Volunteers/Local Missions." It was ten minutes to nine on the morning of Monday, May 5, and Sarabess Coltrane had just become fifty years old.

The file on the top of the stack said "CCSW/ AHCWR," which meant it had to do with the Catholic

Commission on the Status of Women and their Ad Hoc
Committee on Women Religious. Sarabess tucked a
long lock of greying hair behind her ear and pushed
the file to the upper right hand corner of the desk.
That was another reason she didn't want to look into
the mirror. She had always worn her hair long, in spite
of the fact that it had never looked the way it was supposed to. It lay flat against her skull instead of springing out. Now she wondered if it just looked wrong on
a woman as old as she was. Maybe women of fifty
looked ludicrous in waist-length hair no matter what
their politics. Sarabess shifted in her seat and bit her
lip.

"Go back to the beginning," she said to Catherine
Grace. "Now, Joan Esther was in the same convent as
Sister Mary Bellarmine—"

"*Mother* Mary Bellarmine," Catherine Grace said automatically. "And you don't say they were in the same
convent. You say Joan Esther was a Sister in Mother
Mary Bellarmine's house. Anyway, Mother Mary Bellarmine has a great house, in California on the water
with beach all around it and not a lot of hard work to
do—I mean, they run a school but it's no problem—"

"I thought nuns were supposed to like problems,"
Sarabess said. "I thought of it for a while, you know.
Becoming a nun. Although I probably would have
gone to Maryknoll. I mean, the whole point seemed to
be giving service to the poor."

"Why didn't you go to Maryknoll?"

"I couldn't get past all this business of talking about
God as 'He.' I mean, Maryknoll's good, but even they
can't get rid of a Pope."

Catherine Grace finished painting in a stencil of the
letter *M* in red. "Sometimes I wonder why you want to
be a Catholic at all," she said. "You'd be so much more
comfortable in a Wicca church or the Movement Inter-
nationale or something."

"I'm reforming the Church from within," Sarabess
said virtuously.

"Whatever. Anyhow. Joan Esther got transferred out
to California to teach in a program we have there for

immigrants who want to learn English, and as soon as she got out there, Mother Mary Bellarmine started to drive her crazy."

"How?"

"Well," Catherine Grace said, "there was the business of the cold. Joan Esther caught cold on a weekend trip up into the hill country in northern California. So she called in sick and took to bed. And Mother Mary Bellarmine let her, but then she called every half hour to make sure Joan Esther was still in bed. Oh. There was the money for the birthday cake, too. Joan Esther has family out in Oregon or something and her brother came down to visit one Sunday and gave her fifty dollars. And she took the fifty dollars and had a birthday cake made for one of her students, this really old woman who had come out of Cambodia with one grandchild and everybody else in her family dead and Joan thought she needed to be cheered up—you see the kind of thing. Mother Mary Bellarmine had a conniption and a half, from what I've heard, ranting and raving about how that money rightfully belonged to the Order and it wasn't Joan Esther's place to decide what to do with it—"

"But I thought that was true." The next file on Sarabess's stack was the one for the Future Homemakers of America, which she was always tempted to lose. "I thought nuns held everything in common and nobody owned any property. . . . I thought that was what the vow of poverty was all about."

"It is. But even in the old days, Sisters sometimes received presents from their families and nobody screamed at them for not handing them over. And it isn't as if Joan Esther went off and bought herself a mink coat. She just gave a poor old lady a birthday party."

"Maybe the money would have been better used for a soup kitchen or something."

Catherine Grace snorted. "If it was up to Mary Bellarmine, it would have been used to buy new napkins for the refectory. Honestly, I don't know how that woman lasted in this Order. This is really a very sensible Order of nuns, you know. And nice, too."

"Oh, I know you're nice," Sarabess said.

"It just goes to show you how important it is, having a skill nobody else has. My mother used to tell me that all the time. Lisa Marie, she'd say—that was my name, Lisa Marie, me and fifteen million other girls born in the same year, you don't know how glad I was to get rid of it—anyway, on she'd go, about how in the kingdom of the blind the one-eyed man is king. Was your mother really into Elvis Presley when she was young? I think all the women of that generation were, and it's made them warped."

"Mmmm," Sarabess said. Actually, she'd been in to Elvis herself, when she was young, which all of a sudden seemed much too long ago to think about. She pitched the folder for St. Elizabeth's Theater into the pile at the exact center of the desk and said: "So what is it that Mother Mary Bellarmine has? Does she sing plain chant or pray in Aramaic or what?"

"She builds gymnasiums."

"What?"

"She builds gymnasiums," Catherine Grace repeated patiently. "She's built four—except one was an auditorium, I think, but it all comes down to the same thing. She's really good at figuring out financing and finding architects and scrutinizing budgets and all that sort of thing. I don't think she would have been appointed a Mother Provincial if she hadn't been. I mean, she's no good at managing people, is she?"

"I guess not," Sarabess said.

"She's looking over the deal for the new field house here while she's at the convention. I heard Sister Mary Rose and Sister Ann Robert talking about it at lunch yesterday."

"Did she build a gymnasium in California?"

"She built the entire convent. Raised the money for it and everything. Which is part of what makes it all so strange, if you see what I mean, that she'd be so upset about Joan Esther. I mean, Joan Esther decided to leave and made a big point of telling Reverend Mother

General that it was because Mother Mary Bellarmine
was such a pill, but so what? Joan Esther can't build
gymnasiums. It didn't get Mother Mary Bellarmine
into any trouble."

"Are you sure?"

"It didn't get her into any *real* trouble," Catherine
Grace said. "She's still in charge of the whole Southwestern Province. And it isn't Joan Esther who's being
asked to sit in on discussions with the cardinal."

"Maybe it's something personal," Sarabess said.

"Of course it's something personal." Catherine
Grace held the folder in the air and tilted her head.
Sarabess looked up and saw a picture of the Virgin
standing on an oversize rose and the words *May Is
Mary's Month.* "One of the kids in the nursery school
wanted the class to give presents to Mary on Mother's
Day," Catherine Grace said, "but that's Sister Barthol-
omew's operation and you know what Bart's like. Sensible to the death. I wonder why it is the only people
who become nursery-school teachers are the ones
who had their imaginations surgically removed at
birth."

"Maybe you ought to become a nursery-school
teacher and correct the problem."

"Maybe I ought to learn to stop procrastinating so
my posters will come out better. Is this too awful?"

"It's fine."

"If the Church had had to rely on me, the Sistine
ceiling would be full of stick figures."

If the Church had had to rely on me, the Sistine ceiling wouldn't exist at all, Sarabess thought—and then
stopped, because it suddenly all seemed so silly. The
stacks of files on her desk were listing. She put out her
hand and straightened the least stable one. She wondered what would happen if she told Catherine Grace
that it was her birthday and just how old she'd become. Instead, she tucked the file folders from the
stack she had mentally labeled "on-campus extracurricular organizations" under her arm and headed for
the file room.

"You know what Sister Thomasina was saying the

other day?" Catherine Grace called after her. "She was
saying it was all a plot. Somebody's rigged it so that
Mother Mary Bellarmine and that detective from Philadelphia are here at the same time, and then they're
going to bump off Mary Bellarmine because she
knows too much—"

"Knows too much about what?"

"About everything. I mean, she's been around forever, hasn't she? She's not just a pill. She's a pill with
experience. Anyway, they're going to bump her off and
use that detective as a beard, because if he can't solve
it nobody can, and it will be the perfect murder."

Sarabess pulled out the file drawer for "Camp Orgs
A-Ar" and said, "I think somebody tried that on him already. I think the guy got caught."

"Maybe the guy wasn't a Catholic. What do you
think? He is supposed to be an expert on murder."

"I think you're bored to tears in this job," Sarabess
said.

"Of course I am," Catherine Grace said, "but it's for
the greater glory of God."

Sarabess was about to answer that it was more likely
for the greater glory of the bunch of old white men
who ran the richest and most repressive religious organization on earth—but she stopped herself again,
just as she had with the comment about the Sistine
ceiling. She still had a stack of folders in her arms. She
went back to filing them, listening all the while to
Catherine Grace bustling around in the main office,
probably setting up to paint another poster. Sarabess
tried and failed to remember herself ever being that
uncomplicatedly happy, even as a tiny child.

It's just that I'm feeling very tired, she told herself,
putting the folder for the Victorian Society between
the ones for the Via Appia Eating Club and Vincent de
Paul, Friends of in the drawer marked "Camp Orgs
U-W." It's just that I'm feeling old and feeling old gets
me a little confused.

Actually, what feeling old really seemed to be doing
was giving her one of her periodic beef cravings, so
that all she could really think about was a Quarter

Pounder with cheese. Sarabess Coltrane was not doctrinaire. If she wanted a Quarter Pounder with cheese, she had one.

At the moment, she just wished that she could want a murder mystery instead.

5

Father Stephen Monaghan had always loved everything about being a priest, from the obligatory recitation of the Holy Office to the exaltation of celebrating Mass to the petty details of parish maintenance. He had loved it in the 1950s when he had entered the seminary and everybody seemed to be traveling in lockstep to a drummer pounding faintly against an ancient skin in Rome. He had loved it in the years since the Vatican Council seemed to have reduced everything to chaos and confusion. Father Stephen Monaghan had never been confused. Years ago, he had taken Holy Orders to serve God. He was still serving God. In the old days he had served God in a cassock. Lately he did it in Levi's 501 jeans. In the old days, it was the better part of pastoral care to seem to be an autocrat—even if, like Father Stephen, you had no talent for it. He had pretended to be an autocrat and further pretended not to notice that his parishioners were pretending right along with him. In the new days it was the better part of pastoral care to pretend to be a democrat. Father Stephen did that a little better than he had played the autocrat, but not much, and his parishioners were still pretending right along with him. It helped that most of his parishioners these days were nuns. Father Stephen Monaghan liked nuns. He liked modern nuns and traditional nuns, tall nuns and short nuns, old nuns and young nuns. They liked him back.

If there was one thing Father Stephen Monaghan came close to not liking, it was hearing confessions. Some priests didn't like hearing confessions because they thought it was boring. Others didn't like hearing confessions because it got them depressed. Father Stephen didn't dislike it, exactly, because it was so cen-

tral to the role of a Catholic priest and he loved being
a Catholic priest. It just made him uncomfortable.
Sometimes he told himself that this was humility. Too
many priests fell victim to the superiority complex en-
gendered by being put in a position where other people were obligated to reverence you, whether you
deserved it or not. Father Stephen Monaghan was
brought up short every time he had to listen to the
earnest struggles of men and women far more dedicated to the search for perfection than he could ever
be. This morning, he was listening to the struggles of
Sister Domenica Anne, a tall, forceful woman in her
late forties with a face like a Valkyrie and hands the
size of china saucers. He had known Sister Domenica
Anne for years, so he wasn't afraid of her. He had
known from the moment he met her that she was
more intelligent than he was, so he was used to it.
What he couldn't get used to was all this pacing that
went on now that most confessions took place outside
the old confessional box. Father Stephen Monaghan
hadn't been particularly enamored of the old confessional box, but he had to admit now that it had had its
advantages for the concentration. Sister Domenica
Anne kept bopping back and forth, back and forth,
with her arms wrapped across her chest and the veil of
her habit whipping in the wind. It was enough to make
a seasickness-susceptible man dizzy.

It was nine thirty on the morning of Monday, May 5,
and Father Stephen and Sister Domenica Anne had
been out here in the rose garden for over half an hour.
The rose garden always reminded Father Stephen of
the little patch of flowers his mother had grown every
spring in the fifteen-by-fifteen patch of green behind
the triple-decker house in New Haven where they had
rented the middle floor for all the years of his growing
up. Sister Domenica Anne's confession reminded him
of the three other confessions he had heard since just
after dinner last night. There are priests who belong to
religious orders or who are assigned to orders of nuns
on a regular basis. Father Stephen had only begun
shepherding religious women when he was sent to St.

Elizabeth's two years ago. He knew very little about religious orders or how they were run. He knew less about the interior lives of nuns. He was, however, a man of great common sense, and he had a hunch. There was about to be a great deal of trouble on the campus of St. Elizabeth's College.

Sister Domenica Anne had stopped her pacing momentarily. She had her back to the wind, so that her veil was blowing up behind one shoulder and the long skirt of her modified habit pressed against the backs of her legs. Father Stephen rubbed the side of his bulbous nose and wished he wouldn't think of her as a harbinger of the return of the Amazons. The Amazons would probably look like wimps next to Sister Domenica Anne.

"So the thing is," she was saying, "it's not the effect on the Cardinal I mind, because I think the Cardinal could use a little shaking up, I think they all could. But we're in the middle of an enormous project here, costing millions of dollars, and in spite of the fact that we're not a diocesan institution, we've had a lot of help from the Chancery. And I know I'm supposed to have patience, and charity—"

"You keep talking about how it's you who're supposed to have patience and charity," Father Stephen said. "You never mention Mother Mary Bellarmine. Isn't she also supposed to have patience and charity?"

"She isn't my problem."

"What?"

"Her patience and charity aren't my problem," Sister Domenica Anne said helplessly. Then she went back to pacing again. "Father, I know what you're trying to tell me. I know the woman is impossible. Everybody says the woman is impossible. But it's maddening. You think you have control of yourself—"

"Do any of us really have control of ourselves?"

"—you think you can at least be polite to people, and then, there it is, and you can't even figure out what happened. I mean that. There I am, standing in a hallway in full view of I don't know how many students, shouting at this woman, and I don't even know why. I don't know why. I don't know what she did. I'm beginning to think I'm losing my mind."

"How long has Mother Mary Bellarmine been here?"

"For about two days."

"How long is she expected to stay?"

"To the end of the convention, I think. I don't believe Reverend Mother General will need her beyond that."

"What does Reverend Mother General need her for?"

"Oh, to go over the budget for the new field house. Mary Bellarmine is good at that. She's good at running the whole operation, really, the fund-raising and all the rest of it. She's done it a dozen times. Maybe that's why Reverend Mother General had her come in early. So that she could give me some advice on what I'm supposed to do."

"You don't think you need advice on what you're supposed to do?"

"I think I need it desperately. I just categorically refuse to take it from that bitch."

There was a robin sitting on the perch of the birdhouse hanging in the tree branches above his head. Father Stephen Monaghan sighed a little and stretched his legs. He couldn't tell Domenica Anne anything about the other confessions he'd heard, of course, but he couldn't get them out of his mind. *Bitch* was actually one of the milder words the Sisters had been handing him to describe Mother Mary Bellarmine. Last night, a fluffy little old nun—physically ancient, fanatically conservative and almost pathologically repressed—had called the Mother Superior of the Southwestern Province "a world-class cunt." God only knew what kind of well-buried memory bank that had come out of.

Domenica Anne had stopped. She was looking at him expectantly, as if he held the secrets of the universe in the palm of his hand, or in the notes he wrote in the margins of thick books on theology he read when nobody wanted him for anything else. This was what Father Stephen didn't like about hearing confessions, this expectation that he knew what to do better than she did herself.

"Well," Father Stephen said, "I can see how you wouldn't want to lose control in front of your students. We could work on that."

"You don't think anger of this magnitude is a mortal sin?"

"Auschwitz was a mortal sin, Sister. The murder of Lisa Steinberg was a mortal sin. This is more in the line of justifiable homicide—and that does not mean I would condone—oh, never mind. I don't know what I'm talking about. How much longer do you personally have to work with Mother Mary Bellarmine?"

"Oh, I don't really have to work with her. She'll just be around on and off, if you know what I mean. And she's supposed to sit in on meetings."

"On many meetings?"

Domenica Anne considered this. "There's VTZ next week—"

"VTZ?"

"VTZ Corporation gave us most of the money to build the field house, Father. The wife of the founder is one of our alumnae. Actually, I shouldn't say they gave us the money, exactly. They gave us their services. They run a construction company, among other things."

"Among other things?"

"It's a kind of local conglomerate, if you see what I mean. They own a whole lot of different businesses. They'll build a lot of the field house for us and then write it off their income taxes."

"Ah, I see. So no VTZ, no field house."

"Exactly."

"So it would be a good thing for you to keep your temper in any meeting with VTZ executives in attendance."

"Exactly," Domenica Anne said again.

"Then let's work on that."

Domenica Anne blinked. It was so obviously not what she'd expected to hear. Father Stephen understood how she felt. In the old days, he'd never have said anything of the sort. He'd simply have told her to try to keep her temper and then given her an Our Father and five Hail Marys to say as penance. He would have done it in spite of the fact that she hadn't committed any sin that needed to be forgiven. Now he was supposed to provide some real help with her problem, and he was trying.

Actually, the person he'd really like to provide help for was Mother Mary Bellarmine herself, but she hadn't come to see him, and he didn't think she would. It was one of the sad truths of religion that the people who needed it most never came looking for it. It was one of the hallmarks of sin that the world's greatest sinners often thought of themselves as the world's greatest saints.

Saints or sinners, all these confessions about Mother Mary Bellarmine were beginning to make him nervous, and Father Stephen Monaghan didn't like to be nervous.

They're all closed up in here, he thought, looking around the rose garden as Sister Domenica Anne went on pacing. They're all shut up in here together. It can't be a good way to live.

"I keep trying to think of some way to ship her out of here and back to California," Sister Domenica Anne said, stopping at the side of an overgrown bush that seemed to be growing thorns for Sleeping Beauty's castle. "If I could just find some way to get rid of her, I could finally relax."

And that, Father Stephen Monaghan thought, was precisely the sort of thing that made him jumpy.

6

Nancy Callahan Hare liked to tell people that all the girls she'd ever known who'd gone to convent schools had turned out wild, and although that wasn't true—most of the girls Nancy had been with at Sacred Heart and St. Elizabeth's had degenerated into bright-eyed country club wives with three children each in private

schools and a seat on the parish advisory board—most
of the people she knew weren't Catholic, and it worked
out anyway. It at least made a stab at explaining Nancy
herself, who was thoroughly inexplicable otherwise in
the circles in which she moved. The circles in which
Nancy Hare moved had a lot of money, a lot of cosmetic surgery and a fair number of lifetime subscrip-
tions to Paris *Vogue*. They did not have much of
anything else, which made their situation a little am-
biguous in Philadelphia, which was a city that believed
in *old* money. The age of money was not something
Nancy worried about herself. She'd always been an
outsider in Philadelphia. When she was growing up, it
was enough to be Catholic and Irish to be beyond the
pale. She was perfectly happy to have no social cachet
at all, as long as she had money to spend and younger
men to go to bed with.

The young man Nancy had gone to bed with the
night before—that would have been May 4—was a tennis pro at the club her husband had founded with four
other men, when all five of them had been turned
down at every established club on the Main Line. The
new club was shinier and larger and better equipped
than the old ones could ever hope to be, and in no
time at all it had become almost as difficult to get into.
The tennis pro was named Barry Something and on
"sabbatical" from Yale, from which Nancy inferred that
he'd been asked to take a year off and get his act together. Whether this had been caused by too many
drugs or too little studying she neither knew nor
cared. The young man she was going to go to bed with
right this minute—at quarter to ten on the morning of
May 5—was of much more interest to her at the moment. His name was Mark Something and he worked
in a bookstore in downtown Philadelphia. He was supposed to be a novelist, but Nancy had met twenty-two-
year-old novelists before. She had met painters and
poets and composers and musicians before, too. If they
were serious they took off for New York or California.
If they stayed in Philadelphia they were going nowhere fast. Nancy preferred the ones who were going

nowhere. Her husband was going somewhere, and what that meant was perpetual impotence and a head full of calculations and the instructions for hiring a taxi in Riyadh.

Mark had a one-room apartment in a tall grey building within walking distance of Society Hill, with a couch that folded out and a narrow sink full of dirty dishes. He had a boom box the size of Dallas propped up against a found-art coffee table that was pulsing out the last few minutes of Good Old Cultural Norm. Nancy knew Good Old Cultural Norm very well, although not as well as Good Old Cultural Norm had wanted to know her, and the sound of that oily voice bashing the Japanese made her head ache. Nancy was very careful not to allow herself to get headaches, just as she was very careful not to allow herself to smile too much or frown too much or move around too vigorously when she wasn't exercising. She'd had very bad luck with her genetic inheritance. She was only forty-five years old and she'd already had three face-lifts. She'd had breast implants, too, and liposuction. She'd had a nose job when she was fifteen and her teeth capped when she was twenty. She was a very expensive work of art from one end to the other, and she didn't like wrecking herself on the adolescent inanities of Norman Kevic.

What she did like was Mark, and this thing she had thought up with whipped cream. It had taken her a long time to think up this thing with whipped cream, and she was a little proud of herself. Nobody she hadn't told would ever guess that she'd spent so many years at school with the nuns, or that she was even now heavily involved with the alumnae association of her old college, which was forever sponsoring seminars on things like "The Virtuous Woman: Who She Is and How to Become Her." When people asked, Nancy always said her husband insisted. She was supposed to be involved with something that would get her name in the papers and look good in the company prospectus they sent out every year to stockholders and members of the board.

The thing with whipped cream required fourteen pressurized cans of Reddi Wip and six jars of cherries. Mark had bought them and spread them out on his kitchen table, which was a *kitchen* table only by virtue of being shoved off into the corner nearest the half-size stove. Mark was standing at attention next to the trove, looking very proud of himself. Mark was always proud of himself. That was part of what Nancy wanted him for.

What Nancy Hare did not want him for was sex. Nancy Hare did not like sex. She had never liked sex. She was never going to like sex. She engaged in a great deal of it, but that was only because everyone expected her to. If she could have gotten a reputation for being intensely desirable by standing on her head in front of the Liberty Bell, she would have done that.

She took off her sunglasses—she always wore sunglasses, even in winter—and cast a jaundiced eye at the boom box. Cultural Norm was just gearing up for a new assault on all things Japanese. What he had against the Japanese was beyond Nancy's comprehension. Mark saw where she was looking and didn't even have the grace to blush.

"I've been listening to him all morning," he said. "He's been talking about that thing you're involved with. The nun's convention."

"I'm not involved with any nun's convention," Nancy said.

"The thing at the college," Mark told her, speaking very slowly, as if he were talking to an idiot. It was one of his least endearing traits, this fantasy of his that he was brighter than she was.

She picked up one of the cans of Reddi Wip and shook it. "I'm not involved with it," she said. "It's VTZ that's involved in it. I have a place on this committee I never go to except to get photographed for the papers and then I have to show up for a party next week and smile a lot for the Sisters. It's all got something to do with business."

"How could a convention in a convent have something to do with business?"

Nancy shrugged. "Come to the bathroom with me. Were you good? Did you clean out the tub?"

"I got this woman I know to clean it out for me. I'm no good at cleaning things out."

Nancy thought he'd get good at cleaning things out if he had to live for a while with the results of not being good at it, and then she thought this woman must have a very interesting place in Mark's life. She pushed open the door of the bathroom and decided she didn't care, because the bathtub really was cleaned out and it probably wouldn't have been if Mark had stuck to doing it himself. If this worked out she thought she would take him with her to Le Bourget, which was the restaurant all her friends were taking their lovers to lately, and where she had made it a point never to appear twice with the same man. Mark would look good in a suit and a tie and when he talked he would be almost presentable.

"The thing is," she said, "you've got to get into the tub first with your clothes off, and then you've got to wait."

"Are you going to take pictures?"

"Of course I'm not going to take pictures."

"I think it's too bad you're not involved in this nun thing," he said. "It sounds interesting. Hundreds of nuns in one place. Maybe thousands. How are regular people ever going to tell them all apart?"

"Take your clothes off."

"I'm taking my clothes off, for God's sake. I'm just making conversation. What's the matter, dealing with a bunch of nuns gets you spooked?"

"Of course nuns don't get me spooked. I just don't want to talk about them. Why should I? A bunch of homely women who work off their frustrations telling themselves that they're in love with God. I don't believe in God."

"Do you believe in Hell?"

"I believe Hell would be having to spend the rest of my life with those women in that convent," Nancy said. "Now take your clothes off. Norm's just doing his usual bit for employee relations. The boss is supporting the Sisters of Divine Grace, so Norm is making fun of them."

Mark looked startled. "VTZ owns that station? I didn't know that."

"I don't know why you didn't. It's announced practically every half-hour along with the call signal. It isn't a secret."

"I'm not saying it was a secret. I'm saying I didn't know."

"Lie out flat on your back," Nancy said, "and stick your legs up over the rim on this end. Don't fold them. Right. You look very cute."

Mark snorted, but he did what she'd told him to do. He unfolded his legs and lay as straight out as he could in the shortish tub. It was the old claw-footed kind and built for someone much smaller. Mark was six feet two and broad. Nancy waited until he had adjusted himself to her satisfaction, then shook the can of Reddi Wip hard. When she set it off against his belly button, it made a sound like a rocket going off.

"Jesus Christ," Mark said. "That's cold as Hell."

"I'll bring a bunch of cans in this time," Nancy said, walking out on him.

He called after her, "I hope you know what you're doing."

Nancy went back to the kitchen table and began to tuck cans into her arms against her chest. On the other side of the room, the boom box was pounding out Norm's closing theme and being overridden every fifteen seconds by Norm's voice telling another juvenile joke. "What did the Japanese trade minister do when he got to Heaven? Looked out over the angels at work and said, 'The Japanese are more industrious than you.'" "What's the difference between a Japanese teenager and an American teenager? The American teenager doesn't need someone to wind him up in the morning." Nancy made a face at the boom box and headed back to the bathroom.

"Here I come," she called out as she came in, to find the whipped cream beginning to melt against the heat of Mark's skin. "Norm is just going off the air. How can you listen to that idiot is beyond me."

"How you can be married to the idiot you're married to is beyond me. You want to explain that one to me again?"

"It wouldn't matter how many times I explained it. You'd still be too young for me no matter what I did about it. Stop eating the whipped cream."

"I'd rather eat you."

"We'll get around to that later."

"Is your husband going to be back in time to take you to this party you say you've got to go to at the convent?"

"Of course he is. If he wasn't, I wouldn't bother to go."

"If he wasn't, maybe you could take me. I'd love to go."

Nancy waved this away, and started on another can of whipped cream. Nuns. Husbands. Whipped cream. Mark. Under her picture in the high-school yearbook were the words "Nancy's Greatest Ambition: Never To Be A Housewife." She didn't know if she'd made it or not.

She did know that she was sick and tired of hearing about those damned nuns. She'd been sick and tired of hearing about nuns all her life. Ever since her much-older half-sister Megan departed for the Mesdames of the Sacred Heart, Nancy had been getting chapter and verse on how wonderful it was to be a perpetual virgin.

In spite of the fact that sex hadn't turned out to be anything like what she'd expected, Nancy Hare still thought nuns were nothing but trouble.

7

There was a statue of St. Catherine of Siena at the bottom of the rose marble steps leading to the Sisters' Chapel. St. Catherine had a book in her hand and the cap of a Doctor of the Church on her head, perched above the veil of her habit. Mother Mary Bellarmine didn't remember which Order St. Catherine had be-

longed to—she kept thinking it was the Carmelites
and then changing her mind, because Teresa of Avila
had been a Carmelite—but she did know that this
Catherine was not her kind of saint, and never would
be. Mother Mary Bellarmine didn't like intellectual
women, or hysterical ones either, and Catherine had
been both. Mother Mary Bellarmine also didn't like
the Spanish. Sometimes she wondered if there was
something in the air over there that made women join
orders to have visions and live on nothing but the Eu-
charist. Sometimes she wondered if there was something in the air over there that made people stupid in
a more general way. The Good Lord only knew, she
had never met a Spaniard with an ounce of sense.

She stopped at the statue of St. Catherine, looked up
into its face, and shook her head. The doctor's cap
looked pasted on—as it probably had been, in the
1960s or the 1970s when Catherine had been granted
her honor. It was five minutes after ten in the morning
and Mother Mary Bellarmine was at loose ends. It annoyed her. In the old days, ends were never loose.
There were strict schedules governing every moment
of life from rising at four for office to going to sleep at
ten after Compline. In the house she ran in California,
life was almost as well regulated. She couldn't get
away with four in the morning or ten at night—the
new young nuns would have staged a mutiny; they
were impossible these days; they had no sense of religious obedience—but she made it a point to require all
her Sisters to be present at prayers and meals, to walk
in lines when they were all together, to be accompa-
nied by another Sister any time they left the convent
grounds. There were complaints, and Mother Mary
Bellarmine knew it. Reverend Mother General wrote
her a letter at least once a year suggesting that she relax a little. Mother Mary Bellarmine had never relaxed
for a minute in her adult life. She didn't intend to start
now.

The Sisters' chapel was right next door to the Administration Building, exhibiting the kind of simile in
stone that made Mother Mary Bellarmine feel pleased

that the world was such a logical and well-ordered place. The Sisters' Chapel was old, college gothic complete with battlements, as if the good Sisters of Divine Grace would someday be forced to defend themselves by pouring boiling oil on the heads of rampaging peasants. The Administration Building was made of brick and as modern as one of Frank Lloyd Wright's nightmares. Mother Mary Bellarmine could see through the broad front windows on the first floor to a room of women working at computer stations. Unlike a lot of older nuns in the Order, Mother Mary Bellarmine knew a great deal about computers. She had made herself know. As soon as the first one arrived in her house she had seen that it would change the balance of power forever.

Years ago, when Mother Mary Bellarmine was still a small child named Lucy Deegan growing up in Fresno, California, her mother had told her the story of Fatima, when the Virgin came down on a cloud and spoke to three small children in a field in Portugal. She had gone out into her backyard and waited there for a vision, waited and waited, for weeks while nothing came. When she finally got around to entering the convent, she told that story as anecdotal proof of the reality of her vocation, but she left out the ending, which she knew would disqualify her forever. When the Virgin had failed to appear to Lucy Deegan, Lucy Deegan had decided that there was no Virgin to appear. Religion had never been what Lucy Deegan—or Mother Mary Bellarmine—entered the convent for. In these days of short habits and women astrophysicists, she might never have joined the Order at all. But she probably would have. She'd never been much of a feminist, and career advancement had never been the point.

Mother Mary Bellarmine stopped at the directory just inside the front door of the Administration Building and read: "Registrar's Office, G42." The Registrar's Office would be on this floor, the ground floor, in room 42. Mother Mary Bellarmine looked around her and found rooms 4 and 6. She went farther down the central hall looking to her right and left at rooms 10, 12, and 14. She came to an elaborate intersection and read the directional signs, which seemed to indicate less than exemplary planning on the room numberer's part. Rooms 24 to 66 and 91 to 95 could be reached by turning right. Rooms 29 to 41 and 72 to 94 could be reached by turning left. Since there was nowhere else to go, Mother Mary Bellarmine went straight, watching the numbers on the doors she passed jump around in no discernable order.

Room 42 turned out to be the one at the very end of this hall. It took up what had been intended as three separate rooms and, therefore, sat behind three separate doors, only the last of which was marked. Since the doors on the other side of the corridor were not numbered in the forties, Mother Mary Bellarmine had almost turned around and headed back for the directory. If she had, she would have been in a thoroughly foul mood by the time she actually found the room she was looking for. She was in a thoroughly foul mood now. She let herself in the door at the end of the hall and walked up to the gate that separated the tiny waiting area from the row after row of women typing at desks. Some of them had actual typewriters, but most of them were working at the ubiquitous IBM Workstations, tapping keyboards and peering at screens. It was the sort of scene that annoyed Mother Mary Bellarmine no end, because it all looked so space age while being so firmly grounded in the era of quill pens. Mother Mary Bellarmine had no doubt whatsoever that these women went home and peered anxiously at the astrological charts in their newspapers, thinking the predictions made sense.

The new habits weren't as good as the old ones for instilling fear into the hearts of silly women, but they were better than no habits at all. Mother Mary Bellarmine stood at her straightest, made her right hand into a fist and pounded on the countertop. If this had been her operation, there would have been a bell for supplicants to ring. The pounding got the attention of a youngish-looking woman at the one desk set apart from the others, and she frowned. Mother Mary Bellarmine was glad to see her. Every once in a while, Mother ran into an office manager of the old school, grey-haired, steely-eyed, single-minded, and packaged into an armored bra and a suit that had emerged into usefulness when Worth was still a boy. There was no telling how encounters with people like that would go. This woman, though, with her fussiness and her slightly desperate air of wanting to be taken for less than forty—this woman would be a piece of cake. Mother Mary Bellarmine planted the palms of her hands on the counter and waited.

The youngish woman stood up, hesitated, shifted back and forth on her feet, looked at the papers on her desk, looked up at Mother Mary Bellarmine, and seemed to shudder. Mother Mary Bellarmine went on staring at her, as if she were the offending statue of St. Catherine in front of the Sisters' Chapel. The youngish woman took a deep breath and tried to compromise.

"Yes?" she said. "Sister? Can I help you?"

"You can come over here," Mother Mary Bellarmine said. "Where I can hear you without straining my ears and talk to you without shouting. What is your name?"

The youngish woman looked back at the papers on her desk again, seemed to sigh, and then began moving toward the counter. "I'm Mrs. Hobart," she said, hesitating a little on the "Mrs.," as if she'd wanted to use "Ms." and thought better of it. Mother Mary Bellarmine shot a quick look at the fourth finger of her left hand and found no ring there. Mrs. Hobart saw Mother Mary Bellarmine look and hastily shoved the hand into the pocket of her skirt.

"I'm Mother Mary Bellarmine," Mother Mary Bellarmine said. "I've come for the records of Elizabeth Johns. She may be listed as Sister Joan Esther. She joined the Order about twenty years ago."

"Twenty years ago?"

"Eighteen. Sixteen." Mother Mary Bellarmine waved this away. "She finished her college education and came up to Maryville. While she was here she was still Elizabeth Johns. *That* would have been twenty years ago. You do keep records for twenty years?"

"Of course we do."

Mother Mary Bellarmine knew they did. She knew that St. Elizabeth's kept records for longer than that. There were boxes in the basement of the college convent with paper going back to 1896. Every once in a while, the Order's newsletter did a piece on it, as if anyone really cared what happened to a lot of silly college girls at the end of the nineteenth century. The Order's newsletter was called *Friends in Divine Grace*. It drove Mother Mary Bellarmine to distraction.

"Records," Mother Mary Bellarmine repeated, refusing to let her mind be sidetracked by trivialities. "Academic records and social records. For Elizabeth Johns. Class of—I don't know what she was the class of. You'll have to run that through the computer."

"I don't know if we have that on the computer," Mrs. Hobart protested. "And even if we have it, I don't know that we can give it to you—"

"Of course you can give it to me. I'm Mother Superior of the entire Southwestern Province."

"Well, yes, Mother, but you see—"

"And Elizabeth Johns is a Sister now, as I told you. Sister Joan Esther."

"Yes, Mother, I understand that, but—"

"And I don't really have a lot of time to waste. I've wasted far more of it than I should have already. I want those records and I want them immediately. I need to look over them when I go back to the convent."

"But Mother—"

"You shouldn't wear that particular shade of lavender," Mother Mary Bellarmine said. "It makes you seem as if you're trying to look young. You're not young. You're a middle-aged woman and you look it."

Mother Mary Bellarmine had made an art form of creating moments like this, moments when the sudden absoluteness of silence made it clear that people who had not been supposed to be listening had in fact been listening, moments when the psychic electricity went so high it was impossible to ignore the fact that a humiliation had just taken place in public. Mrs. Hobart's neck went as red as frozen carrots and the redness began to spread. It washed up over her chin and into her cheeks. Her eyes seemed to get twice as large and very wet. Mother Mary Bellarmine actually thought she was going to cry.

Mrs. Hobart did not cry. She put her hands together as if she were praying. She stood very, very still. A breeze came in through an open window somewhere and ruffled the jaunty little bow on her jaunty little lavender blouse. Mother Mary Bellarmine finally remembered what Mrs. Hobart reminded her of: the models in *Seventeen* magazine, circa 1964, who always came with everything matched.

Mother Mary Bellarmine cleared her throat. "Excuse me," she said. "I came for some records."

"Yes," Mrs. Hobart said.

"I really have to have them right away. I've got work to do."

"Of course," Mrs. Hobart said.

"Can you get them for me now."

Mrs. Hobart turned around and looked at the other women in the room. The moment had passed. They were all bent over their work, concentrating too hard, to make up for their recent un-Christian curiosity about somebody else's pain. Mrs. Hobart winced at the sight of them.

"Debbie," she said after a while. "Debbie Gross. She can get you what you need."

A very young woman stood up from a Workstation in the front row, looking frightened. Mrs. Hobart motioned her forward and she came.

"Debbie Gross," Mrs. Hobart said again. "This is Sister—"

"Mother Mary Bellarmine," Mother Mary Bellarmine said.

"Mother Mary Bellarmine," Mrs. Hobart repeated. "Yes. Well. I think I'll go back to my desk. I do have the midterm reports to coordinate. Mother Mary Bellarmine. Give Mother the information she needs, Debbie."

"Of course," Debbie said.

"Yes," Mrs. Hobart said again.

Mrs. Hobart drifted back to her desk. Mother Mary Bellarmine watched her go. Then she turned her attention to Debbie Gross, who had gone from looking frightened to looking terrified. Mother Mary Bellarmine took an inventory: skirt too short, hair too long, makeup too thick. Back in the days when Mother Mary Bellarmine was teaching parish school, she'd had a hundred girls just like Debbie Gross. She knew what to do with them.

"Miss Gross," she said. "I need the records on a woman named Elizabeth Johns, who was a student here about twenty years ago. She might be listed under Sister Joan Esther, since she later joined the Sisters of Divine Grace. I told all that to Mrs. Hobart. Did you hear me?"

"I heard some of it," Debbie said faintly.

"Now you've heard all of it," Mother Mary Bellarmine said. "Get me what I need, please. At that point we can discuss your views on artificial birth control."

"What?" Debbie Gross said.

"Artificial birth control," Mother Mary Bellarmine repeated.

Debbie Gross stood up a little straighter and announced, "I am a Jew."

A moment later, Debbie was walking away between the rows of computer stations and Mother Mary Bellarmine was contemplating her second attack, which wasn't obvious but which she knew would come to her soon. It always did. There had been only one woman in her entire life who had been immune from her methods, and that had been Joan Esther. Which was why she was looking for Joan Esther's records now.

Exactly what she would do with Joan Esther's records once she had them, she didn't know, but she was sure that would come to her, too.

There were Sisters in the Order who had a talent for art and others who had a talent for music. Mother Mary Bellarmine had a talent for the clandestine.

She tried to keep it oiled and well.

8

For Norman Kevic, the only thing on earth that needed to be kept oiled and well was himself, and he worked at that, assiduously, until he sometimes thought he didn't do anything else. It was now quarter after ten on the morning of Monday, May 5, and he was exhausted. The show was over and so was his mind, as far as he could tell, drifting out to Venus somewhere and communing with space aliens. Norm had some cocaine in his pocket—usually he was careful not to bring that stuff into the studio; carrying cocaine was a felony in Pennsylvania and he was part-owner of this station; nobody who had been convicted of a felony could own any part at all of a broadcast station—but he had been so bombed out when he came in today he had forgotten all about it. Now he wondered if he ought to find out how much he had and use it, for medicinal purposes only, just to get himself moving in the direction of home. One of the nicer things about being the hottest talk show radio host in the Philadelphia ADI and part-owner of one of the most lucrative radio stations and the man most wanted for supermarket promotions and local people profiles was that he could afford a very nice place, a big house out in Radnor with a swimming pool and three tennis courts and a maid's room that almost never had a maid in it, because Norm couldn't keep help. Actually, Norm didn't blame the help for leaving. His houseboys were offended by his ethnic jokes. Even Norm himself was sometimes offended by his ethnic jokes. His maids had all been intensely Catholic and afraid for their virginity in the onslaught of propositions he unleashed whenever he'd been snorting and drinking at the same time. Norm always wanted to tell them they had nothing to worry about—when he was all hyped up he couldn't get stiff if his life depended on it—but it was too embarrassing to mention and he preferred the reputation he had for being a lecher and a prick and a devotee of sexual harassment. That was how he had approached the Thomas/Hill hearings on the show—as an opportunity to treat sexual harassment as an art form. It had been one of his better brainstorms. By the second day of the hearings, so many people had been trying to call the show to tell him off, the phone lines were jammed and nobody could get through at all. He'd ended up doing it stream-of-consciousness and getting his third warning from the FCC about "borderline language."

Actually, Norman Kevic lived a borderline life and he knew it. He was lying here on the couch in his office because he didn't want to go home, and the exhaustion simply gave him a good excuse. His house was too big and too empty. Because he was who and what he was, he got a lot of sex. It had been years since he had a real relationship, with a woman who would talk to him and be there when he wanted company but didn't want a party. Nice women never liked him for long, and he didn't blame them any more than he blamed his maids. His mouth started running and he just couldn't make it stop. His nerves got to tingling and his body revved up and his mind shifted into high gear and it was all over, nobody could talk to him, nobody to slow him down, he was out and about and on another rampage.

Right now, he was in the middle of another collapse. As soon as the show was over, he had come in here and laid himself out. He wouldn't be able to get up again for hours unless he made an effort at it, which he did not intend to do. He let his hand drop to the carpet and felt around on the floor for his buzzer. It was the kind of buzzer patients are given in hospitals so they can call a nurse. Norm pressed down on it three or four times and then let it drop.

In no time at all, there were footsteps in the hallway outside, sharp little cracks that spoke of stiletto heels on engineered parquet. Norm considered opening his fly and decided against it. Stiletto heels meant Julia Stern, and Julia Stern had no use for him at all. For a while, Norm had taken to insisting on having his buzzer answered only by the women he wanted it answered by, but it hadn't worked out in the long run.

The women he wanted hadn't wanted him and had had a tendency to quit when they were forced to deal with him on a regular basis. There were other things he wanted from his partners and the general manager that trading this sort of favor for was an easy way to get. Julia Stern didn't like him, but she was efficient, and he could use a little efficiency for a time.

The stiletto heels stopped just outside the door. The doorknob turned and the door opened. Julia Stern was a woman in her twenties with too much hair piled too high on her head and too much flab around the middle. Norm wondered what it was like, being a woman this homely and knowing that you were homely. He wondered that about a lot of women, and then sat back in astonishment as they each and every one of them got married and settled down to have a passel of kids. They always married just the sort of men Norm thought would be more interested in someone who looked like Melanie Griffith.

Julia Stern was wearing a short black leather skirt cut halfway up her thigh and a long cotton sweater that reached nearly to the skirt's hem. Norm wondered why it was that heavy young women were always so eager to show off their legs. Julia Stern was chewing gum.

"You buzzed," she said. "I *presume* that means you want something."

"Breakfast," Norm said solemnly.

"What kind of breakfast? Ham and eggs? Pancakes and syrup? Didn't you have breakfast before?"

Norm couldn't remember if he'd had breakfast before or not. The idea of ham and eggs made him ill. The idea of pancakes and syrup made him feel he was suffocating in maple.

"I want three large glasses of orange juice and a pot of coffee," he said. "I think I've got the orange juice in the refrigerator downstairs. I'm dehydrated."

"Right," Julia Stern said.

"Go get him something to eat," the voice of Steve Harald said, booming into the room from the hall. "I've got to talk to him and I want him sober."

Julia Stern made a face and turned away, muttering something under her breath that was probably subversive. Norm paid no attention. If he paid attention to every subversive thing every member of his staff ever said, he wouldn't have any staff. Once the doorway was clear, it was filled with the form of Steve Harald, who was tall and thin and fashionable and the station manager. Norm was almost as curious about him as he was about homely women. When Norm was in high school, it was always people like Steve Harald who were the most important ones, the ones who got elected to things, the ones whose yearbook prophecies were solemn predictions of future success instead of jokey references to adolescent embarrassments. Norm's yearbook prophecy had read "Most likely to be eating a Hostess Twinkie when the world ends."

And yet here they were.

Steve was the station manager, with a salary but no stake in the enterprise, with three thousand square feet in Paoli and his kids in public schools.

Norm was the star with a piece of the action.

Was any of this supposed to make any sense?

Steve leaned against the doorjamb and said, "Fifteen Japanese jokes an hour. I counted them."

"I didn't know I was being that predictable."

"I averaged them. All that crap about the fugu."

"Well, Steve, you have to admit it's pretty weird. Eating a fish that can kill you if you look at it sideways and getting a kick out of putting your life in danger."

"That's not why they do it."

"How the Hell do you know why they do anything?"

"I know why *you* do things, Norm, and I'm telling you it's got to stop. It's really got to stop. We're in mucho trouble with the Japanese-American community as it is. We're going to be in trouble with the FCC before you know it."

"No we're not," Norm said. "It comes under the First Amendment. You know that."

"I know that these are perfectly tasteless jokes with no point to them at all. This is not Detroit. Japan bashing does not go over big here. If you have to get this out of your system, do a show."

Do a show, Norm thought. The room was looking a little fuzzy. The room had been looking a little fuzzy all along, of course, but the quality of it had changed now, it had become tinged with red, and for a moment Norm thought he was having a vision of Hell. Hell was just the way he had always been told it would be, full of red flames and grinning Devils. Then the Devils turned into pink-cheeked troll dolls with neon orange hair.

"Steve?" he said.

"What is it?"

"You know that party I'm supposed to go to, the one for the nuns' convention?"

"Yeah."

"Is anybody else from the station going to be there?"

"Nobody else from the station, as far as I know. Henry Hare is going to be there from VTZ. It was in the press release your own people put out."

"Yeah."

"You can't remember anything anymore."

"Yeah. Listen, Steve. Are you Catholic?"

"Nope. I think my grandparents were Lutheran. My parents weren't anything in particular."

"I'm Catholic."

"I know."

"I just keep thinking about it, you know. A big room full of nuns like that. Thousands of nuns all in the same place."

"So what?"

"So nuns are trouble," Norman Kevic said. "Nuns have always been trouble. They're bad luck if they aren't anything else, and you can't control them. And I keep thinking—you know who else is going to be at that party?"

"No."

"Gregor Demarkian. The name mean anything to you?"

Steve Harald hesitated. Norm waited expectantly. He had always suspected Steve of being functionally oblivious—of paying no attention to anything that didn't relate directly to his job at the station—and now Norm was sure of it.

"Gregor Demarkian," Norm said, "is the guy who does murders. The one the *Philadelphia Inquirer* calls 'the Armenian-American Hercule Poirot.'"

"Oh," Steve said.

"Never mind," Norm said. "But I keep thinking about it, if you know what I mean. I keep thinking about the world's most famous consultant on murder being right there in the middle of all those nuns, and what we could do with that. I hate nuns."

"You've said that," Steve said.

Actually he hadn't, but he'd probably implied it, so Norm decided to let it go. The sound of stiletto heels told him that Julia was coming back. He sat up a little on the couch and got ready to throw a hurricane of orange juice down his throat.

"There was a murder in the Motherhouse of their convent a little while ago," Norm said musingly. "I remember reading about it. Demarkian was in on it."

"On the murder?"

"On the investigation. I wonder what we could make of it."

"Don't make anything of it," Steve said. "You're in enough hot water with the Japanese. All you have to do is insult Henry's wife's alma mater or her best-remembered nun teacher or what the Hell. You may be part-owner of the station, but Henry is still chairman of the board."

And Henry's wife is a little slut with an appetite for nymphomania, Norm thought, but he didn't say it, because it wouldn't have come as news to anybody and there was no point. Besides, Julia really was there, right behind Steve, carrying a plastic tray from the cafeteria. The tray was covered with glasses of juice and cups of coffee and little bowls full of sugar and creamer. Julia hadn't been taking any chances.

Steve stood aside to let Julia through. Norm held out his hands for the tray.

"I hate nuns," Norm said. "I hate them more than I hate the Japanese. At least the Japanese don't think they've got a pipeline right up through the stratosphere to God."

PART 1

CHAPTER 1

1

There was a hand-lettered cardboard sign hanging in the display window of Ohanian's Middle Eastern Food Store, and every time Gregor Demarkian passed it he wondered if there was something about being Armenian that made people a little cracked. Then he thought of the most cracked person he knew—who happened to be a white Anglo-Saxon Protestant named Bennis Hannaford—and decided it wasn't worth worrying about. It was Sunday, the eleventh of May, a bright hot day at the beginning of what promised to be a glorious spring. Gregor Demarkian had spent twenty years of his life with the Federal Bureau of Investigation, ten of them with the Department of Behavioral Sciences. The Department of Behavioral Sciences was that division of the Bureau that helped local police forces coordinate national hunts for serial killers. Gregor had founded it but not named it, the name having been visited on him and all the agents he worked with by some second assistant bureaucrat who had had friends in Congress so long he had lost the knack of speaking English. Bright spring days while he had still been with the division had not been happy. Psychopaths responded to a warming of the weather just like anybody else. When the sun started to gleam, Dagwood Bumstead took his family to the beach and the local nutcase took his victim to a wooded hillside ten miles out of town. Or somewhere. Gregor Demarkian had started his career with the Bureau swearing he was never going to retire. He had ended it at the beginning of his wife's last painful year of battling with cancer. He had never looked back. In the midst of Elizabeth's dying, it had been hard for him to recognize how he'd come to feel about his job—it had been hard to remember he'd ever had a job—but in the years since, he'd been unable to avoid it. By the time Gregor Demarkian had left the Federal Bureau of Investigation, he had come to hate his work with a passion.

The sign in the display window of Ohanian's Middle Eastern Food Store said:

IN FOR MOTHER'S DAY—
HEART-SHAPED HONEY CAKES WITH
GRANNY GLASSES.

Underneath it was a heart-shaped honey cake that indeed had granny glasses, made of silver sugar pearls, and bright eyes with long lashes inside the glass frames, too. Next to the honey cake was a tiny vase of plastic flowers with *MOTHER* printed across the bulbed-out part at the end of it, and another vase with something incomprehensible printed on that. Gregor supposed the incomprehensible thing must be *mother*

spelled out in Armenian, but he couldn't be sure.
There had been times in his life when he'd been able
to do a fair job of dredging Armenian words from the
pit of forgetfulness a life in major cities had confined
them to, but today was not one of those times. It was
hard to tell exactly what today was. It was Mother's
Day, of course. No one walking down Cavanaugh
Street could have mistaken it for anything else. Mother's Day might once have been a sticky-sentimental
gesture by a corrupt Congress looking to do something nobody could cause a scandal over. It might have
metamorphosed into one more shtick for the retail sec-
tor to exploit. On Cavanaugh Street, however, it was
something like a patron saint's feast day. Gregor
Demarkian had grown up on Cavanaugh Street. In
those days it had been an Armenian-American immi-
grant ghetto, the kind of place where bricks fell off the
facades of buildings and plaster crumbled from their
inner walls and social workers arrived with the regu-
larity of bowel movements to berate the population on
how they were doing it all wrong. It was now Philadelphia's jewel of urban renewal, a clean place lined by
town houses and floor-through condominium apart-
ments, trendy restaurants and import boutiques, even
a bookstore and a religious supply house used by all
the priests in all the Eastern rite churches in the city.
That this change had come about was due entirely to
the way the children of Cavanaugh Street felt about
their mothers, which, in Gregor's opinion, was right
up there in both fanaticism and common sense with
the way the people of Jonestown had felt about Reverend Jim. Gregor could just imagine one of the women
of his own generation—Lida Arkmanian or Hannah
Krekorian or Sheila Kashinian—giving the order for a
mass march into the sea. First they'd give the order
for a mass march into rubber boots.

Of course, Gregor didn't want to imply that he didn't
think well of Armenian mothers. He'd had an Armenian mother of his own, once, and an Armenian grandmother, too. They were wonderful women. Bossy,
maybe. A little on the hysterical side when it came to

how much their children ate or how many layers they
wore on perfectly nice days when no layers at all
would probably have made more sense, but still—

He was past Ohanian's Middle Eastern Food Store
now, almost up to the Ararat restaurant. It was eleven
o'clock in the morning, nearly time for the liturgy to
finish at Holy Trinity Armenian Christian Church. Any
minute now, Father Tibor Kasparian would bless the
congregation and Sheila Kashinian would begin to tap
her foot. All the old ladies would rustle and blush and
try to hide the fact that what they really wanted to do
was get out to the vestibule and the front steps as
quickly as possible, where they could get some serious
talking done. It was to avoid church that Gregor had
gone for his walk in the first place. He had nothing
against church—he certainly had nothing against Father Tibor's sermons—but today . . .

Today, today, today, Gregor thought. Today you're
just disgruntled because Cavanaugh Street is celebrating a holiday you have no way to celebrate. In a few
minutes the street will be full of people, Cavanaugh
Street regulars joined by the new immigrants who had
come over since the Soviet Union's fall, and you will be
totally out of place.

Bennis Hannaford often said that if Gregor
Demarkian didn't have a reason to take a despairingly
existential view of life, he would invent one. Young
Donna Moradanyan agreed with her. Donna Moradanyan had the apartment on the floor above Gregor's in
the four-story brownstone that faced Lida Arkmanian's
town house. Bennis had the apartment on the floor below him. Between the two of them, they did a better
than fair job of running his life.

Someday, something unambiguously wonderful is
going to happen in your life, Gregor told himself, and
then you won't know how to behave.

Linda Melajian was standing in the middle of
Ararat's front room, setting a table with restaurant flat-
ware and frowning at the way the yellow linen napkins
were folded. The napkins were yellow because they
went well with Armenia's new flag, a copy of which

was displayed along the side wall in a frame of flowers that always looked so fresh, somebody must have been changing them daily. Gregor reminded himself that old Deena Melajian had fled the Communist invasion in 1946 and then wondered how Linda thought she was going to get away with having skipped church just to set up for the Mother's Day crowd. Everyone who came in this afternoon was going to ask her why she couldn't make time for God.

Gregor tapped on the window. Linda looked up and waved. Gregor went on down the street. The tall front doors of Holy Trinity Church were propped open. Howard Kashinian must have come out while Gregor was watching Linda in the Ararat. Gregor speeded up his steps. It was a good thing he had someplace to go today. It would take his mind off all this hyperbolic celebration of motherhood. It would stop him from wondering what it was all these people thought he was up to—which was a question he often asked about Cavanaugh Street without getting any kind of sensible answer. Gregor didn't even think he'd mind spending the day surrounded by nuns. In Gregor's private cosmology, convents and Cavanaugh Street went together in ways mysterious and divine. They were both largely populated by women with a mission.

Donna Moradanyan's mission was to decorate as much as possible with as little excuse as possible. To that end, she had decorated the front of the brownstone where her apartment and Gregor's were with bright yellow and blue satin ribbons, bright yellow and blue satin bows, and white chiffon hearts sewn into ruffles so enthusiastic they almost seemed alive. Just how Donna Moradanyan had managed to do this, Gregor did not know. It couldn't have been easy getting those ribbons up close to the roof like that. It had to have been nearly impossible to plant that chiffon heart—the one the size of an overgrown twelve-year-old-boy—right in the center of the stones between the third and fourth floors. Did Donna fly? Did she care what having a house that looked like this did to the dignity of her neighbors?

Donna Moradanyan thought Gregor Demarkian had too much dignity, and he knew it.

Over at Holy Trinity, there were rumblings and hiccups. The congregation was beginning to emerge. Gregor hurried up his front steps, determinedly ignoring the gigantic *M* woven out of blue and yellow ribbons that covered the front door. Then he let himself into the foyer and looked around. Since it was Sunday, there was no mail. Since it was a holiday, there was no old George Tekemanian in the first floor apartment—old George would be spending the day with his grandson Martin and his great-grandchildren. Gregor headed on up the steps to the second floor.

It was odd to think about it now, but back when Elizabeth died, the last thing he'd thought he would do was come back to Cavanaugh Street. He hadn't even thought there would be a Cavanaugh Street to come back to.

What would his life have been like without this place?

2

Gregor Demarkian had met Bennis Hannaford in a way he would once have refused to believe he would ever meet anyone—in the course of investigating a murder for whose solution he had no official responsibility. In fact, back in the days when he was still with the Bureau, the idea of getting involved in murder investigations—or in criminal investigations of any kind—as what amounted to an amateur would have sounded to him absurd. Like most professional policemen—and that was what a Bureau agent was, really, a professional policeman—Gregor had scant use for amateurs. Unlike so many professionals, he didn't mind amateurs in fiction much. Bennis gave him novels by Agatha Christie and Rex Stout and he read them with a fair degree of amusement. There was something about the way in which he himself had become involved in other people's murder cases, though, that made him uneasy. It made him uneasier that he had no hold on that part of his life. So far, he had been tangled up in seven of what he called his "extracurricular murders." He had become the darling of the *Philadelphia Inquirer* and *People* magazine. If one more person dared to call him "the Armenian-American Hercule Poirot," he was going to commit a murder of his own. The problem was, if he *didn't* commit a murder of his own, he had no guarantee that he would ever be involved in another case. It was worse than odd. It was like being visited by fairies, or having to rely for your Christmas presents on a very capricious Santa Claus. Of course, he didn't think of murder cases as Christmas presents. It was just that he sometimes wished he had more stability in his life.

"Get married again," Father Tibor Kasparian would have told him. "Marry Bennis," the women said—including Donna Moradanyan, Lida Arkmanian, Hannah Krekorian, Sheila Kashinian, Mary and Deborah Ohanian, Linda and Sylvia Melajian, Christie and Melissa Oumoudian ...

"Get a private detective's license," Bennis Hannaford said.

Bennis's door had a single chiffon heart on it, meaning she had come out early this morning and taken off whatever else Donna had decided to put up. Gregor pressed the buzzer on the door frame and waited.

"Come right in," a voice called from inside. "I've got goddamned plaster of paris in my goddamned hair."

Of course she had goddamned plaster of paris in her goddamned hair, Gregor thought. She's always got something going on that makes no sense and interferes fatally with whatever she's supposed to do next. What Bennis was supposed to do next was to accompany him to this party at St. Elizabeth's College, where the Sisters of Divine Grace would open their first-ever nuns' convention. When Gregor had originally been told about the nuns' convention, he'd thought it was the first ever, but that had turned out not to be the case. The Sisters of St. Joseph of Carondolet had held one in St. Louis back in 1988.

Bennis Hannaford's foyer was taken up in large part

by a plaster of paris model of Queen Zahvea's castle from *Sorcerers of Zed, Witches of Zedalia*. What Bennis Hannaford did for a living was write sword and sorcery fantasy novels, of which *Sorcerers of Zed, Witches of Zedalia* was the seventh or eighth, Gregor couldn't remember which. He wasn't disturbed by the castle because it had been where it was now for quite a while. Bennis had constructed it and then stashed it in the foyer, meaning to throw it out or donate it to one of the fan organizations. That she had never gotten around to either was entirely typical. One of the scale-model knights had fallen off his horse. Gregor put him back on and called out.

"Where are you? Why are you making plaster of paris?"

There was a clank of pots and pans from the kitchen and a not-so-muffled curse. Bennis's language was appalling, and it didn't help any when she told Gregor it was the result of all those expensive girls' boarding schools she'd been sent to. The pots stopped clanging and the door to the kitchen swung open, revealing Bennis in her spring and summer uniform of jeans that had seen better days in 1966, T-shirt that had last been clean for Richard Nixon's first inaugural, and hair that had started out tied into a knot at the top of her head but was now someplace else. Bennis Hannaford was a beautiful woman when she wanted to be, but Gregor had noticed that she very rarely wanted to be.

"Well," he said when he saw her, "you don't look ready to go to a party."

She made a face at him. "I don't have to look ready to go to a party. We don't have to be there until quarter to one and it's not even eleven thirty. Oh, by the way. Sister Scholastica called. She wanted to make sure we knew where we were going."

"Do we?"

"I gave a talk at St. Elizabeth's once. 'The Woman Writer in Fantasy and Science Fiction.' I got a lot of people upset. Come into the kitchen. I've got to finish this idiotic model today or it won't be ready on time."

Gregor was about to ask finished on time for what—

when Bennis made models to help her with her books,
they didn't have any on time to be finished for—but he
didn't. He merely followed Bennis's slight five-foot-
four-inch frame into the kitchen and dusted off a chair
to sit down on. Bennis's apartment was always an un-
holy mess. The cleaning lady who came in twice a
week couldn't seem to get it straightened out, and neither could the cadres of older women who periodically
showed up to "help Bennis out." Stack Bennis's be-
longings neatly away in closets and drawers and they
came right back out again, springing into the air as
soon as one's back was turned, as if all the storage
spaces in the apartment were inhabited by evil genies
with ambitions to be the spirits of jack-in-the-box toys.
The same held true for dust. It didn't matter how diligently one wiped and polished. It didn't matter how
many expensive sprays one used to put a shine on the
woodwork. The shine would be gone and the dust
would be back in less time than it took to put water on
to boil for a celebratory cup of coffee.

The plaster of paris model Bennis was making
seemed to be some kind of pockmarked planetary surface. It looked like the moon, but Gregor couldn't
think of anyone who might want a model of the moon.
Bennis put a cup down in front of him and turned on
the gas under her kettle. Then she set out a spoon and
the sugar bowl and a jar of instant coffee. Bennis's instant coffee wasn't bad. It wasn't Lida Arkmanian's per-
colated variety, but it wasn't bad. It beat what Gregor
and Tibor got when they attacked supermarket sacks
of specially ground coffee beans and put them in a coffeepot.

"In case you're wondering about the plaster of
paris," Bennis said, "it's a topographical map of
Armenia. Or I hope it is. I'm constructing it off a globe
so ancient it might as well still show the world as flat,
but it was the only one Lida could come up with with
the borders of Armenia clearly marked, so here I am.
They need it for the school. Tomorrow."

"Of course," Gregor said.

The school was a parochial school—the first Gregor

had ever heard of in an Armenian-American parish—
set up to accommodate the children of the immigrants
who had come to Cavanaugh Street in the wake of
earthquakes and political revolutions. It had also acquired a little group of children of the native-born res-
idents of Cavanaugh Street, whose parents purported
to like the idea of their children "growing up to know
their heritage." Since most of these parents wouldn't
touch their heritage with a ten-foot pole—unless they
could eat it—Gregor thought that the real draw was
the simple localness of it. The school was housed in a
four-story brownstone right next to Holy Trinity
Church. The children who attended could walk there
in the mornings, and quite a few of them could reach
the school's front doors without ever having to cross a
street.

"Anyway," Bennis said, "I'm practically done except
for the painting, and I'm not really going to do the
painting per se, if you see what I mean. I'm only going
to figure out what color has to go where and then
write a code in pencil on the model and then the kids
will paint it themselves. Did you used to do things like
this when you were in school, Gregor? I don't know. It
doesn't seem to me that all this stuff is really work."

"They're only children," Gregor said mildly. "And
you know how I feel about education. Most of them
won't remember a thing of what they learn two
months after they go out into the real world."

"Well, don't say that in front of Lida. She'll think
you're encouraging the children to drop out."

"Maybe I am."

"Right."

Bennis got up, got the coffee, and poured him out a
cup. She was standing so close to him the plaster of
paris in her hair was clearly visible as flakes. Then she
moved away and Gregor was left wondering why he'd
thought that about the flakes, or felt so compelled to
notice just how close she'd been to him. Standing over
by the stove, a good ten feet away, she was just Bennis
as he always saw Bennis. She was a perpetual thorn in
his side. She was the woman Father Tibor Kasparian

called "Bennis the Menace." She was only thirty-six or thirty-seven, while Gregor was twenty years older than that.

She poured herself a cup of coffee while she was still standing next to the stove, drank it down black—but with enough sugar in it to give diabetes to the Visigoths' invading hordes; Gregor saw her spooning it out of the sugar sack—and put the cup in the sink.

"I'd better go wash my hair," she said. "You know how long it takes to dry and I hate those goddamned little hair dryers. Is there supposed to be anything solemn about this occasion? Can I wear a red dress?"

"I think you should wear a hair shirt and carry a staff," Gregor said. "That way the nuns will know you're serious about atoning for your sins."

"The nuns won't know what sins I've got to atone for, and besides I don't atone. What's the point? There's those I forget what you call them in the refrigerator, the meatballs with the bulgur crusts. Lida brought them. You can heat them up in the microwave."

"I've already eaten. And we're supposed to go up to St. Elizabeth's and have lunch."

"That never stopped you yet."

Gregor was about to say he wasn't the kind of glutton these women liked to make him out to be, twenty extra pounds or no twenty extra pounds, but Bennis was already gone, her bare feet slapping carelessly against the wooden floor of her foyer, on the way to the privacy of her shower. Gregor wondered suddenly if Bennis felt she needed privacy from him—and then he shoved that away, because it made him feel a little crazy. In fact, everything about his relationship with Bennis made him feel a little crazy lately. It was as if, after years of running along on a track on which they were both comfortable, an invisible hand had thrown a switch that got them both off course. He had even started to dream about her.

Gregor Demarkian was a man of that generation that came of age just after World War II. He believed in reason and logic, not intuition and dreams. He felt

nothing but exasperation for people who were forever
exploring their subconscious. He didn't actually think
he had a subconscious.

To prove that he didn't—and that the subconscious
he didn't have wasn't fixated on Bennis Day Hannaford—he got up, topped up his already full enough cup
of coffee, and trained all his attention on the plaster of
paris topographical map of Armenia, that looked like a
vision of Mars at the end of an intergalactic nuclear
holocaust.

3

Exactly forty-four minutes later, Bennis Hannaford
emerged from her bedroom in a rustle of red silk and
a tinkling of gold chains, looking like a short, black-
haired Catherine Deneuve getting ready to do a per-
fume commercial. Her relationship to the Bennis
Hannaford of the plaster-of-paris–filled kitchen was entirely speculative. Her relationship to half of the really
old money on the Philadelphia Main Line was evident.
When Bennis was dressed up like this, Gregor always
thought of her background—complete with dancing
classes, private schools, and a debut that had made the
pages of *Town and Country*—as definitive. When she
wasn't dressed up like this, he didn't think of her background at all.

She turned her back to him and pointed at the base
of her neck. "There's a little button there I can't reach.
I've never understood the designers of women's
clothes. I mean, do they think I've got a husband or a
maid?"

"Both," Gregor said.

"Is your friend the Cardinal going to be at this
party? I mean, here we are, going off to visit the Catholics, and I haven't heard a word about him."

"That's how you think of this? 'Going off to visit the
Catholics'?"

"Well, Gregor, they're not ordinary Catholics, are
they? I mean, they're not Mrs. O'Brien who lived
downstairs from me in Boston and went to Fatima No-

venas all the time and prayed that Michael would break down and marry me. You remember Michael. It was my great good luck that he never broke down and married me."

"You'd have had to have married him at the same time."

"In those days, I didn't have any backbone."

"The Cardinal," Gregor said, "is the Archbishop of the Archdiocese of Colchester, which is in Upstate New York, not here. And he doesn't call me in unless he has a corpse on his hands."

"Would the Cardinal of *this* Archdiocese call you in if he had a corpse on his hands?"

"I don't know if we're in an Archdiocese," Gregor said. "Believe it or not, I'm not an expert on the institutional structure of the Catholic Church in America. And since I have never met the occupant of this see—or the see St. Elizabeth's College is in, if there's a difference—I can't understand why he'd call me in if something embarrassing happened to him. But it doesn't matter, Bennis, because nothing embarrassing has happened to him, in that sense anyway. There are no corpses to discover, and no crimes to ferret out before they cause a nationwide scandal."

"Are you sure?"

"I'm positive," Gregor said firmly. "Sister Scholastica would have said. I have your button buttoned. We ought to go."

"Aren't they building a gymnasium or something? Maybe their contractor is a front for the mob—"

"Bennis."

"—or maybe it's one of the nuns trying to put aside some money so she can make her escape—"

"*Bennis.*"

"—or maybe it's something really sinister, like a plot to supply girls to the white slave trade in Arabia or a clandestine organization with links to the IRA or—"

Bennis had left her pocketbook on the kitchen table while she waited for Gregor to button her. Gregor picked it up and handed it over.

"These are a lot of nice women we're going to see,

a perfectly respectable order of nuns that does a lot of good work in schools and hospitals. They are not prone to committing crimes or collaborating in vice."

"They've already had one murder," Bennis reminded him.

"Considering how that worked out, it proves my point," Gregor said.

"I think of it like an allergy," Bennis told him. "Some people have a tendency to break out in hives whenever they eat strawberries, and some people have a tendency to break out in murders whenever—well, you know, whenever the situation warrants it."

Since Gregor Demarkian couldn't imagine what sort of situation would warrant any group of people in "breaking out in murders," he grabbed Bennis Hannaford by the shoulders, spun her around, and marched her straight at her own front door.

would be stopped for turning the wrong way onto a one-way street from a no-left-hand-turn lane. Sheila Kashinian had won fifty dollars for betting he'd be given a Breathalyzer test. It was embarrassing, but there was nothing Gregor could do about it, except to drive as seldom as possible and allow either public transportation or his friends to take him where he wanted to go.

Bennis Hannaford was a very good driver—she was, in fact, one of the best coordinated people Gregor had ever met—but her idea of time spent not wasted in a car started at approximately one hundred and forty miles an hour. She took the double-nickel speed limit with all the seriousness Carl Sagan took Creation Science. By the time she drove Gregor into the visitors' parking lot at St. Elizabeth's College, he was shaking, and they were a good ten minutes early for the start of the reception. Gregor looked at the tall spires and graceful religious statuary that seemed to be everywhere around him and decided that he was no longer in doubt. There quite definitely was a God, and he could prove it by the fact that *he* was still alive. That there was a Devil he could prove by the fact that they had never been stopped by any agent of the Pennsylvania State Police. It wasn't as if they would have been difficult to spot. Bennis's preferred mode of transportation was a Mercedes 230 SL she had had custom painted a phosphorescent tangerine orange.

According to the map Sister Scholastica had sent them, the visitors' parking lot was directly next door to St. Cecelia's Hall, which was directly next door to St. Teresa's House. St. Teresa's House was the place where the reception and then the lunch were to be held, and therefore the place to which they were headed. Bennis pulled her keys out of the ignition and looked around. From here, as far as Gregor could tell, it was an ordinary enough suburban college campus. The statues of women in long veils marked it as Catholic. The marble arches of its college Gothic buildings marked it as both oldish and expensive. Other than that, it could have been any college at all. Gregor looked around for some sign that 5,264 nuns were now in residence, but couldn't find any. He'd thought the grounds would have been carpeted with women in habits. The grounds weren't carpeted with anyone. From what he could see of the lawns and pathways, they were deserted.

"You'd think there would at least be other people ar-riving for the party. I'm beginning to wonder if we have the wrong date."

"We don't," Bennis told him. "There was one of those plastic letterboards at the gate when we came in. 'Opening Reception, Convocation of the Order of the Sisters of Divine Grace, May 11, 12:45.' And I'm quot-ing. I just think everybody else knows something we don't know about the really good places to park. And there's someone else in this lot, anyway. Over there."

"That pudgy man getting out of the red wreck?"

"The red wreck is a vintage Jaguar. And the pudgy man is Norman Kevic. The one who's on the radio, you know."

"No," Gregor said. "I don't know."

"Well, you ought to. He's got a talk show in the mornings from six to ten. He's very controversial and he's supposed to be very influential. Anyway, I know he's here for the reception because he's been talking about it for a week. When he isn't bashing the Japa-nese."

"What do you mean, bashing the Japanese?"

"He tells really gross, really racist jokes about the Japanese." Bennis shrugged. "I didn't say he was a nice man. I just said he was famous. Get out of the car, Gregor. We really ought to go find out where we're supposed to be. Once we've got that down, we can do what we want."

Since this was eminently sensible advice—and since Bennis so rarely gave eminently sensible advice—Gregor decided to follow it. He opened the door at his side and unfolded his legs from the small car. Since he was six feet four, he always seemed to be unfolding his legs from one place to another. Once he was standing up, he nodded to Bennis, and she used her automatic

door lock. Then she got her cigarettes out of her
pocket and lit up. It was impossible to tell anymore
where cigarette smoking would be allowed and where
it wouldn't be. Since Bennis's habit was deeply in-
grained and passionately defended, she was forever
smoking precautionary cigarettes before entering parties, dinners, speeches, and television studios. Gregor
was used to it. He leaned against the side of the car
and waited.

"I don't understand why you do this," he said. "We
could go over to St. Teresa's House first. That was
what you said we ought to do. You could always nip
out later and light up. And instead—"

"Here comes somebody else," Bennis said.

The somebody else was driving up in an ordinary
maroon Lincoln Town Car, a dowdy second cousin to
Bennis's Mercedes and Norman Kevic's Jaguar.
Gregor watched idly as it maneuvered almost silently
into a narrow parking space and hissed to a stop. Since
the windows were tinted, he couldn't see inside, and
he wondered why not. What made people want to be
anonymous, when they were unlikely to be famous
enough for anonymity to be in question? Then the driver's side door popped open and a man got out, and
Gregor began to revise his opinion. The man wasn't famous. He wasn't anyone that Gregor recognized.
Gregor was willing to bet, however, that he was richer
than both Bennis Hannaford and Norman Kevic com-
bined. The man walked around the back of the car and
up the side to the front passenger door and opened it.
He held out his arm, but the woman who emerged beside him did not bother to take it. She was a thin
woman with overtight skin and the frantic air of the
psychologically desperate. Gregor disliked her on
sight.

"Oh for Christ's sake," she said, leaning over to take
off a shoe and shake it in the air. "Gravel, gravel, and
more gravel. Whatever made you think I liked gravel,
I'll never know."

"I didn't think you liked gravel." The man spoke
with some amusement. "I thought the members of the

Heart Association Committee liked gravel. And I was right."

"I don't see why you think I'll be impressed with the Heart Association Committee," she replied. "If I'd wanted to be on the Heart Association Committee, I could have gotten there myself."

"You didn't get there."

"I didn't want to."

"I think, Nancy, that at some point, you're going to have to stop pretending that you don't care what anybody else thinks of you. It's all you do care about."

Nancy had the shoe back on her foot. She spun around on her heel until her face was almost next to his and said: "I think, Henry, that I'm going to go in and tell the nuns what kind of a son of a bitch you really are, and then we'll see what happens."

At that she turned her back on him and stalked away, toward St. Cecelia's Hall, across a drive so uneven and unpredictable it made her pitch and shudder with every step. The man watched her go for a second or two and then followed.

Gregor looked across the car at Bennis still smoking her cigarette and shook his head. Bennis took a deep drag, leaned closer over the car's roof and said, "Do you suppose they didn't notice we were here, or that they noticed but they just didn't care?"

"B," Gregor said.

"That's what I think, too," Bennis said. "New money. You can smell it all over them. New money fights in public. Old money fights in private. Very old money never fights at all. How's that for social commentary?"

"Finish your cigarette," Gregor said.

Bennis dropped her cigarette on the ground and stamped it out under her heel. Then she picked it up and put it in the flap pocket of her purse. She would throw it away as soon as she found a garbage can.

"I'm finished," she said. "I can't wait to see what those two are going to do when they have a whole order of nuns for an audience."

2

If there was one thing Gregor Demarkian had learned in his short—but very intense—acquaintance with the official branches of the Roman Catholic Church, it was never to anticipate the actions of a nun. He had once gone to Maryville, New York, expecting the Mother-house of the Sisters of Divine Grace to be a quasi-medieval pile complete with bats in the belfry and ghosts in the downstairs back hall. Instead he found a functional building that reminded him of an elementary school. Now he was doing his best not to expect St. Teresa's House to be other than what it was. The facade spoke softly of soaring ceilings and wide hallways inside. It would probably turn out to be a rabbit warren of tiny rooms partitioned with plasterboard. Now that they were this close, he could see all the other people he had expected to see in the parking lot and hadn't. They were coming from somewhere behind the building, which meant Bennis had to be right. There was somewhere else to park. There seemed to be fewer people than he had expected, but he thought it made sense to revise his expectations. This was, after all, a nuns' convention. It was the Sisters who were supposed to be here in force. Seculars could only be guests, not active participants.

The steps to the tall double doored–entrance to St. Teresa's House were wide and deep, but not steep. They were also made of marble. Gregor took Bennis by the arm in the old-fashioned way—it was testament to Bennis's Main Line society upbringing that she neither protested nor stared at him in openmouthed disbelief—and led her up behind a diffident elderly couple in good tweeds who were tottering on ahead of them. Gregor thought the tweeds must have been stifling in this weather. As they got closer to the door he saw that it had been decorated. Whoever had done it had possessed enthusiasm to match Donna Morada-nyan's but more conventionality. There were large baby blue ribbon rosettes fastened to the door frames about shoulder height (for Gregor) on either side. In the middle of each rosette was an embroidered sign that read:

MAY IS MARY'S MONTH.

"What do you suppose that means?" Bennis said, pointing to one of the signs.

"May is dedicated to the Virgin Mary," Gregor told her, "except with Mother's Day in the middle of it all they say that May is dedicated to the Mother of God. There it is."

"There what is?"

"One of the other signs."

Gregor pointed to a large freestanding brass planter full of roses—full, possibly, of a still-rooted rose bush—that was standing just inside the foyer propping back one of the doors. It bore a sign that said:

ON MOTHER'S DAY REMEMBER THE MOTHER OF GOD.

It was exactly the same sign Gregor had seen just last week outside St. Rita's Convent, when he'd helped Father Tibor Kasparian take six cartons of tuna fish to Father Ryan's soup kitchen in the basement of St. Rita's Church. Since the sign had confused him, he had simply asked Father Ryan to explain it.

The crowd ahead of them had turned into a barely moving knot. They were slowed almost to a standstill. Bennis was bobbing up and down on her toes, trying to see over the heads of taller people to what lay ahead.

"There's a receiving line," she reported, as she bobbed back down. "It looks like five or six nuns in not-very-modified habits—you didn't tell me these were nuns who still looked like nuns, Gregor—anyway, there they are. After the receiving line, there's another set of double doors and after that I can't see. Do you know who that is two couples ahead of us? Shayda Marle from *One Life Is Never Enough*. With the character she plays, you'd think she'd be ashamed to show her face in a convent."

Gregor didn't know who Shayda Marle was. He'd never heard of *One Life Is Never Enough*. He did know this wasn't a convent—just an ordinary building on an ordinary college campus being used for this reception—but that hardly seemed a likely topic of conversation when Bennis was in the kind of mood she was in. Gregor recognized the signs. The speeded-up speech. The vocabulary straight out of a particularly bitchy play by Noel Coward. When Bennis got nervous, Bennis reverted to type.

Fortunately, the line had begun moving again, albeit slowly. The tottering little old couple just ahead of them stepped into the foyer. Gregor saw a row of long veils and heard the polite murmur of people who really don't know what to say to nuns, but feel they must say something. He supposed the Sisters were being told they looked well and the weather was fine. Then the tottering old couple moved on. Gregor grasped Bennis firmly by the elbow and led her into the foyer.

"Sister," Gregor said, when he reached the first nun, and then was startled to realize that this was a nun he knew. "Oh. Mother. Reverend Mother. You may not remember me. My name is Gregor Demarkian."

The Reverend Mother General of the Sisters of Divine Grace was not a fool or an idiot or a candidate for the Miss Marple International Ditherers Award—although Gregor had always thought she'd get along with Miss Marple quite well. Reverend Mother General was more of the era when calling the head of a religious order a "general" had more definitively military connotations than it did now. Reverend Mother General would have been an excellent administrator in time of martial law. She would have been an excellent pope in the days when popes had armies. Placed at the head of a European royal house with a mandate for absolute monarchy, she would have taken an upstart like Napoleon or Savanarola and turned him into confetti. John Cardinal O'Bannion—Father Tibor's friend and the person who usually got Gregor involved in Catholic Church–related crime—called Reverend Mother General "a wonderful woman," in a way that made it plain he wished she'd been a wonderful woman in some *other* Archbishop's jurisdiction.

Reverend Mother General looked Gregor up and down. Then she looked Bennis Hannaford up and down. Then she looked back to Gregor again and stuck out her hand.

"I remember you," she said. "I could hardly forget."

"Of course not." Gregor cursed himself mentally for having resorted to that kind of politeness. It wasn't the kind of thing Reverend Mother General liked. He pushed Bennis forward a little. "This is Bennis Day Hannaford. A good friend of mine."

"Bennis Day Hannaford." Reverend Mother General looked thoughtful. "Ah, yes. I've heard a great deal about Bennis Day Hannaford. I'll have to pass you on down the line, I'm afraid. The Sisters beside me here are the Mothers Superior of our Provincial Houses. We have four in the United States—not including the Motherhouse in Maryville—three in Europe, one in Australia and one in Asia. Our Asian house is in Japan. Mother Andrew Loretta beside me here runs it for us."

"How do you do?" Mother Andrew Loretta said, making Reverend Mother General's life easier by clasping Gregor's hand and pulling him determinedly along. She was a round-faced, cheerful-looking Asian woman in her fifties or sixties. Gregor suspected she didn't speak much English. She was trying very hard, though, and Gregor patted her hand with his free one.

"What has Reverend Mother General heard about

me?" Bennis hissed into his ear as Mother Andrew
Loretta passed them along to the next nun in the line.
This was someone named Mother Robert Marie, who
had charge of the Southern Province of the United
States.

"How am I supposed to know what Reverend
Mother General has heard about you?" Gregor asked.
"You're in the papers a lot."

Mother Robert Marie passed them along to Mother
Marie Genevieve, who had charge of the Provincial
House in France. Mother Marie Genevieve spoke nonstop in French, as if it was beyond her comprehension
that anyone on earth could fail to understand the language.

Bennis understood the language. That's what came
of spending four years at Miss Porter's School. She
made polite conversation until they were passed along
to Sister Mary Deborah, who had charge of the house
in Melbourne, and then hissed into Gregor's ear: "The
only time I'm ever in the papers anymore is when I'm
in the papers with you, unless you're trying to tell me
Reverend Mother General reads the fantasy fan press,
which I don't believe—"

"You were on the cover of the *New York Times Sunday Magazine.*"

"That was four years ago. These days I'm only in the
papers with you. Caption under the picture on the first
page: 'Gregor Demarkian with constant companion
Bennis Day Hannaford.' What does that woman *think*?"

"The same thing that everyone on Cavanaugh Street
thinks," Gregor said, "and you don't care."

"Everyone on Cavanaugh Street isn't a nun."

"Tibor's a priest."

"Tibor doesn't think I'm sleeping with you."

"This is Mother Mary Bellarmine," Mother Mary
Deborah said, passing them along one more time but
looking reluctant about it. "Mother Bellarmine is the
superior of our house in the southwestern United
States."

For a moment, Gregor was distracted by Mother
Mary Deborah's obvious confusion. She so plainly had

no idea where "the southwestern United States" actually was or what it might comprise. Then he turned his attention to the next nun in line, and paused. Beside him, Bennis had paused, too. The woman they were standing in front of was not particularly large or particularly small, not especially pretty or noticeably ugly, not different in any significant degree from any of the other nuns in the line. If someone had walked up to him at that moment and asked him what it was that bothered him about Mother Mary Bellarmine, Gregor couldn't have said. She wasn't exactly as accommodating as some of the others. There was that. She had a sour expression on her face. Gregor looked over at Bennis. She had temporarily lost her nervousness. Her head was cocked and her eyes were thoughtful. She might have been looking at a bug.

Mother Mary Bellarmine shook Gregor's hand abruptly. Then she shook Bennis's hand, just as abruptly. Then she folded her arms against her body and said, "Gregor Demarkian. I've heard all about you. You're a friend of Cardinal O'Bannion's. And you cause trouble."

The nun on the far side of Mother Mary Bellarmine must have heard. She jerked into motion, swung toward the little group and said, "Oh! Gregor Demarkian. We've been waiting for you to come through the line. Sister Scholastica is most anxious to speak to you."

"Sister Scholastica," Mother Mary Bellarmine said with contempt.

"I'm Mother Mary Rosalie," the new nun went on, holding Gregor firmly by the arm and dragging him along to her. "I'm in charge of the Northwestern Province—of the United States, that is. I know it must seem as if we're divided up with no good plan behind it at all, and of course that's true, to an extent, we did rather just grow, like Topsy, oh dear, I'm indulging in clichés again. You must be Bennis Hannaford. I'm very glad to meet you too."

"Bennis *Han*naford," Mother Mary Bellarmine said. If it was meant to be a whisper, or a mutter, it failed.

Mother Mary Rosalie still had her hand on Gregor's arm, and Gregor could see she had no intention of letting go. She had no intention of shutting up, either.

"We're all so looking forward to your talk," she was saying, "because of course all that trouble in Maryville last year did upset quite a few of us. We really didn't know what to make of it all. Of course, you'll tell us, and then we'll all feel much better about it. Not better about the fact that the poor girl died. God bless her. That was horrible. Oh. Here she is. Here's Sister Scholastica."

Gregor didn't know how Mother Mary Rosalie recognized Sister Scholastica—now that they were this far down the line and so close to the inner doors, the world seemed to be full of nuns; with the strictly defined habit the Sisters of Divine Grace wore, the world seemed to be full of nuns who all looked exactly alike—but it really was Sister Scholastica that Mother Mary Rosalie had gotten hold of. Gregor had a distinct feeling of relief. Sister Scholastica was someone he knew.

"Sister," Mother Mary Rosalie said. "You remember Mr. Demarkian. And this is his friend Bennis Hannaford." Bennis winced at the word *friend* used in just that way by a woman in a habit. Mother Mary Rosalie went on. "Mr. Demarkian has just been talking to Mother Mary Bellarmine," she said brightly, "and now he's been passed along to me, but I'm sure he's tired of this line. Don't you think?"

There wasn't much of the line left. Gregor watched as Scholastica looked back at Mother Mary Bellarmine and smiled slightly. It was not, Gregor was sure, with amusement. Then Scholastica turned her back on the open front doors and gestured to the open inner ones and the room beyond. In doing so, she turned her back on Mother Mary Bellarmine. Gregor wondered what it was Mother Mary Bellarmine had done.

"Mr. Demarkian," Sister Scholastica said. "And I'm glad to meet Ms. Hannaford after all this time. We'd better get you both away from here."

Gregor moved close and lowered his voice. "What is

it Mother Mary Bellarmine doesn't like?" he asked.
"Armenian-Americans? Former FBI agents. Old men
who show up at parties with much younger women?"

"Gregor," Bennis said.

"Mother Mary Bellarmine," Sister Scholastica said,
in tones so well modulated she might have been leading the Lord's Prayer at the beginning of a parochial-
school day, "is quite simply a royal pain in the ass. And
if you tell Reverend Mother General I said that, I'll
deny it. Why don't I take you in and get you some
food."

"It sounds wonderful to me," Bennis said. "I'm
starving."

"You're always starving," Gregor said.

Scholastica drew them away from the line and led
them toward the inner doors, weaving through the
small clots and collections of nuns dotted only infre-
quently by seculars. *Seculars*, Reverend Mother General had explained to Gregor once, was the proper
term to distinguish people who were not in religious
orders from people who were. Even diocesan priests
were referred to as the "secular clergy." Since nuns
were not clergy, however, they were laypeople, which
meant it made no sense to talk of "nuns and laypeople"
as if there were a difference. Gregor did not remember having asked for this explanation. He hadn't asked
for most of the explanations Reverend Mother General
had given him. Reverend Mother General was like
that.

He let Scholastica lead him into the inner room, going on ahead with Bennis and talking easily with bent
head about he couldn't imagine what. Bennis always
seemed to have a lot to say to women he wouldn't have
expected her to have anything in common with at all.

Scholastica and Bennis slipped into the far room.
Gregor followed them and stopped in the doorway to
look around. Along one wall—the one toward which
Scholastica and Bennis were heading—there was a collection of what looked like long, makeshift conference
tables covered with white tablecloths. The tables were
so long, no single cloths had been found to fit them.

Instead, cloths were layered and dotted with flower arrangements in stoneware vases to hide the overlaps. The stoneware vases were tied with baby blue ribbons, more tribute to May as Mary's month. The paper napkins in the three tall piles next to the plates and the silverware were baby blue, too. Gregor wondered if they were going to get a lot of baby blue food-colored food. There was meant to be a lot of food. There were no chairs anywhere near the tables, or anywhere else in the room. The tables had to have been set up for a buffet. At the moment, only one of them was in use. It had three long silver trays of what looked like cheese puffs on it and one large tureen that might have contained anything. Scholastica and Bennis were headed for the tureen. Gregor headed for them.

He was halfway to his goal, dodging between nuns in identical habits with unidentifiable accents and saying "Excuse me, Sister" almost as often as he drew breath, when he became aware of a very curious fact. The noise had stopped. When he'd first come into this room, the murmur of voices had been like a tidal wave. There were supposed to be more than five thousand nuns here. Some of them were undoubtedly outside. This room had a wall of sliding glass doors on one end that seemed to lead into a garden. Gregor thought most of them were still in this room, waiting for the food, just as he intended to wait for the food. They spoke softly because they were nuns, but even speaking softly could create a wall of sound if five thousand people were doing it together.

At the moment, none of them were doing it at all. No one was even coughing. Gregor looked around for some kind of disturbance and could find none. A second later, the sound began to come back. It came back hesitantly, as it always does when flukes of silence make speakers self-conscious about being overheard.

Gregor revised his estimate of how many people had to be in the room. Publicity or no publicity, there was no way they could have gotten five thousand people in this room. Now that he could see its parameters, he would have guessed it could hold no more than fifteen hundred, and that fifteen hundred would be a squeeze. He trained his attention on the doors leading to the garden. Maybe it wasn't a garden. Maybe it was a field that extended all the way to the Ohio border.

Gregor liked cheese puffs well enough, and he was hungry, but there would be food enough all afternoon. Now he was itching to find out how many people were really here and where they'd all been put. He edged through the crowd toward the sliding glass doors, listening here and there to the sharp-edged sounds of conversations going on just beside his ear.

"She was put in charge of St. Stanislaw's in Cleveland," an older nun said, "but everything just seemed to fall apart—"

"All the old ladies were all worked up because he wanted to change the rule about home visits," a young nun said, "but what are we supposed to do? We don't have sixteen brothers and sisters sitting at home with all the time in the world to take care of business—"

"We kept the Fatima Novena Society going as long as we could," a third nun said, "but it got to the day when it was just old Mrs. Tetrarosa coming to it, and we had to stop."

Gregor got to the sliding glass doors and looked out. What he saw made him feel like one of those Russian nesting dolls. There was a walled garden out there, but there was a gate in the far side of the wall and it was open. Nuns were drifting in and out of it from who knew where.

There was a tall statue of the Virgin standing in one corner of the garden. It had been decked out in roses and baby blue ribbons. There was a woman standing beside it who looked like she was kneeling in prayer. Then she stood up, and Gregor saw that she had neither been kneeling in prayer nor was ever likely to be. She was "Nancy" from the parking lot, complete with too much makeup, too frequent cosmetic surgery and too high heels, and she was clutching a thorny sprig of roses in her hand.

"That little bitch," she said, in a voice that had been

meant to carry, and did. "I'll take care of her. You just *watch* me do it."

She jammed the sprig of roses in her hair—Gregor winced. It must have hurt like hell—and headed for the sliding glass doors. Nuns turned to watch her progress and frowned. Even the ones who hadn't heard what she'd said didn't like the way she was walking. It was more of a stride than a glide, and it was distinctly un-feminine. She came barreling into the reception room, passing through the glass doors so close to Gregor she nearly knocked him over. If she had, she wouldn't have noticed. She marched over to one of the long tables and picked up a large vase of flowers.

"This will do it," she said.

Then she marched out of the room again, through the double doors into the foyer.

Gregor had to move fast to catch up. The room was crowded, even if not with as many people as he'd orig-inally expected, and it was almost impossible to get anywhere without being held up four or five times ev-ery fifteen seconds. At one point he had to grab an el-derly nun by the shoulders and move her bodily out of the way. At another, he had to wedge his hands be-tween two nuns huddled in conference in such a strangely familiar way that he stopped himself just in time from announcing, "Make room for the Holy Ghost."

He got to the double doors just as "Nancy" slid to a stop near the end of the receiving line. There were people actually negotiating the receiving line, but she wasn't about to let them stop her. She grabbed at the back of a man's suit jacket and yanked him out of line. Then she took his place and held the stoneware vase above her head.

"This will teach you," she announced gleefully, in a grating screech that stopped all conversation in the foyer on the spot.

Then she upended the stoneware vase in the air above Mother Mary Bellarmine's head and doused the older nun in plant water and thorns.

CHAPTER 3

1

Sister Joan Esther was not in the foyer when Mother Mary Bellarmine was soaked with water that smelled like chemicals and scratched on the face by a sharp little thorn. It was just as well, because if Sister Joan Esther had been in the foyer then, she would probably have laughed. It was Sister Joan Esther's considered opinion that she had the right to laugh at any misfortune Mother Mary Bellarmine might have, but Reverend Mother General did not hold the same opinion, and Joan Esther had been in trouble once already this trip for what Reverend Mother General called her "attitude." Sister Joan Esther hadn't disputed the description. Lately, she had most definitely had an attitude. She had had an attitude about Mother Mary Bellarmine. She had had an attitude about the Sisters of Divine Grace. She had had an attitude about religion in general. The only thing she hadn't had an attitude about was sleep, because she hadn't been getting any.

While Mother Mary Bellarmine was getting doused in the foyer, Sister Joan Esther was downstairs in the basement kitchen of St. Teresa's House, trying to straighten out what she thought of as "the disaster of the moment." The disaster of this particular moment was actually rather serious, since it involved something that had been announced to the media. Worse, it involved something that the media had decided it liked. The something in question was a series of ice sculptures in the shape of nuns in the old-fashioned, original habit of the Sisters of Divine Grace, one for Reverend Mother General and one for each of the Mothers Provincial, ten in all. Each of these ice sculptures was supposed to have a little hollow dug out in the back of its head, and each of these hollows was supposed to contain an ice cream scoop of chicken liver pâté. Joan Esther, like everyone else, was aware of the fact that what the hollowed-out spaces in ice sculptures were supposed to contain was beluga caviar. It didn't bother her that the Order had neither the money nor the bad taste to go that far. What did bother her was that the ice sculptures had ever existed in the first place and that their existence had been mentioned in a press release. The ice sculptures had been the brainchild of Sister Agnes Bernadette, the Sister Cook for the convent at St. Elizabeth's College, and she was very proud of them. She was also as protective of them as mother bears were supposed to be of their cubs.

Unfortunately, protectiveness had not in this case gotten Sister Agnes Bernadette very far. She had made the ice sculptures. She had put them in the freezer here in the basement of St. Teresa's House. She had gone away expecting everything to be fine. Along had come the little man their benefactor in Tokyo had sent along to deal with the serving of the crates of fugu—and after that, neither Joan Esther nor Agnes Bernadette was entirely sure what had happened. All they were sure of was that one of the statues was smashed.

"He's a very nice little man," Sister Agnes Bernadette was saying, as Joan Esther tried to patch the statue's head back onto its body. "I'm sure he wouldn't do anything like this just to be malicious. . . ."

"He doesn't speak any English?"

Agnes Bernadette sighed. "He says *Hello* and *thank you*. I tried to find one of the Sisters from Japan to translate, but you know what it's been like today. Crazy. You can't find anyone anywhere. And he was so upset."

"And you've got no idea what he was upset about?"

"Not a clue. It seemed to have something to do with the freezer, though. Maybe his fish, his what do you call them—"

"Fugu."

"Yes. Well, maybe the fugu got freezer burn. I don't know, Joanie. He kept pointing to the freezer and getting all agitated. And there was my statue. Maybe I left the statue lying on his fish. . . ."

"His fish were in crates," Joan Esther said firmly. "They were packed in dry ice. I'm sure you didn't do anything to harm them. Mother Andrew Loretta is in the receiving line. Maybe we can haul her down here and get her to translate."

"Well, we couldn't do that," Agnes Bernadette said. "He's gone, isn't he? Took off just after I found him here with the statue and hasn't been back since. Oh, I hope he hasn't gone to commit ritual suicide or something. They do that in Japan, dear, don't they? My little statue isn't worth anything at all like that."

"I think the matter has to be somewhat more serious before it leads to hari-kiri," Joan Esther said drily, "and besides, I think he's a Catholic. Even in Japan, Catholics consider suicide a mortal sin. There. Will this work?"

Agnes Bernadette looked dubiously at the sculpture and sighed again. "She looks like she's wearing a dog collar. Oh, it's terrible. It's really terrible. What are we going to do?"

"We aren't going to be able to do anything if she

melts," Joan Esther said. "Here, we'll take one of those knife things and smooth this out. It won't be perfect but it'll be better than it is. Then all we'll have to do is fill in at the shoulder and reattach the feet."

"Oh, dear," Agnes Bernadette said. "Joanie, you just wouldn't have believed it. It really was the strangest thing."

Joan Esther, who lived in Alaska and taught classes she had to get to for half the year by dogsled, would probably have believed anything, but she'd known Sister Agnes Bernadette for years and liked her. The only problem with Agnes Bernadette was that she was no earthly use in a crisis. Joan Esther pulled a pastry knife out of a drawer and tried it along the now bulging neckline of the ice nun. It worked well enough. There was probably some specialized tool that would have worked better. Joan Esther didn't know what that was, so she didn't have to feel guilty for not using it.

The neckline looked all right. Joan Esther went back into the freezer and got a handful of shaved ice from the bucket of it kept for drinks. She thrust this handful at the gash in the sculpture's right shoulder and stood back to see if she needed any more.

"Fine," she declared. "That's wonderful. What about the rest of the statues? No other damage?"

"Not a thing," Agnes Bernadette said, "but they weren't in the same place."

"What do you mean?"

"Well, I had room for all but one of them on a single shelf. The shelf above the dairy shelf. Usually it's full of frozen cookies because I always make enough cookies so I have extras to thaw for when the girls want them, you know what college girls are like, they spend all their time eating. But I didn't have anything on that shelf this time because I've been keeping the freezer deliberately clear. You know. For things we'd need for the convention."

"But we're keeping the things we need for the convention over at the convent," Joan Esther said.

"I know, Joanie, I know, but I was trying to be pre-

pared. And then I made the statues and, you see, I was
right. I did need the space. So I put nine of the statues
on that shelf and then I ran out of room."

"And you put the other one where?"

"On the other side of the freezer on the bottom
shelf next to the green beans."

"And the fish were there, too?"

"Well, no," Agnes Bernadette said. "They weren't.
They were stacked up in boxes in the far corner."

"Then why do you think this had anything to do
with the fish?"

"Well," Agnes Bernadette said, "the little man has to
do with the fish."

"How do you know this has to do with the little
man? Did you see him break the statue?"

"Well, no, Joanie, but he must have, mustn't he? I
mean, I walked in and he was standing right next to it
and it was smashed. And it was out. If it had been just
lying out, it would have melted."

"Right," Joan Esther said.

"Is this like a detective story, Joanie? Do we have to
figure it out and catch who did it? Maybe we could ask
that Mr. Demarkian who's supposed to be coming and
he could do it for us."

"That's all right," Joan Esther said. "I don't suppose
it matters. I just didn't want to go saying anything to
Reverend Mother General and getting that little man
in trouble when we don't even know if he's responsible. Give me a paper towel, will you please? My hands
are frozen."

"Are we going to be able to use it?"

"I think so," Joan Esther said.

"Oh, good," Agnes Bernadette said.

Joan Esther took the paper towel Agnes Bernadette
handed her and started to rub against the statue's
shoulder. At the rate they were going, this thing was
going to melt just as they carried it up the stairs.

Melted or not, Joan Esther thought she'd be covered.

Reverend Mother General had sent her down here
to fix this thing.

She was fixing it.

It was the first time in forever she'd been able to feel she'd done something right.

2

Norman Kevic had been standing just past the double doors into the reception room when Nancy Hare had dumped the contents of the flower vase on Mother Mary Bellarmine, and right after it happened he'd taken the prudent way out and headed for the garden. He'd been in the garden for less than a minute when he'd decided it was the wrong place for him to be. Norman Kevic had never been the kind of man who loved the great outdoors. The lesser outdoors was always intruding on him. As soon as he got near grass, he got to feeling as if he were crawling with bugs. He'd read once in the *Reader's Digest* that "sexier" people were more assiduously plagued by mosquitoes than unsexy ones, but it hadn't helped. Mosquitoes sucked blood. Ladybugs had tiny, tiny feet that tickled the hair on your arms. Cockroaches were unmentionable. He stood for a while watching a bee go from flower to flower on one of the bushes near the bare feet of the statue of the Virgin Mary, and then he decided he needed to use the john.

Finding a men's john in a building on the campus of a women's college run by nuns is not as easy as it might be elsewhere. Norman Kevic didn't even know who he would properly ask for directions. Nuns had always made him nervous even when they were not paying attention to him. When they were paying attention to him, they shot his anxiety levels into the stratosphere. Then there were all these posters and signs and displays dedicated to Motherhood, virgin and otherwise. Norm wouldn't have guessed nuns could be so hyped on mother love. Several of the nuns he'd bumped into had been wearing little pins that said **"On Mother's Day, Remember the Mother of God"** just the way, at Christmas, they wore little pins that said **"Jesus is the Reason for the Season."** The pins

were very tiny and very discreet. In all likelihood,
Norm was the only one who'd noticed them. The problem was, mothers made Norm even more nervous
than nuns did. Norm's own personal mother had been
a harridan of the first water. If he'd had the sort of
mind susceptible to the recovery movement, he could
have made a career out of going to support groups and
listing the ways in which his mother had alternately
terrorized and suffocated him, never mind the times
she'd simply taken off her belt and let him have it. The
idea of calling a nun "mother," the way he had been
supposed to do in the receiving line, made him physically ill.

He passed into the reception room, looked around,
and saw nothing in the way of doors except the set
that let to the foyer. He approached these cautiously, in
case Nancy's bizarre action might be having a ripple
effect. He found he had nothing to fear. There was a
fuss going on—being made more by the nuns than by
anyone else, which figured—but it was self-contained
at the tail end of the receiving line and not going anywhere soon. Norm peered into the crowd and decided
that the nun Nancy had attacked had not been murdered. That would be Mother Mary Bellarmine, who
was a consultant for the Order on the field house project and whom Norm had met a number of times over
the past week, at publicity meetings or at discussions
of the project, to which Norm had contributed one
hundred thousand dollars. Norman Kevic was no fool.
When he insulted an institution as large and as well
positioned as the Roman Catholic Church, he made a
point of buttering it up as soon as he had an excuse.
He was glad Nancy had handed it to Mother Mary Bellarmine anyway. From what Norm had seen of Mother
Mary Bellarmine, she made his mother look like an
angel of light.

Once into the foyer, Norm looked left and right and
found two doors, set discreetly into corners and cam-
ouflaged with baby blue bunting. The doors had no
signs on them and no signs near them. Norm had no
way of knowing if they were gateways to passages or

simply closets. He could have asked someone, but he didn't want to do it. Norman Kevic had never really been an extrovert. In fact, he'd never really liked people much. They scared him, and—as his mother had told him repeatedly; the very worst thing about Norman Kevic's mother was how often she was right—they weren't *interested* in knowing him. He could get very convivial when he'd had a few snorts. He hadn't had a few snorts in hours. If he could find the bathroom maybe he could take care of that kind of business there as well. Whatever. It was easier to explore on his own. If he blundered into a closet, he could always claim he was looking for his coat. Although who would wear a coat in this weather, he didn't know. He had to get a grip on himself.

The door to his right had on it not only baby blue bunting, but a large oval picture of the Virgin standing on a puffy cloud with her hands held out and a halo around her head. Norm decided to choose that one, because it was his favorite picture of the Virgin from parochial school. Norm hated on principle all pictures of the Madonna and Child, but he was fond of young Marys with dreamy blue eyes in flowing dresses that rippled in the wind. They reminded him of the kind of music video produced by earnest women singers who were serious about Art.

Norm opened the door and peered down into a corridor, which was thankfully not a closet, but wasn't much better, either. It was narrow and dank. Its ceiling was lined with thick, badly painted pipes. Its walls were dark green from the floor halfway up the wall and pale green the rest of the way to the ceiling. Norm felt around on the wall beside the door for a switch. He turned on the light and looked inside some more. Surely, if the men's room was down here, there would be directions? Surely, the men's room *wasn't* down here, because even for a feminist institution this sort of mistreatment would be too much?

Norm went into the corridor and closed the door behind him. He had no idea if St. Elizabeth's was a feminist institution or not. He had no clear idea of what a feminist was. Hell, he had no clear idea who Norman Kevic was. He walked down the claustrophic corridor until he came to a place he had to turn, and hesitated. To his left there was more corridor. To his right there was a heavy fire door. He went to the fire door and opened it up.

"There," a woman's voice said, not so much drifting up to him as flying up, like a rocket. "That ought to be just fine. Now all we have to do is fill the cones with flowers, tie the cones with ribbons, and bring them upstairs."

"I don't know," another woman's voice said, soft and tentative. "I have to tell you, Sarabess. I think we should have started with the flowers and wrapped the paper around them. I don't think we should have made paper cones first."

"Well, we did make paper cones first," the woman Norm took to be Sarabess said. "We're just going to have to live with them. Get me a big pile of roses, Sister, and then we can get started."

There was a breeze coming up from something open down there. Norm went on through the fire door and found himself at the top of a short, shallow flight of stairs. The stairs reached a landing six steps down and then proceeded into the dark. Norm went down to the landing and stopped. Now he could see another door, partially propped open, with light spilling out into the dark under his feet. Every once in a while, the light was obstructed by shadows, which Norm took to be the bodies of women, going back and forth doing whatever they were doing in the room they were in. He advanced a few more steps down, hesitated, and advanced again. It occurred to him that it was a good thing that his quest for the john had been basically on philosophical grounds.

He got to the bottom of the steps and the half-opened door and looked in. He had expected to see a pair of nuns, but what he saw instead was a single young nun and a woman with greying hair who seemed to be some kind of superannuated hippie. They were both working diligently at a line of the kind of paper cones florists used to put bouquets in, except that instead of being green the paper was baby blue, like everything else in this place. Norm peered harder through the door and saw that although the room beyond was strictly functional, with paint that looked like it belonged in a furnace room and bare wooden tables whose surfaces were as splintered as the surface on a cellar door, a certain amount of effort had been put into decorating here, too. On the far wall right in his line of vision was another one of those posters.

Norm moved toward the door, raised his hand, and knocked. He would have walked right in, but he had been noticing lately that women no longer took well to that kind of surprise. He'd walked in unannounced on one of the women in the office once last month and she'd very nearly belted him. He didn't know what had gotten into women these days.

Nobody inside seemed to have heard him. He raised his hands and knocked again. "Yoo hoo," he called, and instantly felt ridiculous. "Can I come in?"

The hippie woman dropped what she was doing and marched over to the door. "Oh," she said, flustered. "It's Mr. Kevic. What are you doing here?"

Since Norm was sure that if he'd met this woman before, he would have remembered it—the grotesque are as memorable as the beautiful—he assumed she knew who he was from his publicity. "I was looking for the—ah—the—"

"The toilet," the young nun in the background piped up.

"Right," Norm said. "I was looking for that. I seem to have gotten lost."

"You're in the basement of St. Teresa's House," the hippie woman said.

"I'm Sister Catherine Grace," the young nun told him.

"I'm Sarabess Coltrane."

Norm gave a little thought to it and decided that no, he had never heard of Sarabess Coltrane and there was no reason why he should have. The high administrators of the college were all nuns and there was no way Sarabess Coltrane was one of those. Norm had only met Reverend Mother General once, and that just half an hour or so ago, but he could just imagine what she thought of Sarabess Coltrane's outfit. Saggy cotton Indian print dress. Plastic barrettes holding back hair that could have used a cut, a conditioner, and a curl. Birkenstock sandals. It was embarrassing.

Norm edged into the room and looked around. There were a pair of industrial sinks along one wall that he hadn't been able to see from outside, and drains here and there in the floor. There was also a freezer whose door had been propped open and that seemed to be filled with flowers. Sarabess Coltrane had even more flowers in her hands. The flowers she had had originally were lying on the long wooden table, badly wrapped in a blue paper cone.

"Here," Norm said. "Let me help with that. I'll probably be faster."

"You?" Sarabess Coltrane sounded doubtful.

Norm took the roses out of her hands and walked over to the table to get a cone. The young nun had been right, of course. They should never have made the cones first. Oh, well. It wasn't that hard to fix if you knew how to fix it.

"I used to work for a florist when I was going to college," Norm said. "That's how I made my spending money before I found a station that would take me on. I used to wrap flowers all the time. Can I have one of those ribbons?"

"Of course," Sister Catherine Grace said.

"The flowers are for the Mothers Provincial," Sarabess Coltrane said. "We're supposed to present them right after lunch."

"Right after lunch may be tomorrow," Sister Catherine Grace said, "because the kitchen is right down the hall from here and we've been listening to poor Sister Agnes Bernadette, having one problem with the food after another."

"If nobody ever presents a bouquet to Mother Mary Bellarmine, nobody will care," Sarabess Coltrane said.

Sister Catherine Grace sighed. "Sarabess had a

run-in with Mother Mary Bellarmine the day before
yesterday. It was very sticky. We've been standing
around down here all afternoon plotting—" Sister
Catherine Grace flashed a look of agony at Sarabess
Coltrane and blushed.

"Never mind," Sarabess said. "We haven't made any
secret of it. Anybody who walked by outside could
have heard us." She leaned over Norm's shoulders and
hissed in his ear: "We've been plotting *murder*."

Catherine Grace giggled.

Norm went over to the freezer and contemplated the
roses. "How many in a bouquet?" he asked. "Twelve?"

"Of course twelve," Sarabess said.

"Roses are Mary's flower," Catherine Grace said.

"You shouldn't be plotting murder with Gregor
Demarkian upstairs," Norm told them. "Don't you
know who he is? The Armenian-American Hercule
Poirot."

Sarabess drew a stool up to the table and sat down
to watch Norm at work. "We know who Mr.
Demarkian is," she said, "but the point we've been
harping on is that it would be perfect. I mean, you
could murder anybody you wanted to today—at least
from down here—and you'd have to get away with it."

"It's because of the food," Catherine Grace said.

"If you go through that door there," Sarabess told
Norm, "you get to the other part of the corridor. This
room straddles it. Anyway, down there there's the
kitchen with all the food for the party just lying
around, and in here there's tons of poisonous stuff,
lye, gasoline, cleaning fluids, all kinds of things."

"And if you didn't want to use something from this
room," Catherine Grace said, "you could use something from the boiler room, because it's between here
and the kitchen. There's kerosene in there."

"And it wouldn't matter how bad the poison smelled,
because there would always be some kind of food that
smelled worse. Let me get you some more roses.
You're *very* good at that."

"Thank you," Norm said. He was very good at it. He
was always very good at everything. Even when he

hadn't had much practice. Even—almost especially—when he was stewed to the gills. People did not get to where Norman Kevic had gotten to without being able to deliver at that level in that way. He considered the proposition the two women had put before him and found an objection.

"What about this room?" he asked them. "If anybody who wants to commit murder by putting poison in the food has to pass through this room to get to the food—"

"But they wouldn't," Catherine Grace said. "There's two more sets of stairs on the other side. One from the first floor and one from the garden—you know, through an outside door."

"Nobody ever comes the way you came," Sarabess said, "except fire marshals when we have a fire drill. How did you ever get into that corridor?"

"I took a door in the foyer and kept on going," Norm said. "But wait a minute. What about your victim? If you poison the food you can't possibly know who'll eat what you poison. Unless you take a very little of it and put it on a cracker and hand it right over, and then somebody might see you and there you'd be. Behind bars."

"We could kill any of the Mothers Provincial," Catherine Grace said.

"Like Mother Mary Bellarmine," Sarabess elaborated. "Because of the ice sculptures."

"What?"

"Sister Agnes Bernadette has ice sculptures made in the shape of nuns, one for each of the Mothers, and there's going to be chicken liver pâté in each one and when they come out each of the Mothers Provincial and Reverend Mother General too, of course, are supposed to eat first from their particular sculpture. It's going to be a big fuss. So you see, all you have to do is poison the right chicken liver pâté—"

"And the sculptures are all going to be marked," Catherine Grace said.

"—and use something that acts quickly so nobody else takes a bite," Sarabess concluded.

"And there you'll be!" Catherine Grace was triumphant. "It's really absolutely perfect, Mr. Kevic. It's like something out of Agatha Christie."

In Norman Kevic's mind, it was something out of Edgar Allan Poe, but he wasn't going to say so.

It just confirmed the feeling he'd had all along that nuns were dangerous, and added to it the conviction that their friends were dangerous, too.

CHAPTER 4

1

Gregor Demarkian was not a religious man. He had been brought up in the Armenian Christian Church—which he described to people as "like the Greek Orthodox, but not really," because it was too complicated to go into the history of millennial Church politics and heresies that might not have been heresies depending on whose side you were on, and he didn't know it all anyway—but once he had become an adult he had given it up. While he had been married to Elizabeth, he had done all the obligatory things. Weddings and funerals, christenings with the infant in antique lace and the godmother in tears: Elizabeth had determined which of those they were obliged to go to, what present they were obliged to bring, and what did or did not constitute an acceptable excuse on Gregor's part. According to Elizabeth's system, Gregor had been forgivably absent from his niece Hedya's christening because he was on kidnapping de-

tail in Los Angeles. His niece Hedya had been chris-
tened in Boston, where Elizabeth's older sister lived
with her husband, and Gregor couldn't be two places
at once. With his niece Maria's christening, though, he
had been in trouble. That had taken place in Washing-
ton, where he and Elizabeth were living at the time. It
had been Elizabeth's opinion that he could have found
a way to make time on a Sunday morning, no matter
what had him tied up in Quantico and the District of
Columbia. As it turned out later, what had him tied up
was the beginnings of what would become both the definitive case against Theodore Robert Bundy and the
establishment of the Behavioral Sciences Department,
but Elizabeth didn't care. Work was never as important
as family, even if "work" meant saving the world. The
world had been in need of saving for several thousand
years. Missing a niece's christening wasn't going to
help him save it.

Mostly, Gregor Demarkian thought of churches as
cultural institutions, like the Boy Scouts and the
YMCA. He didn't know enough about faith to comment on it one way or another, but he could see the
way Holy Trinity operated on Cavanaugh Street, the
way it made it easy for everybody around it to orga-
nize their lives, and he understood the need for something like that. He didn't know if Catholics felt the
same way about the Catholic Church. He expected it
was a bit more complicated, since ex-Catholics were often so obsessional about what had made them leave.
He had noticed, however, that comparing the Catholic
Church with the Boy Scouts was ludicrous. The Penta-
gon, that you could compare it with. Or the State Services Apparatus of the Soviet Union before the fall.
Malachi Martin's International Conspiracy of Everything would be good, too. Gregor meant no disrespect
for the Catholic Church. On an organizational level, he
thought it was a marvel. It was just that he didn't understand how a bureaucracy that big managed to stay
in operation for as long as this one had without stran-
gling itself.

One of the ways it had done that was by making

sure its coordinate parts were as supremely efficient as the central government was reputed to be confused. Gregor Demarkian had heard monologues without end on just how chaotic the Vatican was. Father Tibor's friend Father Ryan couldn't make himself stop once he got started. "Just try to get a request processed through Rome," Father Ryan would say, his eyes beginning to gleam. "Just try it. If it isn't an ordinary annulment appeal or a request for six copies of an encyclical from the publications office, do you know what you get? Forms! That's what you get. Forms!"

Gregor was sure Father Ryan got a lot of forms, but he never had to deal with the Vatican. The Catholic officials he did deal with were priests, bishops, and women religious. They not only did not pass out forms, they took to the field like generals promoted from the ranks who didn't know how to conduct a war without the smell of gunpowder in their noses. It was into this operational mode Gregor saw Reverend Mother General and her Sisters go, after Nancy Hare upended the vase of roses on Mother Mary Bellarmine's head. They went into it instantaneously, and with a precision Gregor would have been surprised to see in a cadre of veteran Bureau agents who had been working together for years. Gregor had seen SWAT teams that worked this well together, once or twice. He had seen an elite unit of the Israeli Army that could do it every time. That these women could do it when they hadn't seen each other for months and only handled a crisis of this sort once every two or three years, astounded him.

"It's because religious obedience is absolute," Reverend Mother General had told him, the one time before this he'd seen such an operation.

Sister Scholastica had demurred. "It's because not one of us wants to mess up and have Reverend Mother mad at us. Not even for one single minute."

In the long moment after Nancy Hare proclaimed Mother Mary Bellarmine a bitch, Reverend Mother General did not look angry. She did not look surprised, either. She simply stepped into the middle of the receiving line, raised her hand, nodded her head, and watched her Sisters go into action.

The Sister who grabbed Nancy Hare was not one Gregor knew. She was tall and broad and athletic in a way that reminded Gregor of girls' high-school gym teachers, and she got Nancy by the shoulders and out of the way in no time at all. Nancy ended up looking more confused than alarmed at being manhandled. She had still been holding the vase when Sister pushed her against the far wall. The movement made her addled and she lost her grip on it. Stoneware isn't china, but if it hits marble from a sufficient height it will shatter. The Sister dived for it and caught it in mid-flight in one hand, keeping Nancy immobile with the other. On the other side of the room, a nun Gregor did know—Sister Mary Alice, Mistress of Novices, whom he'd met in Maryville—was fussing around Mother Mary Bellarmine in that brisk and determined way elementary-school teachers use to calm small boys. Sister Mary Alice didn't look like she much liked doing it, but she did seem to be good at it. Mother Mary Bellarmine's veil was soaked through, and there were trickles of green-tinged water running down her face. The veil had prevented much damage to the rest of her habit. Gregor edged closer in the crowd to get a better look. The modified habit of the Sisters of Divine Grace consisted of the veil—it went over the ears and fastened at the back of the neck—and a long black dress that covered the calf but didn't reach the floor, and a long garment called a scapular. The scapular was a long piece of black cloth with a hole in the middle for the head to go through, that hung front and back from the shoulders to the hem of the habit's dress. There was some religious significance to the scapular. It had something to do with Saint Simon Stock and the Carmelite Order and the Blessed Virgin Mary, the way practically everything in the Catholic Church had to do with the Blessed Virgin Mary. Scholastica had told Gregor about it during the long days they had spent at the Maryville Police Department, doing their parts to straighten out the mess that results in the aftermath of any murder, no matter how successfully solved. Gregor couldn't remember the explanation, but he did remember most of the rest of that conversation, and that had been about just how important the scapular was as part of the habit.

"There were Sisters who wanted to go to really short dresses, knee-length, but they wouldn't have looked right with a scapular," Scholastica had told him, "and if there's one thing the old women in this Order want to express, it's how vital they think it is for Sisters to wear a scapular."

The point now was that Mother Mary Bellarmine's scapular was torn, ripped from the neck hole down the front in one long gash. Gregor couldn't imagine how it had happened. Of course, he hadn't been very close when the incident had happened. It wouldn't have taken long to tear the scapular. It could have been done when his attention was momentarily elsewhere. It still didn't make sense. Nancy Hare had called Mother Mary Bellarmine a bitch. Then she had emptied the vase of roses on Mother Mary Bellarmine's head. Then she had stepped back. She had not taken time to rip Mother Mary Bellarmine's scapular. Gregor was sure of it.

Very young Sisters in long white veils had come into the foyer to clean up. They had a mop and a bucket and a pile of rags. The white veils pegged them as novices. Reverend Mother General emerged from her place in the crowd to supervise their work, nodded a little and said, "Has anyone found Henry yet?"

"Sister Caroline went to get him," a voice called out. "He's in the back garden."

"Oh, for Christ's sake," Nancy Hare said. "Don't bring Henry in on this. He'll act like a jerk."

"She's the one who's acting like a jerk," a voice said in his ear.

Gregor turned and found that the whisperer was not Bennis Hannaford, whom he'd expected, but Sister Scholastica. Her arms were folded in such a way that they were almost entirely hidden by her scapular and

her long dress collar that was so reminiscent of a cape.
Her face was wry.

"This isn't my territory," she told him, "so the lady
is nobody I know, but I have it on good authority that
she likes to make scenes."

"Bennis and I saw her coming in with her husband
when we were in the parking lot. Bennis said she
thought she was the kind of woman who liked to have
an audience."

"I always did think Bennis Hannaford had an intelligent voice. Did you happen to see what started all
this?"

"No," Gregor said.

"I didn't either. It must have been something Bellarmine said in the receiving line."

"Nancy and her husband went through the receiving line before Bennis and I did," Gregor pointed out.
"That was a good while ago—twenty minutes at least.
Do you think it would have taken that woman that long
to react?"

"I don't know," Scholastica said.

"Do you really think there's anything Mother Mary
Bellarmine could have said in the few seconds she'd
have had with the line going past that would have
caused this kind of reaction?"

Scholastica smiled. "Mother Mary Bellarmine," she
said, "could cause World War Three in thirty seconds
flat if she had a mind to. Does that answer your question?"

"Not a nice woman, I take it."

"I absolutely refuse to cause the kind of scandal I
would have to cause to accurately describe that person
while in a habit."

"Right," Gregor said.

"Here comes Henry," Scholastica said. "If anybody
but Reverend Mother were running this show, I'd say
there was about to be a lot of fun."

Somehow, using the word *fun* to describe Henry
Hare didn't quite cut it. He was thin and fashionable
and good looking and athletic, but those qualities
didn't add up to what they were supposed to. Gregor

had thought in the parking lot that Henry Hare had an air of middle-aged stodginess about him. He now found his initial impression confirmed. Henry Hare was angry, and embarrassed, and all the other things a man would be when his wife had just pulled a stunt like this. He should have been generating sympathy by the truckload. He wasn't. He could see the same thought racing through a dozen minds around him. *She behaves like this because he's just so insufferably smug.*

Henry Hare strode into the middle of the foyer, looked at his wife standing against one wall with the tall athletic nun in attendance, looked at Mother Mary Bellarmine standing against the other with her torn scapular, looked at the novices picking up their cleaning things on their way out and said, "Oh, Christ."

Sixty nuns made the sign of the cross and bowed their heads.

"Mr. Hare," Reverend Mother General said firmly, "I believe your wife is feeling unwell."

"Has she been drinking?" Henry Hare demanded.

"Of course I haven't been drinking," Nancy Hare said. "There's nothing to drink. Except mineral water."

"I didn't want to ask if you'd been doing anything else."

"What Mrs. Hare has been doing is feeling unwell," Reverend Mother said in a voice that brooked no argument. Gregor was willing to bet that Reverend Mother's voice almost never brooked an argument. "She needs to go home and lie down," Reverend Mother went on, "and I think you should take her there. The Sisters will, of course, make up a basket so that neither of you will miss any of the lunch we so sincerely wish to provide you with."

"Oh, good," Nancy said, and giggled. "A doggy bag."

"Shut up," Henry told her.

"I'm not going to shut up," Nancy said. "That woman is a bitch and you know it. Everybody knows it."

"I have to do something about my habit," Mother Mary Bellarmine said. "It's ripped."

Reverend Mother General turned. Mother Mary Bellarmine didn't look like a woman who had recently been attacked. She wasn't shaken, and she was paying no attention whatsoever to her attacker. In Gregor's experience, a victim in the same room with her victimizer usually kept a good eye out for another attack, or any sign of irrational behavior.

Reverend Mother General nodded at Mother Mary Bellarmine and said, "You should go change. Is it just your scapular?"

"My veil's wet."

"A veil is no problem. There are scapulars and veils downstairs in the supply room, if I remember correctly. Down near the kitchen. Mary Joachim?"

"That's right, Reverend Mother. There's a subsidiary supply room downstairs right next to the kitchen. We used this building for a convent back in sixty-four when the original convent had a fire and we had to wait for the new one to be built. We've been using that storeroom down there for habits ever since. I don't know why."

"Why," Reverend Mother said, "is the same reason every house in this Order has chicken fricassee every Thursday night. Because once you get started on a path it's practically impossible to leave it. That's what I used to tell my novices when I had Sister Mary Alice's responsibilities. Mary Bellarmine. Do you know your way to the kitchen?"

"Of course I know my way to the kitchen," Mary Bellarmine said. "Sister Agnes Bernadette has had every Sister in the Order running back and forth like laboratory rats helping with the food."

"Gracious as always," Reverend Mother General said. She turned to Nancy and Henry Hare. "What about the two of you? Do you know your way to your parking lot?"

"There's no reason why both of us should miss this reception," Henry Hare said stiffly. "I'm going to call my driver to pick Nancy up."

"I don't think so," Reverend Mother General said.

"But—" Henry Hare said.

Reverend Mother General gave him a look that would have turned stone to dust, and he retreated.

The novices had disappeared with their mops and rags. Mother Mary Bellarmine was headed for a door at the back of the foyer that Gregor hadn't noticed before. Sister Mary Alice had returned to the amorphous crowd and stopped looking as if she were chewing antibiotics undiluted with sugar. Even Nancy Hare seemed to have calmed down—although Gregor had to concede that she'd been calmer all along than almost anybody but Reverend Mother General. No, lack of calmness was not Nancy Hare's problem.

Gregor had turned toward Sister Scholastica, meaning to ask her impressions of the way it had all worked out, when he became aware of the fact that the crowd was parting in front of him, and even Scholastica was stepping aside. He looked in the direction everyone else was looking in and found Reverend Mother General, bearing down on him as if he were a rabbit in the path of a train.

"Mr. Demarkian," she said, in her deep emphatic voice that would have played well as the voice of God speaking from the burning bush, "I have to talk to you for a moment."

From the other side of the doorway, Bennis Hannaford caught his eye and winked.

2

Early in his association with things Catholic, Gregor Demarkian had learned that there were times it was the better part of valor just to shut up. Following Reverend Mother General through a door and down a corridor off the left side of the foyer was one of those times. The door had been decorated with baby blue bunting and a picture of Mary holding out the rosary to the children of Fatima. The corridor was decorated with baby blue bunting and brightly painted posters that looked out of place, as if they had originally been intended for somewhere else. Several of them displayed the message Gregor had first seen in Philadelphia and had been seeing everywhere since, including on the habits of some of the nuns, who wore little plastic pins with the legend,

---

ON MOTHER'S DAY REMEMBER THE MOTHER OF GOD.

Reverend Mother General was not wearing such a pin. She wasn't paying any attention to the posters, either. She was marching them both to the corridor's end, God only knew what for.

What was at the corridor's end were two small studies, each supplied with an overstuffed couch, an overstuffed chair, and a small coffee table. All the furniture had seen better days in the administration of Woodrow Wilson. Reverend Mother General picked the one on the right—she was right-handed; there was nothing to choose between them—and motioned Gregor inside.

"Please excuse us for all that fuss in the foyer," she said. "We really hadn't planned on anything of that sort. Maybe that sounds obvious. But maybe we should have anticipated it. It's so very hard to know. Nancy Hare—that's who that was, Nancy Hare, in case nobody upstairs told you—anyway, we've all known Nancy for a long time. She has a penchant for theatrics."

"Is she someone important?" Gregor asked.

"Important?" Reverend Mother General looked stumped. "She was a student here in a parish school we run—not right here but in Radnor. And then she went to Sacred Heart. And then she came to this college. She's married to Henry Hare. Does the name mean anything to you?"

"No."

"He'd be disappointed. He's the founder and CEO of VTZ. It's a communications conglomerate, I think."

"It's a communications corporation," Gregor said. "I think that in order to be a true conglomerate you have to be at least a national operation, and VTZ as far as I know is still local. Newspapers. Radio stations. A cable channel."

"Also construction," Reverend Mother General said. "I think it may all have started with construction, but don't quote me, because it's not the sort of thing I have an easy time keeping straight. At any rate, VTZ owns a number of companies that supply construction material and do construction work. Mr. Hare has donated a great many materials and services to the building of a new field house for St. Elizabeth's College."

"Ah," Gregor said.

Reverend Mother General gave him a sharp look. "What's that supposed to mean, Mr. Demarkian? Ah?"

"It's supposed to mean that I was wondering why you put up with him. Or with her, either, alumna or no alumna. You don't put up with much, Reverend Mother."

"I wouldn't put up with anything for an ordinary field house," Reverend Mother General said. "No, it isn't that. I'm just finding it more and more difficult in my old age to be as categorically judgmental as I used to be. That is probably God's grace."

"If you say so."

"There is also the problem of Mother Mary Bellarmine," Reverend Mother General said. Then she seemed to think better of it. She sat down on the overstuffed chair and folded her hands in her lap. *Notice all the things the older nuns do,* Scholastica had told Gregor once, *that don't seem to make any sense, but would if they were wearing long old-fashioned habits instead of these new ones.*

"Believe it or not," Reverend Mother General said, "I called you out here to ask you a favor, in spite of the

fact that you did us an enormous favor a little more
than a year ago, and now you're doing another one by
giving this speech. It's a very big favor, Mr. Demarkian. It's going to take a lot of work. And of course we
can't pay you any money."

"Of course you can't," Gregor said. Gregor didn't
take money for involving himself in extracurricular
murders. It was too likely to land him in trouble with
the Pennsylvania licensing agencies. Gregor didn't
have a private detective's license and didn't want to get
one.

"Ever since the—problems—we had in Maryville
last year," Reverend Mother General went on, "those
of us in positions of responsibility in this Order have
been discussing—oh, what am I doing?" Reverend
Mother shook her head. "Sister Scholastica has been
badgering us, that's what's been happening, and I have
to admit I think she's right. I think we could have prevented that murder last year, Mr. Demarkian, if we had
known what we were doing."

Gregor shook his head. "You had two very determined people to deal with. Unless you're asking for
clairvoyance, I don't think you would have been able
to deter either one of them."

"Maybe," Reverend Mother said, looking stubborn,
"but there was that hate mail. You knew the difference
between that and the ordinary kind. We didn't."

"I'd spent twenty years with the Federal Bureau of
Investigation."

"Then there were the simple procedural matters,"
Reverend Mother General went on. "Who to call. Who
to contact. What to report and how. It isn't 1950 anymore, you know."

"Yes," Gregor said, beginning to get lost. "I know."

Reverend Mother General wasn't Bennis Hannaford,
or Sister Mary Scholastica either. She clarified the
point immediately. "What we've got to accept," she
said, "is that with the world the way it is and the way
it's going, we're going to find ourselves dealing with
the sorts of people who make dealing with the police
more and more necessary. There are a lot of lunatics

out there these days, Mr. Demarkian, and a lot of bigots. Just two months ago one of our Sisters was mugged in Boston—in habit, yet. Just three weeks ago, two of our Sisters in Detroit were hospitalized from wounds received from sniper fire. We staff parochial schools in every ghetto in the country and we're proud to do it. Most of the people we deal with would be fine, upstanding citizens of any community they happened to live in, they just don't have much money. Unfortunately—"

"Mmm," Gregor said.

"Cocaine," Reverend Mother General said.

"Mmm," Gregor said again.

"It's not the people who use it you have to worry about," Reverend Mother continued. "It's the people who sell it. So you must see what I mean. You must see what our problem is."

"Actually," Gregor said, "I don't exactly understand how I could be helpful in this sort of ..."

"But of course you do," Reverend Mother General said.

"But of course I don't," Gregor insisted. "The only advice I could give would be to pull your Sisters out of the inner cities because they aren't safe, and I couldn't give you any advice at all about how to guard against the kind of thing that happened in Maryville last year because there isn't any way to guard against it, so just what—"

"What we want you to do," Reverend Mother General said, "is to write a handbook and give a little course. In procedures."

"Procedures," Gregor repeated.

"Procedures," Reverend Mother General repeated. "When to call the police. When to call the FBI. How to preserve evidence. What constitutes evidence. How to handle the press—"

"Oh, no, now, if I knew how to handle the press I wouldn't be the Armenian-American Hercule Poirot."

"Of course you would be. It was brilliant marketing strategy. And, of course, in most places we have the Chancery to help with the press, and sometimes that's very good. Sometimes it's not so good, however. You must know all these things, Mr. Demarkian. This is what you do."

"But a project of the sort you're talking about would really take a very long time—"

Reverend Mother General stood up, beaming. "That's all settled then," she said. "You'll come in and speak to the Mothers Provincial a week from Tuesday. That's aside from the general address you'll be giving this week, of course, we wouldn't deprive you of that."

"But," Gregor said.

"And don't worry about the handbook," Reverend Mother General told him. "We won't need a draft of that for at least fourteen days."

116 *Jane Haddam*

and newly middle-aged parishioners, who seemed to have a highly peculiar idea of what life was about. "Americans," a titled British lady once said, "have somehow got the idea that death is optional." The first time Father Stephen Monaghan had heard that quote, he'd thought it was ludicrous. That was twenty years ago. Now he said Mass on a college campus and in the churches of the surrounding towns when the college was not in session and the churches were short of priests. The people he preached to were either young or nuns. The people he preached to believed they were immortal. It was like talking to children. "Someday you'll die," he'd say, and they'd look at him with contempt so deep it might have bored a hole to the center of the earth. Death was a boogeyman fairy tale, as far as they were concerned.

Today, Father Stephen Monaghan had taken the noon Mass at St. Bridget's in Eddingsberg. Eddingsberg was farther than he usually traveled to say Mass and out of his particular orbit. He'd gone there because the Bishop had asked him to and he always did what the Bishop wanted. He'd had high hopes for the afternoon. After all, Eddingsberg was rust-belt territory. He wouldn't be caught in a clutch of yuppies up there. But he'd underestimated the reach of what he was beginning to think of as the "pernicious doctrine." It must be something they were advocating on television. All he had said—in memory of the fact that his own mother had died on Mother's Day—was that remembering the finitude of life was a good way to keep perspective on the things of this world. That was it. You want a pair of sixty-dollar Reeboks. You have forty-nine, ninety-five. You can walk around convinced your life is terrible, or remember that your life is finite and realize that Reeboks aren't that important after all. That was a little muddled, but not so muddled it was difficult to understand. A four-year-old could have understood it. He'd looked out over the densely packed pews, at the blue ribbons tied into bows on each of the pews' ends, over the heads of the women in their best Sunday hats and the children wiggling and straining against the starch in their clothes. He'd delivered a sermon that was in no way substantially different from the second one he'd ever preached. He'd caused what amounted to a brush fire of indignation. Maybe he'd been a little off in his timing. Maybe this wasn't the kind of sermon good hardworking people wanted to hear on Mother's Day. Maybe he should have said some warm fuzzy things about the Motherhood of Mary and let it go at that. He didn't know. What he did know was that when he was done and standing on the church steps, shaking hands with the people on their way out, a ferociously well-maintained woman in her early thirties had marched up to him, put her hands on her hips and announced: "If you learned to take better care of yourself, you wouldn't have to think about death all the time. You could save your own life!"

Father Stephen Monaghan was himself waiting for the Rapture. He wanted to see the Heavens open up and Christ descending on a cloud. Or however it was done. The Rapture was mostly an evangelical Protestant concept, now seeping into North American Catholicism through various forms of folk religion. He wasn't sure he had it straight.

He was sure he wasn't ready for an afternoon of five thousand nuns, either, but he figured he didn't have a choice. He had told Reverend Mother General at the Sisters' Mass this morning that he would drop in as soon as he got back from Eddingsberg, and he would have to drop in. In the old days, people didn't question priests who turned down invitations or took them up when they hadn't actually been offered. Priests could come and go as they pleased as long as they didn't do anything to offend the Bishop. Now there were a dozen committees to decide every question and at least one person in every group—usually female, usually in her forties, usually with a degree in pastoral counseling or contemporary liturgics from one of the lesser Catholic colleges—ready to jump to her feet at the slightest provocation and start delivering lectures on the necessity of "accountability." "I am accountable only to God," St. Thomas More had said. Father

Stephen Monaghan often wished he had the courage to say the same. Out loud.

It was quarter to two in the afternoon, and there were nuns everywhere, on the walks, in the parking lots, on the steps of buildings. Pulling onto campus from the narrow town road that passed it, Stephen was reminded of the plagues of locusts that showed up at least once in every 1930s picture about agriculture in China or farmers in the frontier Midwest. Of course, nuns were nothing at all like locusts, of course not, but there they were, in those black veils, covering the ground like a living blanket. It wasn't that bad, but it was close. It was very close. And parties being what they were, Father Stephen was sure that they were spreading.

He drove away from the main hub of the party to St. Patrick's Hall, which housed the religion department, where he had an office. He parked in the back and let himself in through the basement door. He didn't think it would do any harm for him to sit in his office for a moment or two, just to catch his breath. He would go over and shake a few million hands in a moment or two.

His office was an eight-by-ten cubicle on the first floor, facing a wall of tree trunks that made viewing any part of the campus impossible. He let himself in, looked over the books he had left on his desk—*Hymns for the Modern Catholic Congregation; Harrigan's Homily Notes for the Liturgical Year*—and sat down in his desk chair. He took his pipe out of the center drawer of his desk and lit up carefully. He always had trouble with his pipe. It wouldn't light. It wouldn't stay lit. The base of the stem got all clogged up and wouldn't let any air through. He'd been smoking this pipe since his ordination, and he still hadn't got the hang of it.

He took a couple of deep drags, decided he was getting a decent stream of smoke with minimal aggravation for once, and wondered if he should wander down the hall to see if anyone had left yesterday's paper out. Father Stephen Monaghan almost never got to the newspaper on the day it was printed, and sometimes didn't get to the paper at all. The Berlin Wall had been lying in pieces on the ground for two weeks before he'd heard of it.

He had just about decided he ought to go over to St. Teresa's House and make his manners and get something to eat—Father Stephen was thin mostly because he was always forgetting to eat; when he remembered to eat he ate like a horse—when he heard a noise out in the hall. It was an unself-conscious, blundering noise, nothing to be worried about, but it was strange. Although St. Elizabeth's was like any other college these days, in that it employed more workaholics than a sane person could stand to be in the same place with for longer than fifteen minutes, on a Sunday like this at the start of a vacation week, those workaholics were likely to be straining themselves to death in the Marabar Caves or the British Museum. Father Stephen wasn't sure what professors of religion did except lose their faith and talk forever about the "symbolic significance of the crucifixion." In fact, Father Stephen admitted to himself, he wasn't sure about much of anything at all. He wasn't a sure kind of man. The only thing he'd ever been willing to bet his life on was the one thing he *had* bet his life on. And that was that Christ had risen on the third day.

He went out in the hall, looked around, heard more blundering, and headed for the stairwell. This was a beautiful building outside, made of stone and gracefully proportioned. Inside, it had been constructed like those ancient parochial schools where Father Stephen had spent his childhood. High ceilings. Heavy doors. Wide tall windows that could only be opened with the help of a long thin pole. Standing in the doorway to his office, Father Stephen could see that the fire door to the stairs at the far end of this hall had been left propped open with a rubber door stopper. Father Stephen assumed that a nun had done it before the weekend sometime, because only the nuns used rubber door stoppers. Everybody else used whatever was handy, like wads of paper and stray books. The sound he was hearing was somebody thrashing around in the stairwell on the basement level, probably with no idea of where he was supposed to go. Or she, Father Stephen told himself. With all the nuns around, it was probably she. He went to the fire door and called down, "Who is it? Can I help you?"

"Oh, thank *Christ*," a man's voice said. "Yes, you can help me. You can get me out of here."

"Just come up the stairs," Father Stephen said, ashamed to be feeling so relieved that the person he was talking to was a man. "How did you get in?"

"There was a door down here that was open, you know, with a book keeping it open, but when I came in I kicked the book out and locked myself in. I mean, for Christ's sake. Haven't you people ever heard of safety locks?"

Father Stephen didn't even know if safety locks had been invented when this building was built. He did know it took a key to get in or out of the building once the locks were set. That was true of every building on this campus. He stepped back and held the door he was standing next to wide open, just to seem welcoming.

"You just come on up," he said, "I can let you out the front door with my key. I hope you haven't been put to too much trouble. Was there something you needed I could get for you?"

"Not exactly." The man emerged in the stairwell, a big young man in overalls creased with what Father Stephen's mother would have called "clean dirt." He's been gardening, Father Stephen thought to himself, and in a moment the truth of that observation was confirmed. The young man was carrying a mud-caked trowel in his left hand, swinging it along as if he didn't even know it was there.

"Hi," he said, looking Father Stephen over with less curiosity than relief. "You don't know how glad I was to hear a guy's voice. I mean, you don't know. I've been up to my neck in them all week."

"Nuns," Father Stephen said solemnly.

"You got it. I'm Frank Moretti. I do groundswork. You know. With the grass. And the gardens."

"You're the groundskeeper?"

"Hell no," Frank said. "The groundskeeper is Ally

MacBurn—Aloyishus, I think. He's sixty-two and about six hundred pounds and he's been here forever. No, I just do work. I plant things."

"Flowers," Father Stephen said helpfully.

"Flowers and grass and bushes. They've got this topiary out in front of the church. Gumdrop hedges. No big deal. I trim that." Frank had reached the top of the stairs. He walked onto the first-floor hall and looked around, no more curious than he had been about Father Stephen. Father Stephen got the impression that Frank Moretti had seen his share of schools and was glad to be quit of them.

"So," Father Stephen said. "What can I help you with? Maybe I can at least direct you to the proper person to be helped by."

"Who'll probably be a nun." Frank Moretti sighed.

"Probably." Father Stephen sighed back.

"Well, I suppose it can't be helped," Frank Moretti said. "It's Sunday, which you probably know, being a priest and all."

"Oh, I know," Father Stephen said.

"Right," Frank Moretti said. "So what I do on Sundays, usually, is I work on the grass. Now the nuns don't like that much, what with Sunday supposed to be a day of rest and whatnot, but the grass is my responsibility and Sunday's really the only day it makes any sense to do it. I mean, it's the only day there aren't six million people walking on it, because you know what these college girls are like. They go anywhere. Forget the signs."

"Mmm," Father Stephen said.

"So I come in and I do the grass, I fertilize, I mix plant food. I do all of it from the back garden beyond the walled garden behind St. Teresa's House to over here and then out again up to the lawns behind the Administration Building. Big area. Of course, I knew I wasn't going to be able to get into that space behind St. Teresa's House today."

"Of course," Father Stephen agreed.

"If you ask me, a nuns' convention is a damn silly idea. Excuse my language. But you know what I mean.

Somebody said there were more than five thousand nuns over there."

"Five thousand two hundred and change."

"Yeah. And they're multiplying. It's a miracle. Forget I said that. The thing is, I knew I was going to have trouble this week, so I packed up my things in a big knapsack last Friday, see, and I put the knapsack on the bench in the gardening shed—"

"Where's the gardening shed?"

"Well, there are six or seven gardening sheds, Father, but the one we use for this part of the campus is right there next to St. Teresa's House on the side like where there's this little alley. So I put all my things in this knapsack and I left the knapsack on the bench and then when I came in today I got the knapsack off the bench and I came over here to work. You follow so far?"

"Perfectly," Father Stephen said.

"Good," Frank Moretti said, "because so do I, because what comes next is first-rate stupid, and I tell you it's because we've got all those nuns around. It's not a good idea. All those nuns. It's enough to give a man the creeps."

"Shades of second grade," Father Stephen said.

"Right," Frank Moretti said, "except in second grade we didn't steal plant food, because there's no damn reason for anyone to steal plant food, I mean if you want plant food all you have to do is go over to the *main* gardening shed and get some, which is a walk of all of about a quarter of a mile, over to the Physical Sciences Building. Or you could go to the store and get it for practically no money at all. And why would you steal it? Because your plant was dying?"

"Somebody stole your plant food," Father Stephen said thoughtfully.

"I didn't discover it until I got over here," Frank Moretti said. "In fact, I didn't discover it until about half an hour ago, which was when I came in here looking for someone to help out, although what anybody's supposed to do about this is beyond me. I mean it. I didn't look in the knapsack before I brought it over here, you see. And I didn't notice about the plant food until half an hour ago because I didn't need the plant food until about half an hour ago. You see what I mean."

"Are you sure somebody stole it? Maybe you forgot to put it in on Friday."

"They didn't steal all of it," Frank said patiently. "They ripped the bag open and took a bunch out. I mean, I figure they took a bunch out. I can't really tell. But you see what I'm saying here. I got a new bag Friday. I remember doing it. And I know I didn't open it myself and none of the other gardeners did either because of the way it was torn. It was ripped right down the side. We'd have used our jack knives and opened it along the top. Where the 'Open Here' sign is."

"Right," Father Stephen said. Then he looked away and frowned. It was so hard to know what this man wanted of him. Father Stephen thought it might be something on the order of "male affirmation" or whatever you called it these days when two men got together and commiserated with each other about women. Then he had an uncomfortable thought. "Frank," he said, "is this stuff that's missing dangerous?"

"What do you mean, dangerous?"

"Well, could someone die from it? Or get very sick? Is it poison?"

Frank looked confused. "I don't think so, Father. We have it all over ourselves all the time and never think anything of it, so it couldn't be too toxic. It's this new organic stuff. Sister Wilhelmina in the biology department switched us to it last year. Said it didn't make any sense to poison the environment just to get greener grass. Saw her point. The old stuff used to be poisonous, though. Bunch of chemicals in it."

"Hmm," Father Stephen said.

"What this stuff would do anybody got ahold of it not paying attention," Frank said, "is it would turn them green. I mean green the color. It's got some kind of natural stain in it and it comes right off on everything. Skin. Clothing. Mix it with water and it's worse. It's like instant dye. Gross."

"Ah," Father Stephen said.

"So the thing is," Frank Moretti said, "I don't want to make a big fuss about it or anything, cause I know how crazy things are all over this place, you know, but what I want to do is, I want to tell whoever I'm supposed to that if any of those nuns want plant food they should come ask us. Instead of ripping open bags and getting it on their own, if you see what I mean. I mean, that kind of thing only causes a lot of trouble."

"Right," Father Stephen said.

"Only now I've told you," Frank Moretti said, "and *you* can tell whichever nun it is that's supposed to know."

Finally, Father Stephen Monaghan knew what Frank Moretti wanted of him.

He wanted to be protected from the nuns.

2

Sister Domenica Anne had entered the Order of the Sisters of Divine Grace at the age of seventeen, right out of high school, and she fully expected to be there until the day she died. She liked being a nun and she liked most of the nuns she met. She hadn't minded the routine prior to Vatican II and she didn't mind the relaxation of that routine now. Stuck on Amtrak or an airplane or some other long trip among strangers, she almost always sought out the other religious women— and there were a surprising number of them on the move these days; since most of them didn't wear habits you simply had to know what to look for—and had a good time discussing the differences in customs among the many orders old, new, flourishing, and otherwise. Domenica Anne would not have believed that she could ever get tired of nuns. She would have been wrong. For almost a week now, the campus of St. Elizabeth's College had been filling with nuns. They had been trickling in like water filling a tide pool. They had become so numerous they had begun to appear as if they were cloning themselves. They were in kitchens and dining rooms, classrooms and living rooms, rectories and convents. They covered lawns and pews. They occupied library carrels and booths at the Bright Day Fountain Shoppe. Some of them even drank beer and ate pizza with tapeplayers blasting out vintage Beach Boys right on the convent's front steps. It was lunacy.

That Domenica Anne was herself going loony had become thoroughly clear immediately after Mass this morning, when she had filed out into the air of the seven o'clock spring morning along with seven hundred other nuns and watched seven hundred more file in. At that point the weather had been considered iffy, so they had had stacked Masses instead of one big Mass on the field behind St. Teresa's House. The weather had been considered iffy all week. Domenica Anne had been filing in and out and out and in with seven or eight hundred other nuns for everything she could think of, sometimes—this was an exaggeration, but not much of an exaggeration—even for a chance at the bathroom. Add to that the fact that she was really not ready to make nice-nice to Mother Mary Bellarmine, and by eight o'clock she'd known that she really couldn't go to this party. Maybe she could come down later, when the receiving line had broken up and everybody was a little addled by too much food. In fact, she probably would, because the food at the party was going to be the only food available for most of the day. In the meantime, however, she thought she would be much more comfortable surrounded by her papers in her own workroom. She might even be able to get something done.

It was now two o'clock in the afternoon. Domenica Anne had been going over her blueprints for five hours, and she was tired. Her workroom was in St. Thomas's Hall, in the attic, in a room that looked down on St. Teresa's House and its garden. All afternoon, Domenica Anne had been able to watch the spillover of the party. When she'd first come over this morning, she'd had her assistant with her. Her assistant was a very young nun named Sister Martha Mary and much too excited by everything to do with the convention to miss the festivities this afternoon. Domenica Anne had sent her over as soon as people began climbing the steps of St. Teresa's House. Now Domenica Anne looked out her window and saw Martha Mary coming back, holding a tray of something covered and seeming to skip.

Martha Mary always seemed to skip.

It made Domenica feel better just to watch her.

Domenica Anne went to stand in the hall near the elevator door to wait. She heard the humming of the elevator machinery and then the humming of Sister Martha Mary. Martha Mary was humming the "M is . . ." parts of the song "Mother" in a kind of reggae beat.

The elevator came to a stop and the doors groaned open. They groaned instead of hissed because the elevator was fifty years old. Martha Mary stepped out without the least sign of surprise to find Domenica Anne waiting for her. Domenica Anne thought Martha Mary might know a great deal about the view out the attic workroom window, since she had to spend so much time hanging around while Domenica Anne got her work done. Martha Mary held the large covered plate out to Domenica Anne and said, "Take it. It's more precious than gold. Nobody over there's gotten anything to eat yet."

"Are you serious?" Domenica Anne asked. She lifted off the paper that covered the platter and found inside more and better food than she'd had since the hordes began to descend on St. Elizabeth's. Roast beef. Turkey breast. Four kinds of olives. A great big wedge of Stilton cheese. Half a loaf of bread. There was more, but Domenica Anne didn't bother to inventory it. She started walking back into her workroom. "What went wrong?" she called back to Martha Mary, knowing that Martha Mary would follow. "Lunch was supposed to be no later than one thirty."

"I know it was supposed to be," Martha Mary said, "but Reverend Mother General seems to have reckoned without the seculars. Or at least without this one particular secular. Nancy Hare had one of her public fits."

"Did she really?"

Domenica Anne put the tray down on the edge of the long worktable where she usually went over the financial records and took the paper cover off for good. Then she made the sign of the cross and said a quick grace. Nuns might be driving her crazy for the moment, but she appreciated convent life. There was no way to forget God when you were in a convent. Even here in this workroom she had a crucifix on the wall, and posters of Mary with blue ribbon bows on them for the month of May.

"Nancy usually has more sense than to have her fits in front of Henry," she said. "I presume Henry was there."

"Oh, yes," Martha Mary said. "He took her home. If you want my opinion, I think she had her fit *because* Henry was there."

"How did one of Nancy's fits hold up lunch?"

Martha Mary grinned slyly. "You remember that thing they were going to do with the ice sculptures, and having them presented to Reverend Mother General and the Mothers Provincial and then each of the Mothers is supposed to take the first bite out of their own chicken liver pâté and blah and blah and it's just the kind of thing Agnes Bernadette would think up except we all put up with it because Aggie's such a dear?"

"Yes," Domenica Anne said. "I know."

"Well, the little ceremony won't work unless all the Mothers are there to take part in it, and the Mothers aren't all there to take part in it right this second because Mother Mary Bellarmine is off somewhere getting changed and the reason Mother Mary Bellarmine is off somewhere getting changed is because what Nancy Hare did was dump a vase of roses on Mother Mary Bellarmine's head and rip her habit somehow or other nobody knows. So you see—"

"Good Heavens," Domenica Anne said.

"I thought it was something you'd want to hear. Anyway, I wanted to get out of there. Ever since Nancy pulled her stunt even the sane people have been tense, and the seculars don't know what they're supposed to be doing. It's depressing. Have you made any progress with the budget yet?"

Domenica Anne sighed. "There isn't any progress to be made with the budget. We need more money. I don't suppose anybody over there threw a fit and wrote us a check."

"Not the kind of check you're talking about. I think it's a good thing Henry Hare signed contracts when we started this project. I think he's about ready to bolt. And I do mean bolt. From the project. From Nancy. From the Church. I'll give you a bet that in less than a year from now, he'll buy himself an apartment in the city and start being seen around town with a model barely out of diapers. Is it a sin to think so badly of a man who's giving the Order so much money?"

"Yes. But not because he's giving the Order so much money."

"I know we're supposed to see Christ in every man," Martha Mary said, "and every woman, too, according to Father Monaghan, but those two remind me of a pair of rutting monkeys. Maybe Darwin was confused. Maybe only some people evolved from the apes. Maybe some other people only seemed to evolve from the apes, but instead—"

"Nobody evolved from the apes," Domenica Anne said, "and you know it. You had Sister Wilhelmina for biology and she's very good at explaining evolution."

"Well, I refuse to believe that Henry Hare and I evolved from a common ancestor. What Nancy sees in him, I'll never know."

"What *Nancy* sees in *him*?"

Martha Mary shrugged. "Give me your razor pen and I'll trim facsimile pictures for a while. If we need so much money, we ought to get started raising it."

"It's on the tool board. I put it away last thing before I left here last night."

"Then you must have taken it out this morning," Martha Mary told her, "because it isn't in its slot."

Domenica Anne had just made herself a sandwich that looked like something out of the "Blondie" comic strip. It had turkey, roast beef, ham, lettuce, tomatoes, and three kinds of cheese on it. She raised it to her mouth and took a bite. Of course the facsimile pictures were important. They were supposed to be assembled into a collage that would be photographed and reproduced for a mailing requesting funds for the new field house. The mailing might make the difference between comfort and debt.

"Look again," Domenica Anne mumbled with her mouth full. "I haven't used it for anything this morning. The last time I had it out was yesterday, like I told you. I was cutting one of the study blueprints along the load-bearing lines to explain why we couldn't put one of the walls where Reverend Mother General wanted us to. I was getting reamed out by Mother Mary Bellarmine for not having anticipated all this when I talked to the architect in the first place. As if I were the one who made decisions about the floor plan with the architect."

"If it had been Mother Mary Bellarmine's project," Martha Mary said, "she would have made decisions about the floor plan with the architect. Dom, really, it's not here. You must have left it out."

"I didn't leave it out," Domenica Anne insisted.

"Well, whatever you did, it's not here now. And we can't leave it lying around loose. It could be dangerous."

"Right," Domenica Anne said.

And, of course, Martha Mary was right. She was always right. Domenica Anne had never had such a responsible assistant. It was just that at the moment, she'd rather eat her sandwich.

She was starving. And she couldn't imagine anything anyone could do with that razor pen that would cause anything like serious trouble.

CHAPTER 6

1

Bennis Hannaford never smoked cigarettes in crowded rooms unless she was very, very nervous—or unless the crowded room in question was a bar, where she was expected to smoke—but when Gregor Demarkian came downstairs after having his conversation with Reverend Mother General, Bennis was sitting in a corner of the reception room, perched on a side table that wobbled under her every time she took a drag, sucking on a Benson & Hedges Light the way mermaids in Florida underwater shows suck on their air hoses. At first glance, Gregor couldn't see what for. The scene in the reception room was actually calmer than it had been upstairs, although it was also more chaotic. All pretense at a reception line had been abandoned. The Mothers Provincial had blended into the crowd. Since their habits were the same as everybody elses', Gregor couldn't pick out a single one of them. There did seem to be even more nuns around than there had been before, and even more baby blue ribbons. There were also a lot of novices Gregor knew had not been there before, because he would have noticed their white veils. He caught sight of Sister Mary Alice, whom he had met in Maryville, and waved. She waved back at him in a distracted sort of way that said she'd just as soon never have met him. Since Gregor didn't blame her for that, he didn't press the point.

What he did do was to make his way through the crowd, deliberately and insistently, in Bennis Hannaford's direction, weaving his way through clots of nuns who sometimes seemed to have been welded together. It was astonishing. None of the nuns was drinking, but all of them were behaving just the way men did at professional conventions, when the liquor flowed like water.

"Listen," one of the older nuns was saying as she jabbed a fingertip in the air in front of a younger nun's face, "I've read everything that's come out in these last few years about school discipline, and I still say nothing is going to get a five-year-old boy to sit in his seat better than putting the fear of God into him."

"But Sister," the younger nun protested, "the problem is that these days you can't put the fear of God into him. And when you try, his parents sue!"

"We put up four AIDS hospices in Cleveland last winter," a cheerfully roly-poly little Sister was saying to another group, "and of course it was a mess with the zoning board, but let me tell you how we got around it—"

"We sent two of our Sisters to the Jesuit seminary to take courses in theology," a Sister with a heavy Australian accent was saying, "and they came back talking about Joseph Campbell and the idea of the numinous. What in the name of all that's holy is the idea of the numinous?"

"I know who Joseph Campbell is," one of the other Sisters said.

"Maybe the idea of the numinous is God," a third Sister said.

The Australian Sister looked skeptical. "Maybe the Jesuits are just as crazy as I always thought they were. Honestly. Such intelligent men and always going to extremes. Do you suppose it's hormonal?"

"Did you hear the one about the Franciscan and the Dominican who were arguing about who was holier, Francis or Dominic?" This was the second nun, the one who had heard of Joseph Campbell. "They argued and argued and argued, and finally they decided to leave it in the hands of God. So they went to the church and they got down on their knees in front of the altar and they prayed and they prayed and they asked God, 'Who was holier, Francis or Dominic?' Suddenly there's a puff of smoke that smacks into the altar cloth right at the front, and the fathers jump to their feet and run up to see what's happened, and sure enough there's a note there where there wasn't any note before. So they pick it up and read it and it says, 'All my saints are equally close to my heart. Stop bickering. Signed, God, S.J.' "

Wonderful, Gregor thought. They even had in-jokes. He pushed by two Sisters who were talking away in French (about Quebec, he could pick up that much) and finally found himself within speaking distance of Bennis Hannaford. He gently removed a tiny nun from his path and went to Bennis's side. The tiny nun—who had to have been ninety—went on lecturing her audience about the proper way to form a First Communion line without a break in her voice of any kind to mark the fact that she'd been lifted into the air and deposited on a different square of rug. There was a poster on a rickety tripod still in his path and Gregor moved that too, in the opposite direction of the tiny nun, so he didn't hit her in the head with it. The poster showed the Virgin Mary on a cloud floating above the entire world in miniature and then the words:

MOTHER OF GOD. MOTHER OF THE CHURCH. MOTHER OF US ALL.

Gregor squinted at the miniature and found the Eiffel Tower, the Taj Mahal, and St. Peter's Basilica in Rome. He thought he might have found the Coliseum, but he wasn't sure.

"Well," Bennis said in his ear, "did you come over to talk or to look at posters?"

"I came to talk. This is a fascinating poster. I think that's supposed to be the Great Wall of China."

"This person says she's somebody you know. Sister Mary Angelus. She says her name used to be Neila Connelly."

"Neila Connelly," Gregor said.

He hadn't been aware that Bennis was talking to somebody. Now he looked at the small girl in the white veil standing by Bennis's side and thought that, yes, she might actually be Neila Connelly, but only a Neila Connelly significantly more grown up than the one he had met in Maryville so many months ago.

"Sister Mary Angelus," he said, feeling a little stupid. What was he supposed to say?

"It's just Sister Angelus," Neila Connelly told him. "Everybody has 'Mary' in their name so almost nobody uses it, except of course old traditionalists like Mother Mary Bellarmine, except it isn't all that traditional because even in the old days almost nobody used it. And I don't think it's fair to call Mother Mary Bellarmine a traditionalist. I don't think she is a traditionalist."

"Mother Mary Bellarmine," Gregor repeated.

Bennis helped him out. "Mother Mary Bellarmine is the woman who got the flowers dumped on her," she explained, "and turned all green and had to go change. She's apparently infamous from one end of this convention to the other."

"She's driving everybody crazy," Sister Angelus said. "Even me, and you know me, Mr. Demarkian. I don't drive easily. And I've only been here for about a week."

"Is she back yet?" Gregor asked. "I didn't see her when I came through."

The three of them looked through the double doors leading to the foyer, but if Mother Mary Bellarmine was around, they didn't see her. They might not have even if she was standing right next to their little group. There were so many nuns. Gregor did see the man Bennis had pointed out to him as the famous Norman Kevic. He had planted himself next to one of the empty cloth-covered tables that were supposed to hold the food when someone decided to get around to it. From the look on his face, he would refuse to budge for anything less than the General Judgment.

"Anyway," Bennis said, "Sister Angelus has been filling me in on Mother Mary Bellarmine, as far as I can be filled in, because we still don't know why Mrs. Hare dumped the flowers on her."

"Mother Mary Bellarmine having problems with Mrs. Hare isn't something I've heard about," Sister Angelus said.

"But the thing is, the other stories are much better, which are all about this woman named Sister Joan Esther—"

"She works in Alaska," Sister Angelus said.

"And Sister Joan Esther's done something to get Mother Mary Bellarmine really furious, so all week the two of them have been fighting."

"It's been worse than fighting." Sister Angelus blushed. "Mr. Demarkian, you must be getting just the worst impression of us. First Brigit and now this. We're really not like this. Most of the time we're a very dedicated, very God-centered community of women—"

"That sounds like a publicity brochure," Bennis said.

"It is." Sister Angelus blushed even harder. "It's from the pamphlet they send you when you think you might want to join."

"Wonderful," Bennis said.

"Never mind," Gregor broke in hastily. "I hope you're not really worrying about the impression you're making. That mess in Maryville wasn't your fault. It wasn't your Order's fault."

"Oh, I know. And good things came out of it, too. The wedding. They write us, you know, and send us things. They're in Tahiti and they're going to Egypt at the end of the summer. But Brigit's still dead. And the way they behave sometimes—"

"Who's they?" Gregor asked.

Sister Angelus turned around and looked doubtfully in the crowd. "I don't see either one of them. Not that I blame Joan Esther. She's not the one who's persecuting anybody."

"Right," Bennis said.

Pronouns, Gregor thought. Neila Connelly had always had a lot of trouble with pronouns. "Who's persecuting whom?" he demanded.

"Mother Mary Bellarmine is persecuting Joan Esther, of course," Sister Angelus said. "At least, it sounds like persecution to me. I don't know. Maybe I'm too thin skinned. Sister Margarita—she was Carole Randolph when you were in Maryville, Mr. Demarkian, you met her—anyway, Margarita says Joan Esther doesn't pay any attention to it at all, that it just rolls right off her back. And maybe it does."

"What does?" Gregor asked.

"Well," Sister Angelus said, "take the night before last at dinner. It's not like the Motherhouse here. We don't all have lunch at the same time and dinner at the same time and we don't all go in to prayers together the way we do up in Maryville. People have too much to do and too many places they have to be, so all that gets made up catch-as-catch can. But that doesn't mean there isn't a dinnertime, if you see what I mean. Sister Agnes Bernadette puts dinner out every night at five thirty and if you're around you eat it, because leftovers are cold unless you've got access to the microwave, and getting access to the microwave around here at night is like the camel and the eye of the needle, if you know what I mean. Everybody wants to use it."

"I have the same trouble in my own house," Bennis said, "and I live alone."

"You live alone in name only," Gregor said sharply.

"The thing is," Sister Angelus said, "Mother Mary Bellarmine always makes it to dinner. She gives this big lecture about how in the old days nobody was ever allowed to skip dinner unless they asked permission, and she thinks all this disorganized nonsense is ruining the Order. Only I don't know, Mr. Demarkian, I mean, there's a fair percentage of our Order that does nursing, you know what I'm saying? What did they do in the old days when they had a woman in labor and the dinner bell rang?"

"Tell her to wait?" Bennis suggested.

Sister Angelus brushed this away. "Of course they didn't. Mother Mary Bellarmine is just being— Excuse me. I was about to be uncharitable. Anyway, she comes to dinner every night and she has this lecture, so she came to dinner two nights ago and she had the lecture ready again, and most of us were just resigned to putting up with it. Especially the novices. You're not allowed to complain about holes in your socks when you're a novice."

"Do you wear socks?" Bennis asked curiously. Gregor shot her a furious look and she shrugged. Her cigarette had been smoked to the filter. She made sure the fire was out and put the filter in her pocket. Then she lit up again.

"Dinner," she said gamely. "The night before last."

"You really shouldn't smoke," Sister Angelus said. "It can kill you."

"I'm counting on it," Bennis said.

Gregor cleared his throat.

"Oh," Sister Angelus said. "Yes. Well. Um. Dinner. So, Mother Mary Bellarmine always comes, Sister Joan Esther never comes, it works out. On purpose, I would say. But the night before last, Mother Mary Bellarmine wasn't supposed to come. She was supposed to be at a meeting about the new field house—I don't know if you've heard, but St. Elizabeth's is in the middle of building a new field house—anyway, Mother Mary Bellarmine has expertise in that area, building things, and she was supposed to be at this meeting with Henry Hare and the Archbishop and I don't know who else, and she wasn't supposed to be back in time for dinner. So it gets to be dinnertime, and who should be in the front of the line waiting to get into the refectory but Joan Esther—"

"Who figured she could have a hot meal for once because her nemesis was going to be out of town," Gregor put in.

"I wouldn't call her a nemesis, Mr. Demarkian. I mean, that would imply that she was in the right, wouldn't it?"

"I don't know," Gregor answered truthfully.

"Well, I don't think she was in the right." Sister Angelus shook her head. "And it's not just because she's nasty to everybody she meets, including me. So. Joan Esther is in the front of the line and she goes in and sits down with Scholastica and Mary Alice and all these other people she knew from formation, and they're talking away about who knows what and letting the postulants and novices get away with murder, when who should walk in at the very end of the line but Mother Mary Bellarmine."

"Did she get back from her meeting early?" Gregor asked.

"It turned out the meeting was canceled. Nobody had heard about it. We would have heard about it if Domenica Anne had come back—Domenica Anne is the Sister who's handling things for St. Elizabeth's College—but Domenica Anne had a lot of work to do and she went to her workroom instead of coming to the convent so nobody saw her. And Mother Mary Bellarmine wasn't around either, but I don't know where she was."

"Maybe she was hiding," Bennis suggested, slipping her extinguished match into her pocket too. "Maybe she was trying to catch this Sister Joan Esther unprepared."

"Maybe she was," Sister Angelus said. "She did catch Joan Esther unprepared, let me tell you that. When she walked in, I thought Joan Esther was going to rise from her place like she was sitting in an ejector seat. She went all red and absolutely furious. Mother Mary Bellarmine looked very smug. If you want my opinion. Which you probably don't. *Anyway.* There wasn't any room at the table where Joan Esther was sitting, and Mother Mary Bellarmine wouldn't have sat there anyway, because it was a secondary table. There's always one table in the refectory reserved for Sisters Superior and guests, that's assuming there's more than one table in the refectory at all, and besides, with all the new people in residence—oh, I should have told you."

"Told me what?" Gregor asked.

"Well, Mr. Demarkian, with all the Sisters in attendance, the dinner I'm talking about isn't the only dinner. We go in shifts. And not all in the same place, either. I mean, about twenty-one hundred of us go to the refectory here in three sittings, about seven hundred each, which is what the refectory can hold when the folding doors are opened up and they use the rooms on either side of it. We go at five thirty, six thirty, and seven thirty. Then the rest of everybody eats in the all-college dining hall. That seats about eleven hundred. They go at five thirty, six thirty, and seven thirty, too. You're assigned a place and a time and you aren't allowed to go in at any of the other places or times because it messes everything up. If you miss your seating you have to wait until eight thirty or eat out. They're really strict about it."

"Do you mean they'd turn you away at the door?" Bennis asked. "If you got held up by your bus breaking down in Philadelphia and didn't make it until an hour later, they'd just make you wait some more?"

"Sister Justin Martyr spent two days straight without any sitting with Sister Dymphna because Sister Dymphna was dying, and after Sister Dymphna was dead and Justin Martyr stumbled in practically dead herself they turned her away from the seven-thirty

over at the dining hall because she was supposed to be
at the six-thirty. And the seven-thirty at the dining hall
is undersubscribed. Reverend Mother General had to
intervene."

"If it was some sort of subscription, you'd think your
Sister Joan Esther would have known better," Bennis
said. "She should have found out which sitting in
which place Sister Mary Bellarmine was signing up
for, and signed up for something different."

"She wouldn't have known," Sister Angelus said. "It
was all done by mail. Everybody signed up to sit with
their friends from formation. Of course, Sister
Scholastica is Sister Joan Esther's closest friend in the
Order, even though Joan Esther was a couple of years
ahead or something, maybe I've got that wrong, but
Scholastica would have to be at the sitting she was at
which is the same sitting Mother Mary Bellarmine is
at because that's when all the administrators eat. Together. You know. And us. They like to keep an eye on
us." She tapped her white veil.

"Back to what Mother Mary Bellarmine did,"
Gregor said.

"She did what she always does whenever Joan Esther's in earshot," Sister Angelus said promptly. "She
started talking in this really loud voice about loyalty
and commitment and religious obedience, and about
how some people these days don't understand what it
really means to be a nun. Well, Joan Esther had heard
all that before. Mother Mary Bellarmine is supposed
to be incredibly furious that Joan Esther requested a
transfer out of her province and up to Alaska. So Joan
Esther didn't react at all. She just went on eating and
at least pretending to talk to the other Sisters at her table."

"That seems calm enough," Bennis put in.

"Oh, it was," Sister Angelus agreed. "It was all par
for the course. Mother Mary Bellarmine had pulled
the same sort of thing half a dozen times during the
week at recreation or just around where she and Joan
Esther happened to be together. It's what happened
next that got everybody talking."

"What happened next?" This was Gregor.

"Well, Mother Mary Bellarmine started to say how they had just started their five-year audit out on the coast, except that she wasn't letting it rest in the hands of the accountants anymore because she didn't trust them. She knew more about fraud and flimflam than any second assistant bookkeeper from Deloitte ever would, so she was going over the books just as soon as Deloitte got finished with them. And that it had already paid off, because she'd caught two pieces of petty fraud the accountants hadn't noticed. And of course there would be more to come."

"And?" Bennis asked.

"And she went on and on like that for a long while, and then Joan Esther raised her voice so loud her people back in Alaska could probably have heard her and said, 'People shouldn't go searching under rocks if they don't want to be bitten by snakes.' And then everybody in the entire place shut up."

"I'll bet they did," Bennis said. "What happened next?"

"What happened next was that Mother Mary Bellarmine lost it," Sister Angelus said. "She rose right up out of her chair, looked straight at Joan Esther and said, 'If I go searching under rocks, the only snake I'm going to get bitten by is you.' And then Joan Esther stood up and said, 'You can bet it's going to be me.' And then Reverend Mother General stood up and made us all observe silence for the rest of the meal."

"Whoosh," Bennis said. "What do you suppose all that was about?"

"Oh, we all know what it was about," Sister Angelus said. "Mother Mary Bellarmine thinks Joan Esther made her look bad when she requested the transfer, and now she's doing anything she can to make Joan Esther look even worse. And of course Joan Esther did make Mother Mary Bellarmine look bad. She told Reverend Mother General that Mother Mary Bellarmine was such an impossible woman to work for, she'd rather show religious obedience to a squirrel. And that got around."

"There is also another possibility," Gregor said carefully. "There is the possibility that Mother Mary Bellarmine, unpleasant though she may be on a personal level, may have a point. There may be something wrong with the books. And Sister Joan Esther may be the one who made that wrong."

Sister Angelus shook her head. "Impossible," she said definitely. "Sister Joan Esther doesn't know one end of a quarter from another. She's a Sister without pence."

"What?" Bennis asked.

"It's a kind of religious discipline," Sister Angelus explained. "Some of the Sisters take a kind of corollary vow with the vow of poverty and they go without money. Literally. No change in their pockets, not even for the bus. No checking accounts. Nothing. When Joan Esther goes off to those small villages she serves in Alaska, somebody has to go with her to carry the money, because she doesn't carry any at all. And sometimes there isn't anyone to go with her, so she has to go by herself. She's got the most remarkable stories about getting stuck. In fact, she took that discipline because of the first fight she ever had with Mother Mary Bellarmine. Over a fifty dollar birthday gift."

"It's enough to make you ill," Bennis said.

"It's just a lot of bad feeling over silliness," Sister Angelus declared. "Mother Mary Bellarmine is like that. Everybody says so. Everybody says that if our Reverend Mother General had been Reverend Mother General when Mother Mary Bellarmine was a postulant, Mother Mary Bellarmine would never have made it through formation. It isn't just Joan Esther she's got it in for. You should see the things she does to Sister Domenica Anne. Just yesterday it got so bad, Domenica Anne came *this close* to slapping Mother Mary Bellarmine in the face, and we all thought she was going to do it, too, because that was about money as well. Mother Mary Bellarmine was saying that Domenica Anne was going to cost the Order a million dollars

with her bungling if it was bungling, and that was the
point when Domenica Anne—"

"Wait," Bennis said. "Look. I sense deliverance. I
think it's the food."

2

Gregor didn't know what Bennis wanted deliverance
from—hunger or Sister Mary Angelus—but he was
starving, and as the crowd pressed back away from
the double doors that led to the foyer and let the long
procession in, he felt a good deal of relief himself.
When he was younger he used to go without food for
considerable periods of time. When he was first in the
Bureau and doing kidnapping stakeouts he would
sometimes forget to eat for more than an entire day.
Since he'd been back on Cavanaugh Street, such non-
chalance had not been possible. The women on
Cavanaugh Street cooked and so did some of the men.
Both men and women thought it part of their Christian
duty to feed any stray human being who might not be
getting enough to eat. This resulted in some very desirable outcomes. Father Tibor Kasparian had managed to set up an excellent soup kitchen and a food
basket distribution network in a downtown Philadelphia neighborhood not as fortunate in urban renewal
as their own. He had also organized a relief effort for
the victims of the Armenian earthquake and to help after the political upheavals that resulted in Armenian in-
dependence that had been rewarded by a letter from
the Armenian government that came very near to can-
onizing everyone on Cavanaugh Street. What this attitude also resulted in, however, was the fanatical
determination of every woman in the neighborhood
over the age of fifty that neither Gregor Demarkian
nor Bennis Hannaford should be allowed to "starve."

Bennis burned it off with cigarettes and late nights.
Gregor didn't burn it off at all. Bennis sometimes described him as "a Harrison Ford with twenty pounds
too much weight on him," but any day now she was
going to have to increase that number to forty, or

worse. Gregor was no longer used to going without meals. He didn't want to be.

The procession coming through the double doors was truly a procession. It was headed by a cheerfully plump middle-aged nun with nothing in her hands at all, followed by nuns in a two-by-two row. At the front of that row was Reverend Mother General with a Sister whom Gregor didn't recognize. The Sister was carrying a tray on which there was an ice sculpture of a nun in a very old-fashioned habit and a lit candle. Gregor couldn't imagine why the candle didn't melt the ice. After Reverend Mother General came the woman Gregor thought he remembered as Mother Deborah, from Australia. The Sister walking next to her—with an identical ice sculpture and an identical candle—was the one Gregor had been introduced to as Peter Rose. That had been in Colchester, in the first case he had ever handled for the Catholic Church. He looked down the line—snaking through the hushed crowd with ease now—and found Mother Mary Bellarmine, looking clean and pressed in what he assumed must be a fresh habit. At least that scapular thing had been changed. Even with that long collar that fell halfway down the arms like a cape, the torn scapular could not have been pinned up without looking pinned up. This didn't look pinned up.

Bennis whispered in his ear, "You know what Sister Angelus just told me? That woman carrying the ice sculpture for Mother Mary Bellarmine is the unfortunate Joan Esther. How do you think that came about?"

"Coincidence," Gregor said firmly.

"I say it was deliberate," Bennis said. "Joan Esther has had enough, so she's got herself taken on as Mother Mary Bellarmine's temporary lackey. Only the thing is, she's poisoned the whatever it is—"

"Bennis," Gregor warned.

"—as soon as Mother Mary Bellarmine takes the first bite, *wham*. What do you think of that?" Bennis said this with relish.

"I think you ought to be locked up," Gregor said.

"My father thought that, too, and he tried, but even

with his money he couldn't make them do it. Look at
Norman Kevic. If that man gets any closer to that table, his molecules will merge."

Gregor looked at the last ice sculpture in the row.
There was a hollowed-out part at the back of its head
that was indeed filled with food. "What do they have in
those things?" he asked Sister Mary Angelus. Sister
Mary Angelus shrugged.

"Chicken liver pâté," she said. "It's not something I
like, but nobody thought to give us any caviar. I suppose they think it isn't suitable for nuns. That's Sister
Domenica Anne at the end there, by the way, carrying
the tray for Mother Andrew Loretta. Mother Andrew
Loretta is from Japan."

"Who's the woman who looks like Woodstock revis-
ited in old age?" Bennis asked.

Gregor looked in the direction she was pointing and
decided that her description was more than apt. The
grey-haired woman looked painfully awkward and ex-
cruciatingly out of date, as ridiculous as a man would
have if he'd shown up in this place wearing plus fours
and spats. She was not, however, any one Sister Angelus knew.

"I think she works for the college somewhere," Sister Angelus said. "I've seen her around. What's she
carrying?"

"She's got a lot of roses wrapped in paper," Bennis
said. "She's with a nun."

"Oh, the nun," Sister Angelus said. "That's Catherine Grace. She works in the Registrar's Office. I knew
that woman looked familiar. She works in the Registrar's Office, too. I don't remember her name. But we
all had to go over there to get our room keys, and I
met her."

"Room keys through the Registrar's Office," Bennis
said. "What a concept."

"Oh, my Heavens," Sister Angelus said. "That's
Nancy Hare."

Gregor swung around to find Nancy Hare, but he
didn't have a chance. The crowd was impenetrable and
there was too much going on at the tables. Reverend

Mother General stepped forward. She clapped her hands together sharply and silenced everyone in the room. Gregor told himself it happened because the nuns were used to those clapping hands, but it seemed eerie to him nonetheless.

Reverend Mother General raised her hand to her forehead. "In the name of the Father and of the Son and of the Holy Spirit. Bless us O Lord—"

The nuns finished. "—and these thy gifts which we are about to receive from thy bounty.

"Through Christ our Lord, who lives and reigns with You in unity with the Holy Spirit. Amen."

"Amen."

"Sister Agnes Bernadette," Reverend Mother General told the crowd, "who is Sister Cook for the convent here at St. Elizabeth's, has made for all the Mothers Provincial and for myself these ice sculptures in our honor, and she has done us the great favor of making them all alike. Not one of us has to be reminded of her imperfections. When I look at this sculpture of myself, I am not old. When Mother Maria Hilde looks at hers, she is not fat. This is what God has promised to do for us all at the Resurrection of the Body, except of course not in ice. I for one very much appreciate this intimation of immortality as provided for me by Sister."

All the nuns laughed. Gregor didn't know what for.

"Now," Reverend Mother said, "I know you're all hungry—"

A good-humored groan went up from the crowd.

"And I know Sister Agnes Bernadette is anxious to feed you. She's got enough food coming up to feed the greater metropolitan area. So let's get started. If the Mothers Provincial are ready—"

"Oh, we're ready," Mother Mary Deborah said in her thick Australian drawl.

The crowd laughed again.

"Mother of God, give us food," someone in the back prayed, and the crowd laughed again.

"I'm sure the Mother of God was a very good cook,"

Reverend Mother General said. "Mothers, if you will, please."

The Mothers Provincial raised their hands in the air. Gregor was fascinated to see that each hand held a cracker. He supposed that each cracker was smeared with chicken liver pâté. This was the oddest spectacle he had ever witnessed. He hadn't the faintest idea what to think of it.

"Now," Reverend Mother General said.

At the sound of "now" all the Mothers Provincial bit down on their crackers, and the crowd cheered. At that moment more nuns began to come through the double doors from the foyer, a long line of them, with each carrying a heavy silver tray. This was lunch for real coming on. The semimilitary precision of the scene at the tables broke up. Gregor looked at Bennis and found her just as astonished as he was.

"Wasn't that strange?" she demanded.

But Sister Angelus barged in. "It was silly, but we had to do it. Sister Agnes Bernadette was so proud of her sculptures. And it's not so wonderful being a convent cook, you know. You're stuck in a kitchen all day. Reverend Mother General just wanted to make Agnes Bernadette feel good."

"Well," Bennis said, "I hope she managed."

"That's a pile of Italian sausages they just put out," Gregor said. "I'm going to go eat."

Of course, everybody else was going to go eat, too, so he had to wait. Norman Kevic's strategy now seemed to be eminently sensible, since he was the first person in line and supplied with a plate and utensils almost before anyone else had collected himself enough to get started. Gregor took his place behind two giggling novices and in front of a pair of Sisters chattering away in German. The line inched forward slowly and he went with it, catching glimpses now and then of what looked like the world's most complete collection of food.

"They're putting all the really ethnic stuff out in the garden," one of the novices ahead of him said. "Hello,

Mr. Demarkian. You probably don't remember me. I'm Sister Mary Stephen."

"Mr. Demarkian?" the other novice said. "Really? Who came to Maryville and investigated Brigit?"

"He didn't investigate Brigit," Sister Mary Stephen said scornfully. "He investigated the murder."

"I was sick that whole week and I never met him," the other novice said.

"This is Sister Francesca," Sister Mary Stephen said. "And I meant what I said about the ethnic food. If you like that kind of thing better you probably wouldn't have to wait in so long a line. There's a Japanese table out there with a chef from Japan. And a French one with a Sister who was a graduate of Cordon Bleu before she entered the Order. There are a couple of others out there, too."

"Aren't Italian sausages considered ethnic?" Gregor asked.

"These at the tables here are Italian-*American* sausages," Sister Mary Stephen said.

Sister Francesca laughed.

"There's some Polish-American kielbasa up there, too," Sister Mary Stephen said, "and being a Polish-American myself you know how I feel about—what's that?"

That was disturbance well far up the line, but not as far as it could have been. Gregor tried to get a handle on the position so he could concentrate on the incident and had a hard time doing it. There were so many nuns milling around and there was so much general confusion. Then somebody gasped and somebody else cried, "She's turning blue!" and Gregor leaped out of the line into the relatively less choked area to the side of it to see what was going on.

What was going on was a death. He knew it as soon as he saw the woman's face.

She was clutching her throat and staring straight ahead. Her eyes were bulged wide and her skin was a color that was halfway between blue and white. It seemed to be made out of glass.

"Something that affects the nervous system," Gregor thought automatically.

Then he stepped forward and let the nun fall straight into his arms.

It was the one Sister Angelus had pointed out to him as Sister Joan Esther.

PART 2

CHAPTER 1

1

The police took Mother Mary Bellarmine in for questioning. Gregor would have been willing to bet they were going to long before they arrived, just as he would have been willing to bet he knew what had poisoned Sister Joan Esther long before anyone had done the tests to confirm that she'd been poisoned at all. Gregor was good at poisons. In the Bureau, everybody had to specialize in something. What else there was to specialize in hadn't interested him much. Back in the days when he'd joined, the Bureau demanded that each of its agents have a law or an accounting degree. Gregor had opted for accounting and become a CPA just to qualify for agent training. After that, he'd done his best to forget everything he knew about business and finance. Both bored him. He'd been offered a chance to specialize in firearms, but they made him nervous. He had driven his instructors at Quantico positively nuts. In the end, he had opted to become the resident—and only—expert on poisons, acquiring an encyclopedic knowledge of acid and alkali, lethal mushroom, and distilled chemical, that made him an object of curiosity from one end of the Bureau to another. When he was a young agent in the field, his station supervisor in Los Angeles would call him up at all hours of the night to find out if the poison in the latest Perry Mason or Ed McBain would "really work."

Just by looking at her, Gregor knew that Sister Joan Esther had died from something that affected the central nervous system. The signs were obvious, from the paralysis of the lungs to the twitching of the extremities. He knew what something because of the conversation he'd been having with the two young Sisters just before Joan Esther keeled over. That conversation stuck in his mind so strongly, he could barely wait to get his chance to check it out. Wait, however, he had to, because he had hold of Joan Esther's head. The big reception room was brightly lit, but like all large rooms overfilled with people, it had many shadows. One of those shadows seemed to have fallen across Joan Esther's face, making her look oddly quasi-decapitated. It was not a comfortable sight. Gregor had caught her around the tops of her shoulders. Now he lowered her gently to the floor. The circle of people around them had gotten bigger and bigger. Nobody wanted to get too close. Gregor heard one woman say "she's fainted" and another protest that no, no, she was dead. The protesting woman had a high tight voice just this side of hysterical. Gregor checked the pulse in Joan Esther's wrist and then in the side of her neck. He had known it was going to be futile before he started, but its futility still depressed him. He stepped back away from her and stood up.

"Mr. Demarkian?" Reverend Mother General said.

Trust the nuns, Gregor thought. They might not understand procedures. They might think they need a course to tell them what to do in cases of sudden death. They at least don't disappear. He couldn't count the number of disappearing friends, relatives, and colleagues he had had to put up with in the aftermaths of various suspicious deaths.

Gregor's hands felt dusty. He brushed them absently against the panels of his suit jacket and said, "She's dead, Reverend Mother. She was dead before she keeled over."

"I don't suppose this could be some kind of heart attack," Reverend Mother General said. Her face was very pale.

"I doubt it. You should check, of course."

"Of course. What do you think it is?"

Gregor looked up at the doors leading out to the garden. "Something that affects the central nervous system," he said. "Reverend Mother, you'd better go call the police."

"I sent Scholastica to call the police before you put Sister Joan Esther on the ground. They were very close friends, you know, Scholastica and Joan Esther. Scholastica is distraught." Reverend Mother General paused. "In the old days," she said, "Sisters were forbidden by the Holy Rule from forming what were called particular friendships. In the sixties, that rule was labeled homophobic, as if the founder of this Order were worried that her charges would all turn into lesbians if they were allowed the least bit of latitude. It wasn't that, of course. It was things like this that worried the founders of orders of women religious. I don't think Scholastica is going to be of any use to anybody for the next week."

"Mmmm," Gregor said.

"You should tell us what's happening," a woman's voice demanded from the crowd, and this time it wasn't on the right side of hysteria. "You should tell us what's going on!"

Reverend Mother General had never had the least tolerance for hysteria, in herself or anyone else. Gregor watched in admiration as she rose to her full height—which she managed to make look much taller than the four feet eleven or so she actually was—and took control of the Sisters of her Order with more assurance, and to better effect, than Montgomery had

had control of his forces on the march to liberate
Paris.

"Sisters," she said, "there has been a death. Sister
Joan Esther has died. We need a priest in here right
away, if one of you near the door might look into the
garden and find one willing to come in. Other than
that, we need calm. I want this room cleared of all Sisters and I want it cleared now. There's the back garden
to go into. Do not wander off. The police have been
called—"

A little ripple of shivers went through the crowd.

"—and since we don't yet know why or how Sister
died, the police will probably want to ask questions.
You have nothing to worry about. All you need to do
is tell the truth. You will be happy to know that our
own expert on matters of sudden death and police contact, Gregor Demarkian, is with us now, and has
agreed to be of help."

Gregor hadn't agreed to anything, of course. For all
Reverend Mother General knew, he was due in Tahiti
in an hour.

"Now," she went on, "I want people to move and I
want them to move right away. That includes the
Mothers Provincial, if they wouldn't mind—"

"Of course we wouldn't mind," Mother Mary Deborah said.

"Where's Agnes Bernadette?" someone in the crowd
asked.

"She's down in the kitchen," Mother Mary Deborah
said. "I saw her go. Oh, dear. I suppose somebody
should tell her what's happened here, and tell everybody else in the kitchen, too—"

"I'll go," Scholastica said, arriving at the scene looking red-eyed and breathless. "The police have been
called, Reverend Mother. They'll be here in a minute.
I'd just as soon talk to Aggie, if you don't mind."

"I think it's a very good idea," Reverend Mother
General said, "unless for some reason Mr. Demarkian—"

"It's fine with me," Gregor said.

"Fine," Reverend Mother said. "Go."

Scholastica went.

Reverend Mother looked around. The room had already begun to empty out. Religious obedience might not be what it used to be, but Gregor thought it was good enough, at least in this Order with this woman at its head. He looked through the thinning crowd and spotted a few familiar faces. Norman Kevic had retreated from the food—although Gregor didn't know if "retreated" was the word he wanted. After all, Norm had been at the head of the line. He had probably had a good deal to eat before the fuss started. Gregor made a note to find out just what it was Norm had eaten. He couldn't imagine that he was wrong about what had killed Joan Esther and how it had been administered, but it was always good to cross-check. Sister Mary Alice was standing next to the doors leading out to the garden, shepherding shaken-looking novices into the garden. One of those novices was Sister Mary Angelus. He swung around to let his gaze make a circuit of the room. He found neither Nancy Hare nor Mother Mary Bellarmine.

He didn't see Bennis Hannaford, either, but he wasn't really worried about that. There had been a sudden death. Bennis Hannaford would show up. He turned back to Reverend Mother General.

"What I want to do," he said, "is to secure the table next to which Sister Joan Esther was standing when she died. I believe that was the table where the ice sculpture for Mother Mary Bellarmine was set up."

"Probably," Reverend Mother General said. "What do you mean, you want to secure it?"

"I mean I want to stand somebody next to it to make sure that nothing on the table is touched."

"You can't imagine that the Sisters are going to want to eat after all this," Reverend Mother General said. "Maybe they will want to eat at that, but you can't think they'd want to eat from any of the tables in here, under the circumstances—"

"Under what circumstances?" Gregor asked. "You and I both saw Joan Esther fall. So did a couple of dozen other people. That group suspects food poison-

ing or just plain poisoning. Nobody else has the least
idea what is going on. For all they know, Sister Joan
Esther died of natural causes."

"Oh," Reverend Mother General said.

"Besides," Gregor went on, "I'm not really worrying
about your Sisters eating what's on that table. I'm
much more worried that something on that table will
simply disappear."

"Disappear?" Reverend Mother General looked
blank.

"If this is what I think it is, there's something on
that table somebody is going to want to get rid of very
quickly."

"Oh," Reverend Mother General said again. She
blanched, but the loss of color in her face was not reflected in her voice or posture. She said, "Now you understand what I was telling you earlier, Mr. Demarkian,
we really are appallingly uneducated in matters of this
kind." Then she marched them both in the direction of
the table where Joan Esther had set the statue in
honor of Mother Mary Bellarmine. There wasn't much
on it but the statue even now, and that was melting.

Bennis Hannaford was talking to two nuns and edg-
ing toward the tables. Gregor caught her eye and
waved. She waved back and seemed to use the wave to
settle some kind of argument. A moment later she was
at their side, puffing on a cigarette as if her life depended on it. Gregor periodically attempted to con-
vince her that her life depended on *not*, but it never
did any good.

"I know we're all supposed to go out in the garden,"
she said apologetically to Reverend Mother General,
"but I wanted to talk to Gregor for just a minute
before—"

"That's quite all right," Reverend Mother General
said. "My instructions weren't aimed at you."

"I don't want you to go out into the garden anyway,"
Gregor said. "I want you to do me a favor."

"What's that?"

"Stand by this table over here and make sure nobody touches anything."

"This table over here?" Bennis looked at the table curiously and then walked up to it. She looked at the melting ice sculpture and the tablecloth and the single basket of rolls that had made it here on the first wave of food service. She looked at the candle, still lit, and at the small picture of the Virgin framed in ruffled blue ribbon near the candle's base. Then she walked around to the other side of the table and looked some more.

"Gregor?" she asked. "What is it I'm supposed to be guarding?"

"Everything," Gregor said.

"Every what?" Bennis insisted. "I mean, what have I got here? A picture framed in a ribbon. A lot of rolls I don't think have been touched. At least, they're still wrapped up in a napkin and the napkin is all tucked in. A candle. And an oddly shaped ice cube."

"The oddly shaped ice cube has chicken liver pâté in it," Gregor said.

"No it doesn't."

Bennis lifted up the ice sculpture and held it out for Gregor to see.

And she was right, of course.

There was a deep hollow in the back of the ice sculpture's head, but there was no chicken liver pâté in it.

There wasn't anything in it.

The hollow was so clean, it was hard to believe there had ever been anything in it, ever.

2

He should have been prepared for it, of course. If he'd been out to commit a murder under the circumstances under which this one had been committed—assuming one had been committed here at all—his window of opportunity to cover his tracks would have come while Joan Esther was keeling over, or in the long minutes immediately following, when everybody would be so intent on looking after the dying nun that a bull ele-

phant could sweep through on roller skates without
anyone noticing a thing.

Of course, Gregor thought, he did know a murder
had been committed here. A murder had to have been.
He didn't know a single poison that could have produced the effects he'd seen in Sister Joan Esther that
could also be mistaken for something benign. He
didn't know a single form of natural death that could
mimic those effects, either. He supposed there had to
be something out there. A rare tropical disease. A
highly unusual genetic abnormality. There was always
something. He preferred to go for the commonplace.
The commonplace was so often the truth.

Bennis leaned back against a wall with her arms
crossed over her chest. Reverend Mother General
stood at the end of the table, looking strained. Gregor
paced back and forth in front of the ice sculpture, wondering what he was supposed to do next. Finally, Reverend Mother General said, "Mr. Demarkian, I don't
want to intrude on your thoughts, but this doesn't
make any sense to me. Why would anyone want to
take the chicken liver pâté out of the sculpture's
head?"

"To get rid of it," Bennis said from her place at the
wall. "That's where the poison was. Presumably."

"Well, that's simply not possible," Reverend Mother
General said. "The poison couldn't have been in the
chicken liver pâté, because if it had been Mother Mary
Bellarmine would have been poisoned first."

"Ah," Gregor said, straightening up a little.

"She wasn't poisoned first," Bennis said, "unless she
was and it's taking the Devil's own time to take effect.
I saw her going out to the garden just before I came
over here."

"No," Gregor said.

"No what?" Bennis asked him.

"No, it isn't taking a long time to take effect. Not if
it's what I think it is. I have to go out to the garden."

"If you want Mother Mary Bellarmine, I can call her
in here," Reverend Mother General said. "It's going to

take you an age to find her out in that crowd of Sisters."

"I'm not going to find Mother Mary Bellarmine," Gregor said. Then he turned to Bennis. "You stay here and guard just the way I told you. We don't want something else to go missing."

Bennis made a face at him, but Gregor ignored it. In a way, she had a right. He really didn't need her to guard the table anymore. Reverend Mother General could have guarded it herself, or—if she had something else to do, which she probably did—she could have detailed one of the Sisters from Japan or the Philippines to do it. There had to be hundreds of nuns in this crowd who didn't know either Mother Mary Bellarmine or Sister Joan Esther. Gregor simply wanted to make sure Bennis was out of his hair until he was ready to deal with her, which wouldn't be for a while yet. There was a lot he needed to find out.

He went through the doors at the back into the garden, pausing for a moment on the threshold to get his bearings. The crowd before him was thick and uneasy, but not heavily distressed. From what he could hear of the conversations going on around him, most of the Sisters still thought they had been presented with a case of unfortunate, untimely, but perfectly natural death. Gregor hoped they'd go on thinking that way. It would make them a lot more tractable in the short run, and in the long run it didn't matter what they'd thought when. He peered through the clots and collections of chattering nuns in habit, to the statue of the Virgin in her rock garden grotto, festooned in blue ribbons. There was another statue of the Virgin, this time as Madonna with Child, at the back near the rear gate. That was festooned in blue ribbons, too. The nun standing just in front of him had one of those blue plastic pins on which seemed to be spelling out the tried-and-true sentiment: *ON MOTHER'S DAY REMEMBER THE MOTHER OF GOD.* It only seemed to be, to Gregor, because it was in German. Gregor gave the probably German Sister a small smile and pushed past her, into the center of the garden.

Actually, to call this enclosed space a garden was misleading. It was at least an acre worth of land, extending back far beyond the point where thick hedges marked the end of the rear yard of St. Cecelia's Hall. Aside from the two statues of the Virgin in their miniature hand-made grottoes, there were three small gazebos and a half a dozen extra-long picnic tables with benches to match. The picnic tables were occupied, mostly by Sisters drinking coffee or picking at plates of food. Only the older nuns were eating well. Maybe they were more comfortable with the idea of dying because they were closer to it than the younger Sisters were. Maybe they'd just seen more of it.

Gregor drew close to the nearest gazebo and saw that it was occupied by a flurry of young nuns helping a middle-aged one with large trays of Chicken Cordon Bleu. This must be the French food Sister Mary Stephen and Sister Francesca had been talking about inside. Gregor moved along to the next gazebo, which turned out to be Spanish, and then to the third and last, so far across the lawn to the back he could see past the rear gate to the field beyond. The field was full of nuns, too. Fortunately, this gazebo was the one he had been hoping to find. He recognized Mother Andrew Loretta right away. She must have come out to give the news to her nuns. Her nuns were scurrying around a sushi bar, smiling graciously at the few people who spoke to them and tending to the food in their care as if it were alive.

Gregor went up to the side of the gazebo and leaned in. "Mother Andrew Loretta?" he asked. "Could I talk to you for a moment?"

Mother Andrew Loretta had been speaking to one of her novices in Japanese. Mother Andrew Loretta was Japanese, although with a name like that Gregor found it hard to remember unless he was looking straight at her. She said one last thing to the young Sisters and then stood up, walking over to where he stood as if she were gliding.

"Mr. Demarkian," she said. "Have you come for food? With the tragedy people aren't eating much."

"Has the word got around already?"

"Oh yes." Mother Andrew Loretta nodded. "It got around in ten seconds flat, if you ask me. Of course, nobody knows what to make of it. Neither do I. Are you sure you wouldn't like something to eat?"

"Postive." Actually, Gregor was starving. It just didn't seem right to be chowing down at the start of a murder investigation. In fact, it was what his nieces would call "gross." "Actually, I came over here because I thought I'd heard something—but I must have been wrong."

"Heard what?" Mother Andrew Loretta said.

"Heard that somebody sent you a lot of fugu and a fugu chef all the way from Tokyo," Gregor said.

Mother Andrew Loretta went white. "Do you think that's what it was? Fugu poisoning? But it couldn't have been, could it? Where would Joan Esther have gotten the fugu?"

"I don't know where," Gregor said, although he thought he did, "but it doesn't matter if there isn't any to be had. The symptoms of her death were consistent with fugu poisoning. Didn't you notice?"

"I've never seen anyone die of fugu poisoning." Mother Andrew Loretta shook her head. "But you're wrong about there being none of it around, Mr. Demarkian. We have boxes of it down in the freezer. And we have that fugu chef you heard about. He's supposed to be here right this minute."

"Why isn't he?"

"I don't know."

"Do you have any idea where he might have gone to?"

"Not a one." Mother Andrew Loretta took a deep breath. "It's all very complicated, you see, Mr. Demarkian. Japan is not like the West."

"I've noticed," Gregor said.

Mother Andrew Loretta ignored him. "Japanese men—Japanese men who have been reared in Japan—don't take orders from women. And I mean they simply don't take them. In this country, my position is enough to guarantee my authority. In Japan it would not be. So, as far as I can figure out, Mr. Yakimoto had something of a temper tantrum this afternoon—"

"About what?"

"I'm not sure," Mother Andrew Loretta said desperately. "I wasn't there. He spoke to Sister Agnes Bernadette and caused some kind of terrible problem in the kitchen. Really, Agnes Bernadette was not clear and I didn't have a lot of time and Agnes Bernadette being the way she is . . ." Mother Andrew Loretta hesitated. "You know, it might have been about the fugu. It was about someone tampering with something. I did understand that much. At the time I simply assumed . . . well, fugu chefs are so temperamental. It's part of their . . . well, part of their job, in a way, I suppose. And there was this temper tantrum and Mr. Yakimoto took an ice hatchet or something to one of Agnes Bernadette's statues and then he just disappeared, and he's been gone ever since. I suppose because he's been sulking."

"That was this morning," Gregor repeated.

"More or less," Mother Andrew Loretta said. "I was at the nine thirty Mass, so I didn't get back until late, you see. And then I had so much to do . . . but it could have been the fugu. It could have been. Maybe someone opened one of the boxes and Mr. Yakimoto is upset."

"Maybe," Gregor said.

"But if Sister Joan Esther died from fugu poisoning, it would have to have been deliberate," Mother Andrew Loretta said. "Unless . . . oh, dear. You don't think Agnes Bernadette could have used it for something, do you? I mean, that she might not have understood what the problems with it were and she'd run out of fish and then she used some—"

"Were the problems explained to her?" Gregor asked.

"I don't know," Mother Andrew Loretta said.

"Would she be likely to want fugu to put in chicken liver pâté?"

Mother Andrew Loretta blinked. "Chicken liver pâté . . . that sounds terrible. Oh, I remember. That was what was in the ice sculptures. I had some. It wasn't so bad. But there couldn't have been fugu in the chicken liver pâté, Mr. Demarkian, because here I am. Still alive."

"There couldn't have been fugu in the general recipe of anything else," Gregor said, "because here is everybody, still alive."

"Except Joan Esther," Mother Andrew Loretta said.

"Who didn't have access to anything somebody else hadn't eaten," Gregor pointed out.

"Oh yes she did." Mother Andrew Loretta shook her head. "She had access to that chicken liver pâté—if you bring it down to the chicken liver pâté that was in the ice sculpture on Mary Bellarmine's table. Mary Bellarmine didn't eat any. I was standing right next to her at the very next table and I could see that her cracker was empty. Mary Bellarmine being Mary Bellarmine, I'm surprised she didn't announce to the room how much she hated ... oh, dear."

"Did Mother Mary Bellarmine hate chicken liver pâté?"

"I don't know," Mother Andrew Loretta said. "I was being uncharitable and I was speculating and I was ... oh, dear. You can't really think that, Mr. Demarkian. Not about any nun. Not even about Mother Mary Bellarmine."

What Gregor was thinking about Mother Mary Bellarmine at the moment was that she was much too smart a woman to pull the sort of obvious stunt this seemed to be. Of course, he'd only met her for a moment. He could be very wrong. He had been very wrong at times in his life. Still, at the moment, he didn't like the way this was setting up.

Neither did Mother Andrew Loretta. To say she was distressed was to euphemize. She looked sick.

"Mr. Demarkian," she protested one more time, "I know how, to someone in your profession, this must look—"

At just that moment there was the sound of squealing breaks in the distance and the intermittent whoop that told Gregor some cop somewhere was operating his siren by hand.

"Excuse me," Gregor said. "I think the cavalry has arrived. I'd like to talk to you later, if you wouldn't mind."

"Of course I wouldn't mind," Mother Andrew Loretta said. "I'd be happy to talk to you any time. But you must understand—"

Gregor never heard what it was he had to understand. He was already halfway across the back garden to the doors of the reception room.

3

He reached the doors from the reception room to the foyer just as a wedge of plainclothesmen came through the front door. He stopped and let them come to him, giving himself a chance to look them over. He was fairly sure he'd never met any of them before, in spite of the fact that he knew a good portion of the police personnel on the Main Line. The leader of this group was reasonably young—maybe in his early thirties—and very aggressive. He had an ethnically Italian face that reminded Gregor unpleasantly of Mario Cuomo. He seemed to be looking for trouble. Once he spotted Gregor, he seemed to have found it.

Gregor stood his ground. The young man came across the foyer and into the reception room, walked around Gregor the way a child might walk around a maypole, stopped so close that his nose and Gregor's were very nearly touching and said: "Oh, my *God*. If it isn't the Armenian-American Hercule Poirot."

CHAPTER 2

1

There was an emaciated figure of Christ on a crucifix on the wall of the foyer closest to the right-hand outside door, and Gregor Demarkian stood looking at it for a long time after he'd been called "the Armenian-American Hercule Poirot." "The Armenian-American Hercule Poirot" was the name the *Philadelphia Inquirer* had given him in the middle of their somewhat overenthusiastic coverage of his first extracurricular case, and it was the name that had been picked up gleefully by everybody from *People* magazine to *Oprah*. By now, Australian aborigines and Trobriand islanders knew enough to call him that. Gregor had given up showing that he minded. It was useless to show that he minded. The description was now as closely connected to him as his hair. What he had every intention of showing that he minded was the tone in that young man's voice, and the quick dismissal that made it clear that the young man regarded Gregor

Demarkian as nothing better than an amateur. Gregor Demarkian had never been an amateur. As for the young man, anybody who looked that much like Mario Cuomo ought to be careful about the kind of fun he made of other people.

At the moment, the young man was not making fun of anybody. He was just standing five feet in front of Gregor's face, looking past Gregor's shoulder into the reception room. Gregor would have thought he was eager to get on with it, except that he looked so smug.

This was not going to be easy. Back in the Bureau, when Gregor had a title and a recognized line of authority, he had been able to command respect without ever raising his voice. Since then, he'd been able to command it without the title or the line of authority, just because he was that kind of man. "Believe you have the right," one of his instructors at Quantico had said, "and everybody else will believe it, too." That worked 99 percent of the time. Gregor didn't think it was going to work here.

Still, he had to try. Reverend Mother General was expecting him to. He looked away from the crucifix and held out his hand. The young man was really very, *very* young. Gregor thought he had to be a good two to five years younger than most men would be when they made detective on a major suburban force.

"My name is Gregor Demarkian," Gregor said, with his hand still out. "What's yours?"

"I am Lieutenant Jack Androcetti." The young man ignored Gregor's hand. "I'm in charge here."

"So I gathered."

"You are not in charge here."

"I never said I was."

"You are not necessary to this investigation."

Gregor cocked his head. "Not even as a material witness? I did catch the body as it fell."

"Fell?"

"Sister Joan Esther. She was standing up and then she fell over. I caught her."

"I think we ought to discuss this," Reverend Mother General said.

She had been in the reception room when the police arrived, still hovering around the table where Sister Joan Esther had died. Now she came out under the arm Gregor was using to steady himself against the reception room door and glared nunnily at Jack Androcetti. "Mr. Demarkian is a friend of this Order," she said severely. "Mr. Demarkian acts for us in many capacities. Mr. Demarkian is certainly authorized to act for us in dealing with *you.*"

Jack Androcetti was not impressed. "Is Mr. Demarkian a lawyer?" he asked.

"No," Gregor said.

"Then Mr. Demarkian has no standing here," Jack Androcetti said, smirking. "This is a murder investigation. We will therefore—"

"How can you possibly know it's a murder investigation?" Sister Scholastica demanded.

Where she had come from, Gregor didn't know. People seemed to be crowding in from everywhere, even from the front walk, behind the police. With the exception of Bennis—whose frenzied smoking and frantic whispering Gregor could hear coming from behind him into his left ear—and Norman Kevic, the crowd was entirely composed of nuns. Scholastica stepped forward from the sea of habits and drew herself up to her full height, looking all the more Valkyrie-like because strands of bright red hair were escaping from her veil. Even Jack Androcetti started to look a little impressed.

"How can you possibly know it's a murder investigation?" Scholastica repeated. "*We* don't know it's a murder investigation. We just know that Sister Joan Esther died."

"Fine," Jack Androcetti said. "But you called us. This Sister Esther must have died in somewhat unusual circumstances."

"Sister *Joan* Esther," Reverend Mother General said.

"She could have died from anything," a little nun piped up. "I saw it happen. One minute she was fine and the next minute she was falling over. It could have been a heart attack."

"It couldn't have been a heart attack," Gregor said, "because she was turning blue."

"People turn blue from heart attacks," another Sister said. "I've seen them. I'm a nurse."

"They don't turn *that* kind of blue," Gregor said gently.

"I think somebody ought to call the Archbishop," Sister Mary Alice declared. "Maybe if we get someone from the Chancery down here the police will start to make sense."

"Oh, for Heaven's sake, Mary Alice," another nun said. "Get your consciousness raised. We don't need a priest to take care of us. We can take care of ourselves."

It was beginning to get to him. Gregor could see it. The big liquid eyes were glazing over. The hangdog face was freezing into rigidity. The hands were opening and closing, opening and closing, like Captain Queeg's in *The Caine Mutiny*. Lieutenant Jack Androcetti was coming very close to losing it.

"Just a minute," he said finally, when the babble had risen high enough so that he could no longer be accused of interrupting anyone in particular. "In the first place, we're going to secure the scene. That's what we do when we get to a scene. We're going to secure it. Where *is* the scene?"

"In there," Sister Scholastica said, pointing to the reception room doors.

"There are ten long tables set up against one wall," Gregor said. "Sister Joan Esther was standing next to the one third in from this door."

"The one without any chicken liver pâté in the statue's head," little Sister Angelus offered up.

"Shh," one of the other novices said.

"But I heard them," Sister Angelus said.

Jack Androcetti took a deep breath. "Chicken liver pâté. The statue's head. Sergeant Collins?"

"Right here." A young black man in uniform stepped forward. Gregor noticed that he wasn't young enough. He was older than Jack Androcetti.

"Sergeant Collins," Jack Androcetti repeated,

"please take a couple of men and go into that room and find the scene if you can manage it—"

"Well, of course he can manage it," a nun in the crowd said. "Her body's still lying right there on the floor."

"Fine," Jack Androcetti said. "Sergeant Collins—"

"I'm on my way," Sergeant Collins said.

Sergeant Collins moved forward, with a small army of men following along behind him, and Gregor began to relax a little. It wasn't true that there was always one man in every police investigation who knew what he was doing, but if you were lucky it was. This time they were lucky. Sergeant Collins waited politely for Gregor to move his arm and then went on through into the reception room. As he was going past, he winked.

"All right, ladies," Gregor heard him say in the next room. "We have to clear this room. Everybody out. I'm going to post an officer at the back door. Leave your name with him."

"I say we shouldn't be doing any of this until we know what Sister died from," a nun in the crowd said, but everybody ignored her. They were concentrating on Jack Androcetti, who seemed finally to have made up his mind to do something besides cast aspersions on the general character of Gregor Demarkian. He was casting his eyes around the foyer in dissatisfaction.

"Is there anywhere I could set up an office?" he asked. "A small room with a desk and some chairs?"

"I could get you a small room with chairs," Sister Scholastica said. "No desk. This isn't that kind of building."

"I'll take it," Jack Androcetti said.

"It's through that door at the back to your left," Sister Scholastica said, going forward to show him the way. "There's a hallway there with some rooms off of it."

Gregor watched Jack Androcetti take in the decorated door, the picture of the Virgin, the blue ribbons. Then he turned around and looked at the door on the right, which was even worse. If Jack Androcetti had

been that kind of man, Gregor thought, he would have
fainted dead away.

2

If Jack Androcetti had been a halfway decent policeman, Gregor wouldn't have spent the next two hours
wandering around the back garden and along the strip
of grass that allowed passage from the back garden to
the sidewalk at the front. Androcetti knew Gregor had
caught the body as it fell. Any policeman worth his
service revolver would have taken that and run with it.
Gregor had never liked the kind of detective story
where the police were made to look like absolute idiots. To his mind, they exhibited a particularly obnoxious form of class snobbery and a total disregard for
reality. Even the Nero Wolfe books—which he liked
because Wolfe was fat and proud of it—annoyed him
because of their portrayal of the police. What he was
supposed to do with a case where the police really
were idiots, he didn't know. He consoled himself with
the knowledge that Sergeant Collins at least seemed to
have a brain in his head. How much good that was going to do anyone, Gregor didn't know.

Lieutenant Jack Androcetti set himself up in the
room Sister Scholastica had found for him and began
summoning witnesses. He still didn't know he had a
murder on his hands, but he was determined to pro-
ceed as if he did, which was standard policy in most
police departments. Nobody wanted to be caught in
the middle of an investigation that had been ruined because it had never been properly started, although
God only knew it happened all the time. Unfortunately,
in his zeal not to have anything to do with Gregor
Demarkian at all, Androcetti was calling every nun
anyone had seen anywhere in the reception room at
the time, and those interrogations were going to take
hours. Gregor looked around the foyer and saw that
Bennis had disappeared. She was probably out smoking another cigarette somewhere, which was what she
always did when she got agitated. He looked for Sister

Scholastica, but failed there, too. Scholastica was so
tall and that hair of hers was so red, Gregor had
thought he might be able to pick her out even in the
middle of all these habits. If she was here, he didn't
see her. He looked through the crowd for anyone at all
he might know, and found no one. All the habits had
begun to blend together and take on the visage of one
enormous nun.

Gregor went to the front door, looked out on more
crowds of nuns on the sidewalk and a couple of television crews unloading Minicams, and went down the
steps in search of Bennis. It wasn't true that there
were nothing but nuns in the tight little groups that
dotted the sidewalk like misplaced clusters of decora-
tive shrubbery. Seculars had been invited to this reception, and as soon as Gregor started looking for
Bennis, he saw lots of them. He dodged an elderly
woman with a handbag that seemed to be made entirely of seashells and a young man in a pink and
green tie that clashed outrageously with his electric
blue shirt. Both the old woman and the young man
were wearing those little pins that said *ON MOTH-
ER'S DAY REMEMBER THE MOTHER OF GOD.*
Gregor had read that message so often lately, he was
ready to say a Novena. He pushed through the crowd
some more, careful to stay to the building side of the
pavement so that he wasn't too flagrantly exposed to
the newspeople.

He had just decided to try going around to the back
when he got held up by a knot of nuns with their
heads together, whispering frantically to each other
and ignoring everything going on around them. He
was about to excuse himself and push past when his
gaze lit on a face he was sure he knew. It took him a
while to retrieve it, in spite of the fact that he had seen
this woman more than once today and recognized her
before. That was what looking at thousands of habits
could do to the mind's ability to recognize anything at
all. Then the name came to him and he brightened.
Sister Mary Alice. That's who that was. Sister Mary Alice, good friend of Sister Scholastica and Mistress of

Novices at the Order's Motherhouse. Gregor abandoned his attempts to get by the knot of nuns and made his way in the other direction instead.

Sister Mary Alice was standing by herself, almost all the way down the sidewalk to St. Cecelia's Hall. Gregor walked up to her and cleared his throat. She seemed a million miles away, and throat clearing didn't get her attention. He drew up closer to her and said, "Sister?"

Sister Mary Alice came to with a start. "Oh," she said. "Oh. Mr. Demarkian. I'm sorry. I was thinking of something else."

"I could tell."

"I could hardly believe what a really terrible man he was," she said. "That policeman, I mean, that Androcetti. And stupid, too, if you want to know what I think. Was Joan Esther murdered?"

"My guess is yes," Gregor said carefully. "But it is a guess. They'll have to do an autopsy."

"If she was murdered, I'll bet she wasn't murdered on purpose," Mary Alice said. "No one would murder Joan Esther on purpose. I bet the poison or whatever it was was intended for somebody else."

This was interesting, Gregor thought. He never got over his surprise at how much nuns were willing to tell him. Maybe he reminded them of a priest. "Intended for whom?" he asked Sister Mary Alice.

"Intended for Mother Mary Bellarmine." Sister Mary Alice was prompt. "I know half a dozen people who would like to murder Mother Mary Bellarmine, religious and lay. She's an equal opportunity annoyance. Anyway, from what I heard, it must have been intended for her. The poison. It was poison?"

"I think so," Gregor said carefully.

"Well, what I got from Scholastica was that there was poison in the chicken liver pâté—"

"Not exactly," Gregor said hastily. "You really mustn't do that, Sister. We don't have proof of the sorts of things you're assuming. That Sister Joan Esther was poisoned. That the poison was in the chicken liver pâté—"

"Where else could it have been?" Sister Mary Alice demanded.

"It could have been on something discrete—a canapé, for instance, that someone made up special and handed to Joan Esther in person. In fact, that's a far better speculative explanation than that the poison was in the chicken liver pâté, because the chicken liver pâté would have been eaten by Mother Mary Bellarmine first, unless of course you're assuming that Mother Mary Bellarmine is herself—"

"—no it wouldn't have—"

"—Joan Esther's killer, which would make this a far cruder murder than I think it is. What do you mean, she wouldn't?"

"Mother Mary Bellarmine wouldn't have eaten the chicken liver pâté," Mary Alice said, "because she has gout. Do you know about gout?"

"Only what I've read in eighteenth-century novels," Gregor said.

"Well, I don't know much about it either," Mary Alice said, "but I do know it's very painful and Mother Mary Bellarmine has it in her foot. And the thing about gout is, if you've got it you can't eat organ meats. They make it worse."

"You can't eat organ meats at all? Not even a bite from a cracker just to take part in a celebration?"

"Well, Mr. Demarkian, if it was anybody but Mother Mary Bellarmine we were talking about, I'd say you were right. She'd have taken a bite just to be polite to Agnes Bernadette. But this is Mother Mary Bellarmine we're talking about here. She doesn't bend for anybody."

Gregor considered the possibilities. "Who else knows about this?" he asked.

"If you mean about the gout," Sister Mary Alice said, "the answer is practically everybody. She complained about it very loudly and very clearly whenever it flared up. I'd say anybody who's been around her for any time at all—say on and off for a couple of months—would have heard about it. About her not be-

174 *Jane Haddam*

ing able to eat organ meats, though, that's a different thing."

"You don't think many people knew about that," Gregor said.

"The only reason I knew about that is because one of my novices told me. Her father's got gout in his legs. And I told her not to tell anyone in case it got back to Sister Agnes Bernadette, because Aggie had gone through so much trouble to set all this statue thing up. I don't think it's general knowledge."

"I don't think it's general knowledge either."

Mary Alice was warming up. "It really would make much more sense if somebody had been trying to kill Mother Mary Bellarmine and the plan had just gone wrong. I mean, why would anybody want to kill Joan Esther? Even Mother Mary Bellarmine wouldn't want to kill Joan Esther, just put her in the stocks and humiliate her because of going to Alaska. I mean, you don't kill somebody just because they didn't like working for you and went to Alaska. But Mother Mary Bellarmine ... Even if there wasn't anything else, there would be all that about the money."

"All that about what money?"

"The money for the field house," Sister Mary Alice said. "Mother Mary Bellarmine has been going over the plans and the books and all the rest of it for days. There's at least a million dollars involved, if not more. Somebody could be stealing and Mother Mary Bellarmine could have found out about it. Or there are a million other things. Goodness only knows what she did to get Nancy Hare so upset—"

"Nancy Hare," Gregor said. "Did you see Nancy Hare in the reception room when the sculptures were being brought in?"

"Then? No, of course I didn't. She'd gone home by then. Hadn't she?"

"It was just something somebody said," Gregor told her. "Go on with what you were saying."

"Well, there isn't much more to say. It just seems so rational. If I'd wanted to kill Mother Mary Bellarmine, I'd have done it that way. The pâté would have been there and she would have taken the first bite and that would have been that. Don't you think so?"

"Maybe," Gregor said.

"Well, I like it," Mary Alice told him. "It makes a lot more sense than what we have now. How can you deal with things like this all the time? I barely survived after Brigit."

"This still may turn out not to be a 'thing like this' at all," Gregor reminded her. "We're still only speculating."

"I think I was right and we should have called the Chancery," Mary Alice said. "I think this is going to be one big mess." She peered around in the crowd and sighed. "That's a television reporter heading our way, Mr. Demarkian. Unless you're looking for publicity, you'd better get out of here."

"I'd better get out of here," Gregor said.

"Hey!" A young woman called out from behind a Minicam. "Isn't that Gregor Demarkian?"

The only avenue of escape was the strip of lawn leading to the back garden. Gregor took it, all too aware that in a sea of nuns, he must be as clearly identifiable as the bull's-eye on a target.

3

"Hey," Bennis Hannaford said three minutes later, when Gregor had finally made his way out the back gate and into the field and discovered her sitting on a low stone wall. "You look positively frazzled. Is that lieutenant still giving you a hard time?"

"You saw all that," Gregor said.

"I saw enough of it. Is that man as stupid as he appears to be?"

"Stupider."

"I was afraid of that."

"I don't know if afraid is what I am," Gregor said. "Obviously, I'm not going to be called in as a consultant on this case."

"Do you think not? Not even by the Order or the Church or whoever?"

"Androcetti had a point in there. I am not a lawyer. I have no official standing. If I am asked to consult by the Order or the Church, what will I do? My effectiveness depends on the police. I've always had their cooperation. I don't think I'd get much of anywhere without it."

"So what do you think will happen?"

"I don't know." Gregor sighed. "I suppose Androcetti will do something dramatic, especially now that the television cameras are here. I even have a suspicion I know what the stupid something will be."

"What?" Bennis asked.

"Arrest Mother Mary Bellarmine."

"What?"

The low stone wall was very close to the gate to the garden of St. Teresa's House. The gate's opening was stuffed full of nuns, much as every other inch of ground in this place seemed to be stuffed full of nuns, but with less room to move. Now one of the nuns closest to them turned around and peered into his face. She was not a nun Gregor knew, but from the way she was looking at him he surmised that she knew him at least by reputation. She had the wrinkled, very soft skin of old women who have never worn much makeup.

"Mr. Demarkian?" she ventured.

"That's right," Gregor said. "This is Bennis Day Hannaford."

"I'm Sister Mary Celestine. I hope you don't mind. I overheard what you said. About that policeman arresting Mother Mary Bellarmine."

"It was just a speculation," Gregor said quickly. "It hasn't actually happened."

"Oh, I know that," Sister Mary Celestine said. "I know that. There would have been much more fuss if someone had been arrested. But if it does happen it will be wrong. I hope you realize that. Especially if it happened the way everybody says it happened. Because poison was put in the pâté."

"I think I just had this identical conversation with Sister Mary Alice," Gregor said.

"I don't think so," Sister Mary Celestine told him.
"You see, I was standing right next to her. To Sister
Joan Esther, I mean. When she died. I was standing
right up against that table the whole time the sculptures were being brought in and Reverend Mother
General was making her speech and—well, everything. Do you see?"

"I don't know," Gregor said.

"I think I do," Bennis jumped in. "I think Sister saw
something."

"Well, I didn't see anything sinister." Sister Mary
Celestine shook her head. "I didn't think anything of it
at the time. I mean, I'm assigned to St. Elizabeth's. I
live and work here. I've met Norman Kevic a dozen
times."

"What has Norman Kevic got to do with it?" Gregor
asked.

"He picked up the ice sculpture," Sister Mary Celestine said promptly. "I saw him do it. He was weaving
in and out among the tables, trying to get something
to eat. You know how he is. And he's good at that, at
insinuating himself in places where he's not supposed
to be. Not that anyone was paying any attention to
him. I mean, Norman is Norman. And there was such
a crowd."

"But he picked up the statue," Gregor prompted.

"That's right."

"When?"

"While Reverend Mother was making her speech.
All the sculptures had been put down on the tables,
and he was at the table closest to the door. When Reverend Mother started talking he picked that statue up
there—I forget who that belongs to—and then he
started working his way down the line of tables. He'd
just got to Mother Mary Bellarmine's table when Reverend Mother started to wind up her remarks, and he
stopped."

"But he picked up the statue."

"Oh, yes."

"By the head?" Gregor asked. "By the feet? How?"

"Oh, by the feet," Sister Mary Celestine said. "It

was most definitely by the feet and by the shoulders, if you know what I mean. He picked it up the way you'd pick up any statue and turned it over in his hands."

"And then what?"

"Then he put it down again," Mother Mary Celestine said. "Oh, dear. This all sounds so trivial. And it probably was trivial. Norman was probably just being Norman. He's like that."

Gregor considered everything she had told him. He didn't like it. It was too complicated, and it seemed to rest too much on chance. Granted, there was a huge crowd. If Norman Kevic had been intent on poisoning the pâté and killing someone, he couldn't have counted on going unseen. He had been, after all, a man in a crowd of nuns.

"Did Norman Kevic know the Sister who died? Sister Joan Esther?"

"I wouldn't think so," Sister Mary Celestine said. "Joan Esther lived in Alaska, and before that she lived in California, at the Provincial House. I don't think she's been out East since her formation."

"What about Mother Mary Bellarmine? Would Norman Kevic have known her?"

"Well, they certainly would have met. Norman has been very involved in our field house project, and Mother Mary Bellarmine was a consultant on that. That's because she's built similar things for our Order in other places. They must have been at meetings together off and on all last week."

"I thought you said you weren't going to be involved in this case," Bennis said.

"Involved or not involved, I like my world to make sense," Gregor told her.

Bennis raised an eyebrow. Sister Mary Celestine was still standing patiently before them, her hands clasped next to her waist and her face expectant. Gregor tried to concentrate on her.

"Well, Sister," he said, "I'm glad you told me all this. I hope you understand that you also have to tell the police."

"I'll tell the police," Sister Mary Celestine said, "and when I do I'll give him a piece of my mind."

"Yes," Gregor said. "Well. My point here is that this is very significant information, even if it comes to nothing, and you shouldn't think you don't have to say anything to Lieutenant Androcetti because you talked to me—"

"I don't think that," Sister Mary Celestine said, "but I tried to talk to three different police officers and none of them would listen to me. I suppose they were the wrong police officers, but what was I to do?"

"I don't know," Gregor said. "Did you notice the young black officer giving orders in the reception room?"

"Oh, of course. The smart one."

"Try him. His name is Collins. Sergeant Collins. You'll still have to talk to Lieutenant Androcetti, but at least you'll have given your story to one officer who will listen to you."

"Listen to me," Bennis said suddenly. "Here comes the fuss you were talking about."

Gregor turned in the direction in which Bennis was pointing—toward the gate to the back garden, through the gate and into the lawn beyond—and saw a swirling mass of movement that looked like a black ocean in the middle of a storm. The black ocean resolved itself into nuns' black veils and the storm into the white veil of a novice. Under the novice's veil Gregor recognized Sister Mary Angelus.

"Let me through," she was shouting, "let me through! I've got to find Mr. Demarkian."

Gregor climbed up on the low stone wall where Bennis was still sitting. It made him more visible, although it also made him look ridiculous.

"I'm over here," he called out to Sister Angelus. "Come this way."

She must have heard him. She pushed two older nuns out of her way—Gregor could hear her "excuse me"'s because they were loud in spite of being distracted—and barreled through the gate into the field. Once on open land, she stopped, looked around,

and trained her sight on Gregor. Then she took off
again at a full run. Her veil flapped in the breeze. Her
calf-length black habit flapped up to expose her knees.
Her long rosary slapped against her side. She got to
Sister Mary Celestine out of breath and panting wildly.

"Oh, Mr. Demarkian," she said. "Oh, I'm sorry, Mr.
Demarkian, you have to come quick. Reverend Mother
General said to get you and tell you to come right
away."

"But why?" Gregor asked. "What's happened?"

"What happened is that they've taken Sister Agnes
Bernadette away in handcuffs." Sister Angelus
wheezed, still breathless. "And there are cameras out
there from all three networks watching them do it."

Sister Agnes Bernadette.

Cameras from all three networks.

Gregor Demarkian groaned.

How bad was all this going to get?

CHAPTER 3

1

There was a bottle of Johnnie Walker Black behind the copy of *Anna Karenina* on Henry Hare's bedroom bookshelf, and when Nancy Hare decided she wanted to go to bed that evening, she went right to it. Nancy didn't sleep in Henry's bedroom, and hadn't for years, but she still treated it as her own turf. She borrowed his shirts to sleep in and his bathrobes to lie around the house in and his ties to try out various things she read about in *The Joy of Sex*. She never tried out anything from *The Joy of Sex* on Henry, because Henry didn't think sex was a joy. He thought it was more of a responsibility. He thought it was like working at the office or paying his taxes, something he didn't like to do much but was much too honorable to try to get out of. Of course, Nancy didn't like to do it much, either, but there was something about *Henry* not wanting to do it that she found insult-

ing. It was as if she lacked something fundamental that
would make him behave like a normal human being.

Was it one of the ordinary duties of a wife, to make
her husband behave like a normal human being?

The Scotch was in an unopened bottle. The bottle
was unopened because Henry's valet checked it every
morning and replaced it if a drink had been taken out
of it. A drink was taken out of it once or twice a month,
when Henry wanted to make himself feel like James
Bond. Nancy took one of the clean crystal drinking
glasses out of Henry's private bathroom—Henry had
to have clean crystal drinking glasses to fill with water
to clean his mouth out after he brushed his teeth, he
also had to have brand new, never before used socks
to wear every morning, because he'd heard that
J. Paul Getty never wore a pair of socks twice—and
filled it to the brim. She drank half of it down and
topped it up again. Then she took a cigarette out of the
gold box on Henry's bureau and lit up with a gold
Dunhill lighter. It was crazy. This bedroom was like
some fantasy out of *Penthouse* magazine, except not so
gross. The bed was the size of California and up on a
platform. There was a switch in the bedside table that
could make the ceiling panels turn until the ceiling
had become a mirror. There were pillows the size of
outboard motors tossed randomly on furniture and carpet the way the loaves of manna had been tossed from
the Heavens. It was all calculated to seduce someone,
but Nancy didn't know who. Henry certainly wasn't interested in seducing her.

She turned on the television and sat back to watch
the eleven o'clock news. She didn't expect to hear
much more than what she had heard at six. It was all
over town now, that a nun had died at St. Elizabeth's.
She'd even had phone calls about it. And Henry was
furious. Henry was taking it personally. Henry thought
it was all her fault, because she'd thrown those flowers
on that nun.

That nun.

Nancy took a drag—they were English cigarettes,
much too strong and much too harsh—and tapped her

ash into the crystal ashtray in the shape of a fish that Henry kept on top of the TV set. Since he didn't smoke, Nancy didn't know who it was for, either. Living around Henry was eerie. It was as if he weren't himself at all, but an alien from outer space who had occupied the body of a much gentler, much more sophisticated man.

"A nun accused of deliberately murdering one of her Sisters at a Main Line convent is out on bail," the woman on the TV said. "News coming up at eleven, right after these messages."

The bedroom door opened and Henry stood in the doorway, his shirt off and his belt unbuckled, looking blank. That was eerie, too. If Nancy did something outrageous, Henry looked annoyed. If she didn't—if she was nice, or neutral, or just not sufficiently obnoxious to get attention—Henry looked blank. Nancy had the odd feeling that she was never really there for him.

She had put the bottle of Scotch on the night table. She picked it up, topped her drink off again, and went back to watching the news.

"They let Sister Agnes Bernadette out," she said, pointing at the set. It wasn't necessary, but it was conversation. If she didn't start one, he never would. "I wonder what happens now. Does she go back to the convent and act like nothing ever happened? Does she still cook?"

"How do you know she cooks?"

"She was cook at the convent when I was at St. Elizabeth's," Nancy said. "She's been there forever. And if you want to know the truth, I don't think she'd have had the heart to deliberately kill Hitler, never mind some nun everybody says she actually liked."

"I thought it was some nun nobody knew," Henry said. "Some nun from Alaska. I thought the point was that this Sister Agnes had gone off her nut."

"Sister Agnes Bernadette."

"I wish you wouldn't drink at this time of night. When you drink, you always make a scene."

Nancy's cigarette was burned almost to the filter. That was something you really didn't want to do with these cigarettes, because the closer they got to the butt the worse they tasted. They were supposed to be the most wonderful cigarettes in the world and they made her gag. She got up, got another one, and lit up again. She almost never smoked when Henry wasn't around. She was addicted to nicotine only in his presence. It had something to do with the fact that when he saw her smoke he always worked around to lecturing her. She wished he would work around to something else, but he wouldn't and she wasn't going to ask for it. There was a time in this marriage when she had asked for it a lot and been turned down too often.

"There," she said as she got back to the bed, "there's Sister Agnes Bernadette. She looks miserable."

"You'd look miserable, too, if you'd just been arrested for murder." Henry had moved in from the doorway now and was standing next to his built-in wardrobe. He would leave his clothes over a chair and his valet would take them away in the morning. Someone would iron his underwear and someone would put creases in his trousers and someone else would make sure he found only the tie that went with the suit he was supposed to be wearing that morning.

"I'm surprised they haven't come here asking to talk to you," Henry said, "with that stunt you pulled and then disappearing on me so I couldn't find you for better than half an hour—"

"I didn't disappear on you. I just went to talk to someone."

"Well, you were missing and you were still at St. Teresa's House, and we were supposed to be gone. You don't *know* how that burns me. She shouldn't have asked me to go. She should have gotten rid of you and left it at that."

"Why? Because you're giving them umpteen jillion dollars?"

"Yes."

"Some people don't operate on a totally cash basis, Henry. Some people have other considerations."

"I don't give a damn what she considers for herself,"

Henry said, "I only care what she considers for me, and I shouldn't have been tossed out of that reception like a gate-crasher. I'm not a gate-crasher. I'm the man who made it all possible."

"You didn't have anything to do with the nuns' convention."

"That's not what I meant. I've donated six million dollars in goods and services to this project of theirs. That college wouldn't survive without me."

"The college wouldn't survive unless you built them a field house?"

"You really shouldn't talk about money, Nancy. You don't understand the first thing about it. You're not competent."

"I don't see why anybody from the police should have wanted to talk to me," Nancy said. "I don't know that I've ever met this Sister Joan Esther. And nothing happened at all to the nun I threw the vase on."

"Except that she got wet. And green. And ripped."

"I know she got ripped, but I didn't rip her."

"You must have ripped her," Henry said. "You were the only one there. You were probably so far out of control, you didn't know what you were doing."

"I am never that far out of control."

"You're that far out of control all the time. It's your life. It's what you do instead of working for a living."

I couldn't have ripped the scapular because I couldn't have got to the scapular to rip it, Nancy thought, and it was true. The top of the scapular was concealed under the sweep of the long collar that covered the shoulder and part of the arms and all of the chest until the breast line. She couldn't have gotten to the top of the scapular without ripping the collar off first—it ought really to be called a cape—or doing something so outrageous everybody would have remarked on it, like grabbing at Mother Mary Bellarmine in such a way that it would have looked like she was about to commit rape.

Her cigarette was burned halfway down. That was enough. Nancy put it out and went to get another one. Across the room, Henry was standing in nothing but a pair of Christian Dior underwear, looking more like the tall, handsome boy she had married than he had in years.

I used to be happy in this place, she thought. Then she lit the cigarette she was holding in her hand and turned away.

It was all indicative, really it was.

He had asked her for an explanation of what she had done to Mother Mary Bellarmine and she had given him an answer calculated to make no sense and he had not pursued it.

He considered her such a flake that it wasn't worth his time to unravel why she did what she did, when or to whom.

He was so wrapped up in himself, he didn't have time to puzzle out anyone else's behavior or to consider it even for a moment in any light but the one that reflected on himself. To Henry, what Nancy had done to Mother Mary Bellarmine was to commit an act that got Henry Hare thrown out of a reception given by the Sisters of Divine Grace.

It all went around and around and it never got any better, and Nancy was sure it wouldn't get better if she told him she hadn't had a reason at all for throwing those flowers on Mother Mary Bellarmine.

"What are you *staring* at?" Henry demanded now.

Nancy decided to let that one ride, too.

If she started getting the hots for Henry Hare again, she was only going to come to grief.

2

It was eleven fifteen on Mother's Day night, and Sarabess Coltrane was worried. She was worried about where she was—which was on a dark street in downtown Philadelphia, alone, standing under a street lamp that seemed to have been dimmed down in front of a door that seemed to be lit by a spotlight—and about what she was about to do. She was afraid that when she went upstairs in this building somebody—a security guard or a secretary or somebody—would make her go away again. She was worried that when she saw Norman Kevic, he wouldn't remember who she was. Most of all, however, she was worried about the conversation she had had with Sister Catherine Grace that afternoon, and with Norman Kevic too, when they were all working on the roses.

Sister Joan Esther was lying dead, and it had all happened exactly the way Sarabess and Catherine Grace had imagined it would. Norman Kevic had to remember that. They had gone into it all in detail. So far he hadn't told the police, but Sarabess was sure he was going to. He would have to. He was famous and he probably had a stake in being a good citizen. Once he told, Sarabess was sure she'd be in all sorts of trouble, and Catherine Grace, too, because that police lieutenant was a real loose cannon, as Sister Scholastica had been saying all afternoon. Actually, Sister Scholastica had been saying a few other—and stronger—things, but it embarrassed Sarabess to remember them. Nuns weren't supposed to talk like that.

If I don't go in now, I'll never go in at all, she thought.

She forced herself away from the lamppost and into the puddle of shadow just beyond it—surely it was much too small a puddle to contain a murderer or a rapist or a mugger or anything else human—and went to the door. The door was made of glass and framed in brass with the WXVE lightning logo etched into the glass just above the brass handlebar. Sarabess pushed against the handlebar, holding her breath. The door could have been locked. She had been listening to Norman Kevic live all the way into the city from St. Elizabeth's. She had been listening to him while she parked her car and while she walked down the street to this door. She had been listening to him through the earphone of her little Japanese radio right up until about ten minutes ago, when she had started to work up her courage to go inside. Norman Kevic had to be in this building, but that didn't mean the building wasn't locked.

It wasn't locked. Sarabess pushed her way into the

foyer. She stopped at the little desk that blocked the way to the elevator and looked around. There was supposed to be a security guard or somebody. There was a clipboard on the desk with a signup sheet on it and people's names and floors written in little squares in pencil. Sarabess looked around and saw no sign of a uniformed man or a gun-toting woman or anyone else. Whoever it is has probably gone to the bathroom, she thought. It wouldn't be fair to just go on up. She went on up anyway. She went around the desk and to the elevators and jabbed at the buttons. The elevator doors opened immediately and she stepped inside.

This was the point at which things might have gotten sticky. Sarabess had never been in the WXVE building before, but since it was such a large building she was sure it wouldn't be *just* for WXVE. There would be other businesses with offices on these floors, architecture firms and certified public accountants, and she had absolutely no idea who was where. If there was a directory in the lobby, she hadn't seen it. Even if she had seen it, she wouldn't have taken the time to read it. If she had, the security guard might have come back, and then God only knew what would have happened. Now she pushed a button at random— "fourteen" because it was really "thirteen" and Sarabess liked to be counterphobic—and prayed for rain. If it wasn't the right floor, it could at least be a neutral one. It could be one where the security guard wasn't roaming around looking for trouble.

The fourteenth was a floor belonging to Martin, Debraham, Carter, and Allenkoski, attorneys at law. The elevator opened onto a darkened foyer with a large oak desk in it. The desk had a rose pink felt blotter in the middle of it and a brass nameplate next to the phone that said, "Tiffany Moscowitz." Sarabess pressed the button for twenty-two and held her breath.

On "twenty-two" she had a little luck. It didn't belong to WXVE, but it wasn't deserted, either. It belonged to a magazine called *Greek World*, and they must have been meeting a printer's deadline for an issue. Sarabess knew all about printer's deadlines. She had worked for an underground newspaper in college, and what she had come away from it with was the conviction that some members of the working class were worse than the capitalist class, and among those members were all printers. It was disgusting. If you went so much as a half hour over deadline they charged you all kinds of penalties, and then they made you pay time and a half on top of it. Sarabess was sure that every printer drove a Cadillac and smoked thick cigars, conspicuously consuming the environment.

Greek World had a logo that looked like a whirling dervish dancing on the top of the Parthenon. It was tacked to the back wall of their foyer in the form of an enormous oakboard poster painted in acrylic primary-colored paints. When the elevator doors opened, a young man was running by with a huge stack of mechanicals badly balanced in his arms. Sarabess hated to stop him. She knew the look on his face. It said he'd lost any control he'd ever had over his panic hours ago.

She had to stop him. She had no choice. She stepped out of the elevator, grabbed at the sleeve of his shirt and said, "Excuse me?"

The man with the mechanicals stopped. He looked around the foyer as if he had never seen it before. He looked at Sarabess as if he had never seen her before. In the second instance, he was right.

"Excuse me," Sarabess said again. "I seem to be lost. I'm supposed to be going to WXVE—"

"That's downstairs," the young man said promptly.

"Downstairs where?"

"Depends what part of them you want. Reception's downstairs on 'twelve.'"

"Good. I'll go to reception."

"Except nobody's there. Only nine to five. Broadcast is on ten."

"Fine," Sara said desperately, "I'll go—"

"They'll never let you in there," the young man said. "You don't have one of those passes on your shirt."

"But—" Sarabess said.

"You'd better go to 'nine,'" the young man said.

"Nobody knows that's part of WXVE at all. The elevator opens on a little dinky foyer and the foyer leads to all the office warrens and nobody ever wants to go there if they don't have business. Try 'nine.'"

"Yes." Sarabess stepped back into the elevator.

"Greeks are crazy," the young man told her. "I thought I knew that because my mother is Greek, but I never really knew that until I got here."

"Yes," Sarabess said again.

The doors to the elevator closed again. Sarabess checked to make sure she had pressed the button for 'nine'—it was lit up, in all that crazy talk she couldn't remember doing it—and sank back against the wall. Her stomach felt full of glass. Her heart felt hollow. Now she was supposed to wander around through a warren of private offices, looking as if she belonged somewhere in them, which she didn't, and trying to get—where? Were there internal staircases? Was Norman Kevic wandering around himself? In all this time she had wasted, he might have finished up and gone home. They'd said on the radio it was a special appearance just to talk about the murder. Sarabess didn't know if you called time on the radio an "appearance."

The elevator doors opened on 'nine.' The foyer really was dinky. It was also unmarked. Sarabess stepped into it and looked around. Nobody seemed to be in the offices beyond the foyer, if what they were were indeed offices. Sarabess couldn't hear the sound of a single conversation or a hollowly buzzing phone.

There were three openings off the foyer, not doors but archways of a sort, badly made, like the ones in cheap tract houses. Sarabess went through the middle one and looked around. She was on a long corridor lined with cubicles. It was the kind of place she had always been afraid she'd get stuck working. She went on through as quickly as she could without feeling as if she were running, which was not very quickly. When you're frightened, you always feel as if you were moving faster than you are.

The corridor of cubicles came to an end at a kind of intersection, with new corridors going to the left and to the right. Sarabess peered in each direction and thought she saw a light to the left of her. It was all so dark and sterile here and so hollow. She was suddenly reminded of the story Norman Kevic had told that afternoon of his search for a men's room. The parallels were unmistakable and she started to laugh.

There was somebody down there in a cubicle, light on and all. Whoever it was—female, Sarabess thought—called out "Who is it?" in a voice twice as scared as Sarabess thought she could manage on her own.

"I'm sorry," Sarabess called back. "I'm lost. I'm supposed to find a man named Norman Kevic."

"Oh, Norman. Good old Cultural Norm. Norm isn't here this time of night."

"Yes he is. He was a witness to the murder—"

"What murder?"

"There was a murder at a reception at St. Elizabeth's College this afternoon. Really. I'm not a nut. You can check it out."

"Norm was a witness?"

"Well, he was there. You know. He's doing some kind of special broadcast right now all about it."

"Just a minute."

Sarabess listened to a set of beeps and wonks that she supposed was a phone, then to a murmuring voice whose words were unintelligible but whose tone rose by the minute. Then there was a sharp click and the cubicle voice called out: "What's your name?"

"Sarabess Coltrane."

More murmuring. There was another sharp click.

"That was Norm," the cubicle voice said. "He said I was supposed to take you right up. Just a minute and I'll be ready to go. You must have really made an impression."

"What do you mean?"

An actual person emerged from the single lighted cubicle, a woman so young Sarabess could barely believe she was out of high school, wearing jeans and a T-shirt and a pair of hot pink plastic flip-flops that slapped against the soles of her feet.

"You must really have made an impression," the young woman repeated. "I've never heard Norm talk like that about a woman. You don't look like I expected you to."

"Oh," Sarabess said.

"Usually Norm is such a smarm," the young woman said. "I take it you haven't been to bed with him."

"What?" Sarabess said.

"Never mind," the young woman said. "Of course you haven't been to bed with him. If you had, he'd have made you sound like a taxi dancer. Never mind. Let's go."

The young woman started down the corridor away from the intersection and Sarabess followed, feeling more confused than ever and wondering what she was supposed to make of it all. Apparently, Norman Kevic had rather liked her, or something. What was that supposed to mean?

At the moment, it was supposed to mean that he would let her in to talk to him, which was vitally important. Sarabess had to do something about that conversation she'd had with Sister Catherine Grace.

For the moment, she thought it would be just as well to get that done and see what came next.

If anything did.

3

It was quarter to twelve, and at St. Elizabeth's Convent, almost everything was quiet. Compline had been sung. Final prayers had been said. A rosary had been started for the succor of Sister Joan Esther's soul. If the habits had been longer and the Office sung in Latin, Sister Scholastica might have thought she had been transported to 1953—or 1553. That was part of what she loved best about being a Catholic and being a nun. She liked to think of all the women before her who would find her life utterly familiar and be able to live it themselves without hardly any adjustment at all. Even having a murder in the house might not have been too much of an adjustment. Religious life in the

Middle Ages and the High Renaissance was not the placid and well-regulated thing it became later. Sister Scholastica sometimes wondered if she would have found it more interesting than what she had now.

She went down the back hall of the visitors' wing—visiting Sisters only, here; secular visitors got rooms in St. Francis of Assisi Hall—and let herself down through the door at the back there and then through the back door of the chapel. The light inside was very dim, but she could see Sister Agnes Bernadette nonetheless, kneeling close to the front with her back hunched over as if she'd acquired a bad case of osteoporosis in a matter of hours. Scholastica dipped her fingers in holy water, made the sign of the cross and went inside. When she reached the center aisle she genuflected in the general direction of the tabernacle and then hurried up to the front. If Sister Agnes Bernadette had been praying, Scholastica wouldn't have interrupted her. Sister Agnes Bernadette wasn't praying. Sister Agnes Bernadette was in tears.

Scholastica sat down on the pew and put an arm around Sister Agnes Bernadette's broad shoulders.

"I thought this is where you'd be. I checked your cell to see that you were in bed, and you weren't."

"I couldn't sleep," Sister Agnes Bernadette said. "I don't know what I'm going to do."

"Whatever you're going to do, you can do it a lot better if you've had some rest."

"But it's all so impossible." Sister Agnes Bernadette raised her teary face to Scholastica. "I didn't kill Joan Esther. I didn't kill anyone. I don't even think I killed them by accident, Sister, because then a lot of people would have died, wouldn't they? Mother Mary Deborah ate almost all her chicken liver pâté by herself and there was nothing wrong with *that*."

"I know," Scholastica said.

Sister Agnes Bernadette sat up a little straighter. "I don't think that poisonous man cares what's true or not," she said. "That Lieutenant Androcetti. I think all he cares about is getting on the television news."

"Well, I'll agree to that."

"I don't think he thinks I killed her either. I heard that man, that Gregor Demarkian, say that they weren't absolutely a hundred percent sure there had been a murder. There had to be lab tests and an autopsy—oh, dear—an autopsy on Sister Joan Esther—"

"Now, Sister—"

"But you must understand what I'm saying," Sister Agnes Bernadette said. "Nothing matters to that man except making an arrest and making news because as long as there's a trial he'll look good. I was thinking all this out while I was sitting in jail. As long as there's a trial he'll be fine, because when the trial comes out not guilty it's just the prosecutor who will look bad. Not him. Sister, I—"

"It's all right."

"I keep trying to offer it up," Sister Agnes Bernadette said. "I keep telling myself there's no help for it, I've been arrested and things will go along from here and there will be a trial, and because I'm not guilty of course I won't be convicted, but in the meantime it will all be so awful, so awful, and so I keep trying to offer it up—"

Offer it up, Sister Scholastica thought. This was terrible. She hadn't heard of anyone "offering it up" for years. Schoolchildren "offered up" the pains of scraped knees or the humiliation of not being chosen for the baseball team in a childish attempt to identify with the sufferings of Christ. Grown women were not supposed to "offer up" totally unfounded murder accusations and full-blown media-hype trials. At least, Scholastica didn't think they were. Scholastica's God was a good deal more sensible than the One worshiped by so many other people.

"Don't you worry," she told Sister Agnes Bernadette. "We'll take care of it. We'll get Gregor Demarkian to take care of it."

"But Gregor Demarkian said he wouldn't take care of it," Sister Agnes Bernadette pointed out. "He said that because the police didn't want him there as part of the investigation—"

"I know what he said."

"But how are you going to make him change his mind?"

"I'm not going to make him change his mind."

"But—"

Sister Scholastica stood up. "Come on," she said. "Get some sleep. We'll have Mr. Gregor Demarkian on our side in the morning. I promise."

"Sister—"

Scholastica held up a finger. "*First* I'm going to wake up Reverend Mother General." She held up another finger. "*Then* Reverend Mother General is going to wake up John Cardinal O'Bannion."

"John *O'Bannion?*"

"Then," Scholastica held up her third and last finger, "Cardinal O'Bannion is going to wake up Gregor Demarkian. Trust me. It will work."

"But what about *our* Cardinal?" Sister Agnes Bernadette asked wildly. "What about the Archbishop of Philadelphia?"

Sister Scholastica shrugged. "I wouldn't worry about him. I think Reverend Mother General can take care of him."

And since that was true, Sister Agnes Bernadette meekly agreed to be escorted to bed.

CHAPTER 4

1

It was Donna Moradanyan's idea to build a maypole in the middle of Cavanaugh Street, but there were objections—the two young men who occupied the local cop car, for instance, felt it would have a deleterious effect on the logical nature of traffic—so in the end she put it up in the window of the Ararat restaurant. Gregor Demarkian saw it for the first time on the morning of Monday, May 12, when he went to meet Father Tibor Kasparian for breakfast. He saw a few other things, too, but he was in so foul a mood they almost didn't matter. The maypole was a good six feet tall and wrapped around with ribbons of every possible color. May might be Mary's month and blue might be Mary's color, but if the symbolism held, Mary was only one of a number of aspects of spring being celebrated here. Gregor tried to remember what a maypole was for and couldn't. He had vague memories of Elizabethan England and royal picnics and cus-

toms stretching back to a pagan mist, but that might
have been some movie he saw with Glenda Jackson in
it. He stopped on the street and looked the maypole up
and down anyway. Then he said the Armenian-
American equivalent of "bah, humbug" and bought a
copy of the *Philadelphia Inquirer* from the metal pull
dispenser at the curb. The front page of the *Inquirer*
was full of the murder of Sister Joan Esther but not,
Gregor was happy to see, full of him. There was a picture of the front of St. Teresa's House with the hundreds of nuns milling around it and another of a
tensely smiling Jack Androcetti. Gregor looked long
and hard at Androcetti's picture and just restrained
himself from sticking his tongue out at it. The ribbons
of the maypole rippled and winked, blown about by a
breeze inside the restaurant. Gregor folded his paper
under his arm and went to look for Father Tibor.

Tibor was inside, sitting in a wide booth in the back,
with the remains of five or six strong Armenian cof-
fees spread out across the table and an ashtray full of
the butts of the dark brown Egyptian cigarettes he
smoked. He was looking at the paper, too, but opened
to an inside page, and as Gregor slid into the other
side of the booth he looked up and shook his head.
Gregor was in the kind of mood when he gave lectures
about how calling Turkish coffee Armenian coffee because you couldn't say the word *Turkish* in an Armenian neighborhood for any reason except to start a riot
was taking it all too far, but just as he was about to get
started Linda Melajian came up with coffee and a bowl
of fried dough. Gregor was embarrassed that he
couldn't remember the Armenian name for the kind of
fried dough this was. Linda Melajian was very young
and very polite to older people, the way the very
young are very polite to creatures they consider only
recently landed here from Mars.

"Good morning, Mr. Demarkian," she said. "I read
all about you in the paper this morning. You want your
usual scrambled eggs?"

"I want my usual scrambled eggs," Gregor said,

"thank you, Linda. Tibor? What was there to read
about me in the paper this morning?"

Tibor looked up, shrugged, and turned the paper
around so that it was right side up for Gregor and
Gregor could read it. His little bald head gleamed in
the light, and his shoulder seemed less hunched than
usual. Tibor was younger than Gregor by almost ten
years, but he looked older. A couple of years in Siberia
and a half dozen more in one Soviet prison or another
could do that to you. Tibor was a cheerful man, but he
often looked physically tired. This morning, he looked
less so.

Gregor looked down at the two-page spread of paper
Tibor had turned for his inspection, caught his own
picture—standing next to Bennis, looking hot and di-
sheveled while Bennis looked as close to perfect as
Bennis usually did—let his eye travel up to the headline and winced. The *Inquirer* had done it to him again.
It never failed. It was a kind of vendetta. The main
headline read: **DEMARKIAN OUT.** The subhead
sounded less like baseball news: **NO ROOM FOR
PHILADELPHIA'S OWN ARMENIAN-AMERICAN
HERCULE POIROT, ACCORDING TO POLICE
LIEUTENANT.** Gregor turned the paper around so it
was right side up for Tibor and sighed.

"Has Bennis seen that yet?" he asked.

Tibor shook his head. "Bennis is not awake, Krekor,
you should know that. She is never awake until very
nearly noon. Are you very upset about this police lieutenant?"

"I'm getting very interested in just how bad a repu-
tation he's got. Look at that subhead. 'According to
Police Lieutenant.' Newspapers never say it like that.
They say 'According to Police.' "

"It is Donna Moradanyan you have to watch out for,"
Tibor said. "She is very worked up this morning. She
has decided we have to hold Mother's Day again."

"What do you mean, hold it again?"

"Hannah Krekorian's children and grandchildren
could not come, Krekor, and Hannah was disconsolate,
and there was no one to cheer her up because every-

one was having Mother's Day but Hannah was not, so
now Donna Moradanyan thinks we should hold it
again. Mother's Day. For Hannah. To make her feel as
if she's had one."

"Right," Gregor said.

"We will do this next Sunday, Krekor, and it will require a party where people play games. Donna and
Lida Arkmanian were planning it this morning. During
a party where people play games, I would like to be in
Florida on vacation."

"I don't blame you. What about the refugees? Don't
they need anything from you that could keep you
away?"

"The refugees will all be invited, Krekor. You know
what these women are like. There are no refugees, just
people who are probably fifth cousins twice removed if
you look back far enough but nobody wants to bother
so you let them stay on the living room couch just in
case. I wish I had come to Cavanaugh Street when I
was first a refugee. It would have saved me a bout of
dysentery in Jerusalem."

"Considering what else could have happened to you
in Jerusalem, I think you got off easy with the dysentery."

"I do not think it is natural for someone as young as
Donna to be so close to someone as old as Lida. Not
like this. Lida is old enough to be the mother. Donna
is old enough to be the daughter. They should fight."

Linda Melajian had come back with Gregor's scrambled eggs—three of them, on a big plate that also contained four Jimmy Dean spicy breakfast sausage
patties and a pile of hash browns the size of a small
dog. None of this was Armenian food, but the Ararat
served it anyway because the Melajian women were
convinced that if they didn't, people like Gregor and
Father Tibor would never get any breakfast at all. It
was Cavanaugh Street's one complaint about Bennis
Hannaford that she seemed never to have cooked
breakfast for anybody, even for herself. That was tem-
pered by reports from Lida Arkmanian and Sheila

Kashinian about what happened when Bennis *did* cook.

Gregor thanked Linda for the plate, grabbed the salt and began to pile it on. He ignored Tibor's fretted *tsk*ing—Tibor ate pastry for breakfast, pastry so sweet it could make Gregor's teeth curl—and picked up a triangle of toast to add more butter to it. It already had enough butter on it to qualify it as a bona fide outpost of a dairy state.

"If you keep that up, you will give yourself an illness," Tibor said.

Gregor looked up to tell him what a crock that was—this *was* the man who fried his own chicken in bacon fat—but as he did he caught sight of Ararat's front door out of the corner of his eye, and turned to see who it was opening to let in. The door had opened and shut again and the young man had been standing near the table nearest the cash register for half a minute before Gregor's mind was able to put it all in place. It wasn't the sight of a black man on Cavanaugh Street that was the surprise, or even a black man in the Ararat for breakfast. There was a time when that would have been a shock, but not anymore. Gregor knew every detective in the Philadelphia police force's homicide division, and a number of them had been to Ararat to eat breakfast with Gregor Demarkian. (The tourists, white or black, weren't supposed to know about breakfast.) It wasn't the color of this man's skin but the arrangement of his features that gave Gregor Demarkian pause. The man looked so damn familiar but Gregor just couldn't place him.

The man looked around the restaurant once or twice, found Gregor and Tibor in their booth, squinted in their direction and then looked relieved. He came striding over from the cash register with the air of a man who has finally—*finally*—reached his destination. He came up to their booth and stopped, his hands deep in the pockets of his short jean jacket. Tibor put down the coffee he was holding and looked polite.

"Well," the young man said. "Mr. Demarkian. You don't know how glad I am to have found *you*."

"Good morning," Gregor said.

The young man sighed. "You don't remember me. I'm not surprised. In all that crap yesterday, you probably wouldn't remember much of anybody but Jack and we all know how Jack affects the public."

"Jack," Gregor repeated. He was fairly sure the young man meant Jack Androcetti, but he couldn't be sure.

The young man confirmed it for him. "Lieutenant Androcetti," he said patiently, "my supposed boss of the moment. My name is Collins. Rob Collins. I'm a sergeant with—"

"I remember you," Gregor said. "The intelligent one."

"Thanks," Rob Collins said.

"Does Jack Androcetti know you're here?"

"Of course he doesn't. I'm looking to get fired. Or something. God. Jack Androcetti doesn't know his— Never mind. Look, could I talk to you?"

"Does this mean you want me to leave?" Father Tibor asked.

"No," Gregor said.

"Is he your partner?" Rob Collins asked.

"He's my priest," Gregor told him.

Rob Collins said, "Right."

That was the moment when Linda Melajian came over with a new placemat and a new place setting and pushed Rob Collins toward Tibor's side of the booth.

"You want one of Mr. Demarkian's cholesterol specials or would you prefer something healthy?"

"Coffee?" Rob Collins suggested.

"The coffee in this place is not healthy," Gregor said.

"I'll get coffee," Linda said to the world at large.

Rob Collins sat down next to Father Tibor Kasparian. "Mr. Demarkian," he said, "you've got to listen to me. We're in a lot of trouble."

2

The coffee in Ararat was very definitely not healthy,
and Linda brought a pot of it, on the principle that if
Gregor was meeting someone at the restaurant for
breakfast, that someone had to be there on business.
Gregor knew that Linda had already read through the
Inquirer. She had probably decided that this had something to do with that. She would be right if she had, of
course, but what Gregor worried about was what
something she might have decided this had to do with
that. The people on Cavanaugh Street had only the
vaguest notions of what went on during a murder investigation, and those came chiefly from television.
Even Bennis Hannaford, who had actually been present at more than one such project, tended to romanti-
cize the whole business. Father Tibor was better, but
nobody really listened to Father Tibor. They treated
him as an unworldly and utterly holy local saint with
no practical intelligence whatsoever. Gregor always
wanted to point out that a man with no practical intelligence whatsoever could never have made his way
from a Siberian prison camp to an East German safe
house to Jerusalem to Rome to Paris and then to the
United States. The sheer logistics of something like
that were paralyzing. The people on Cavanaugh Street
apparently thought Tibor had been lifted up by an angel and set down on the doorstep of the nearest Bishop of the Armenian Christian Church. They would
probably also think that Gregor had a secret deal going with the police investigating the murder of Sister
Joan Esther.

Rob Collins thought that what he had going was an
unqualified disaster, which was usually what he had
going when he got stuck with Jack Androcetti.

"Lot of guys in the department want to say it was
racism got Jack his promotion," Rob said, "but this
time I think it was good old-fashioned politics. I mean,
they promoted him ahead of two white guys who were
ahead of me on the list, if you see what I mean. The
name Capeletti mean anything to you?"

"Sure," Gregor said. "Philadelphia Democratic machine in the forties and fifties. Some kind of party boss."

"Some kind, yeah. Party chairman for Philadelphia and functional kingpin for the entire Main Line. Good old ward politics, buy the votes and rig the voting machines. Capeletti was Jack's grandfather on his mother's side. You beginning to get the picture?"

"I take it there are still a lot of Capelettis in politics on the Main Line."

"A lot."

"Does this mean they had to make him a *homicide* detective?"

"Homicide was what he wanted." Rob Collins sighed. "You heard about how he arrested the nun, Sister Agnes Bernadette?"

"Yes, I did. Everybody did. It was on the news."

"Right. Well, it's a crock. A total crock. Androcetti's got absolutely no reason to think she killed anybody except that she was the cook who handled the food, and even that's crazy because the nun who was helping her handle the food was the nun who died."

"Sister Joan Esther."

"Right. And the thing is, he knows it's crap. He knows it. He pulled it out of thin air as soon as he heard the television people were there. I think he was afraid you'd get a jump on the publicity."

Gregor speared a piece of sausage and leaned back, contemplating the ceiling fan, contemplating the situation. "Let's start from the beginning here," he said. "Do you actually know you have a murder yet? Do you have the lab reports back?"

"I don't have the lab reports back, but I talked to the medical people. A guy on our team named Ben Bowman heard you talking to that lady—"

"Bennis Hannaford?" Tibor suggested helpfully.

"No, not her. Some nun. About fugu. You know, Japanese puffer fish."

"Mother Andrew Loretta," Gregor said.

"Maybe." Rob Collins sipped his coffee and winced. "Anyway, when Ben told me about it I went to the doc and gave it to him as a possibility, and what he said was that it sounded perfect and he'd test for it. The symptoms or whatever, I mean. If it turns out to be fugu, does it mean we don't have a murder?"

"It would depend on where she got the fugu. From what I understand, the fugu was supposed to be prepared by a special fugu chef sent especially from Japan at a gazebo in the garden. It wasn't to be left around for anyone to pick up anytime—which would have been a bad idea because fugu is extremely dangerous if it's not handled properly. Since I know from talking to Sister Andrew Loretta that no fugu was being served yesterday at all—because the fugu chef was having a temper tantrum—my guess would be that Sister Joan Esther would have had to have been given it deliberately. Did anyone check the ice in the hollow of the ice sculpture's head?"

"It melted," Rob Collins said. "Somebody's testing the water."

"What about the chicken liver pâté in the other ice sculptures? What about the food that was already on the table?"

"Oh, we got all those. But Mr. Demarkian, couldn't it have been a mistake? With the fugu, I mean. Couldn't someone have picked some up by accident and then used it—"

"—in the chicken liver pâté?" Gregor shook his head. "I'm willing to bet anything that the pâté was made as a single enormous batch, and none of the rest of it was poisoned. I don't know how the fugu was kept. I asked yesterday, but Mother Andrew Loretta wasn't clear and I didn't have the mobility I would have had under other circumstances—"

"Jack," Rob groaned.

"*Mmm.* I think if you have fugu poisoning here you also have a murder here. I take it if you didn't have a murder here, you'd be rid of Jack Androcetti."

"You got it."

"Sorry," Gregor said.

Rob Collins shrugged. "It was a long shot in any case. I was pretty much resigned. Now that we do have a murder, though, I'm damned if I believe it was committed by that weepy nun we arrested yesterday. I bet she doesn't even put out traps for mice."

Gregor waved at Linda Melajian. Astoundingly, the pot of coffee was already drained. They needed more. Linda knew from across the room what they wanted and went to get it.

"The two questions that interest me the most," he told Rob Collins, "are who would have known that fugu was poisonous, and whether or not it was Sister Joan Esther who was supposed to be killed. The first is the kind of question that has no really hard answer."

"Yes, it does," Father Tibor said. "The answer is, 'everybody in Philadelphia.' It is on the radio, Krekor, it is on the radio all the time. From a man named Norman Kevic."

"Good old Cultural Norm," Rob Collins said.

"I'm beginning to wish I'd heard this Norman Kevic. What does he say about fugu?"

"He just makes a lot of racially offensive jokes about Japanese people dying from it," Rob said. "If you're asking does he say what it looks like or what part of it is poisonous, the answer's no."

"Mmm," Gregor said. "Well, that leaves things up in the air, which is where I thought they'd be. Let's get on to question number two. Was it really Joan Esther who was meant to be killed?"

"She's the one who's dead," Rob pointed out.

"I know." Gregor sighed. "I was in law enforcement for twenty years. She's the one who's dead, and that should be definitive in most cases. But in this case it bothers me. The pâté was put in the ice sculpture on the assumption that Mother Mary Bellarmine would take the first bite of it on a cracker during a kind of half-ceremony that was supposed to open the buffet. Did Jack Androcetti get that much?"

"He did," Rob Collins said, "but somebody told us that this Mother Mary Bellarmine had gout and couldn't eat the chicken liver pâté—"

"But not everybody knew that, don't you see? And if you didn't know that, and if you were intent on killing

Mother Mary Bellarmine, you would have had a fairly clear shot—or you would have thought you had. And I can think of half a dozen reasons why someone would want Mother Mary Bellarmine dead. I can't do the same with Sister Joan Esther."

"Well, I can't find any reason for that Sister Agnes Bernadette to have killed Sister Joan Esther," Rob Collins said. "Jack seems to be treating this like a psychotic break. Sister went a little nuts. Sister put some poison in the lunch pâté. Chalk it up to sexual repression."

"Did he really say this thing?" Tibor asked.

"Jack chalks *everything* up to sexual repression," Rob Collins said. "But you know, Mr. Demarkian, it's odd what you said, about Mother Mary Bellarmine. Before Jack pulled his stunt with the arrest, I was doing a lot of hard looking at Mother Mary Bellarmine."

"Why?"

Rob Collins picked his jean jacket up from where he had dropped it on the bench between Tibor and himself and rummaged around in the pockets. He came up with a small stenographer's notebook and began to flip through it.

"Sister Joan Esther," he said slowly, coming to rest on a page full of what looked like the tracings of chicken entrails, "was a nun in the Provincial House in southern California that Mother Mary Bellarmine is the head of. I'm making a hash of the hierarchy, I know, but bear with me. Nuns get assigned to houses and work out of those houses under religious superiors. Mother Mary Bellarmine was Sister Joan Esther's religious superior in this place, that was up until about a year ago. Anyway, at about that time Sister Joan Esther requested a transfer, and when a posting came up in Alaska she took it. The posting in Alaska was the only one that came up, and the first one, but if she had waited a month or two she could probably have gotten something else—"

"Possibly she was interested in going to Alaska," Gregor suggested.

"Not according to my sources," Rob Collins said. "According to my sources, she was interested in getting away from Mother Mary Bellarmine, pure and simple. She—Joan Esther—was at this Provincial House for about a year and a half, and in all that time she and Mother Mary Bellarmine did nothing but fight."

"About what?"

"About everything, as far as I was able to tell. The way a habit should look. How to teach a class in English as a second language. If it was a nice day."

"All right," Gregor said. "This sounds classic."

"It got even more classic. One day, Sister Joan Esther writes to Reverend Mother General at this main house they've got in Maryville, New York—"

"Motherhouse," Gregor said.

"—and she makes it a very long letter, and the next thing anybody knows, this Reverend Mother General goes out to California to pay Mother Mary Bellarmine a visit and apparently to give her a dressing down. According to one of the women I talked to—not a nun, a secretary at the college—anyway, according to her, the rumor is that this Reverend Mother General threatened to start proceedings to have Mother Mary Bellarmine removed from her post if Mother Mary Bellarmine didn't start to behave, and Mother Mary Bellarmine responded to this by blowing up at Sister Joan Esther. Then Sister Joan Esther went to Alaska, and everything calmed down until they met again last week. At which point, my secretary claims, it became perfectly obvious that Mother Mary Bellarmine hated Sister Joan Esther with a passion. Which leaves me with a couple of very interesting questions.

"The first one being, why was Sister Joan Esther the one to carry the ice sculpture to Mother Mary Bellarmine's table when Mother Mary Bellarmine hated her so much? You know what the simple answer to that is, don't you? It was sheer coincidence.

"I was wondering if it could be a backfire," Rob Collins said. "I was wondering if Sister Joan Esther could have been trying to murder Mother Mary Bellarmine, and then when Mother Mary Bellarmine didn't die maybe she thought she'd done it wrong and not poisoned the pâté at all, and then she took a taste and—wham."

"Would you have taken a taste?" Gregor asked.

"No," Rob Collins said.

"Good," Tibor put in. "I know the criminal is supposed to be quite stupid, Krekor, but that would be too much."

"The other possibility," Gregor said, "is that Sister Joan Esther did it on purpose, to annoy Mother Mary Bellarmine. But you see, we always come down to this one point. The poison—fugu or whatever—was in *that particular* pâté. I can't see it there waiting to knock off Sister Joan Esther. There was no way the murderer could know that Sister Joan Esther would be the one standing next to that particular ice sculpture. The question is, was there any way for anyone to know that Mother Mary Bellarmine would be standing next to that particular statue?"

"I don't know," Rob Collins said.

"That's another thing that would be nice to find out," Gregor said.

"Yeah." Rob Collins shook his head. "Except maybe we won't ever find anything out, because Jack's already made his arrest. The prosecutors are furious, by the way. They know they've been handed a really bum case. Hell, even the newspapers know it's a really bum case."

"You ought to check into the financial arrangements for this field house they're building," Gregor said. "I don't know anything about this Henry Hare, but I didn't like what I saw of him, and I liked even less what I saw of his wife. And you know what multimillion dollar projects are like. The potential for white collar crime is enormous."

"I can't investigate Henry Hare," Rob Collins said gloomily. "Not while Jack has got that little nun on the leash. I can't investigate anyone."

"Mmmm," Gregor Demarkian said.

"I don't like this," Father Tibor Kasparian said. "This is not a positive attitude."

Tibor still had his paper open to the pages with the Armenian-American Hercule Poirot story on them. Gregor contemplated his own face upside down and watched Rob Collins do the same. This was definitely not a positive attitude, but he didn't know what to do about it. This was definitely not a positive situation. He looked up and watched the maypole in Ararat's front window. It would have looked gay and bright if Tibor hadn't ruined it, by letting him know that it portended a party where not just people, but Actual Armenian-American Adults, would have to submit to pushing potatoes with their noses and acting out charades.

"Well," Rob Collins said after a while, "what do you think we should do? Maybe we could hire somebody to break both of Jack Androcetti's legs and take him out of the picture."

"I don't think so," Gregor said. "Maybe we could arrange to have him called out of town."

"Do you have friends who will do that for you from the FBI?" Rob Collins asked.

"Of course I don't," Gregor said. "I think movie producers ought to be shot. The Federal Bureau of Investigation has to be the stodgiest organization in the United States government. The Bureau does not go around playacting to make life easier for former agents. And when they try, they blow it."

"Yeah," Rob Collins said. "I've dealt with the Feds before. They always blow it."

"Well," Gregor said, "I wouldn't say always."

"Listen," Linda Melajian said, rushing up to their table. "You've got to go see. There's a big car parked right in front of your house with three men in it dressed all in black and I think they're looking for you."

Since Father Tibor lived behind Holy Trinity Church and Rob Collins didn't live on Cavanaugh Street at all, Gregor Demarkian presumed that Linda was speaking to him. With that assumption, he got up from the table and went to stand beside the maypole in the window.

He looked up Cavanaugh Street and found just what he'd been told to look for. There was most certainly a big black car parked on the street in front of his house, and there were most certainly a couple of men dressed in black inside it. That they were looking for him—and not for Donna Moradanyan, Bennis Hannaford, or old George Tekemanian—was tautological.

Gregor strode to the door of Ararat, pulled it open, and went outside.

3

Less than two minutes later, Gregor was standing on the sidewalk between the black car and his own front stoop, knocking politely on one of the smoked glass windows nearest the street. Behind that window there was some movement to and fro, and then the whirring sound of the electric window opener bringing the glass down. The young man just on the other side of that window was wearing a clerical collar. He looked Gregor up and down and said, "Are you Mr. Demarkian? Mr. Gregor Demarkian?"

"That's right," Gregor said.

"Good," the young man said. "We've been calling your number for hours. We're from the Chancery. From the Archbishop's office?"

"I know what a Chancery is," Gregor said drily.

"Well, the Archbishop would like to see you," the young man said. "Right away. He says it's very urgent."

"I'm sure it is."

In fact, Gregor Demarkian was more than sure it was. He would have staked the fate of his immortal soul on it.

With Roman Catholic Archbishops, everything was always urgent.

CHAPTER 5

1

The three young men in clerical collars did not take Gregor Demarkian to the Chancery, or to the Archbishop's informal residence out on the Main Line, but to St. Elizabeth's College. Since Gregor had been expecting it, he was neither panicked nor annoyed, only a little curious. Would the Archbishop himself actually be at this meeting? Gregor had only met one Roman Catholic archbishop, John Cardinal O'Bannion, up in Colchester, New York. John was an ex-sailor, an ex-boxer, and an ex-the Lord only knew what else, but considering the difficulty he had remembering not to swear it was probably something interesting. What Gregor had heard about the Archbishop of Philadelphia was very different. What he had seen of him—on television and in the newspapers—was very different, too. Tall, elegant, the product of one of the country's richest and most socially prominent Irish Catholic families, he had been educated at

Groton and Harvard before deciding to enter the seminary. Having decided to enter the seminary, he had
been immediately recognized as a young man with ex-
traordinary potential and channeled into the heavier
academic tracks. After ordination he had spent a year
at a university in Rome, another two years working in
the Curia, and another year and a half after that writ-
ing a book on canon law. His first *Explanation of the
Catholic Faith*, a catechism for adults, had been published when he was thirty-two. A twenty-fifth edition,
with an appendix detailing the intricacies of Vatican II,
had been published the year before last. He was a
Prince of the Church of the old school, a throwback to
the days of the Counterreformation, the kind of Archbishop laypeople automatically thought of whenever a
pope died. His name was David Law Kenneally, and
from what Gregor had heard he liked being called
"Your Eminence" very much. Gregor couldn't imagine
Kenneally in the same room with John Cardinal
O'Bannion. It was a stretch imagining those two in the
same church.

The car went through the gates of St. Elizabeth's as
Gregor remembered them, but turned off almost immediately in an unfamiliar direction. Gregor looked out
the windows and saw lawns covered with nuns. There
were nuns everywhere and then more nuns again, as
if, just out of his line of sight, they had begun cloning
themselves. Gregor wondered if this is what it had
been like, back in the days when the Sisters of Divine
Grace had had enough vocations to staff a college like
St. Elizabeth's entirely with nuns. He supposed even
that had been less disconcerting, because even a staff
full of nuns couldn't create the effect he was now seeing. The black car pulled up in front of a tall building
with a discreet carved wooden plaque planted in the
ground cover on the lawn in front:

CONVENT.

Gregor peered up at the double-doored front entrance to see Sister Scholastica pacing back and forth, her arms folded across her chest under the long black collar of her habit, her veil held to her bright red hair by what seemed to be a single bobby pin. Or maybe nuns didn't use bobby pins to hold their veils on their heads. Gregor didn't know. He did know what he meant.

The three young men had not said much on the trip in to St. Elizabeth's, but they had been unfailingly polite, and they were unfailingly polite now. As soon as the car came to a full stop, the one in the front passenger seat hopped to the curb, grabbed the handle of Gregor's door and opened it. Then he held out an arm to help Gregor to his feet and didn't look offended when Gregor didn't use it. Up at the convent's front door, Sister Scholastica hesitated, looked hard to make sure she was seeing what she was seeing, and then came down the steps toward them. The young man at the curb asked Gregor if there was anything he could do, shook his head a little when Gregor said there wasn't, and backed away when Sister Scholastica came striding toward them.

"Gregor," Sister Scholastica said. "You don't know how happy I am to see you. You don't know how happy all of us will be to see you. Especially Sister Agnes Bernadette. She's been hysterical. And Reverend Mother General. Come with me."

"Sister?" the young man at the curb said.

"It's all right," Sister Scholastica told him. "The Archbishop is with my Reverend Mother. You weren't asked to bring Mr. Demarkian right to His Eminence himself?"

"Well, no," the young man said. "We were just supposed to get him here."

"He's here," Sister Scholastica said.

She put her arm through Gregor's and began tugging him toward the convent's front door.

"You won't believe what's been going on here," she told him. "You'd think the police would have been crazy enough for anybody, but we had to get together and make it worse. What do you think about that?"

Gregor didn't think anything about that. He was still a little surprised to be here on such short notice—and a little embarrassed, because it was a public indication of just how much he wanted to be involved in this case, and Gregor made a point of never admitting that he wanted to be involved in a case at all. He let Sister Scholastica lead him up the steps and through the convent door, saying as little as possible.

Scholastica was talking like a woman just released from a sixteen-year vow of silence. Her strong voice with its Upstate New York accent filled the tall-ceilinged foyer; she bounced up the stairs to the second floor.

"The nuns have been bad enough," she told him, "but we've got more than nuns here this weekend, and the other people have been just plain impossible. I don't care what you say about appreciating other people's cultures, give me Americans every time."

2

Gregor Demarkian had never been in a convent before Vatican II. He had no idea if convents had been structured differently then, or if a conservative order like the Sisters of Divine Grace still did things basically as they had always done. He was fairly sure that he would never have been allowed in the convent's private rooms—which he had been in Maryville, when he had gone to the Motherhouse of the Sisters of Divine Grace to look into the death of a postulant named Brigit Ann Reilly—but that was something else again. Scholastica led him up one hall and down another, stopping every once in a while to make the sign of the cross with holy water and say a quick prayer near a statue or a picture. She came to a halt in front of a tall, antique wooden door with a crucifix covering it that started two inches above the floor and ended two inches below the ceiling. Gregor found the effect—an emaciated, suffering Christ as tall as Gregor was himself, a set of nail wounds that could have come out of a medical school textbook—distinctly disconcerting. Scholastica stepped in front of the door, opened it, and went inside.

"Your Eminence?" she said. "Reverend Mother? I have Mr. Demarkian."

"Mr. Demarkian," Reverend Mother General said. She slipped past Sister Scholastica and came out to meet Gregor, pushing the door back wide as she did so. Gregor noticed that she managed to make her habit look more conservative than it actually was. She took his arm and began tugging at him much as Sister Scholastica had done. Nobody in this Order seemed to think they had time for anything but hurrying this morning.

"Mr. Demarkian," Reverend Mother General said again as she ushered him into what turned out to be a massive office, complete with a football-field-size desk, carved oak built-in bookcases, and a crucifix at least as large and well detailed as the one on the door. There was a tall man standing behind the desk, wearing a pair of clean blue jeans and a cotton sweater. He managed to make clean blue jeans and cotton sweaters look as if they ought to cost a hundred dollars apiece at Brooks Brothers. Reverend Mother General stopped in front of the desk and motioned to the man behind it. "Mr. Demarkian, this is David Kenneally, the new Archbishop of Philadelphia—new these last four months, I believe—and of course the de facto religious superior of the nuns in this house—"

"What Reverend Mother is trying to say," David Cardinal Kenneally said drily, "is that I have no influence in this place at all. How do you do, Mr. Demarkian. I've heard a great deal about you from John O'Bannion."

"I'm a little surprised I haven't heard *from* John

O'Bannion," Gregor said. "Right at about this point in the proceedings, I usually get a phone call that starts, 'I know you're probably busy but—'"

"We tried," Sister Scholastica said. "The Cardinal called you four times this morning. You were out."

"I was eating my breakfast," Gregor said. "In peace."

David Kenneally cleared his throat. "Yes. Well. I assume you must know why we've asked you here. It seems we've gotten ourselves in a great deal of trouble."

"I taught David in the eighth grade," Reverend Mother General said. "He used the royal *We* then, too. David, *you* haven't gotten yourself into a great deal of trouble. The Order has gotten itself into a great deal of trouble, and in the process put the Archdiocese in a very difficult position—"

"She used to talk like this back when she was teaching the eighth grade," David Kenneally said. "Seriously, Mr. Demarkian, Reverend Mother has explained to me your reluctance to involve yourself in this matter under the circumstances and I can hardly say I blame you—"

"But I'm not reluctant to involve myself in this matter," Gregor said. "I'm not reluctant at all. I spent all of last night making notes about what I saw happen, what I think happened, and how it might be all worked out. My problem is that I don't know how I could possibly be of any help to you or to the Sister who was arrested, given the fact that—"

"That the police are being entirely too uncooperative," David Kenneally interrupted. "Yes, I see. But you can consult, can't you? That's what you do. You consult. And we seem to need some consultation."

"At least you could talk to Agnes Bernadette," Reverend Mother General put in. "She really is distraught. She has every right to be distraught. Unless you think she actually was the one who—"

"No," Gregor said. "I don't think that. Let me ask you something. If I was to—consult, as you put it—do you think you could get some people to talk to me? Some very specific people?"

"I could probably deliver any practicing Catholic in this Archdiocese," David Kenneally said, "appealing to courtesy if nothing else."

"*I* could deliver the Pope," Reverend Mother General said.

"The Pope won't be necessary," Gregor said faintly. "What I'd like to do first is to talk to Sister Agnes Bernadette, not here but over at St. Teresa's House. I want to go down to the kitchen where the food was prepared—I did understand that rightly, the food was prepared at St. Teresa's House?"

"That's right," Sister Scholastica said. "The cold food, anyway. There were some hot dishes that were made other places and then brought over to be microwaved up."

"But the chicken liver pâté was made there," Gregor insisted, "and the fugu fish was stored there—"

"That is quite correct, Mr. Demarkian," Reverend Mother General said. "And as for the fugu fish, possibly you should talk to the chef—"

"He only speaks Japanese," Scholastica reminded her.

"Perhaps you should speak to Mother Andrew Loretta," Reverend Mother General corrected. "That's what I'll do. I'll get Sister Agnes Bernadette, Mother Andrew Loretta, and that chef over there at the same time. That way, you can question them all. Is there going to be anybody else you're going to want?"

"I'm going to want quite a lot of people," Gregor said, "but the only one you might have difficulty getting hold of is Nancy Hare."

"Nancy Hare?" Scholastica looked shocked.

"I'll get on the phone to Henry," David Kenneally said with a sigh. "Oh you don't know how I don't like to get on the phone with Henry. I'll try to have Mrs. Hare here in an hour."

"Tell her she's been granted an ecclesiastical annulment," Scholastica said acidly. "She'll be here in twenty seconds flat."

Reverend Mother General ignored her. "Come," she said to Gregor Demarkian. "Help me over to St. Teresa's House. I like to watch you operate."

The last time, Reverend Mother General had several times threatened to make sure he couldn't operate at all, but Gregor didn't think this was the time to mention it. With nuns, there were a lot of things there would never be time to mention at all.

3

Like Cavanaugh Street, St. Teresa's House seemed to have decided not to let go of Mother's Day. Gregor didn't know if he was noticing more of the decorations today because the place was relatively deserted, or if little elves had come in the night and tied baby blue ribbons to every available surface, but the general effect was one of almost maniacal mother worship. Of course, Catholics didn't "worship" Mary any more than Armenians did, but Gregor would have been hard put to make that point to anyone whose first experience of Catholicism was the long hall leading to the basement kitchen of this particular place.

> ### MAY IS MARY'S MONTH,

one poster after another proclaimed. The relentless message was relieved only by variations, like the blue-and-white concoction that declared

> ### THE MOTHER OF GOD IS THE MOTHER OF US ALL.

Sister Scholastica saw Gregor staring at the posters and whispered in his ear, "They were made by the elementary-school children in all the parish schools run by this Order in Philadelphia and on the Main Line. The deal was there was going to be a contest, and the winners were going to get their posters put up here during the convention, except nobody wanted to disappoint any of the children and besides the teaching Sisters were all worried about self-esteem—"

"In my day we didn't have self-esteem," Reverend Mother General said from Gregor's other side. "We had self-respect. And no more of it than what we had earned."

Sister Scholastica went on ahead, opened a door covered with a picture of Mary holding a child wearing a gold crown, and said, "Oh, Aggie, there you are. And Mother Andrew Loretta. Do you know—"

"Mr. Yakimoto will be here in just a minute," Mother Andrew Loretta sang out.

Gregor got a little ahead of Reverend Mother General and went into the kitchen. It was much as he had expected, the picture of church basement kitchens everywhere, in spite of the fact that this was not the basement of a church. It was a little more elaborate than it might have been, but just as spare, with long plastic-topped counters and laminated shelves, mismatched as to color and material, as if whoever had put them in had consciously decided not to take trouble with what nobody in the public was ever supposed to see. Gregor noticed a tall door at the back with a heavy metal handle and asked the nun whose face was familiar from last night's news broadcasts, "Is that the freezer?"

Sister Agnes Bernadette nodded.

Gregor went over to the freezer and peered inside. It was a standard commercial walk-in freezer, the kind of thing small-town hamburger joints put in as a matter of routine. The air inside was frigid. There were a pile of large boxes on the floor in one corner with Japanese characters written across them in red and black. Gregor nodded perfunctorily in their direction and then stepped back out of the cold. He closed the freezer door and turned to look at the people who were waiting for him.

"Well," he said. "Let's start from the beginning, shall we? I take it you're Sister Agnes Bernadette."

Sister Agnes Bernadette was near tears. Gregor had the feeling that Sister Agnes Bernadette had been near tears since she'd been arrested, and maybe before. Sister Agnes Bernadette was the kind of woman who was often near tears. "Oh, Mr. Demarkian," she sniffled. "I'm so glad you're here. I'm so glad you changed your mind—"

"Don't be glad yet," Gregor told her. "I haven't done anything. I just want to get a few things straight. Is that all right?"

"Of course it's all right," Reverend Mother General said.

"Let's start with how you and Sister Joan Esther ended up here putting chicken liver pâté into ice sculptures. Was Sister Joan Esther assigned to help you? Was it known in advance that she'd been doing this job? Was this an organized thing?"

"Oh, no." Sister Agnes Bernadette shook her head. "I was supposed to do it all on my own—the pâté, that is, and the ice sculptures. I mean, the ice sculptures were already done. I did those last week when I had a spare minute from the other cooking, which wasn't easy to find, you know. And then yesterday morning I was supposed to come down here and make chicken liver pâté in the food processor and use the ice cream scoop to fill the heads, but when I did one of my statues was broken—"

"Broken?" Gregor asked.

"With the head and the feet knocked off," Mother Andrew Loretta said. "Mr. Yakimoto—oh, good, here comes Mr. Yakimoto now."

Mr. Yakimoto was a small Oriental man with wild eyes. He had been angry on Sunday and he seemed to be angry still. He took up a position near Mother Andrew Loretta that suggested that he'd just as soon take off for Borneo, or go into a fit that would leave more than a statue in pieces on the ground. The door to the corridor opened behind him. Gregor and Reverend Mother General looked up at the same time, just catching Mother Mary Bellarmine as she slipped in behind Mr. Yakimoto. Reverend Mother General started to say something sharp, but Gregor stopped her.

"It's just as well Mother Mary Bellarmine is here," he said. "We can get to phase two without having to wait for her to come. Now. For phase one. Let me go over this carefully. Sister Agnes Bernadette, you came down here to work on the chicken liver pâté when?"

"About an hour before the reception," Sister Agnes Bernadette said. "I went to a late Mass, you see, and then I had other things to do, and really, this thing with the chicken liver pâté isn't supposed to be very complicated. And then I came down here and opened the freezer and there it was. There they were. Mr. Yakimoto and the statue. Broken."

"Mr. Yakimoto didn't mean to break the statue," Mother Andrew Loretta said. "It was an accident."

Mr. Yakimoto began to speak very rapidly in Japanese. Mother Andrew Loretta nodded at him vexedly. "I'm sorry, Mr. Demarkian, I know we talked about this yesterday and I didn't know anything, but we have all been asking around. We really are trying. According to Mr. Yakimoto, what happened was that he came downstairs yesterday afternoon to get the fugu out to prepare it for serving. It had to be defrosted. The first thing he noticed was that the top box in the stack had been cut into—slit open is the way he's been putting it—"

Mr. Yakimoto jumped in with another cascade of Japanese.

"Yes," Mother Andrew Loretta said. "One of the fish was gone, missing, and Mr. Yakimoto was rightly very concerned about it. He hoped that it might be still stored somewhere in the freezer, and so he began to look through everything there, and after a while he began to get a little excited—"

"I know exactly what happened," Sister Agnes Bernadette said. "I get that way all the time myself.

You try to fix things and you try to fix things and after
a while you just get crazy."

"One of the statues dropped when he was looking
behind it," Mother Andrew Loretta said, "and at just
that point Sister Agnes Bernadette came in, and he
tried to get across to her how serious a thing had happened, but of course she doesn't speak Japanese, so he
decided to go out and try to find one of the Sisters
here from Japan, but they were all in chapel—"

"And in the meantime, I was getting frantic," Sister
Agnes Bernadette said, "because it was getting late. So
I went rushing out into the corridor and there was
Joan Esther—"

"Did that make sense?" Gregor asked. "Was that
someplace Sister Joan Esther should have been?"

"It made sense for anybody to be anyplace yesterday," Sister Scholastica put in. "There was so much going on."

"I think Joanie was doing a little hiding out," Sister
Agnes Bernadette said. "I think it had all begun to get
to her, and I couldn't blame her for that because it had
all begun to get to me, too. Nuns, nuns, nuns. It's all
very strange."

"It used to be normal," Reverend Mother General
said.

Agnes Bernadette ignored her. "Joanie was there so
I got hold of her and dragged her in, and she was one
of those take-charge people so it was all right. She saw
what the problem was right away and started to help
me—to put the statue back together, I mean. And she
did, too. The statue did get put back together."

"What about after that?" Gregor asked. "What about
putting the balls of chicken liver pâté in the statues'
heads?"

"Joanie didn't do that," Sister Agnes Bernadette
said. "I did that myself. Joanie got the trays set up for
me instead."

"All right," Gregor said, "what about those trays?
Who decided who was going to carry which one
where?"

Sister Agnes Bernadette looked confused. "Nobody

decided anything. We got the trays all set up, but there weren't any differences in the sculptures. Then we needed people to carry them, so Joanie went up to the stairs and opened the door and called up, and eventually somebody answered and she got some Sisters to come down and help. Then we each of us took a tray and went trooping upstairs."

"In no particular order," Gregor said.

"That's right," Sister Agnes Bernadette said.

"So it was just coincidence that Sister Joan Esther ended up carrying the ice sculpture that was destined to be placed on the table assigned to the one woman she disliked most in this Order."

Sister Agnes Bernadette looked confused. "Mother Mary Deborah? Joanie didn't dislike Mother Mary Deborah. Nobody dislikes Mother Mary Deborah."

"It was Sister Mary Sebastian who brought the ice sculpture to Mother Mary Deborah," Reverend Mother General said.

"But that can't be right," Sister Agnes Bernadette said. "I know I'm not a very organized person, Reverend Mother, but I can count."

"She got called out of the line," Sister Scholastica said suddenly. "I'd forgotten all about it. It was only for a second—"

"*I* called her out of the line," Mother Mary Bellarmine said. "Her veil was unfastened. It looked like a handkerchief stuck to her head."

"What was she supposed to do about it with a tray in her hands?" Scholastica demanded.

"Oh, dear," Sister Agnes Bernadette said. "I see what happened. I see where Joanie ended up."

"Where Sister Joan Esther ended up was the grave," Mother Mary Bellarmine said crisply. "She ended up there early and badly, as might have been expected. I came down to watch you, Mr. Demarkian. I came down to see how a great detective works."

At the moment, Gregor didn't feel much like a great detective. He felt like a small boy being scolded by an adult he has no respect for. He looked Mother Mary

Bellarmine up and down and considered his possible moves.

"It occurs to me," he said, "that you might have been in a position to see something nobody else did. You did come down here in the middle of the reception, didn't you?"

"Well, yes," Mother Mary Bellarmine said. "I did. How did you know that?"

Gregor hadn't known it. He'd known Mother Mary Bellarmine had had to go somewhere to change after her run-in with Nancy Hare, and he'd hoped it was down here, and God had smiled.

He said only, "I saw what happened, in the reception line, with Mrs. Hare. Do you know *why* she threw a vase of roses on you?"

"I haven't the least idea," Mother Mary Bellarmine said.

"Neither does anybody else," Gregor told her. "Well, we've got Mrs. Hare coming in to talk, maybe she'll tell us. Let's get back to you. It was a pretty violent attack."

"Was it? I've known Nancy Hare for years. Since the days when she was Nancy Callahan and I was teaching at this college. She's always been violent—*emotionally.*"

"She was being more than emotionally violent, yesterday."

"I noticed."

"She tore your habit."

Mother Mary Bellarmine shrugged. "My habit got torn, yes. I don't remember Nancy tearing it deliberately. I suppose she must have."

"She had to have," Gregor said. "It couldn't have simply snagged on a stray nail. It was protected by your collar. Look."

Gregor turned to Sister Scholastica—for some reason, she seemed a more likely candidate for this demonstration than Mother Mary Bellarmine or Reverend Mother General, and Gregor was terrified that Sister Agnes Bernadette would blush—and lifted up the long capelike collar until it exposed the top of the scapular. The scapular fit closely around the front of the neck and was fastened at the back with a small button. Gregor let Scholastica's collar fall again.

"Your collar wasn't torn," he pointed out. "Only your scapular was."

"Yes," Mother Mary Bellarmine said. "But what I really remember is being so wet."

"So once you were wet, what did you do?"

"I went downstairs and changed. We store habits in a room in this basement, I don't remember why, it goes back to the days when St. Elizabeth's was still building buildings or something of the sort. At any rate, there are supplies down here and I came to get them."

"Did you go into the kitchen?" Gregor asked.

"I had no need to go into the kitchen."

"Did you see Sister Joan Esther? Or Sister Agnes Bernadette?"

"No."

"Did you see anybody else?"

Mother Mary Bellarmine considered this. "Sister Catherine Grace and that foul woman from the Registrar's Office were in the plant room. The woman whose name I can never remember who's still some kind of hippie—"

"Sarabess Coltrane," Sister Agnes Bernadette said. "She's really very nice, even if she is something of an anachronism."

"She's *totally* ridiculous," Mother Mary Bellarmine said. "They were doing something with flowers, Ms. Coltrane and Sister Catherine Grace. That was on my way down. On my way up I saw that man. The one who makes all the racial jokes on the radio."

"Norman Kevic?" Gregor was surprised.

"That's it," Mother Mary Bellarmine said. "I remember wondering what he thought he was doing, wandering around like that. Of course, he's got a tremendous financial interest in the field house—"

"I wouldn't call it a financial *interest*," Reverend Mother General said.

"Then let's just say he's got a lot of money invested," Mother Mary Bellarmine said, "and he's got

stock in Henry Hare's companies and I've been looking over those books and I don't like them. You know
I don't like them, Reverend Mother. I've been saying
so for a week."

"Yes," Reverend Mother General said. "You have
been saying so for a week."

"He was skulking around down there, looking into
cupboards, doing I don't know what. If I hadn't been in
a hurry, I would have demanded an explanation. As it
is, you're going to have to get an explanation directly
from him."

"I'll go tell His Eminence," Sister Scholastica said.

Gregor beat his finger against the scarred surface of
one of the wooden tables. "Go get His Eminence," he
agreed, "but while we're waiting for the delivery of
Nancy Hare and Norman Kevic, I'd like to talk to—
what are their names again? Sarah Elizabeth—"

"Sarabess Coltrane," Reverend Mother General corrected. "And Sister Catherine Grace."

"I'm on my way," Sister Scholastica said.

"I don't see that he's doing anything we couldn't
have done ourselves," Mother Mary Bellarmine said.

Gregor was glad to see that even Reverend Mother
General herself ignored that.

CHAPTER 6

1

When Norman Kevic got off the phone with Sarabess Coltrane, he spent a minute listening to Roger Miller singing "My Uncle Used to Love Me But She Died," another minute contemplating the buying of a pack of Benson & Hedges Menthols, and a third minute deciding there was nothing for it but to go out to St. Elizabeth's College. By then, Roger Miller had stopped singing and Steve was pacing back and forth outside the booth, absolutely furious, which was what Steve always was when Norm did the least little thing out of the ordinary. In this case, "out of the ordinary" meant playing music instead of talking for the last two and a half minutes of his show. Norm had done that because he'd wanted to talk to Sarabess and because, for God's sake, he'd been talking on the air now for over a decade and you'd think the great American public would be sick of it by now. Steve was not sick of it, but Steve was not one of his

most faithful listeners, either. Steve only turned on the
radio when somebody warned him that the worst was
about to happen. In Steve's mind, "the worst" was anything that caused an advertiser to pick up the phone
and call the station. In Norm's mind, "the worst" was
anything that might cause the *Philadelphia Inquirer* to
say he was losing his edge.

But he was losing his edge. That was why the night
with Sarabess had worked out the way it had, instead
of ending up in bed, which was where Norman
thought nights with women should always end up. He
hadn't stayed up talking until six o'clock in the morning since he was in college. He had never stayed up
talking until six o'clock in the morning with a girl. He
still wasn't sure what it meant. He was just glad that
Sarabess had felt perfectly comfortable calling him up
in the middle of the morning. He wasn't entirely sure
why.

"Listen," she had said, when he'd put Roger Miller
on and signed himself off and guaranteed Steve's bad
mood for the rest of the day. Or maybe the rest of the
week. "He's here, that Demarkian man, and he's asking the oddest questions. It's like he's psychic."

"Psychic how?" Norm had asked her. "Did you tell
him anything?"

"I didn't tell him anything," Sarabess said, "but
Catherine Grace did. I'd forgotten all about Catherine
Grace. She's such an innocent."

"She's a child."

"Well, maybe. But here he is, and he's odd. Do you
know what he did just a minute ago?"

"No."

"He went down to the potting room and asked me to
show him how we put the flowers in the vases before
we put the vases on the table—isn't that odd? I mean,
how many ways can you put flowers on the table?"

"I don't know."

"Then he put a little bunch of daisies in a vase just
the way you're supposed to, with a little water at the
bottom and then he held the vase in the air, and then
do you know what he did?"

"No."

"He turned the vase over on the one tablecloth we have down there. I mean, it's an awful tablecloth and really old and stained and everything, but of course now it's completely ruined."

"Why?"

"Because of the plant food they put in the water for it, or whatever it is. Don't you know about that? At St. Elizabeth's you never fill vases just with water. The flowers die too soon. You mix in a little plant food and put that in, and the only problem with that is that the plant food turns everything it touches green—"

"What?"

"Green," Sarabess said impatiently. "Norm, are you all right? I heard Mr. Demarkian talking to the Archbishop—the Archbishop is here, as if things weren't bad enough—and they were saying they were going to call you up and ask you to come here. To talk, you know. For questioning."

"I was questioned by the police," Norm said quickly.

"Well, now you're going to be questioned by the Catholic Church. Norm, I'm beginning to get very, very—I don't know. But I am. Are you going to go into hiding?"

"Of course I'm not going to go into hiding," Norm said. "I'll be there in less than half an hour."

"You will?"

"Of course I will. I just have a couple of things I have to do first."

"I'm glad you're coming," Sarabess said. "I want you to come. When he was asking questions like that, I didn't know what to do."

"Mmm," Norm said.

"He's a very strange man," Sarabess said. "He keeps walking around muttering to himself that he needs a knife. Sometimes I wonder if he isn't a little cracked. Crazy, I mean. Dangerous."

"Gregor Demarkian is always dangerous," Norm said.

"I'm glad you're coming," Sarabess said.

Norm was glad he was coming, too. He was also

glad he had an automatic lock button on his console that worked the door, because without it he would never have made it out of his chair in time to make sure Steve couldn't get into the booth. His phone had three separate lines, too, which meant that he didn't have to answer the one Steve was going to call him on any minute now just to get a line free to call out. He picked up his phone and called his car, from which his driver answered in a sleepy voice that indicated he'd been camped out in the driver's seat waiting to go home. Norm considered the fact that staying up all night on no cocaine at all was practically as tiring as staying up with all you could snort, and what that fact meant for his future. It might mean nothing. Sarabess was organic, but Norm thought he could talk her out of that. He thought he could talk her into a haircut, too.

He told his driver to be at the south elevator door to the garage in fifteen minutes. Then he hung up, waited for a dial tone, and punched in the number for the local police. He had that number—along with the fire department, the FBI, the state capitol, the Roman Catholic Chancery, and the offices of the Philadelphia branch of White People's Liberation—on an automatic dial pad. He kept them on an automatic dial pad because he sometimes used them on his show. He could still remember the day he had called the Chancery pretending to be the Pope and caused a scandal so bad, the Papal Legate had come to visit him at the studio.

The phone was picked up on the police end by a young woman with a voice like strawberry syrup. Norman Kevic contemplated the ceiling of his booth and thought of green stains on white tablecloths and flowers wrapped in tissue paper and tied up with bright blue bows. The young woman went through her patented spiel about which branch of which government service he might actually be looking for, and then Norm told her.

"I'm looking for Jack Androcetti? I have some information for him about a homicide he's working on?"

That, of course, was not entirely accurate, but it would get him put through to Androcetti, and that was really all Norm cared about.

After he'd had his little talk, he could go out to the car and get driven over to St. Elizabeth's, where he would do his best to protect Sarabess and be on hand for any breaking developments at the same time.

Jack Androcetti, he thought, and made a face.

At least Jack Androcetti was better than Gregor Demarkian.

2

Father Stephen Monaghan had seen many odd things in his day, but he thought the oddest was certainly this gathering of the tribes that had begun taking place on the sidewalk outside of St. Teresa's House and was now spilling into the foyer and out the back of the reception room door. It wasn't a gathering of the Order. The Order was still as large as it had ever been, and still as ubiquitous on this campus. Coming over to St. Teresa's House from the little landscaping shed where he had finally found Frank Moretti, Father Stephen had seen dozens of them, in pairs and triples, walking on every available walkable surface. Their black veils flapped in the wind and their rosaries made an odd clacking noise whenever they were brushed by the wind. Father Stephen was reminded of the days before Vatican II, when he had said Mass every other Sunday at the chapel of the Motherhouse of a large Order of religious women based in Bethlehem, Pennsylvania. The Sisters had come to and from chapel, to and from meals, to and from sleep, in perfect ordered rows, clacking all the way.

Frank Moretti didn't remember the Church before Vatican II. Frank was only twenty-three, and he thought of all nuns as sort of odd. There was no religious awe in all of this. The young gardener thought of all virgins as odd as a matter of course.

They found Gregor Demarkian in the foyer, lying flat on the floor with his ear to the tiles, squinting into the dust in that place where the wall and floor joined. Since Reverend Mother General was also squinting into that same joint—although she was still standing; Father Stephen didn't think Reverend Mother would ever go crawling around on the floor—Father Stephen didn't think the dust would be there very long. Father Stephen waited while Demarkian sighed, stood up, and brushed off his suit. Father Stephen got the distinct impression that Gregor Demarkian was the kind of man who put on a suit as soon as he got up in the morning, no matter what he expected to do with his day. Demarkian looked around, looked at Father Stephen and Frank, and sighed.

"I don't suppose you two have come to tell me about how you lost a knife," he said.

"A knife?" Father Stephen said.

"I don't deal in knives," Frank Moretti said. "I don't deal in guns, either, and I'm not exactly fond of blunt instruments. People can get hurt."

"I suppose they can," Father Stephen said. Then he did his best to put this conversation back on track. "We heard you were here," he said, "and you were asking about anything that might have gone on that day—it was yesterday, I can't believe it was only yesterday—that was odd. And there was something odd. Frank can tell you."

"It was odd but it wasn't important," Frank said.

"What was it?" Gregor Demarkian looked interested.

Father Stephen nudged Frank in the elbow. Somehow, this wasn't working out the way he'd expected it to. He'd been all excited when he'd heard Demarkian was here, and the Archbishop, too. It had felt as if they were all finally beginning to get their own back, after the way that dreadful young man had behaved to everyone and then gone off and told the newspapers about it. Now they were standing in the middle of the foyer with nuns all around them and other people, too, and it was—well, disorganized.

Gregor Demarkian had gone to the doors that separated the foyer from the reception room and was muttering under his breath. Father Stephen marched up to him and touched him on the shoulder.

"It was only the theft of some plant food," he said bravely, "but that's very strange, isn't it? Who would want to steal plant food?"

"Plant food," Gregor Demarkian said. He looked straight at Frank Moretti. "Where was this plant food stolen from?"

"Right across the way there," Frank said. "There's a shed, a landscaping shed, out behind St. Patrick's Hall. It's not far."

"What goes on in St. Patrick's Hall?" Demarkian asked.

"Classes, mostly," Father Stephen said. "But this was Sunday, Mr. Demarkian. No one was there."

"Was the plant food stolen on Sunday?" Demarkian asked. "Could you be sure of that?"

"It could have been Saturday afternoon or Saturday night," Frank Moretti said. "I saw the thing just after lunch Saturday and it was all right. But it's like I told the Father, Mr. Demarkian. It was probably one of them nuns. I mean, they're everywhere, aren't they? And one of them probably has a plant that's not doing too well because she overfeeds and overwaters it and overeverything elses it, too, if you see what I mean, and—"

"Does either one of you know anything at all about the new field house?"

Father Stephen looked at Frank Moretti. Frank Moretti looked at Father Stephen. It was one of those questions and neither of them knew what to do with it. Father Stephen looked helplessly around the foyer and his eyes came to rest on Reverend Mother General and Sister Scholastica and Mother Mary Bellarmine.

"Oh," he said. "If you want to know about the field house, you should talk to Mother Mary Bellarmine. She's some kind of expert."

"All I know about the field house is that they're digging a hole for it out on Sunset Hill, and it's playing Hell with my grass," Frank Moretti said.

"I don't want an expert," Gregor said. "I want your

impressions. Has either of you ever heard of a man named Henry Hare?"

"Oh, dear, yes," Father Stephen said.

"He's a jerk," Frank Moretti said.

"Frank," Father Stephen said.

"He *is* a jerk," Frank Moretti insisted. "I don't think it matters so much if he cuts a few corners, if you know what I mean, everybody does these days or nothing would ever get built, but he kids himself about it. It's like he's got to con himself worse than he's got to con everybody else."

"I thought that was the point of Mother Mary Bellarmine," Gregor said. "I thought she was supposed to be impossible to con."

"That's certainly what I've heard," Father Stephen said. "Oh, yes. She is supposed to know everything there is to know about building campus buildings. There is that."

Gregor Demarkian folded his arms across his chest and seemed to go off into his own little world. This was not criminal detection the way Father Stephen wanted criminal detection. This was not Nero Wolfe in his chair or Sherlock Holmes with his magnifying glass. It was Sister Joan Esther who was dead and it was Sister Joan Esther that Father Stephen thought they should be concentrating on. He watched as Demarkian started pacing, stopped, and started again. By the time Demarkian stopped the second time, Father Stephen was so tense, he jumped.

"Let me ask you two something," Demarkian said. "There's been a suggestion made, in more than one quarter, that the wrong woman was murdered here yesterday afternoon. Does either of you think that's possible?"

"Anything's possible," Father Stephen said, "with God."

"Fine. The projected victim—in case Sister Joan Esther was not meant to be the victim—would be a nun named Mother Mary Bellarmine—"

Frank Moretti started to choke.

"—and the reason for her choice as a victim would

be what she knows or may know about the financing of the new field house and Henry Hare's possible involvement with unjustifiable aspects of that financing. Does that scenario sound plausible to you?"

Father Stephen thought immediately of the confessions he had heard, the stream of frustration and hate that flowed in Mother Mary Bellarmine's direction the way the needle of a compass flowed north, and blushed.

"Well," he said. "If it had been Mother Mary Bellarmine who had died, I do believe I would have found it less—less outrageous."

"I don't know Mother Mary Bellarmine," Frank Moretti said.

"But there hasn't been any suggestion that there is anything wrong with the financing of the field house," Father Stephen pointed out. "Really, Mr. Demarkian, I've only heard good things about that project."

"Mmm," Gregor Demarkian said.

"And Henry Hare isn't a crook," Frank Moretti pointed out. "I didn't say he was. I just said he cut the usual corners and lied to himself about it."

"Mmm," Gregor Demarkian said again.

Father Stephen looked at Frank Moretti and found Frank looking back. This was really too much. It really was. Sister Agnes Bernadette was distraught, and that awful young policeman was likely to come back at any moment. Father Stephen had heard wonderful things about Gregor Demarkian, but now he wasn't sure he believed any of them.

"I don't understand what you're doing," he said querulously. "You can't believe Sister Agnes Bernadette committed a murder. You can't believe— well, I don't know how to go into what you can't believe."

"I don't believe Sister Agnes Bernadette committed a murder," Gregor said pleasantly.

"Well, then," Father Stephen said. "Why don't you find out who did?"

"But I already know who did."

"What?" Father Stephen said.

"I already know who did," Gregor repeated patiently. "I knew who did yesterday. There was only one possible explanation. But that doesn't get us anywhere, does it?"

"Why not?"

"Well," Gregor said, "I have a knife to find, for one thing. And then I've got to talk to Nancy Hare. And then I've got to find some way around Lieutenant Androcetti, and then—well, you see what I mean."

"No," Father Stephen said, and it was true. He didn't see anything. He didn't understand the first thing about what was going on. Had somebody really tried to kill Mother Mary Bellarmine and killed Sister Joan Esther by mistake? And what did it mean if somebody had?

Father Stephen could certainly see someone murdering Mother Mary Bellarmine more easily than he could see someone murdering Sister Joan Esther, but then he hadn't really known Joan Esther except to wave hello to and she might have been a harridan when she was out of public view. He did think that before Vatican II, she wouldn't have been murdered at all. It was all very confusing.

On the other side of the foyer, Mother Mary Bellarmine was standing alone, contemplating the proceedings with a malevolent eye, and Father Stephen shuddered.

3

". . . already knows who did it," Martha Mary was saying, looking out the window of St. Thomas's Hall to the front steps of St. Teresa's House. "I heard him say so myself. And he's looking for a knife. Oh, Domenica, really, we've got to tell him—"

"Tell him what?" Sister Domenica Anne demanded in annoyance. "That I lost a razor?"

"An X-Acto knife," Martha Mary said. "I bet it's just the kind of thing he's looking for. And you know what it's going to be about, don't you? It's going to be about the field house. I heard him. It wasn't Joan Esther who was supposed to be murdered at all. It was Mother Mary Bellarmine—"

"Well, there certainly would have been enough suspects if that had happened." Domenica Anne shook her head.

Martha Mary sparkled. "And guess what," she said. "Guess what it's all going to come down to. The field house!"

"What do you mean?"

"The field house," Martha Mary said. "I heard them, Dom, I really did. It's all going to come down to some kind of financial hanky-panky Henry Hare has been pulling with the field house and Mother Mary Bellarmine found out about it and now—"

"Bull*shit*," Sister Domenica Anne said.

Martha Mary was shocked. "Dom," she said, "you said, you said—"

"I said *shit*," Domenica Anne said, "and I meant *shit*. There isn't a single thing wrong with the financing for that field house except that we don't have enough of it and we never do so so what?"

"But Dom—"

"But Dom nothing," Domenica Anne said. She looked at her regulation habit shawl thrown over the back of the director's chair she used for drafting and decided the day was too hot for it. Heaven only knew why she had brought it over here to begin with. She grabbed her keys and hooked them onto her belt instead.

"I have," she told Martha Mary, in as calm a tone as she wanted to manage, which was not calm at all, "put up with the intolerable, the impossible and the outrageous for over a week now in order to let that woman go over the plans for my field house project. *My* project, Martha, remember that, I've been working on it for two solid years. I know every dime we've spent or promised to spend. I know every foot of lumber we've bought or promised to buy. I think Henry Hare is a slug that belongs under a rock—and I dearly wish his own wife would put him there—but he hasn't been cheating us because I've made sure he hasn't been cheating us. I have taken all I am going to take. If that woman thinks she's going to use Joan Esther's dead body and my work as opportunities for self-aggrandizement, she's got another think coming."

"But Dom," Martha Mary wailed. "It isn't Mother Mary Bellarmine who was saying those things. It was Gregor Demarkian."

"And who do you think put those things in Gregor Demarkian's head?" Domenica Anne demanded. "Oh, I could just—well, I'm not going to tell you what I could just do. Let's go."

"Where?" Martha Mary looked frantically around the large attic room, panicked. "Where can we go?"

"To Gregor Demarkian, of course," Domenica Anne said. "To get all this straightened out."

"To get what straightened out? Are you going to tell him about the X-Acto knife?"

"Why not? Martha, in the name of our Lord Jesus Christ, will you please move it?"

"Dom." Martha Mary was even more shocked than she had been before.

Outside there was the sound of squealing tires and the heavy bump that meant a pair of cars in slow collision. Domenica Anne strode to her window and looked out on the road in front of the sidewalk in front of St. Teresa's House, where a pair of long black limousines had rammed into each other, front to front, just hard enough to cause broken headlights and minor crumples. Behind the white limousine a small Mercedes had pulled up and braked just in time not to be damaged. Nancy Hare was emerging from the undamaged car with a smile on her face that had a great deal in common with the smile on the Mona Lisa's.

"Wonderful," Domenica Anne said sourly. "Nancy Hare, Henry Hare, and Norman Kevic."

"What?"

Martha Mary rushed to the window and looked out.

The two men were standing face to face, raising their fists in the air. Nancy was standing off to one side, doubled up with laughter.

"Come on," Domenica Anne said. "Let's go join the war."

CHAPTER 7

1

There was an alcove that jutted out over the front door from the second floor of St. Teresa's House, and when Gregor Demarkian was finished looking through broom closets he stood in it. From the windows there he could see the cars pulling up to the curb outside and the people getting out. He noted the separate arrivals of Nancy and Henry Hare with some amusement. This whole situation made him feel a little uneasy, in spite of the fact that it was the way it was supposed to be. Maybe it was the fact that nothing before had ever been the way it was supposed to be that gave him pause. Reverend Mother General and the Archbishop had come out on the steps. Reverend Mother General paced back and forth the way school principals will when they have to think of something awful to do to someone and can't. Gregor couldn't remember how many lectures he had given about how murder cases had to be solved in the first forty-eight hours, about how physical evidence was much more important than the psychological kind, about how what must be true must be true no matter how strange it might seem. In his career, he could remember fewer than three men who had been convicted on physical evidence, and fewer than half a dozen whose guilt had been determined in the first forty-eight hours. As for the strangenesses, that was something else. Everything was strange. Just behind him, at the head of the narrow flight of steps leading down to the equally narrow corridor off the foyer, there was a gigantic poster, the one Gregor thought of as the granddaddy of all posters for Mother's Day as Mary's Day. Maybe he should have put that as the "grandmother" of all posters. It was at least as tall as he was, propped up against a wall with a rubber door stopper at its feet to keep it from falling over. It showed the Madonna standing on a cloud and holding the Child in the air. The Child had a crown and a scepter and a face that was at least fifty years old. Gregor wondered if women had once looked on their sons in this way, or if this was a male distortion of memory, what men thought their childhoods had been about. At the bottom of the poster were the words,

> ### ON MOTHER'S DAY REMEMBER THE MOTHER OF GOD,

which Gregor was getting sick of. Gregor was getting sick of mothers and nuns and everything else he could think of connected to this case that was not a case. What it really was was a mess he had stumbled into that he was going to have a very difficult time cleaning up. He would have felt better if it had been Cardinal O'Bannion he had to deal with, and not this genteel Archbishop. Gregor knew what to expect from Cardinal O'Bannion. He looked back down at the walk and saw Nancy and Henry fighting, standing only a foot or two apart and screaming at each other. Gregor was safely enclosed behind his window. He couldn't hear so much as an intonation from the people down below. He knew more or less what they were saying from the way they stood and the way they moved. Nancy was probably calling Henry a lot of very rude names. Henry was probably appealing to his honor. Gregor was sure Henry was the kind of man who appealed often to his honor. As for Reverend Mother General and the Archbishop ... Gregor gave them one more look and shook his head. They thought they were going to make things better, but they were wrong.

Gregor searched around in his pockets until he found a crumpled piece of paper and a small pencil. Donna Moradanyan put the pencils in his pockets—just in case—and he crammed himself full of paper, because he hated to throw the stuff out. He flattened out a wadded up American Express receipt on the window-sill and wrote

a small knife

in badly formed script. His handwriting was atrocious. Then he realized that the receipt was small and that if he wanted to get it all in, he'd have to cramp. He made his letters very much smaller and wrote

plant food

fugu

chicken liver pâté

flowers

thorns (too sharp)

timing

Then he rubbed his face. It was the timing that made him sure—given the timing what other solution could there be?—but that was neither here nor there. It wasn't as simple in this case as telling the police what he knew and sitting back to let them handle it. The mere thought of Jack Androcetti made him wince. Gregor looked back at the front walk, saw that Norman Kevic had joined the war and a half dozen nuns in habits had signed on as spectators, and decided his suspects could wait. There was one more thing he wanted to find out for sure. To do that he had to make a phone call.

The second floor of St. Teresa's House didn't consist of much. It certainly didn't contain a phone that he could see. The lobby downstairs did contain a phone, but he didn't want to use it. It was in a place anyone might walk in on him at any time. There was a public pay phone in the lobby of St. Cecilia's Hall, and he was going to have to use that. It was incredibly annoying. If there was one thing Gregor Demarkian had never been interested in doing, it was playing the kind of hide-and-seek, private-spy games so beloved of the fictional detectives Bennis Hannaford was so crazy about. Bennis was always giving him volumes in the adventures of Mike Hammer and the Continental Op. Gregor preferred Nero Wolfe, who sat in a chair and only got out of it to go to the dinner table.

Gregor went down the narrow flight of steps to the corridor off the foyer and stopped to listen. If anyone was in the foyer, they were keeping so still they weren't even breathing. He opened the door and looked out. The foyer was empty. He rushed across it to the door on the other side and slipped into the corridor beyond. Now it was just a question of making it across the two thin strips of lawn and through the hedge that divided the two buildings, and he would be safe. He paused at the side door of St. Teresa's House when he got to it and listened to the sounds out in the street. There was no mistaking what was going on now. Henry Hare was furious. Nancy Hare was furious. Norman Kevic was furious. The Archbishop seemed to be struck dumb. Gregor stopped at the hedge and peered around as best he could to see what he could

see. Mother Mary Bellarmine was standing off to one
side, watching Henry and Nancy with a tight, malicious look on her face. Norman Kevic had sidled up to
the grey-haired hippie Gregor remembered as Sarabess Coltrane and was holding her by the arm. Gregor
rushed the rest of the way to St. Cecilia's Hall, grasped
the knob of the side door and was relieved when it
opened without a hitch. All he would have needed was
to be locked out of his refuge.

Norman Kevic had put his arms around Sarabess
Coltrane's waist. Mother Mary Bellarmine had turned
her attention to them, and now *she* was furious. It had
to be something in the air. Gregor slipped through the
door into St. Cecilia's Hall and headed for the bank of
pay phones on the other side of the building. He hated
delaying action like this, but he didn't think there was
anything he could do. He didn't want to be like Jack
Androcetti, jumping to conclusions and ruining his
own case with haste and mindlessness. Assuming he
had a case. He stepped into the first of the phone
booths and felt around in his pockets for a quarter.

He especially didn't like delaying action to call Bennis Hannaford, but with Androcetti behaving the way
he was and Gregor's FBI contacts useless, he was
stuck.

2

Bennis Hannaford screened her phone calls, so instead
of a voice, Gregor got a tinny tinkling in his ear and
then an off-key rendition of "Mother," starting with the
M and moving on through the rest of the letters, but
with different lyrics than originally written. Bennis was
apparently in a mood. The lyrics were filthy, and she
almost never did that anymore now that she was living
on Cavanaugh Street. Gregor waited until the singing
stopped and then said, "Bennis? Bennis, pick up. This
is me. It's *important*."

There were a couple of clicks in his ear and then the
sound of Bennis's voice saying "Oh, damn." The next
thing he heard was a match being lighted, and that

was reassuring. Bennis was always ready to talk when she settled down with a cigarette. That was why she settled down with a cigarette. Gregor waited until he heard the frantic puffing that announced that Bennis had her cigarette actually lit. Then he said, "Are you ready to talk now? This really is important."

"I'm ready to talk," Bennis said. "Are you all right? There have been rumors about you up and down the street all morning. That some big black car came and took you away. That you've been kidnapped. That that fool police lieutenant arrested you—"

"Nobody has arrested me. A big black car came and took me away. It belonged to the Archdiocese of Philadelphia—"

"Uh, oh."

"—and if I've been kidnapped, it's because I want to be. I've returned to the scene of the crime. I'm at St. Elizabeth's."

"Are you."

"I need some information."

"What information could you possibly need? You're the one who told me you couldn't get involved in this case. Because of Jack Androcetti."

"Yes," Gregor said. "Well."

"Well, nothing," Bennis told him. "I never want to hear from you a little lecture about how I should mind my own business. Never again. Not when the police have specifically told you to stay out of it and you're still—"

"Bennis."

"God, I can't believe it. All the times you've told me what a nudge I am. All the times you've told me I can't mind my own business. All the times—"

"*Bennis.*"

"Right. I'll shut up. What do you need?"

What Gregor Demarkian needed was an aspirin, or maybe even two Excedrin, like in the television commercials. Why was it that Bennis Hannaford always ended up making him feel this way? The booth he was in had one of those half-size seats that would have been inadequate for an undersize dwarf. Gregor sat down on it the best he could.

"Do you remember the invitations we got to the reception yesterday?" he asked her. "They came in a big packet—"

"I remember. But those weren't the invitations. I mean, the invitations were in with all the rest of the stuff, but the rest of the stuff was about the Order—"

"Fine," Gregor said. He didn't need a description. "Do you still have that stuff?"

"Of course I still have that stuff. Somewhere. Lida's daughter's husband has been laid up. She hasn't had time to get in here and clean out my papers for at least two months."

"You could always clean out your own papers," Gregor said.

"I could, but that would only deprive Lida of an occupation. It would be like learning to cook. If I learned to cook, who would Hannah Krekorian bring casseroles to? Oh, speaking of Hannah Krekorian—"

"I know," Gregor said. "We're supposed to hold Mother's Day all over again next Sunday so she doesn't miss it. Go find that packet."

"I really think you ought to get into the spirit of this thing," Bennis said. "It's going to be good. Donna's going to make a cake for Hannah's granddaughter Lisette to jump out of—she's three—and then—"

"Bennis."

"I'm going. Honestly, Gregor, sometimes you're impossible. Donna was only trying to be—"

"*Bennis.*"

"You say my name a lot, Gregor, have you noticed that? You say my name a lot."

Gregor was about to recite the words of an ancient curse, but as it turned out he didn't have to. Having had her say, Bennis disappeared from the line and came back moments later, rustling.

"We got lucky," she said. "The whole thing was right where I thought it was in the refrigerator—"

"In the refrigerator?"

"In the crisper drawer, where I keep important papers. Even though you really couldn't call these important papers. What's usually in the crisper drawer is my current contract. Never mind. Here they are. What do you want to know?"

The crisper drawer, Gregor thought, feeling slightly dizzy. "What I want to know," he said, "is about that field house they're building. Wasn't there a brochure on the college or something—"

"Not a brochure on the college," Bennis told him, "a little pamphlet about buildings. All the buildings. Just a second. Here it is. It starts with the Motherhouse in Colchester. Building overseen by the Blessed Margaret Finney. Isn't that the woman who started the Order?"

"Yes. Go forward. Find the field house."

"I will." There was the sound of paper being paged through. Bennis started muttering. "Mother Mary Bellarmine, Mother Mary Bellarmine, Mother Mary Bellarmine. There are a lot of these projects built by Mother Mary Bellarmine. Isn't she the awful woman from the line yesterday?"

"She most certainly is."

"Well, she spends a lot of her time erecting architecture. Big projects, too. There's a picture of her here in front of a boarding school in 1965, five brand new buildings at a cost of over twelve million dollars. I wonder where the Order got the money."

"People gave it to them," Gregor said impatiently. "Get to the field house."

"I've gotten to the field house. What do you want to know?"

"Who's building it, for one thing. Who's in charge of the building."

There was more paper rustling. "It says here the project director is someone named Sister Domenica Anne. Is that someone you know?"

"No."

"I think I remember hearing yesterday that Mother Mary Bellarmine was consulting on the project or something. I'm trying to remember. Maybe Sister Anselm told me that. Didn't you hear that, too?"

"Yes, I did."

"Well?"

Gregor paused. "What about the pamphlet," he said again. "It doesn't mention Mother Mary Bellarmine?"

"Not in connection with the field house."

"What about Henry Hare?"

"Oh, it mentions Henry Hare a lot. Henry Hare has a big stake in this project. There's a picture of him here at the groundbreaking, shoveling dirt out of the ground, with the caption 'The field house project was made possible by the generosity of Henry Hare and the VTZ Corporation. Mr. Hare has been more than generous with both his time and his money, and VTZ is supplying the majority of the building materials and construction crews for this project.' That's a very iffy proposition, you know, Gregor. I mean, it looks like charity but it isn't, really. He's expecting to make money on it."

"Mr. Hare?"

"That's right. He'll sell the Order their lumber and their nails and their heating ducts and whatever and take a cut. It's not necessarily dishonest. Interior decorators work that way all the time. It's just not a way I'd want to do business."

"Mmm," Gregor said. "Is there anybody else you recognize in those pictures? Or anybody whose name we know in the copy?"

"There's Norman Kevic," Bennis said. "VTZ owns the station he's on, or a good part of it, anyway. I think I remember hearing that Norm owned part of it himself. Anyway, there's a picture of him here with Nancy Hare, of all people, and she looks positively calm. I suppose it's some kind of obligation. She has to play Lady Bountiful every once in a while to keep up the image of VTZ."

"She didn't seem to care much for the image of VTZ yesterday," Gregor said. "Are you sure that's it? There aren't any cameo appearances by somebody strange, like Sister Scholastica or Sister Agnes Bernadette?"

"Not a thing."

"How about any mention of a big donor, an anonymous source of significant cash?"

"Nope. Are you sure it would be here?"

"No, I'm not," Gregor said. "And the fact that it's not there doesn't mean it doesn't exist. There might be a very secret benefactor someplace who just doesn't want his benefaction called attention to. That's unusual, though. My feeling is that if there isn't any mention of such benefaction, there isn't any such benefaction."

"Is that bad?" Bennis asked. "Do you need something like that for your theory to be correct?"

"I don't deal in theories, I deal in facts. And no, I don't need a benefaction. If there was something like that, it would throw a monkey wrench into everything. I still wouldn't be wrong, mind you, but I'd have a lot harder time proving it."

"Marvelous," Bennis said. "Do you want to tell me what's going on? Would you like to clue me in to who and what and where and why and when? I mean, I'm only the person with the most interest in this sort of thing that you know."

"It's easy," Gregor said pleasantly. "All you have to know is not only who is dead but who was supposed to be dead."

"You mean you think it was supposed to be Mother Mary Bellarmine who was killed after all?"

"I mean I hear police sirens."

"What's that supposed to mean?"

"It's supposed to mean that one of my suspects seems to have called Lieutenant Androcetti. I'll talk to you later, Bennis."

"But—"

"I'll talk to you later."

"If I had a penny for every time you promised to tell me later and didn't, I'd be richer than my father was."

Bennis's father was dead. Gregor hung up the phone and walked out of the phone booth to the front door of St. Cecelia's Hall. From there the siren sounded too loud and too urgent, better suited for an air raid than a college campus. The nuns had heard it

just as surely as he had and had come out to look.
When he'd first come over, Gregor had imagined St.
Cecilia's Hall to be empty, but it most surely hadn't
been. Nuns were coming out of doors and out of corridors, down stairs and out of rooms. Their habits
were all virtually identical, mostly black, and disturb-
ingly mobile, so that each and every nun looked like a
flag blowing in an unseen breeze.

Gregor wormed his way past the nuns standing in
the doorway and onto the front steps. Now he could
see nuns coming at him from every side of campus,
moving across the lawns and sidewalks with eerie
grace, looking like nothing so much as the reconsti-
tuted pod people in the first version of *Invasion of the
Body Snatchers*. Since nuns were nothing like pod people, at least in Gregor's experience, he ignored the image and concentrated on the patrol car.

It was a patrol car, too, not an unmarked one, with
a flashing bubble light on its roof and a pair of uniforms in the front seat. It pulled to a stop in the midst
of the arguing Hares, practically knocking Nancy Hare
to the ground. She jumped back and bumped into
Mother Mary Bellarmine. Mother Mary Bellarmine
jumped back, too, then tottered forward and seemed to
grab Nancy Hare around the throat. A second later,
she had righted herself again and begun to brush off
her habit in a furious attempt to retrieve her dignity.
The patrol car's two front doors popped open and a
pair of glum looking uniforms got out. A second later,
one of the back doors opened and Jack Androcetti cat-
apulted himself onto the pavement. He was wearing a
lightweight wool summer suit with very tiny red lines
on a grey background. He reminded Gregor of the
kind of kidnapper who went into office-supply stores to
type his ransom notes on IBM Selectric demonstrator
models.

Androcetti shoved his hands in his pockets and began to bellow.

"Demarkian," he shouted. "Demarkian, where are
you?"

Gregor Demarkian sighed. Every nun in the area

knew where he was. They were looking straight at him. Jack Androcetti was staring up into the branches of the tree that spread out above his head. It could have been a metaphor for the man's entire career.

Gregor decided to give him a break of sorts.

"I'm right here," he said, as he walked down the front steps of St. Cecelia's Hall and started down the sidewalk to the patrol car. "I'm coming."

It was one of those mistakes you can make only once or twice in a lifetime. It was one of those mistakes that can kill you.

Jack Androcetti was not interested in conversation, or in solving the case, or in finding out what was really going on here. Jack Androcetti wasn't interested in anything but solving problems the way he'd always been able to solve them before.

As soon as Gregor Demarkian got into range, Jack Androcetti pulled back his fist and let loose with a right-upper cut.

3

One potato, two potato, three potato, four.

Gregor felt the impact on his jaw and that was what he thought.

One potato, two potato, three potato, four.

It was crazy.

Jack Androcetti had a big fist. His aim was terrible and his technique was nonexistent, but that didn't matter. He was huge and he was fierce and he connected. Gregor's ears rang and rang, like a car alarm going off in the night. On the other side of the little crowd of people now gathered around them, Gregor saw Norman Kevic begin to fade carefully out of the group, headed for safety, headed for open space.

"Wait," he said, through what seemed to be blood filling his mouth. What if he'd lost a tooth? "Wait," he said again. "Stop—"

"For Christ's sake," somebody said. Gregor took a minute to recognize the man as Rob Collins. "What are you doing? You've made him bleed."

"That son of a bitch has no business in this case," Jack Androcetti said.

"He's not in the case," Rob Collins said. "He's at the college. And he's got a perfect right to be here."

Norman Kevic was still sliding away, sliding away. It seemed to be taking place in slow motion.

"Wait," Gregor said again, this time wondering if he was making any sense at all. A Sister he didn't know planted herself in front of him and handed him a glass of ice water. He took it and rinsed out his mouth. "Wait," he said for the fourth time, when the blood was mostly gone. The problem was, the blood came back again. Gregor shook his head.

"That son of a bitch," Jack Androcetti said again. "I told him to stay out of it. I meant for him to stay out of it. He's going to stay out of it."

"Stay out of what?" Sister Scholastica demanded, barreling out of nowhere. Nowhere was really a gaggle of nuns. What did you call groups of nuns? Gaggles were for geese. Pods were for whales. Schools were for fish. It was maddening. "I think you're a jerk and a bully," Scholastica said, "and if I were you I'd get off this campus now, before you get thrown off. I don't care if you are the police. This is private property and Church property and all the rest of it. I have half a mind to kick you in the shin."

"Sister," the Archbishop said, sounding alarmed.

"Sister is exaggerating," Reverend Mother General said. "But I know how she feels."

"You can get suspended for hitting a civilian," Rob Collins said. "You can get canned."

The pain was so bad, Gregor couldn't stand up. He kept gulping down ice water, but it didn't seem to help. He got down on his haunches and put his head between his knees. He was down there with his eyes closed when whatever happened happened.

That's how he thought of it later. When whatever happened happened.

He caught only the result of it.

He felt some of his pain ebbing away.

He stood up.

He looked blindly through the crowd at nothing in particular and focused when he detected movement.

The movement was the collapse of Nancy Hare, falling forward onto Norman Kevic and grabbing his tie in the process, so that Norman looked choked.

Nancy had a shiny thin X-Acto knife sticking out of her side.

CHAPTER 8

1

Nancy Hare was not, of course, dead. Of course she wasn't dead. She'd keeled over from shock, that was all, and Gregor Demarkian knew it as soon as he saw the X-Acto knife sticking out of her side. X-Acto knives were what agents in the Bureau called "secondary weapons," meaning they could work, but only in aid of something else. The one case he knew of where an X-Acto knife had been the instrument, its blade had been smeared with cyanide. There would have been no chance to smear this blade with cyanide. This was a spur of the moment thing. This was an attempt to distract attention. Gregor didn't know if it would ever go further than that. Maybe, given enough time, their murderer would home in on Nancy Hare for real—find some more fugu and slip it in Nancy's breakfast eggs, find a real knife and stick it in Nancy's back. If Gregor had been this murderer, he would have found it necessary. What's the point of kill-

ing if you can't get away with it? How can you get away
with it if somebody knows what you did? He watched
Norman Kevic wriggling around on the floor, half
pinned under Nancy Hare's limp body and being
helped very little by the ministrations of Sister
Scholastica and Henry Hare. It was hard to tell what
Sister Scholastica and Henry Hare were actually trying
to do. Maybe they weren't trying to do the same
things. Gregor looked up and across the room and
found Sister Agnes Bernadette with her back pressed
to a far wall, looking terrified. Then he found Jack
Androcetti and smiled. Androcetti was looking from
Agnes Bernadette to Nancy Hare and back again, ap-
palled and furious. Even he could figure out what all
this meant.

"Wait a minute," he said. "Wait a minute now."

"I've taken the knife out," Sister Scholastica said. "Is
that what I should have done, Mr. Demarkian?"

"I don't want anyone asking questions of Gregor
Demarkian," Jack Androcetti said.

"Oh, for God's sake," Rob Collins said.

"Don't swear in a convent," the other uniformed officer said.

"This isn't a convent," Scholastica said automatically.

Gregor pushed himself through the crowd to Nancy
Hare's side and knelt down. He could smell liquor on
her breath, but it was faint. She'd probably had a cock-
tail to work up her courage to come down here, but
that was all. He moved her body gently and saw that
she was bleeding badly, but didn't seem to be having
any other trouble of any kind.

"Somebody ought to call a doctor, just in case," he
said. "There seems to be a little tear. She may need
stitches."

At the mention of a doctor, Archbishop Kenneally
seemed to come to life out of a long sleep. He snapped
to attention and looked fierce, fiercest of all in the direction of Jack Androcetti, whom he apparently didn't
like. That was no surprise, as far as Gregor was concerned. Nobody liked Jack Androcetti. He was too big
an idiot.

"Doctor," Archbishop Kenneally said. "We've got a Catholic hospital right here in Radnor—"

"We've got a Catholic doctor right across the lawn in St. Catherine of Siena Hall," Reverend Mother General said, stepping in. "Sister Mary Joseph took her medical degree at Yale and she practices in Harlem, so I'm sure she knows something about knife wounds."

"This is hardly a knife wound of that sort," Sister Scholastica said.

"Why doesn't she get up?" one of the other nuns asked. "If she's all right, why is she just lying there?"

"I'm not going to have any nun doctor in here looking at this victim," Jack Androcetti said. "It's a conflict of interest. She'll try to cover something up. Maybe she'll off the patient right when I'm looking—"

"Oh, Jesus H. *Christ*," Rob Collins said.

"Shh," the other uniformed man said. "Rob. You gotta stop that. These are nuns."

Gregor thought it was about time to put a stop to all this nonsense, but he never got a chance. Reverend Mother General had reached the end of her rope. He had seen it happen before. Once you caught that glint in the Reverend Mother's eye, you got out of the way, fast. She had been kneeling on the other side of Nancy Hare from Gregor. Now she stood up and advanced on Jack Androcetti. Androcetti was an Italian name. Most Italians are Catholic. Maybe there was something deep in the recesses of Jack's memory that told him he was about to be in a lot of trouble. He stepped back as Reverend Mother General marched in his direction, and stepped back again, and stepped back again. In the end, the lieutenant had his back to the foyer wall and a semicircle of very censorious nuns around him. That was when Reverend Mother General reached up and grabbed his lapel.

"Young man," she said, "I don't know what mental defective in the Radnor Police Department approved your promotion to detective, but that person ought to be taken out and shot. You are rude, overbearing, irresponsible, immature. But most of all, you are stupid. You haven't done a single bit of good for anybody since the moment you arrived at St. Elizabeth's and you have done a great deal to make matters worse. I no longer care whether you are supposed to be here in some official capacity. I no longer care about the laws of Radnor, Pennsylvania. If I have to, I will ask His Eminence the Cardinal Archbishop here to demand your reassignment. I want you out of my life."

"I'm the investigating officer in charge of this case!"

"Nobody calls me the Cardinal Archbishop," David Kenneally said into Gregor's ear. "Not even the Pope."

Gregor was willing to bet Jack Androcetti would never again call David Kenneally anything else. Androcetti was looking around the room wildly, from one implacable nun face to another. His eyes came to light on Sister Agnes Bernadette and he flushed. Agnes Bernadette hadn't moved from her place on the far wall.

"She's got an accomplice," Jack Androcetti said, sputtering a little. "She's got some other nun in this place helping her out."

"Why?" Sister Scholastica demanded.

"I thought your explanation for what had happened here was insanity," Reverend Mother General said coldly. "I thought your entire rationale was that Sister Agnes Bernadette went off her head and tried to poison everybody at the reception."

"And it isn't true," Sister Mary Alice said, "because there wasn't any poison in any of the food except the scraps they took from the statue that went on Mother Mary Bellarmine's table. I know because Sister Mary Sebastian has a cousin in the police lab and she called him up and asked."

"I'll get him fired," Androcetti said.

"You won't have a chance," Reverend Mother General said.

"She was over here when it happened," Jack Androcetti said. "I saw her. She was standing right next to this woman—"

"Nancy Hare," Henry Hare said sharply. "Mrs. Henry Hare."

"—and she moved back after she stuck the knife. I

saw her." Androcetti looked triumphant. "I *saw* her," he repeated.

Gregor Demarkian sighed. He had been kneeling down next to Nancy Hare—who seemed to be peacefully asleep, which wasn't necessarily such a good sign—and keeping an eye on Norman Kevic. He could have dispensed with keeping an eye on Norman Kevic because Norm no longer seemed interested in leaving. Norm had a curious, speculative look on his face, as if he'd seen something he should have been ready to tell the police, but wasn't. Gregor supposed he had. That was the way he read Norman Kevic. He wouldn't have put it past Norm to have seen the murderer put the fugu in the chicken liver pâté and just not reported it. God only knew what people like that did with that kind of information.

Gregor stood up and brushed off his pants. "You didn't see Sister Agnes Bernadette put a knife into Nancy Hare's side," he said, "because I saw her standing right there against that wall in the moment Nancy Hare fell. She wouldn't have had time to make the circuit."

"You're imagining things," Jack Androcetti said tightly. "Eyewitness testimony is notoriously unreliable."

"I am not your ordinary eyewitness," Gregor pointed out. "I spent twenty years in the Federal Bureau of Investigation."

"It doesn't matter if you did or not," a young nun piped up. They all turned to look at her and she blushed. "I was standing right next to Aggie the whole time. I really was."

"You were distracted," Jack Androcetti said.

On the floor at Gregor's feet, Nancy Hare stirred, and moaned, and fluttered open her eyes. It was something of a shock. They had been talking about her for so long as if she weren't there, it took an adjustment to understand that she was. Henry Hare had gotten to his feet to argue with Jack Androcetti. Now he dropped to his knees to look into his wife's eyes. Gregor couldn't decide if the expression in Henry

Hare's own eyes was concern or contempt. Maybe, for Henry Hare, the two emotions were one.

Nancy groaned again and tried to move. A spasm of pain crossed her face and Gregor heard a muttered "Oh, shit." The nuns must have heard it, too, but they gave no indication that they had. Maybe they felt about it the way Gregor did—that at this point Nancy had earned a little profanity. Nancy moved again, winced again, swore again. She looked at the faces staring down at her in astonishment.

"What the Hell is going on here?" she demanded.

Henry leaned closer to her. "Nancy," he said, "you've been badly hurt—"

"I can tell I've been badly hurt," Nancy pronounced with withering scorn. "Would you get out of my face?"

"You're not yourself," Henry said.

"Now that she's awake, we ought to do something about that wound," Mother Mary Bellarmine said. "I know Sister Mary Joseph is supposed to be on her way, but for simple hygienic purposes—"

At the sound of Mother Mary Bellarmine's voice, Nancy Hare's head had swiveled around. Her eyes grew wide. Her lips pressed down into a thin line. She tried to get up and couldn't. The wound in her side was small, but it was painful enough to make sitting up impossible. Nancy settled for lying back and turning her face in Mother Mary Bellarmine's direction.

"You," she said. "What's the matter with you? You were supposed to pretend to knock me out, not go ahead and stab me."

2

It was one of those moments Gregor always thought of as epiphanous. It wasn't a surprise—he had known who had killed Sister Joan Esther and caused all the rest of the trouble yesterday—but it made motives clear in a way he wouldn't have been able to do for himself. He didn't think he had ever seen a woman with less respect for her husband than Nancy had for Henry Hare. It went beyond disrespect to a kind of visceral hatred that had no starting point and no end. As for Mother Mary Bellarmine, she was what Gregor had always thought she was, one of those people it isn't good to cross, one of those people with no sense of proportion. She also had a great deal more to lose than Nancy Hare.

"I do not," she said carefully, drawing herself up to that height only nuns in habit can reach, "know what you're talking about. I most certainly did not stab you."

"You most certainly did," Nancy Hare said. Then she made a face. "Don't give me this shit. You know perfectly well—"

"I know you're a woman who wants to be rid of your husband," Mother Mary Bellarmine said sharply. "That's all I know."

"You could have had the knife," one of the nuns said suddenly. As always when a nun spoke unexpectedly, all the others turned in her direction. This nun was older and more sophisticated than the last one, though. She didn't blush. "Excuse me," she said. "I'm Sister Domenica Anne."

"And I'm Sister Martha Mary," a younger nun said.

"Are you the Sister Domenica Anne who's in charge of the field house project?" Gregor asked her.

Domenica Anne nodded. "Yes, I am. I came over—I came over because I heard you were working on an explanation that depended on—that you thought there was something wrong with the financing of my project—some fraud or something I hadn't caught but Mother Mary Bellarmine had—but it isn't true, it really isn't. There isn't anything like that at all."

"I know," Gregor said.

Sister Domenica Anne looked bewildered. "You know?"

"He can't know," Mother Mary Bellarmine said. "I know. I've been over and over those books. I've seen them. If he wasn't a damn fool like all the rest of them he'd be trying to find out who tried to murder me."

"Nobody tried to murder you," Gregor said patiently. "Nobody had the chance—or, at least, nobody with any known motive did. The only person who had an opportunity to put fugu in that pâté was you."

"Horse manure," Mother Mary Bellarmine said. "You don't even know if it was fugu in the chicken liver pâté. Just because Sister's cousin or whatever he was—"

"I don't have to worry about Sister's cousin or Lieutenant Androcetti's favorite lab technician," Gregor said. "I have the scapular. Your scapular. The one that was torn yesterday."

"It was torn," Mother Mary Bellarmine said, "because this woman tore it."

"She couldn't have." Gregor looked around. "Sister Scholastica? Could you come here for a moment?"

Sister Scholastica came forward. "Is this going to be an occasion of scandal?" she asked dubiously.

"Not if I'm right."

Scholastica looked as if she were none too certain she wanted to trust in Gregor's being right, but she stood still anyway. Gregor walked around her once or twice and stopped facing her.

"This habit," he said, "consists of a black dress topped by a black scapular topped by a black collar that's what I would call a cape. The collar comes about midway down the upper arms and flutters. All right so far?"

"We all know what our habits are like," Mother Mary Bellarmine said coldly. "We've been wearing them for years."

Gregor nodded. "Right. Now yesterday, I stood in this foyer and watched Nancy Hare walk up to Mother Mary Bellarmine with a vase of flowers in her hand, dump those flowers over Mother Mary Bellarmine's head, and generally cause a disturbance. Are we all agreed on that?"

"Of course we are," Reverend Mother General said. "I wish we weren't."

"I'm glad we are," Gregor said. "My point here is this. In order for Nancy Hare to have torn Mother Mary Bellarmine's scapular without also tearing the collar, she would have had to reach up under the collar to get at the scapular's neck hole. I didn't see her do anything remotely like that. Did any of you?"

"She didn't go near the collar," Sister Scholastica said suddenly. "She dumped the roses from up high—I saw her—and then she dropped the vase and stepped away."

"Why should I have gone near the collar?" Nancy Hare demanded. "I wanted to get her wet, not rip her up."

"I don't think it would have mattered if you had gone near the collar," Gregor said. "I don't think you could have torn the scapular. Sister?"

"I'm ready," Sister Scholastica said.

Gregor put his hand up under Sister Scholastica's collar and hooked his fingers over the tight neck of the scapular. Then he pulled as hard and as violently as he could. Nothing happened.

Gregor flipped the collar up and showed the assembled company the neck of the scapular.

"Not a rip or a tear," he said with satisfaction, "and I'm far stronger than Mrs. Hare. I'm far stronger than Mother Mary Bellarmine, too."

"I don't understand what all this is supposed to mean," Mother Mary Bellarmine said stiffly. "Obviously, my scapular was torn. Therefore, Mrs. Hare must have torn it. Unless you're trying to say I tore it before Mrs. Hare attacked me—"

"I didn't attack you," Nancy Hare said weakly.

"You couldn't have torn it before Mrs. Hare doused you with roses, because if you had I would have noticed and so would everyone else. That was a long, dramatic tear. It went right down your chest. What happened to the scapular after you changed out of it?"

"I threw it away," Mother Mary Bellarmine said. "It wasn't of any use to anybody anymore."

"We recycle cloth," one of the Sisters in the crowd said. "If one of the groundsmen found cloth in the trash he'd put it in one of the recycling bins."

"Maybe we should send somebody out to look for it," Gregor said. "We'd find two things, I think. One is that that tear was not a tear at all, but a cut—"

"With the X-Acto knife," Sister Domenica said suddenly.

"And the other is that there's a big green stain all across the front of the habit. I don't know how that would show up against black—"

"It did show up," Reverend Mother said. "I remember seeing it. I remember thinking that someone had put too much plant food in with the flowers."

"Someone had," Gregor said.

Mother Mary Bellarmine was still not having any. She was a proud woman, Gregor thought, proud and furious, like the ancient queens and duchesses who had once run their husbands' estates when their men had spent too much of their lives drinking. Catherine de Medici. Berenice. Medusa. Her spirit was too mean for the best of those, but she was crazy enough.

"Exactly what was it I was supposed to be after," she demanded, "in all this nonsense and subterfuge? Why would I want to tear my habit to shreds?"

"So that you could go change it."

"I did go change it," Mother Mary Bellarmine said.

"I know you did. You took a long time doing it, too. The little ceremony with the ice sculptures was held up for half an hour. Nobody thought it was particularly odd, however, because everybody knew you had to clean up after Nancy Hare's attack."

"And I did."

"I'm not denying that you did," Gregor said. "I'm saying you gave yourself time. To get hold of the fugu—"

"Are you trying to tell me I ground up a fugu fish right there on the very afternoon—"

"You did it the day before, I'd guess. You know, this isn't going to be that hard to put together. Once we know what we're looking for, we will be able to find people who saw you—near the kitchen downstairs, near the ice sculptures, handing a cracker with chicken liver pâté smeared all over it to Sister Joan Esther—"

The corners of Mother Mary Bellarmine's mouth twitched upward. "Try it," she said.

"I will," Gregor told her.

"Try it," she said again. "Try it all you like, Mr. Demarkian. You'll never find a single thing."

At that moment, the front door opened and a little phalanx of nuns came bustling in. One carried a doctor's big black bag. That one looked at Nancy Hare on the floor and sighed out loud.

"Nancy, Nancy," she said. "What kind of trouble have you gotten yourself into now?"

Nancy Hare had been fading all the while Gregor talked to Mother Mary Bellarmine. Already weak with shock, she was getting weaker with loss of blood. The nun with the black bag—whom Gregor assumed was Sister Mary Joseph—knelt down beside her and began to cut cloth away from her bloody side. Bloody but not bleeding. Sometime when Gregor wasn't looking, somebody had stanched the flow of blood.

"Nancy went to college here," a nun Gregor hadn't seen before told him. "A lot of the Sisters have known her forever."

Mother Mary Bellarmine had moved. Gregor picked her out of the crowd and saw that she was looking amused, grim and amused, as if she fully expected to lose every battle and still win the war. Gregor wondered if she was right.

She could be right.

It bothered him.

He was still enough of a policeman to hate the idea of guilty people who got away.

3

In the end, he sidled over to Reverend Mother General, tapped her on the shoulder, and whispered in her ear.

"I've got to talk to you," he said.

And she nodded.

EPILOGUE

1

Food poisoning," Bennis Hannaford was saying, waving the Sunday *Inquirer* in the air like a tattered flag. "*Food* poisoning? Gregor, for God's sake. What's going on here?"

It was now Sunday, the eighteenth of May, and from what Gregor could see, what was going on here was a surprise party that wouldn't be a surprise to anyone less physically challenged than a blind and deaf mole the way things were going. He was standing at the long windows that took up most of the Cavanaugh Street side of his living room. From there he could look across the street and down one flight into Lida Arkmanian's party room, and what did the woman think she was doing? Gregor and Lida had been in grammar school together. Lida had been a friend of Gregor's late wife. Gregor had been the first to warn Lida that Johnny Arkmanian was too much of a wild man to make a good husband. As it turned out, Lida

liked wild men and Johnny was very, very, very good
at business. Now that he was dead, Lida was bored
and had a huge town house and a lot of money to
make mischief with. What *seemed* to be going on down
in that party room was a Mexican hat dance per-
formed by four girls in Armenian peasant costumes,
but that couldn't be right.

The doorbell rang. Bennis dropped the paper, said
"Just a minute," and went to answer it. Gregor heard
Donna Moradanyan's voice in the hall saying, "Lida
said to stuff these in your refrigerator but you weren't
home so either you have to go downstairs with me or
we'll have to put them in Gregor's, but I put the honey
cakes in Gregor's for the Halloween party and he ate
them so maybe—"

"He won't eat them today," Bennis said. "He won't
have time. I have to get him into this bow tie."

Donna Moradanyan's son Tommy came scooting
into the living room and up to Gregor's side. He was
just a little over two years old and very serious in the
way two-year-olds are. "Strychnine," he said to Gregor,
as soon as he saw him.

"Absolutely," Gregor said. "Except in this case, it
was a fugu fish."

Tommy Moradanyan considered this and shook his
head. "Strychnine," he said again.

Gregor nodded. "I'm with you. It's a much better
word."

Donna stuck her head through the living room door.
"Tommy, honey, we've got to go. Auntie Lida has a big
red party hat for you to put on. Hello, Gregor. I read
all about you in the paper this morning. It's too bad it
didn't work out."

"Right," Gregor said, and let it go at that. For one
thing, he didn't want to get tangled in explanations
with Donna Moradanyan, which was a little like trying
to play cat's cradle with a string that had been dipped
in honey. For another, he didn't want to unravel the
sentiment. What was too bad? That bodies hadn't
dropped like flies from one end of Radnor to the other?
That the cause of death hadn't been blatant enough to

win him another cover story in *People* magazine? Gregor had been the cover story in *People* magazine three times now, and he had had enough. True crime was to *People* what the centerfold was to *Playboy*. Be the photographic subject of either one, and your life was ruined.

Tommy Moradanyan said "Strychnine!" one more time, nodded solemnly, and ran off to join his mother. Bennis started murmuring all the things she always murmured when she was showing people out, some of which seemed to have to do with apologizing for his "gruffness." It was at times like these that Gregor thought Tibor and Lida and old George Tekemanian were wrong. He didn't have to marry Bennis. On some astral plane, he had *already* married Bennis.

Bennis came back into the living room. "The front of the building still looks like a gift box," she said, "and so does the front of Hannah's, but we've just been saying Donna wants them that way, they took so much work she just wants to look at them a little longer. What do you think?"

"I think Hannah is over in her kitchen right this minute humming 'I'm Going to a Surprise Party' under her breath."

"You're such an optimist."

"I'm such a realist. Not more than ten minutes ago, Mary Ohanian went marching down the middle of Cavanaugh Street carrying a pile of wrapped packages the size of the Christmas window display in Saks and holding four ribbon bows in her teeth. What do *you* think Hannah thinks is going on?"

"Well, Gregor, she might think there's a party, but that's no reason she'd think it was for her."

"No? There's a huge party she hasn't been invited to but everybody else has—"

"Maybe we hurt her feelings," Bennis said.

"Maybe you tipped your hand. What bow tie? I don't wear bow ties."

"Well, you have to wear some kind of tie, Gregor. Old George Tekemanian is coming in his tuxedo. It's that kind of party."

In the first place, Old George Tekemanian's tuxedo had been bought to celebrate the end of the Ottoman Empire in World War I. In the second place, the way Lida threw a party, it was impossible to tell what kind of party it was without directly asking somebody, and these days she couldn't possibly throw one on Cavanaugh Street without inviting the refugees, and the refugees didn't have a lot of clothes. In the third place, the bow tie Bennis was holding out to him had bright red polka dots on a black background. Gregor Demarkian had never worn polka dots on anything.

"Bennis," he said warningly.

But Bennis's mind was on something else. She had abandoned the bow tie to the coffee table. She had picked up the paper again and was frowning at it.

"Food poisoning," she said under her breath. "It's impossible. *Food* poisoning."

"Bennis—"

"Oh, don't *Bennis* me," she said. "Just talk."

2

Gregor Demarkian sometimes thought that doing business with the Catholic hierarchy was a little like doing business with God Himself. You were always being very careful not to say the wrong thing or do the wrong thing or even think the wrong thing. Of course, in other ways it wasn't like doing business with God at all, and might be like doing business with the other side. They had a lot more experience than he did in the way the world operated. In this case, there were three considerations: the death of Sister Joan Esther, the guilt of Mother Mary Bellarmine, and the functional impossibility of Jack Androcetti. All three had to be cleared up for the case to be resolved in a way that would allow any of them to call it successful. Gregor allowed Bennis to get him a cup of coffee—she made better coffee than he did, and it postponed the bow tie—and tried to explain.

"In some ways," he said, "it was the simplest and most straightforward case I've been on since I left the

Bureau. It went by the book, really. Cleared up in less than twenty-four hours. Solved on physical evidence—"

"Physical evidence?"

"That's what I said. And the motive. Ah, the motive. You don't know, after all the financial chicanery and convoluted political and religious nonsense I've been put through over the last few years, you have no idea how pleasant it was to find a good old station-house motive for a murder."

"Which was what?"

"Fear, loathing, and revenge," Gregor said promptly. "The woman was a murderer in the tradition of every street assassin in every midsize town in the country. The neighbor's daughter makes the cheerleading squad and your daughter doesn't. You take a thirty-eight and blast your neighbor right out of her living room. The guy at the station next to yours at work reports you for smoking marijuana on the job. You wait around one night when he's working late and when he goes out to his car you blow him away—"

"Gregor, be serious. People don't do things like that."

"Of course people do things like that," Gregor said. "They do them all the time. Most murder cases are either that sort of thing or drug war fatalities. The sort of murderer you and I have had to do with is actually very unusual. Of course, Mother Mary Bellarmine is also very unusual in her way—"

"I noticed," Bennis said drily.

"I meant that she was a good planner," Gregor said, "and that she held her emotions with a certain amount of stubbornness. Most of these people are not very well integrated, as the psychologists say. They get all worked up for a couple of hours, but then they calm down and they can't remember what they were worked up about. Mother Mary Bellarmine was definitely not like that. Sister Joan Esther had done her what she considered—what Mother Mary Bellarmine considered—a grave injustice, by requesting a transfer out of Mother Mary Bellarmine's house and by making it perfectly clear to Reverend Mother General and anyone else who would listen that she was requesting this transfer because Mother Mary Bellarmine was a grade-A, number one bitch—"

"I doubt if that was the word she used," Bennis objected.

"I'm sure it wasn't," Gregor agreed. "The point is that Sister Joan Esther said what she said and did what she did quite publicly, and that it was, as far as I was able to determine, the only time any such thing had ever been said publicly about Mother Mary Bellarmine. Not that it hadn't been said, mind you. It had been said over and over again. Sisters talking among themselves. Even Sisters talking to seculars, which is unusual in a matter of criticism. But all those things were said privately."

Bennis looked thoughtful. "You know, you're right. I was talking to Scholastica at the reception that day and she made a couple of very pointed comments about Mother Mary Bellarmine and then we got into the background, why a woman like that would be a nun, why the Order would have kept her—honestly Gregor, you wouldn't believe it, but once a nun gets past formation it's practically impossible to get her out, or it used to be—anyway, we went on and on, but she never said anything about actual complaints to Reverend Mother General except for Sister Joan Esther's."

"There were complaints to Reverend Mother General," Gregor said, "but they weren't formal ones, and because they weren't formal ones, they didn't result in what Sister Joan Esther's complaint did. Meaning that after Sister Joan Esther left for Alaska, Reverend Mother General told Mother Mary Bellarmine in no uncertain terms that if she didn't get her act together, she was going to lose her position as Mother Provincial of the Southwestern House. And that got around, too, of course. In convents, everything seems to get around."

Bennis had finished her cup of coffee. She got up and got some more, pouring out from Gregor's Revereware coffeepot as elegantly as if she'd been using her mother's Georgian silver service. "Was she planning it all along?" she asked. "Before she got to St. Elizabeth's for the convention, I mean. Did she come East knowing she was going to kill somebody?"

"I don't think so," Gregor said slowly. "I'm sure she didn't come East thinking she was going to kill somebody with fugu. I know how she got that idea. You told me."

"I did?"

"It was Cultural Norm," Gregor said. "The Japanese jokes. One of the ones he told over and over again went 'Do you know how to save a Japanese from fugu poisoning? No? Good!' "

Bennis winced. "Well, that's awful enough."

"It's awful enough, but it was an idea that couldn't miss. All those fugu fish in the boxes in the basement of St. Teresa's House. It was fairly easy to get one and grind it up."

"In advance?"

"Well in advance, I'd say. On the day of the reception, the kitchen would be occupied. Sister Agnes Bernadette would be there, and she'd probably have a helper. As it turned out, the helper was Sister Joan Esther, but it didn't have to be."

"That's something I don't understand." Bennis stopped to sip her coffee. "So much of this seems to depend on it being Joan Esther who carried Mother Mary Bellarmine's statue into the reception room, but Mother Mary Bellarmine couldn't know she would, could she? How did she arrange for it?"

"She didn't."

"She didn't?"

"Of course she didn't," Gregor said. "You're going on the assumption that there was fugu in the ball of chicken liver pâté in the statue on Mother Mary Bellarmine's table. But there wasn't. There couldn't have been. Sister Agnes Bernadette made the pâté just that morning in a big bowl—and it stayed in a big bowl, to be doled out with an ice cream scoop at the very last minute. Didn't it bother you that the scoop of chicken liver pâté from Mother Mary Bellarmine's statue disappeared after Sister Joan Esther died?"

"I thought it disappeared because it was full of fugu," Bennis said.

"Why would anyone bother?" Gregor asked. "We all assumed there was fugu, or some other poison, in the pâté. Why get rid of it? Unless there *wasn't* any, of course."

"There were traces of fugu in the statue's head," Bennis pointed out. "It was in one of those lab reports Sister what's-her-name got from her cousin."

"Rub a little fugu on the inside of the statue's head when nobody's looking, which shouldn't be hard because Sister Joan Esther is dying and half an international Order of nuns are being shocked out of their minds. Mother Mary Bellarmine simply picked up the ball of chicken liver pâté and chucked it someplace, outside probably, in that little brook or under some shrubbery where she could grind it into the dirt. And she was the only one who could have done that, by the way. She was the only one close enough to the table."

"But where was the fugu?" Bennis asked. "What did Sister Joan Esther eat?"

"A cracker she thought had chicken liver pâté on it," Gregor said. "A cracker Mother Mary Bellarmine had made up and stashed in the basement before the reception started. Because of the smell."

"Smell?"

"It's May," Gregor pointed out. "It's hot. While I was discussing all this with the Archbishop, I kept thinking that we might never have been able to pin it on her at all if the weather had been colder, because if it had she could have made up the fugu on the cracker and either kept it on her or kept it somewhere convenient, like hidden on a windowsill off one of the reception room windows. But she couldn't, you see, because the fugu would go bad in the heat and go bad very quickly. She had to keep it someplace cool. And the most obvious place to keep something cool is—"

"In a refrigerator, and there was a refrigerator in the basement. But Gregor," Bennis said, "you just told me how the fugu couldn't have been in the chicken liver pâté because Mother Mary Bellarmine wouldn't have had time with Sister Agnes Bernadette and whoever else running around the kitchen—"

"Yes, I know, it would have taken too much time. But think what actually did happen. First, Nancy Hare came storming into the foyer with a vase of roses and poured the contents all over Mother Mary Bellarmine's head. Then Mother Mary Bellarmine went downstairs to change and—"

Bennis sat up straight. "Took forever. That's it. She took *forever.* She *waited.*"

"Exactly," Gregor said. "By the time she came back up again, all dressed and ready to go, everyone was chomping at the bit. The Sisters who were supposed to carry the statues in were all lined up and waiting at the door—"

"And that's another reason she couldn't have put the fugu in the pâté," Bennis said. "It was too late. She did take an awfully long time getting dressed."

"She had to wait for the kitchen to be mostly clear. And she gave herself an out, after all. Her habit was torn, stained, a mess."

"About her habit . . ." Bennis said.

Gregor held up his empty coffee cup. Bennis refilled it. "She stole a little extra plant food from one of the landscaping sheds and put it in the bottom of each of the vases. When the police began looking through all of them they found plant food on the bottoms, thick as grit. That ensured stains. She stole an X-Acto knife from Sister Domenica Anne, to make sure her habit got ripped enough to cause a major disaster. She didn't want Reverend Mother General to deliver one of her patented pronouncements on 'you look all right for the moment, let's get on with it.' She did all of this on Saturday, the day before, so she didn't have to be running around— What's the matter?"

Bennis shivered. "She's a cold woman," she said. "Doesn't she make your skin crawl?"

"People who kill people always make my skin crawl. And don't start singing. My point here is that practically everything that seemed like a carefully crafted plot was nothing of the sort. The woman didn't use a rapier. She used a bludgeon. She just made it *look* like she was using a rapier."

"But what about Nancy Hare? How could she know Nancy Hare would dump that vase of roses on her?"

"She knew because she asked Nancy Hare to do it."

"What?"

Gregor shook his head. "Nancy Hare is the kind of person Lida is always saying 'needs professional help.' I'm just not too sure what kind of professional. Nancy Hare's entire life is driving Henry Hare crazy, and especially driving him crazy in ways that interfere with his work because she hates his work. Mother Mary Bellarmine told Nancy Hare—this is according to Nancy Hare—that she was on the trail of someone who was making financial graft out of the field house project, and she needed a diversion created to allow her to search this man's car—"

"Norman Kevic," Bennis said automatically.

"Exactly. Norman Kevic. Nancy saw a way to get at Henry in the process and agreed. That was Saturday. She'd worked herself into a proper frenzy by the time we saw her Sunday. Then, when Sister Joan Esther died, Mother Mary Bellarmine pointed out the obvious—which is that Nancy has a very bad record, that it was Nancy and only Nancy who was seen making a huge fuss at the reception, that Nancy hadn't actually gone home when she was supposed to but hung around a few moments, I saw her and so did one of the nuns, briefly, and on and on in a way that made it seem as if the most likely suspect was going to be Nancy Hare. And given Jack Androcetti, that constituted a threat. That's why Nancy agreed to let Mother Mary Bellarmine 'deck' her, as she put it, the day after, when I wanted to talk to her. The idea was to create enough of a diversion so I wouldn't get to talk to her."

"What about the X-Acto knife? Did Mother Mary Bellarmine really mean to kill her?"

"I don't know," Gregor said. "Certainly not then. Certainly not with an X-Acto knife. As to later—" He shrugged. "Who knows? At this point I don't have to know."

Bennis had brought her copy of the *Inquirer* into the kitchen with her. Now she picked it up. "Food poisoning," she said, pointing to the headline. "This says food poisoning. Not murder."

"I know," Gregor said.

"Well?"

Gregor sat back in his chair. "Well, Bennis," he said, "sometimes you go by the book and sometimes you do what works. Do you know what I mean?"

"No."

"The first thing we wanted to do was to make sure Mother Mary Bellarmine got put away, right?"

"Right."

"The Order has a rest home—an insane asylum, really—that they run up in New Hampshire. They've made her a deal she can't refuse. She's committed herself voluntarily. Next week, someone will commit her involuntarily. Reverend Mother General will take care of the rest, and when she retires, there won't be a Sister in the Order eligible for her position who won't know the whole story. So far so good, yes?"

"Okay." Bennis sounded dubious.

"It's a method that has the added virtue of not making a group of very remarkable women who do very necessary work look any worse than they have to. It's not the fault of anyone now in charge of the Sisters of Divine Grace that once long ago some formation team made a mistake in letting Mother Mary Bellarmine through, or that in the 1950s it seemed more important that Mother Mary Bellarmine was good at finances but not good at personal relations. Things change. People change. Times change. I like the nuns."

"I like the nuns, too. What about Jack Androcetti?"

"The Cardinal Archbishop is having a little chat with the town of Radnor."

"What about Nancy Hare?"

"She's talked Henry into going to a sex therapist in New York City."

"What about Rob Collins?"

"He ought to be out of uniform in a month and a half—Bennis, what's all that noise?"

"Noise." Bennis Hannaford leaped to her feet. "Oh. I almost forgot. Now, look, Gregor, be reasonable. I mean, it's no day to get upset."

"What are you talking about?"

3

What she was talking about was very quickly clear. His front door popped open. His tiny entry foyer was filled with people. More people spilled through his front door and into his living room and his kitchen and his hall and probably his bedroom. At the front of this group of people was Hannah Krekorian, theoretically the party girl, with a big white orchid corsage on her chest.

"Krekor!" Hannah said gaily. "We *surprised* you!"

"Bennis," Gregor said.

"Now, Gregor—"

"It's not my birthday," Gregor said.

"You won't tell anybody your birthday," Lida said. "We had to make it up."

"You had a surprise party for me *last month*," Gregor said.

"The theory is, if we drive you crazy enough, you'll *have* to tell us," Bennis said.

Father Tibor came up and wagged his finger in the air. "If you had not stolen your baptismal certificate we would know, Krekor. That was not an honest thing to do."

"It was a matter of self-preservation," Gregor said grimly.

And it might have been, but it didn't matter, because Sheila Kashinian had just come through the door with a ten-tiered cake that looked like something once bound for a wedding and now afflicted with multiple personality disorder. It had blue-and-white icing and a little statue of a nun on the top layer and then different colors and different statues all the way down.

"It's to celebrate your cases," Howard Kashinian

said with immense satisfaction, and Gregor considered the fact that, Howard being Howard, this was exactly the kind of thing he'd get satisfaction from.

Sheila put the cake down on the kitchen table and stood back to admire her creation.

"Now," old George Tekemanian said. "We will sing. Krekor very much likes to hear us sing."

It was a crock, but Gregor couldn't very well say so.

They might be driving him crazy, but they surely meant well.

Maybe next month he could stow away on a tramp steamer and not be found again until Christmas.

About the Author

JANE HADDAM is the author of thirteen Gregor Demarkian holiday mysteries. *Not a Creature Was Stirring*,
the first in the series, was nominated for both an An-
thony and the Mystery Writers of America's Edgar
awards. *A Stillness in Bethlehem, Precious Blood, Act of
Darkness, Quoth the Raven, A Great Day for the Deadly, A
Feast of Murder, Murder Superior, Festival of Deaths, Dear
Old Dead, Bleeding Hearts, Fountain of Death* and *And One
to Die On* are her other books. She lives in Litchfield
County, Connecticut, with her husband, her son, and
her cat.

If you enjoyed
Murder Superior,
you will want to read the latest
Jane Haddam hardcover,
AND ONE TO DIE ON.

Here is a special preview of
AND ONE TO DIE ON,
available at your favorite
bookstore now!

And One To Die On

**A Birthday Mystery
by Jane Haddam**

Sometimes, she would stand in front of the mirror and stare at the lines in her face, the deep ravines spreading across her forehead, the fine webs spinning out from the corners of her eyes, the two deep gashes, like ragged cliffs, on either side of her mouth. Sometimes she would see, superimposed on this, a picture of herself at seventeen, her great dark liquid eyes staring out from under thick lashes, her mouth painted into a bow and parted, the way they all did it, then. That was a poster she was remembering, the first poster for the first movie she ever starred in. It was somewhere in this house, with a few hundred other posters, locked away from sight. She had changed a lot in this house, since she came to live here, permanently, in 1938. She had changed the curtains in the living room and the rugs in the bedroom and all the wall decorations except the ones in the foyer. She had even changed the kind of food there was in the pantry and how it was brought there. She had felt imprisoned here, those first years, but she didn't any longer. It felt perfectly natural to be living here, in a house built into the rock, hanging over the sea. It even felt safe. Lately she had been worried, as he hadn't been in decades, that her defenses had been breached.

Now it was nearly midnight on a cold day in late October, and she was coming down the broad, angled stairs to the foyer. She was moving very carefully, because at the age of ninety-nine that was the best she could do. On the wall of the stairwell posters hung in a graduated rank, showing the exaggerated make-up and the overexpressive emotionalism of all American silent movies. TASHEBA KENT and CONRAD DARCAN in BETRAYED. TASHEBA KENT and RUDOLPH VALENTINO in DESERT NIGHTS. TASHEBA KENT and HAROLD HOLLIS in JACARANDA. There were no posters advertising a movie with Tasheba Kent and Cavender Marsh, because by the time Cavender began to star in movies, Tasheba Kent had been retired for a decade.

There was a narrow balcony to the front of the house through the French windows in the living room, and Tasheba went there, stepping out into the wind without worrying about her health. They were always warning her—Cavender, the doctors, her secretary, Miss Dart—that she could catch pneumonia at any time, but she wouldn't live like that, locked up, clutching at every additional second of breath. She pulled one of the lighter chairs out onto the balcony and sat down on it. The house was on an island, separated by only a narrow strip of water from the coast of central Maine. She could see choppy black ocean tipped with white and the black rocks of the shore, looking sharp on the edges and entirely inhospitable.

Years ago, when she and Cav had first come here, there was no dock on the Maine side. She had bought the house in 1917 and never lived in it. She and Cav had had to build the dock and buy the boat the first of the grocery men used. They had had to make arrangements for the *Los Angeles Times* to be flown in and for their favorite foods, like caviar and pâté, to be shipped up from New York. They had caused a lot of fuss, then, when they were supposed to want to hide, and Tash knew that subconsciously they had done it all on purpose.

Tash put her small feet up on the railing and felt the wind in her face. It was cold and wet out here and she liked it. She could hear footsteps in the foyer now, coming through the living room door, on their way to find her, but she had expected those. Cavender woke up frequently in the night. He didn't like it when he found the other side of the bed empty. He'd never liked that. That was how they had gotten into this mess to begin with. Tash wondered sometimes how their lives would have turned out if Cavender hadn't been born into a family so poor that there was only one bed for all six of the boy children.

The approaching footsteps were firm and hard-stepped. Cav had been educated in parochial schools. The nuns had taught him to pick his feet up when he walked.

"Tash?" he asked.

"There's no need to whisper," Tash said. "Geraldine Dart's fast asleep on the third floor, and there's nobody else here but us."

Cav came out on the balcony and looked around. The weather was bad, there was no question about it. The wind was sharp and cold. Any minute now, it was going to start to rain. Cav retreated a little.

"You ought to come in," he said. "It's awful out."

"I don't want to come in. I've been thinking."

"That was silly. I would think you were old enough to know better."

"I was thinking about the party. Are you sure all those people are going to come?"

"Oh, yes."

"Are you sure it's going to be all right? We haven't seen anyone for so long. We've always been so careful."

Cav came out on the balcony again. He reminded Tash of one of those Swiss story clocks, where carved wooden characters came out of swinging wooden doors, over and over again, like jacks-in-the-box in perpetual motion.

"It's been fifty years now since it all happened," Cav said seriously. "I don't think anybody cares anymore."

"I'd still feel safer if we didn't have to go through with it. Are you sure we have to go through with it?"

"Well, Tash, there are other ways of making money then selling all your memorabilia at auction, but I never learned how to go about doing them and I'm too old to start. And so are you."

"I suppose."

"Besides," Cav said. "I'll be glad to get it all out of here. It spooks me sometimes, running into my past the way I do around here. Doesn't it spook you?"

"No," Tash said thoughtfully. "I think I rather like it. In some ways, in this house, it's as if I never got old."

"You got old," Cav told her. "And so did I. And the roof needs a twenty-five-thousand-dollar repair job. And I've already had one heart attack. We need to hire a full-time nurse and you know it, just in case."

"I don't think I'll wait for 'just in case.' I think that on my hundred and third birthday, I will climb up to the widow's walk on this house, and dive off into the sea."

"Come to bed," Cav said. "We have a lot of people coming very soon. If you're not rested, you won't be able to visit with them."

Cav was right, of course. No matter how good she felt most of the time—how clear in her mind, how strong in her muscles—she was going to be one hundred years old at the end of the week, and she tried easily. She took the arm he held out to her and stood up. She looked back at the sea one more time. It wouldn't be a bad way to go, Tash thought, diving off the widow's walk. People would say it was just like her.

"Tell me something," she said. "Are you sorry we did what we did, way back then? Do you ever wish it could have turned out differently?"

"No."

"Never? Not even once?"

"Not even once. Sometimes I still find myself surprised that it worked out the way it did, that it didn't turn out worse. But I never regret it."

"And you don't think anybody cares anymore. You don't think anybody out there is still angry at us."

"There isn't anyone out there left to be angry, Tash. We've outlasted them all."

Tash let herself be helped across the living room to the foyer, across the foyer to the small cubicle elevator at the back. She came down the stairs on foot, but she never went up anymore. When she tried she just collapsed.

She sat down on the little seat in the corner of the elevator car. Cav's children. Her own sister. Aunts and uncles and nieces and nephews. Lawyers and accountants and agents and movie executives. Once everybody in the world had been angry at them. When they had first come out to the island, they'd had to keep the phone off the hook. But Cav was probably right. That was fifty years ago. Almost nobody remembered—and the people who did, like the reporter who was coming for the weekend from *Personality* magazine, thought it was romantic.

Good lord, the kind of trouble you could get yourself into, over nothing more significant than a little light adultery.

The elevator came to a bumping stop.

"Here we are," Cav said. "Let me help you up."

Tash let him help her. Cav was always desperate for proof that he was necessary to her. Tash thought the least she could do was give it to him.

Hannah Kent Graham should have let the maid pack for her. She knew that. She should have written a list of all the clothes she wanted to take, left her suitcases open on her bed, and come out into the living room to do some serious drinking. Hannah Graham almost never did any serious drinking. She almost never did any serious eating, either. What she did do was a lot of very serious surgery. Face lifts, tummy tucks, liposuction, breast augmentation, rhinoplasty: Hannah had had them all, and some of them more than once. She was fifty-seven years old and only five foot three, but she weighed less than ninety pounds and wore clothes more fashionable than half the starlets she saw window-shopping on Rodeo Drive. Anyplace else in the world except here in Beverly Hills, Hannah would have looked decidedly peculiar—reconstructed, not quite biological, made of cellophane skin stretched across plastic bone—but she didn't live any-place else in the world. She didn't care what hicks in Austin, Texas, thought of her, either. She was the single most successful real estate agent in Los Angeles, and she looked it.

So far, in forty-five minutes, she had managed to pack two silk day dresses, two evening suits, and a dozen pairs of Christian Dior underwear. She was sucking on her Perrier and ice as if it were an opium teat. In a chair in a corner of the room, her latest husband—number six—was sipping a brandy and soda and trying not to laugh.

If this husband had been like the three that came before him—beach boys all, picked up in Malibu, no-table only for the size of the bulges in their pants—Hannah would have been ready to brain him, but John Graham was actually a serious person. He was almost as old as Hannah herself, at least fifty, and he was a very successful lawyer. He was not, however, a divorce lawyer. Hannah was not that stupid. John handled contract negotiations and long-term development deals for movie stars who really wanted to direct.

Hannah threw a jade green evening dress into the suit-bag and backed up to look it over.

"What I don't understand about all this," she said, "is why I'm going out there to attend a one hundredth birth-day party for that poisonous old bitch. I mean, why do I want to bother?"

"Personally, I think you want to confront your father. Isn't that what your therapist said?"

"My therapist is a jerk. I don't even know my father.

He disappeared into the sunset with that bitch when I was three months old."

"That's my point."

"She murdered my mother," Hannah said. "There isn't any other way to put it."

"Sure there is," John told her. "Especially since she was in Paris or someplace at the exact moment your mother was being killed on the Côte d'Azur. It was your father the police thought killed your mother."

"It comes to the same thing, John. That bitch drove him to it. He went away with her afterwards. He left me to be brought up by dear old Aunt Bessie, the world paradigm for the dysfunctional personality.

"There's your father again. That's it exactly. What you really want to do, whether you realize it or not, is brain your old man. I hope you aren't taking a gun along on this weekend."

"I'm thinking of taking cyanide. I also think I'm sick of therapy-speak. You know what all this is going to mean, don't you? The auction and all the rest of it? It's all going to come out again. The magazines are going to have a field day. *People. Us. Personality.* Isn't *that* going to be fun?"

"You're going to find it very good for business," John said placidly. "People are going to see you as a very romantic figure. It'll do you nothing but good, Hannah. You just watch."

The really disgusting thing, Hannah thought, was that John was probably right. The really important people wouldn't be impressed—they probably wouldn't even notice—but the second stringers would be all hot to trot. The agency would be inundated with people looking for *anything at all* in Beverly Hills for under a million dollars, who really only wanted to see her close up. If this was the kind of thing I wanted to do with my life, Hannah thought, I would have become an actress.

The jade green evening dress was much too much for a

weekend on an island off the coast of Maine. Even if they dressed for dinner there, they wouldn't go in for washed silk and rhinestones. What would they go in for? Hannah put the jade green evening dress back in the closet and took out a plainer one in dark blue. Then she put that one back, too. It made her look like she weighed at least a hundred and five.

"What do you think they have to auction off?" she asked John. "Do you think they have anything of my mother's?"

"I don't know. They might."

"Aunt Bessie always said there wasn't anything of hers left after it was all over, that everything she had was in their house in France and it was never shipped back here for me to have. Maybe he kept it."

"Maybe he did."

"Would you let him, if you were her? Reminders of the murdered wife all around your house?"

"You make a lot of assumptions, Hannah. You assume she's the dominant partner in the relationship. You assume that if he has your mother's things, they must be lying around in his house."

"*Her* house. It was always her house. She bought it before she ever met him."

"Her house. Whatever. Maybe he put those things in an attic somewhere, or a basement. Maybe he keeps them locked up in a hope chest in a closet. They don't have to be where your aunt is tripping over them all the time."

"Don't remind me that she's my aunt, John. It makes me ill."

"I think you better forget about all this packing and go have something to drink. Just leave it all here for the maid to finish with in the morning, and we can sleep in the guest room."

"You only like to sleep in the guest room because there's a mirror on the ceiling."

"Sure. I like to see your bony little ass bopping up and down like a Mexican jumping bean."

Hannah made a face at him and headed out of the bedroom toward the living room. She had to go down a hall carpeted in pale grey and across an entryway of polished fieldstone. Like most houses costing over five million dollars in Beverly Hills, hers looked like the set for a TV miniseries of a Jackie Collins novel. The living room had a conversation pit with its own fireplace. It also had a twenty-two-foot-long wet bar made of teak with a brass footrail. Hannah went around to the back of this and found a bottle of Smirnoff vodka and a glass. Vodka was supposed to be better for your skin than darker liquors.

Hannah poured vodka into her glass straight and drank it down straight. It burned her throat, but it made her feel instantly better.

"You know," she said to John, who had followed her out to get a refill for himself, "maybe this won't be so terrible after all. Maybe I'll be able to create an enormous scene, big enough to cause major headlines, and then maybe I'll threaten to sue."

"Sue?"

"To stop the auction. You're good at lawsuits, John, help me think. Maybe I can claim that everything they have really belongs to my mother. Or maybe I can claim that the whole auction is a way of trading in on the name of my mother. Think about it, John. There must be something."

John filled his glass with ice and poured a double shot of brandy in it. This time, he didn't seem any more interested in mixers than Hannah was.

"Hannah," he said. "Give it up. Go to Maine. Scream and yell at your father. Tell your aunt she deserves to rot in hell. Then come home. Trust me. If you try to do anything else, you'll only get yourself in trouble."

Hannah poured herself another glass of vodka and swigged it down, the way she had the first.

"Crap," she said miserably. "You're probably right."

For Carlton Ji, journalism was not so much a career as it was a new kind of computer game, except without the computer, which suited Carlton just fine. Two of his older brothers had gone into computer work, and a third—Winston the Medical Doctor, as Carlton's mother always put it—did a lot of programming on the side. For Carlton, however, keyboards and memory banks and microchips were all a lot of fuss and nonsense. If he tried to work one of the "simple" programs his brothers were always bringing him, he ended up doing something odd to the machine, so that it shut down and wouldn't work anymore. If he tried to write his first drafts on the word processor at work, he found he couldn't get them to print out on the printer or even to come back onto the screen. They disappeared, that was all, and Carlton had learned to write his articles out in longhand instead. It was frustrating. Computers made life easier, if you knew how to use them. Carlton could see that. Besides, there wasn't a human being of any sex or color in the United States today who really believed there was any such thing as an Asian-American man who was computer illiterate.

Fortunately for Carlton Ji, his computer at *Personality* magazine had a mouse, which just needed to be picked up in the hand and moved around. It was by using the mouse that he had found out what he had found out about the death of Lilith Brayne. He didn't have anything conclusive, of course. If there had been anything definitive lying around, somebody else would have picked it up years ago. What he had was what one of his brothers called "a computer coincidence." The coincidence had been there all along, of course, but it had remained unnoticed until a computer program threw all the elements up on a screen. The trick was that the elements might never have appeared together if there hadn't been a program to force them together, because they weren't the kind of elements a human brain would ordinarily think of combining. Computers were stupid. They did exactly what you told them to do, even if it made no sense.

Carlton Ji wasn't sure what he had done to make the computer do what it did, but one day there he was, staring at a list of seemingly unrelated items on the terminal screen, and it hit him.

"FOUND AT THE SCENE," he screen flashed at him, and then:

GOLD COMPACT
GOLD KEY RING
GOLD CIGARETTE CASE
EBONY AND IVORY CIGARETTE HOLDER
BLACK FEATHER BOA
DIAMOND AND SAPPHIRE DINNER RING

Then the screen wiped itself clean and started, "TASHEBA KENT IN PARIS." This list was even longer than the previous one, because the researcher had keyed in everything she could find, no matter how unimportant. These included:

SILVER GREY ROLLS ROYCE WITH SILVER-PLATED TRIM
DIAMOND AND RUBY DINNER RING
BLACK BEADED EVENING DRESS
AMBER AND EBONY HOOKAH
BLACK FEATHER BOA
VIVIENNE CRI SHOES WITH RHINESTONE BUCKLES

If the black feather boa hadn't been in the same position each time — second from the bottom — Carlton might not have noticed it. But he did notice it, and when he went to the paper files to check it out, the point became downright peculiar.

"It was either the same black feather boa or an identical one," Carlton told Jasper Fein, the editor from Duluth House he was hoping to interest in a new book on the death of Lilith Brayne. Like a lot of other reporters from *Personality* magazine, and reporters from *Time* and *Newsweek* and *People,* too, Carlton's dream was to get a really spectacular book into print. The kind of thing that sold a million copies in hardcover. The kind of thing that would get his face on the cover of the *Sunday Times Magazine,* or maybe even into *Vanity Fair.* Other reporters had done it, and reporters with a lot less going for them than Carlton Ji.

"You've got to look at the pictures," Carlton told Jasper Fein, "and then you have to read the reports in order. The police in Cap d'Antibes found a black feather boa among Lilith Brayne's things just after she died. That was on Tuesday night—early Wednesday morning, really, around two-thirty or three o'clock. Then later on Wednesday morning, around ten, they interviewed Tasheba Kent in Paris, and *she* was wearing a black feather boa."

Jasper Fein shook his head. "You've lost me, Carlton. So there were two feather boas. So what?"

"So what happened to the first feather boa?"

"What *happened* to it?"

"That's right," Carlton said triumphantly. "Because after the black feather boa was seen around Tasheba Kent's neck at ten o'clock on Wednesday morning, no black feather boa was ever found in Lilith Brayne's things in the South of France again. That feather boa just disappeared without a trace."

Jasper Fein frowned. "Maybe the police just didn't consider it important. Maybe it's not listed because they didn't see any reason to list it."

"They listed a lipstick brush," Carlton objected. "They listed a pair of tweezers."

"Twice?"

"That's right, twice. Once at the scene and once again for the magistrate at the inquest."

"And the only thing that was missing was this black feather boa."

"That's right."

Jasper Fein drummed his fingers against the tablecloth. They were having lunch in the Pool Room at the Four Seasons—not the best room in the restaurant, not the room where Jasper would have taken one of his authors who had already been on the bestseller lists, but the Four Seasons nonetheless. Carlton had no idea what lunch was going to cost, because his copy of the menu hadn't had any prices on it.

"Okay," Jasper conceded. "This is beginning to sound interesting."

Carlton Ji beamed. "It certainly sounds interesting to me," he said, "an I'm in a unique position to do something about it. I'm supposed to go up to Maine and spend four days on that Godforsaken island where they live now, doing a story for the magazine."

"Love among the geriatric set?"

"I can take any angle I want, actually. My editor just thinks it's a great idea to have Tasheba Kent in the magazine. Hollywood glamour. Silent movies. Love and death. It's a natural."

"Did you say those feather boas were identical?"

"They were as far as I could tell from the photographs, and there are a lot of photographs, and most of them are pretty good. The descriptions in the police reports are identical, too."

"Hmm. It's odd, isn't it? I wonder what it's all about."

"Maybe I'll have a chance to find out when I go to Maine. Maybe I can get someone up there to talk to me."

"Maybe you can," Jasper said, "but don't be worried if you don't. They're old people now. Tasheba Kent must be, my God—"

"One hundred," Carlton said.

"Really?"

"Among the other things that are going on during this weekend I'm supposed to attend is a hundredth birthday party for Tasheba Kent."

"There's the angle for *Personality* magazine. That's the kind of thing you want to play up over there. Not all this stuff about the death of Lilith Brayne."

"To tell you the truth," Carlton said, "I'm going to have to play up the death of Lilith Brayne. My editor's going to insist on it."

Jasper Fein looked ready to ask Carlton how that could, in fact, be the truth, when Carlton had said only a few moments before that his editor would take any angle he wanted to give her. Jasper took a sip of his chablis instead, and Carlton relaxed a little. At least they understood each other. At least Jasper realized that Carlton was going to hang onto his ownership of this idea. Now they could start to talk business for real, and Carlton had a chance of ending up with what he wanted.

Carlton wasn't going to talk money now, though. He wasn't going to talk details. He was going to wait until he got back from Maine. Then he'd have more to bargain with.